THE
JASPER
FOREST

THE JASPER FOREST

Book Two of
The Guardian Cycle

JULIA GRAY

An *Orbit* Book

First published in Great Britain by Orbit 2001

A CIP catalogue record for this book is available from the British Library.

ISBN 1 84149 057 1

Typeset in Ehrhardt
by Palimpsest Book Production Limited
Polmont, Stirlingshire
Printed in Great Britain by
Mackays of Chatham PLC, Chatham, Kent

Orbit
A Division of
Little, Brown and Company (UK)
Brettenham House
Lancaster Place
London WC2E 7EN

For Gemma, Luke, Rebecca and Yvette,
four of the most wonderful, talented and inspiring young
people in the world!
With much love.

PROLOGUE

The mountain was still growing.

Although the movement could no longer be seen by the naked eye, Kerin Mirana could still feel the earth's adjustments through the soles of his well-worn boots. He had *jasper feet* – an invaluable asset for a traveller in the stone forests. He felt the rock grinding beneath him, and was aware of even the smallest variations, while his eyes could only measure the mountain's progress from one hour to the next.

Even in Macul, a land where – as Kerin knew better than most – little could be taken for granted, there had never been anything like this before. Earthquakes were common enough, even in the country's most stable regions. In certain areas the land rose or fell steadily – though gradually – so that where a man had once fished, now his grandson planted crops. Rivers changed course, broke their banks or dried up; victims of the movements of the earth, the vagaries of the weather and, closer to the coast, the suddenly unpredictable tides. Subsidence and avalanches altered the shape of the landscape. Little remained static. During his travels, Kerin had witnessed much that had left him in a state of wonder. He had seen many awe-inspiring sights, but this . . .

Little more than one long month ago, this had been a valley, with a small lake, recently increased in size and fed by several streams from the surrounding hills. From where Kerin stood, he would have looked down over gentle green slopes to the placid surface of the water. Now he had to tip his head back in order to glimpse the upper reaches of the new-born mountain. The distant summit was too high to be seen, and the black rock towered over everything around it. And the forces that had created its unnatural bulk were driving it still. Before the prospector's disbelieving eyes, the mountain was growing higher yet.

The dark extrusion had erupted from the earth like a gigantic creature emerging from its chrysalis, splitting the skin of soil and vegetation and slewing it aside like an old husk as the black mountain made its shuddering reach for the heavens. It brought to mind ancient legends – of dragons and giant worms who lived beneath the world of men, in caves deep inside Nydus, and who came to the surface every so often, breathing flame and smoke into the air and making rocks flow in red waves or explode into the sky. But no one believed in those tales any more. In any case, there had been no fire here. The mountain's rise had been astonishing but, by human standards, its movement had been almost stately. Nevertheless, it was still an unprecedented event – a geological disturbance so vast that the term 'earthquake' hardly seemed adequate.

The few people who had been nearby had fled in terror as the upheaval devastated the valley and shook the land for miles around.

There had been no warning. There had not even been a major conjunction of the moons during the time of its growth. Kerin glanced at the sky reflexively, even though he knew what he would see. No traveller in such inhospitable regions could afford to be ignorant of the prevailing lunar influences. The only visible moon was a pale sliver of amber, low in the eastern sky. In any case, Kerin knew that neither he nor the land was false-dreaming. He would have no need to plant a new prayer-flag – although many would, pointlessly in his view, from fear.

The mountain awed Kerin, but it did not frighten him. He was certain that he had been the first to return to the area, once the initial convulsions had slowed a little, and he knew that they would soon be over. And then he would move.

He had spent all but the earliest years of his life trekking over the region's forbidding terrain. He knew its secrets and its dangers better than any man alive. The faint trails, the hidden signposts, and the bizarre plant life of Vejar Province were all familiar to him. It was a remote, barren area of water and melting rock: of deeply-fissured plateaus, of pools studded with stone towers, of sinkholes, caverns and crevasses, and of rivers that plunged underground only to reappear many miles away. Near-vertical cliffs, conical peaks and crags that had been carved into improbable shapes by wind and water all contributed to the reputation of the province as a place of mystery and peril, but they held no terrors for Kerin.

Indeed, he had earned his due-name by being the first – and so far the only – man brave enough to walk through the Tzi Gate. This was a huge hole in one particular ridge, formed when the old course of an underground river had been exposed by erosion and an earth tremor. Although Kerin had recognized it as a natural formation, others had been intimidated by the massive structure, and linked its existence to supernatural powers. No one had dared tempt fate by entering the so-called gate until Kerin had decided to do so, simply because he'd wanted to see what was on the other side. Staring up at the roof of the stone archway, half a mile above his head, had been a humbling experience, but the view from the other side had been disappointingly ordinary and Kerin had returned without mishap. After that he had known that there was no part of Vejar that was forbidden to him – provided, of course, that he always obeyed the dictates of the sky – and he had been travelling ever since, only seeing his wife and young sons for a few days each year.

Even so, he had never seen anything like this before. And yet he knew where the black rock had come from – even if he did not understand why – and was already studying its formations. He was shrewd enough to realize that such opportunities came only once in any lifetime, and he was determined to take his chance when the mountain finally grew still. He would be the first to climb the new peak. Excitement vibrated within him, in time with the trembling of the earth, but Kerin's eyes were calm and his gaze never shifted from the mass of dark stone.

PART ONE

FENDUCA

CHAPTER ONE

He could hear a voice. It sounded familiar, but he couldn't tell where it was coming from, or see the face of the man who spoke.

'I remember it now as I remember dreams; in fragments that make no sense by themselves; in the feeling that I have seen or experienced something before, without knowing when or where.'

There were faces then. Dozens of them, curious or indifferent, smiling or angry. So many faces – but never hers. Not even here, not even now.

'But it was not a dream. I wasn't even asleep.'

The voice droned on, a monotone. Boring. And yet he couldn't stop listening. He was trapped.

'If I had been, the pain in my arm would have woken me.'

Why couldn't he see her face? Hadn't he been punished enough without that?

'No, I was not asleep. I know that now.'

The voice was growing quieter as it neared the end. But he knew that sooner or later it would begin again, another cycle in the endless round.

'I was waiting to be born.'

The fear came then, clutching at him with red fingers, pulsing in his blood, that other ocean. Thunder from within as well as from below. He was helpless in both tides. He knew that the voice, *his* voice, was trying to tell him something, but he couldn't understand what it was. And then he forgot everything again. No memory. Just movement, gentler now, and the faces. None of them real. Not even real ghosts.

He laughed at the thought before it was lost once more – until the next round.

'Farewell, brother.'

A new voice, one he *did* recognize. The enchanter was still pursuing him. But that didn't matter. Nothing mattered any more. Not even time. A circle has no end.

'I remember it now as I remember dreams . . .'

The raft drifted slowly on the sluggish tide, its single occupant curled up on the rough wooden planks. Water slopped lazily around him, and the parts of his clothing that were not sodden were encrusted with salt. His matted hair was stiff with the same gritty substance; even his eyelashes were rimmed with white, as if too many tears had evaporated there.

His eyes were open but glazed – not blind, but unseeing. He twitched sometimes, like a sleeping dog when it dreams of chasing rabbits, but otherwise he lay still. Whatever life he still possessed lay hidden deep within his crumpled frame, behind the dwindling fire of those pale, diamond-fever eyes.

Lamplight bent and twisted around him. He was floating, swimming in darkness, surrounded by an ancient loneliness. There was a star burning. Released, he fell *upwards*, landing awkwardly on the roof of the cave. A bird perched next to him. *What's going on?* Spiral winds carried her voice away, and a vast roaring deafened him as the darkness shifted.

Two skies, two mountains. The Dark Moon swallowing the sun, the winged huntress devouring her prey. A sword raised. More ghosts. Brother?

I was waiting to be born.

The star-maze glowed, beckoning. Hurry. Hurry!

The reason for haste eluded him. A circle has no end.

Terrel could no longer tell when he was dreaming or when he was awake. Both worlds seemed equally bizarre. Occasionally, something – usually a spasm of pain – reminded him that he must still be alive, but even that seemed doubtful now. Surely there were no animals of such gigantic size in his world. They towered over him, moving with a regular swaying rhythm that was both hypnotic and vaguely menacing. He could feel their eyes fixed upon him. The creatures were colourless for the most part, their skin hard and grey-looking, almost as if they were made from stone. But no rock could ever have contorted itself into such varied and fantastical shapes – it could not move, as these monstrous presences did. Rock did not grow patches of green fur or hair, nor did it whisper with the echoing voices of a gulping, hissing tongue. He had tried to listen to what they were saying, but he could make no sense of their wordless murmuring.

At least now there *was* something to see and hear. Until the animals came he had been alone for what seemed like a lifetime, riding on the waves of magic with only the sky above him and the sea below. Blue upon blue, striped with the reflections of the sun and moons, blinding glitter and heat balanced by the cold stars and the Amber, Red and White. He had been aware of the Dark Moon too, though he could not see it. He felt the invisible pull of the sky-shadow, and knew that its blind face would look down upon him at the moment of his death.

In his isolation, Terrel had peopled his world with ghosts – even with those whom he knew, or hoped, were still alive. They had all come eventually, friends and foes alike, all except one. Dreaming or awake, Alyssa's face eluded his thoughts and visions, even though he heard her voice sometimes or saw her spirit encased in other forms. Of all the cruelties he had to bear, that was the worst.

The dragging ache in his twisted limbs was something he had coped with all his life, but now it seemed irrelevant, unnoticed amid other torments of body and mind. He could hardly move the fingers of even his good hand without the muscles cramping and every joint being lanced by pain. His breath rattled in his lungs and he felt nauseous almost all the time, even though his stomach was empty. His lips were bloated and cracked, and his tongue was now like a dry clump of rough leather, so swollen that he could only just prise it away from the roof of his mouth. Thirst raged within him, although he only occasionally recognized it for what it was. For the rest, it was just one more helpless yearning among all the others.

His meagre supply of fresh water had run out several days ago, and now – in a rare lucid moment – his fluttering gaze fell upon the empty bottle, and he felt the Dark Moon draw closer. He was about to surrender, to answer the siren call of oblivion, when a stray thought emerged from the chaos of his disordered mind. At first he did not know what it was, but it nagged at him, as relentless as the ocean, until meaning followed. His promise. From the moment those words had been uttered, they had ruled his every action – and while there was still breath in his body they would not allow him to give up. *I will come back for you.* The words seemed empty now, but he could not set them aside. The struggle had to continue. Even if it was to a bitter end.

Ignoring the renewed protests of his body and the weary groan that escaped from his parched lips, Terrel forced himself to sit up and look around. The giant creatures crowded about him, seeming to lean inwards as they encircled his flimsy raft, and he shrank into himself, fearing that he would be crushed. But the animals had grown still, just as the waves that propelled him on his journey had now left him becalmed.

Understanding came slowly, fighting its way through the tangle of his delirium. The looming giants were indeed made of rock, lifeless but for the tufts of grass or fern that clung to their sides. Terrel could not imagine what forces had carved these outlandish and sinister shapes, but their movement had been an illusion brought on by the rise and fall of the gentle swell and languid currents that lapped around the bases of the overhanging cliffs. He had drifted into a labyrinth of stone, that rose from the ocean to form a water-born maze.

When the second realization came, it sent a desperate surge of energy pulsing through his mind and body. The rocks, no matter how strange their shape, represented *land*, the first he had seen since the Floating Islands had left him floundering in their massive wake. He might yet survive this ordeal.

Even though his dreams still tugged at the edges of his vision, Terrel could see one thing clearly now. The sides of the rocks were so precipitous that there was no chance of him disembarking there. What was more, there would be no point in even making the attempt. These stone pinnacles were clearly barren, devoid of any source of sustenance. The sparse vegetation might suck life from cracks in the surface, but he could not, and in any case, it was far above him, out of reach.

The next thought that came brought another spark of hope – and one on which he forced himself to act. If this was some part of a foreign land, then it was possible that the water below him was not the ocean that had propelled him into exile. If this was a river, then he might be able to drink.

Leaning down to the edge of the raft was a slow and arduous task that made his head spin and his vision blur, but hope lent him the power to persevere. Dipping a finger into the water, he brought it to his mouth and dribbled a few drops onto his swollen tongue. Pain stung him, filling his cheeks, his teeth and eyes as well as his lips, but that was nothing compared to the wretchedness that filled him as his half-dead senses recognized the dread taste of salt. He retched convulsively, his empty stomach heaving. He knew better than to try to drink any more. He might as well have swallowed poison.

Exhausted by his efforts, and his spirit crushed, Terrel lay where he was and fell into another feverish hour of sleep. When he awoke, it was to find that the raft had not moved. Whatever current had been pushing him along had been caught up by the enveloping spires of grey stone, so that he was travelling round in slow circles, going nowhere. He would have cried out then – if he'd had either the strength or the voice for it – because it seemed that he was doomed to stay in that rock-bound lagoon for ever. A pointless end to a pointless journey. The final nightmare – and the death of his promise.

'Alyssa!'

In his mind he was shouting, crying out in futile misery. But the only sound that came from his ruined mouth was a choking hiss of agony that echoed from the cliffs about him, then died away into silence. He fell back into the shadow of the Dark Moon.

A new ghost, a new voice, crept into his dreams. He recognized neither. Nor could he understand what it said. The words were gibberish; meaningless sounds sent to taunt him.

A second interloper was talking now, but he made no more sense than the other. They seemed to be calling. Was it to him? Terrel had no idea what they were saying, but he could recognize the urgency in their tone. Was this new torment in this world or the next?

The voices persisted, overriding the other delusions in his fevered mind, giving him no rest. At last, reluctantly, he opened his salt-encrusted eyes. And saw two men in canoes, watching him from the edge of the lagoon.

CHAPTER TWO

For a few moments, Terrel assumed that the two men were simply more of his strange delusions. He just could not believe that they were real. But he eventually realized that there was something substantial and resolute about the look of them, and this gave him hope. The men had fallen silent now, aware that he was looking at them, but they made no move to approach him. Terrel knew that if he were to be rescued, he would have to initiate the contact.

As he struggled into a sitting position, and raised his left hand in greeting, he wondered what was causing their hesitation. They were only some thirty paces away, in one of the lagoon's many entrances, and from that distance it must have been obvious that he posed no possible threat. Why then, given that they were clearly intrigued by his presence, were they not making any effort to come any closer? In fact, the two men were making small strokes with their paddles, to avoid moving any further forwards.

Their response to his feeble wave was to glance at each other, and to exchange a few words that Terrel could not hear. They still did not move.

'Please,' Terrel croaked, trying to beckon to them with his shaking hand. But he managed only to exaggerate the trembling of his fingers, and could not be sure that they'd understand his signal. He was about to call for help, but realized that his first word had come out as no more than a hoarse sigh, which they could not possibly have heard. His tongue, long unused for speech and bloated by his ordeal, was useless. Sign language was his only hope.

He gazed at the strangers, his eyes imploring them to come to his aid, and tried to wave again, hoping to draw them to him. This provoked further conversation between the two, more animated this time, but Terrel could understand none of what they said. He waved until his strength gave out and he was forced to drop his arm again.

The newcomers' argument had become vehement now. One of the men pushed his paddle into the water, and was about to move forward when his companion – the younger of the pair – barred his progress by thrusting his own oar across the other's chest. At the same time he shouted something, and the elder of the two abandoned his attempt to move. Then the more cautious sailor turned back to Terrel and called out to him. The boy understood none of the strange language, but it was clear that they were not going to come to his aid.

Frustrated and angered by this turn of events, just when he had been granted a last flicker of hope, Terrel felt despair leach away the last of his resistance, and he collapsed on to the damp boards.

*

'We can't just sit here!' Olandis muttered.

'We've no choice,' Aylen replied firmly. His conviction had not wavered for an instant, even in the face of his brother's fierce disagreement. 'This is Anador, remember. The red lagoon. Have you forgotten last night's skies?'

'But he's no more than a boy – and he's ill. He could die.'

'If we go in there, we'll bring ruin on ourselves and all our clan. Is that what you want? He has to get out by himself.'

'Oh, come on, Chute!' Olandis exclaimed. 'He's too weak. Anyone can see that. And the current's taking him round in circles.'

'Maybe that'll change when the tide begins to ebb,' Aylen suggested.

'And take him out to sea again? And us with him, if we're not careful. We could all end up dead then.'

'There's no alternative,' Aylen stated grimly. 'We'll manage somehow.'

'Moons!' Olandis hissed. 'I wish Pa was here.'

'He'd only tell you the same as me. He'd never go against moon-lore, especially in a place like this.'

Olandis fell silent, wondering why he could never win an argument with his brother. At nineteen he was Aylen's senior by two years, and was much stronger physically, but that counted for nothing when it came to a war of words. Even as an infant Aylen had always been able to get the better of him that way. And the most galling thing of all was that Olandis knew his sibling was almost always right.

The previous night had seen the rebirth of the Red

Moon, so that now it was just beginning to wax again, and that – together with the fact that the unseen Dark Moon had been full at the same time and was now beginning its slow decline – made Anador a place of peril. None of their people would dare enter the lagoon until the heavens were realigned in a more favourable way.

'There was something strange about his eyes,' Aylen said quietly.

Olandis had seen that too. The castaway's gaze had been unnerving, and his eyes had seemed to glitter in an unnatural way.

'Fever?' he guessed.

'Maybe,' Aylen replied, though he sounded unconvinced. 'I wonder how he got here.'

It had not occurred to Olandis to be curious about this. He had simply seen another human being in trouble and wanted to help him out. It had been his sharp ears that had picked up the earlier hissing cry, above the shuffle and lapping of the swell, and he who had insisted on going to investigate. He hadn't really believed that there would be anyone there, but as soon as he glimpsed the flimsy raft he had turned to his brother, meaning to say 'I told you so' – but then he had seen the expression on Aylen's face and had kept quiet. This was a place the brothers normally avoided, even when moon-lore allowed navigation in the area. There was something about the unusual colours in the water that made them nervous. Dreams hung heavy within this part of the coastal maze.

'Maybe he's a sharakan,' Olandis suggested. He meant it as a joke, wanting to lighten the mood, but – to his astonishment – Aylen seemed to take the idea seriously.

'Perhaps,' he murmured, nodding slowly. 'This

would be a good place to trade, if his magic was strong enough.'

'*Nothing* about him looks strong!' Olandis exclaimed. 'Besides, he's no more than a child.'

'Age is no barrier to talent – or ambition,' Aylen remarked sagely, glancing at the sky. As dusk fell, the only moon visible was the White, three days past full and still bright and pure against the fading blue. Under other circumstances he might have been content to stare at her delicate face, asking for her dreams to guide his way, but that was impossible now.

'Is he asleep?' Olandis asked, peering at the huddled figure on the raft.

The brothers stared, both wondering if it was a sleep from which the boy would ever awake, and then, with one accord, they began shouting again.

The suddenly renewed noise, and the unearthly echoes it set up, roused Terrel from his stupor. He cursed silently, then forced his eyes open and glanced at the source of the din. What could they want now? The two men had still not moved, and their words meant nothing, but their urgent tone and the meaning of their beckoning gestures were unequivocal this time. They wanted Terrel to go to them.

Their faces were set in serious expressions, not mocking or threatening, and Terrel wondered why, if they were really so anxious to help him, they could not simply move to his side. It would only take them a matter of moments to paddle their way across the intervening distance, but for Terrel it might as well have been a full mile of open water. In all the time he had been adrift, he had not once tried to influence the raft's course. In the open sea that would have been pointless; the strong swell had been impossible to fight, and one direction had been as good as another. Now that he was in relatively calm waters, and was in desperate need of purposeful motion, he had neither the strength nor the means to achieve it. Even if he'd had a wooden blade, like the strangers, he would have had difficulty lifting it, let alone using it to any effect. Moreover, the square raft was crudely built and moved awkwardly, unlike the streamlined canoes. It was hopeless. He closed his eyes again, and gave himself over to the ghosts.

'He's not listening,' Olandis said.

'Or he is, but can't do anything about it.'

The brothers fell silent, each lost in their own thoughts.

'The tide's turning,' Aylen said eventually.

'It can't be. It's too soon.' Olandis glanced at the sky, but on this occasion there were no answers to be found there.

'It's the Dark Moon,' his younger brother said. 'Farazin said it's not where it's supposed to be.'

'But that's impossible,' Olandis objected. 'Cutter said—'

'Cutter's a fool,' Aylen interrupted. 'Who would you rather believe? In any case, the tide *is* turning. Look.'

They both knew what this latest development meant. The currents within the maze could be treacherous in themselves, and if the brothers stayed too long and were caught by the ebb tide in full spate, together with the flow from the river, they'd be in danger of being swept out into the ocean. If that happened, it was possible that they'd never get back. Their lightweight boats were built for inland waterways, not the open sea.

'At least we might be able to fight it.' Olandis pointed out. '*He* won't stand a chance.'

'I know,' Aylen agreed soberly.

'We could go round to the far side. Catch him when he drifts out of the lagoon. If we time it right, we should be able to reach him and get back.'

'And if we don't?'

'We've got to do *something*.'

'All right,' Aylen conceded reluctantly, 'but there's something I want to try first.'

Terrel was dreaming of a beautiful crystal city that rose into the sunlight from the depths of the ocean. He was making his way towards it, knowing that – in a sense – he would be going home, when he realized to his horror that his longed-for sanctuary was under attack. Glowing meteors were raining down from a hostile sky, wreaking untold havoc among the delicate facets. He tried to move more quickly, to get there before the onslaught destroyed everything, but the dream held him back no matter how hard he fought.

He woke up when one of the smaller meteors hit him painfully on the side of his head.

'Did it catch?' Aylen asked.

'I think I hit his head,' Olandis replied anxiously.

'That's the least of his worries. Have any of the hooks caught?'

Olandis tested the line.

'I think so.'

The brothers' fishing lines were designed for trailing behind their canoes rather than for casting, but by tying a metal weight to one end they had been able to fashion something usable. Their hope was that, even if the castaway was unable to grasp the twine, one or more of the several hooks attached along its length would dig into some part of his raft or clothing. Olandis's throw had been more accurate than he'd dare hope for, and now, as he pulled carefully on the line, he felt it snag firmly. However, as he tried to pull it in, all that happened was that he moved forward, coming too close to the forbidden lagoon.

'We'll have to row backwards, pull him out that way,' Aylen decided. 'Tie the line to your canoe.' As Olandis did as he was told, Aylen attached his own craft to his brother's with a piece of rope. 'Ready?'

'Yes.'

Both men began to paddle steadily, feeling the line grow taut. To their relief it held as they edged backwards.

'Moons! It's heavy,' Olandis complained. 'Why did he put to sea on a piece of junk like that?' They were fighting against an increasing current, and the shape of the raft meant that it pulled awkwardly against the flow.

'It's coming,' Aylen breathed. 'Keep going.'

Something was dragging at Terrel's sleeve and pricking his arm. Still struggling to free his mind from the disintegrating shards of his dream, and wondering why his head hurt so much, he could not work out what might be causing this strange sensation. His every movement took a colossal effort now, but when he could at last touch his arm, he found that a piece of twine had been drawn across both him and the raft.

Opening his eyes, Terrel saw a shining beam of light dipping in and out of the water between him and the strangers' canoes. After a few moments, he realized that this was in fact a solid cord, and that he was being towed along. However, even as a glimmer of hope returned, he realized that his would-be rescuers were still keeping their distance, and he wondered if they suspected him of carrying some sort of contagious disease. Then, too exhausted to try and make sense of any of this, Terrel closed his eyes again and let fate take him where it would.

Every time Olandis tried to shorten the line, they lost ground and began to drift back towards the lagoon. Having hooked their catch, they seemed unable to reel him in. And time was growing short.

Eventually, the brothers decided to keep rowing until the raft was well outside the lagoon, then – while Olandis tried to hold their position – Aylen would go back to the stranger and transfer him to his own boat. Although the canoe had been designed for one person, and would ride perilously low in the water with an extra passenger, they knew that this was the only chance for them to help the stranger and for them all to escape.

'Nearly there,' Olandis gasped. 'Ready?'

'Yes. Will you be able to hold him?'

'I'll have to, won't I? But not for long.' The two men were tiring now.

'I'll be as quick as I can.'

'Go, then.'

As Aylen leaned forward to untie the rope, Olandis increased his efforts and managed to keep the craft still. His brother moved fast then, going with the tide to run alongside the stranger's makeshift boat. Untangling the boy from the fishhooks and then dragging his almost life-less body into the canoe was an awkward business, but determination – and his brother's exhortation to hurry – lent Aylen strength. At last, just before they were about to cross the border of Anador, he was able to yell to Olandis to cast the line adrift.

As the cumbersome raft swirled back into the lagoon, on its way out to sea again, Aylen began to row against the current, the crumpled form of the castaway sprawled across his legs.

By the time they reached more placid waters, the brothers were almost exhausted, but their success filled them with a shared sense of triumph, and they knew they were safe enough now. Their camp for the night was not far away, on a flat sandy shelf above the high-tide line, and once there they'd be able to rest and recover. Their passenger's immediate prospects were less certain. He was in a very bad way, clearly dehydrated and barely conscious. His twisted form made him seem even more pitiful.

'Give him some water now,' Olandis said. 'He may not last till we get to camp.'

Aylen nodded and, while his brother held his canoe steady, he unstoppered his flask and held it to the stranger's lips, trying to support his lolling head at the same time. The first few drops trickled down over the boy's chin, but then some dormant reflex took over and his lips parted. Aylen was able to direct the flow into his mouth, and the two men both saw and heard him swallow painfully. A little life seemed to seep into his body with the precious liquid and Aylen smiled, feeling hopeful for the first time. A moment later he cried out and almost dropped the flask, his heart suddenly full of both amazement and fear.

The stranger had opened his eyes to look at his saviour, and Aylen found himself ensnared, looking into their colourless, crystalline depths. He no longer knew whether the crippled boy they had rescued was a miracle or a monster.

CHAPTER THREE

'What is it? What's the matter?'

At the sound of the older brother's voice, the stranger turned his head to look at him – and Olandis saw immediately what had so disconcerted Aylen. The castaway's eyes were extraordinary. Even in the fading sunlight they flashed and glittered like multi-faceted jewels, their only colour coming from brief rainbow flickers as the light moved within them. To Olandis, whose own eyes were a deep brown, there was genius or madness in those orbs – perhaps both. Either way, it was obvious that the dreams behind such eyes would be beyond his comprehension, beyond the grasp of most ordinary men.

'Do you really think he's a sharakan?' he asked, finding himself talking in a whisper.

'I don't know,' his brother replied. 'He hasn't any tattoos.'

'Too young?'

Aylen shrugged.

'Maybe he'll tell us. When he can.'

The stranger's eyes closed again then, and Aylen laid him back down in the canoe. The brothers were both secretly relieved that they no longer had to look into that unnerving gaze.

'Let's get back to camp,' Aylen said. 'We need to get some food into him.'

That night they took it in turns to watch over their patient, while the other slept as best he could. The stranger had been persuaded to take more water, and in fact he had done so eagerly, to the extent that their supplies were now running low. But they hadn't been able to get him to eat anything. The brothers had made their own meal – from fish they'd caught themselves, and hard bread that Ysatel, their stepmother, had packed for them – but neither had had much of an appetite. They were more concerned with the welfare of the boy they had rescued.

His recent ordeal – however it had come about – had obviously taken its toll on him, but it seemed that he'd hardly been in perfect physical health even before that. His right arm was withered, the hand little more than a clenched claw, and his right leg was twisted, the foot bent up at an unnatural angle so that the boot he wore must have been specially made to fit its awkward shape. Unlike the sores on his calves and forearms – which had almost certainly been caused by long exposure to seawater – these deformities evidently dated from a much earlier time.

'An accident, do you think?' Olandis asked quietly, during one of their changes of shift deep in the night.

'I don't know,' Aylen replied. 'I've never seen anything like this before.' Growing up in Fenduca, the brothers had been witness to injuries of all kinds – and seen the often distressing consequences for the victims – but the stranger's skewed form was outside their experience. 'If it was an accident, I guess it must've happened when he was very young.'

'Perhaps he was born like that,' Olandis suggested.

'Perhaps. I'll keep an eye on him now. You get some rest.'

Olandis nodded, but seemed in no hurry to lie down. Instead, he sat beside his brother, watching their patient sleep. Since the rescue the boy had been barely conscious, though his sleep seemed to give him little rest. He frowned often, and his limbs twitched frequently in response to some invisible prompting. Although he mumbled to himself occasionally, the brothers could make no sense of what he said.

'He's dreaming,' Olandis said.

'All the time. But they're not *true* dreams. He can't trade with them.'

'Most of us can't,' the older brother commented sombrely. 'Do you think we should set a prayer-flag?'

Aylen shook his head.

'We don't have the right cloth.'

'I could find something.'

'No. His dreams can take care of themselves. It's his body we have to help now. We'll take him back to Fenduca in the morning. He needs someone with proper healing skills.'

As if to confirm Aylen's diagnosis, the patient gave voice to a rasping cry of pain, no louder than a whisper, but no less agonized for that. At the same time his face contorted into a mask of unutterable misery as his cracked lips parted again, in an elongated hiss that was full of regret and longing.

'A-yssa.'

They had heard him say something similar a few times now, but this was the clearest yet – and the yearning tone was unmistakable. However, the word itself meant nothing to them.

'Could it be someone's name?' Olandis wondered.

Before Aylen had the chance to reply, the stranger began muttering again, his voice husky and deeper this time, but his words still made no sense.

'He's raving,' Olandis said. 'Do you think he's lost his mind?'

'What was that last word?' Aylen asked sharply, ignoring his brother's question.

'Sounded like "badanis". Or "bajanis". Why?'

The castaway was silent again now, apparently lost in a calmer part of his dreaming.

'Could it have been "vadanis"?'

'I suppose so,' Olandis replied, still puzzled.

'I've heard that somewhere before,' Aylen said, his brow creased as he tried to remember.

'It doesn't mean anything to—' Olandis began, but got no further as his brother exclaimed aloud.

'Vadanis! It's from the wanderers' tongue.'

'What does it mean?'

'It's the old name for the Cursed Islands. You know, the ones that move.'

Olandis stared at Aylen in astonishment.

'He can't have come from there,' he said eventually. 'That's insane!'

*

When morning came and Aylen roused Olandis to begin the preparations for their journey home, their patient appeared to be sleeping peacefully. His skin tone was healthier and – with his eyes closed – he looked normal enough, or at least as normal as anyone with his disabilities could look. The brothers' earlier speculation had made them both wary and intrigued. The people of Macul had long believed that the Cursed Islands were either unpopulated or – if it was possible for anyone to survive in such unnatural circumstances – then the islanders must either be madmen or live like wild beasts. It was obvious that no true civilization could exist in a land where you could not even be sure where you were from day to day, and where the entire country must be inherently unstable. If the stranger really *did* come from Vadanis, it might explain his outlandish appearance and his tendency to spout gibberish – but the notion still seemed very far-fetched.

When they had done everything possible to break camp, short of dismantling the tent itself, the brothers looked in on their patient. He woke then, and seemed a little more alert than before. He drank eagerly once more, and was even able to eat a small amount of mashed fish, although swallowing was obviously very difficult and made him wince with the pain. Neither Aylen nor Olandis was able to look him in the eye for long – which seemed to puzzle or disappoint him – but when they tried to talk to him he responded more readily than before.

'Can you speak?' Aylen asked.

The boy's reply was incomprehensible, but his voice, while still hoarse and little more than a whisper, was at least working rather better now. As he spoke he glanced back and forth between his two saviours, as if hoping for some reaction.

'That's not the wanderers' tongue,' Olandis observed.

'No, it isn't,' Aylen agreed. 'So he really is a foreigner.'

Macul was a vast country, and the brothers had never met anyone from beyond its borders.

'Either that or he's crazy.'

'I don't think so. He's trying to talk to us.'

At this, as if to prove the point, the stranger spoke again. Unfortunately, what he said was just as unintelligible as his earlier efforts.

'This is hopeless,' Olandis grumbled.

'Not necessarily,' Aylen replied. Turning back to the castaway, he pointed to his own chest and said clearly, 'Aylen Mirana.'

'What are you doing?' Olandis whispered.

'We've got to start somewhere. Might as well be with our names.' He touched his chest again and repeated his name, then pointed to his brother and said, 'Olandis Mirana.' After that he gestured to the boy and raised his eyebrows in query.

The stranger hesitated, then mimicked the other's action and pointed to himself.

'Terrel.' It came out as a harsh grating sound.

'What did he say?' Olandis asked.

'Sounded like "Terel".'

'Is that his name?'

'I'm not sure. It could be, or it could just mean he's got a pain in his chest.'

'Oh, great. This is getting us nowhere.'

'"Terel" means "moonlight" in the wanderers' tongue, doesn't it?' Aylen asked thoughtfully.

'Don't ask me.'

'Farazin would know.'

'Perhaps he's named after the light in his eyes,' Olandis suggested.

The subject of the speculation merely looked from one to the other, his face a picture of incomprehension.

Terrel lay back in the cramped space in the bows of the canoe, and tried to make sense of this latest turn of events. So much had changed since he'd left the haven, but his present predicament left him more confused than ever before. Knowing that he must have been very close to death, he was immensely grateful to his saviours. Their fresh water and food – even though the tiny portion of fish he'd managed was sitting heavily in his abused stomach – had revived his spirits as well as his body. However, he was still very weak and, although he now felt as though he was going to survive, his increased awareness made the other unknowns of his current position all the more alarming. He felt lost and without hope. Even when he was awake – he still slipped in and out of consciousness – he had no idea where he was. In his more lucid moments, he was sure there could be nowhere like this on Vadanis. That meant the horror of his exile, which he had hoped was only a nightmare, was all too real. The fact that he was unable to communicate with the men who had rescued him was frustrating, and confirmed that he was in a foreign country. A barbarian country. And if that were true, then the land to either side of the river they were travelling along did not move. It stayed where it was, stagnant and prey to untold evils.

It was true that his new companions had not behaved

like barbarians, but he had no way of telling where they were taking him, or what plans they had for him when they reached their destination. When they had helped him into the canoe that morning he had gone reluctantly, but had been unable to resist. Going out on to the water again had set all sorts of horrors loose in his head, but it soon became clear that the two men had no intention of heading out to sea. Instead they were travelling inland, against the flow of the wide river, which ran between clusters of extraordinarily steep-sided, conical hills. The hills reminded Terrel of the 'animals' he had encountered earlier, but these were much larger and the vegetation that clung to their slopes and summits was much more verdant. With a cloudless blue sky giving the calm surface of the water an almost metallic sheen, it was a breath-taking, beautiful landscape – but for Terrel it was a friend-less, alien realm. Everything he had ever loved or cared about was immeasurably far away. The idea that he might ever be able to return to the Floating Islands seemed ridiculous, but that was what he had sworn to do, and somehow he had to try to get back. And unless he made a start by learning something of the land he was now entering, his quest would be over before it began.

He glanced up at the young man whose boat he shared, and saw him look away after a few moments. Terrel was aware that his rescuers were unnerved by his eyes, but he was used to that. Before he'd been taught to use the glamour to disguise them, most people had reacted in a similar way to his 'enchanter's eyes'. Using the glamour now was impossible; his mind was incapable of sum-moning the necessary resolve and belief. Until that moment it hadn't even occurred to him to try, and at this stage it would have been pointless. They had seen the true nature of his eyes, and having them change to blue now would only make matters worse. As a result Terrel resorted to an earlier stratagem that had seemed to lessen their impact, and half closed his lids. Squinting like that did him little good, but it made it easier for others to ignore the strange nature of his irises.

Terrel's earlier 'conversations' had produced almost nothing of use. A few words here and there had seemed vaguely familiar, but he had been unable to grasp their meaning. The one possible step forward had been their exchange of names. At least that was what Terrel supposed it to have been. At the time he'd had to think before remembering his own name, and those of his rescuers had seemed very complicated. Even so, it was the best chance he had of beginning another dialogue. If he was ever to learn anything, he had to start somewhere. Terrel cleared his throat.

'Aylemirana?'

Aylen's eyes widened in surprise and Olandis, who was paddling steadily alongside, glanced at the stranger.

'Yes? That's me.'

Although their patient's response was meaningless, it was at least clear that he was trying to communicate with them. Once again Aylen thought that one or two words seemed familiar, but he could make no overall sense of it.

'I'm sorry,' he said, shaking his head. 'I don't understand.'

The stranger's disappointment was obvious, and he fell silent for a while. Then his expression changed, and it seemed that another idea had occurred to him. His next question consisted of a single word – one the brothers *did* recognize.

'Macul?' As he spoke, he jerked his good hand from side to side, presumably indicating the hills on either shore.

Aylen nodded vigorously.

'Macul. Yes. Macul.' He pointed with his paddle to emphasize his agreement.

'At least he knows where he is,' Olandis commented.

'Seems like it,' Aylen replied. Then, suddenly inspired, he switched his attention back to the boy. 'You. Are you from Vadanis? Va-dan-is?'

His passenger looked up as if the word was indeed familiar, but his expression was unreadable. He tried to reply, only for his tongue to betray him and his voice to creak into silence. A drop of blood ran from the corner of his ravaged mouth and, as his eyes closed again, his head lolled back.

'The sooner we get home the better,' Olandis said.

When Terrel next emerged from the inexplicable images of his still feverish dreams, he found that the canoes were navigating a much smaller river, with both men having to labour to drive their heavily laden craft against the stream. The land about them was less spectacular now, the slopes more manageable and the greenery not so lush.

Fleeting memories disturbed him when he tried to move his tongue and found it parched and swollen once more. He wanted to ask for water, but remembered his last attempt at speech and decided not to try again just yet. He also recalled their most recent attempts at conversation, and the memory made him feel very uneasy. Confirmation that he was indeed in the barbarian land of Macul had come as no real surprise, but dread had risen within him nonetheless. On top of that, his companion's reference to Vadanis had confused and troubled him. What did they know? Were they trying to tell him something?

His rescuers were talking to each other now and, judging from the tone of their voices, they seemed to be relieved about something. Perhaps they were nearing their destination.

With some considerable effort, Terrel twisted round to look ahead. What he saw took his breath away and made him wonder anew about his fate.

Dwarfing everything around it, and with its colour contrasting starkly with its surroundings, the black mountain rose above him like a monster trying to swallow the sky.

Chapter Four

A woman's face drifted out of the mist that seemed to surround Terrel permanently now. He recognized her as one of several people who came to look at him from time to time. He associated her with kindness, with the comfort of a cool damp cloth wiped over his face, or food offered on a crude wooden spoon. The thought of food made bile rise in his throat, but he fought against that, knowing he must eat if he was ever to escape the mist.

'Meha va'ac aloua, Terel?'

She had a gentle voice. She did not shout or grow angry when he could not answer, like some of the others. Her smile, whenever he gave any response, was a reward he sought. But her question was incomprehensible, and it took him a few moments to realize that she had used his name – which sounded strange in her unfamiliar accent. When he did, it made him want to remember hers. Even his recent memories were blurred now and, although he was certain that he knew what she was called, it was a struggle to bring her name to mind. He had heard others talking to her . . . What was it? Her name . . .

His eventual success felt like a triumph.

'Ys-a-tel,' he whispered, stumbling over the alien syllables.

The smile that replaced her concerned expression lit up her face. She said something that he did not understand, then held up a small wooden cup so that he could see it.

'Aloua?'

Since Terrel had been in the village, he had learnt a few words of his hosts' language, almost without realizing it. 'Aloua' meant water, and he tried to nod to indicate that he would like some. He had no idea how long he had been lying in the hut. It sometimes seemed as though he had only just arrived; at other times he seemed to have been there for ever. But no matter how long it had been, he was almost always thirsty, even now.

For all his efforts his head hardly moved, but Ysatel had obviously seen enough to know what he wanted. She held the cup to his lips and tipped it back and forth, allowing him to take a small mouthful and then swallow several times, rather than gulping it down. The water was brown in colour, and its oddly metallic taste had made Terrel gag at first, but he was used to it now, and grateful for the way it revived his spirits each time he drank.

After he'd finished a second cupful, Ysatel offered him some soup, and he forced himself to accept a few mouthfuls before he had to stop. His stomach had rebelled too many times to allow him to continue. The food he'd been given had been mostly plain fare, but to his ravaged senses it often tasted and smelled very strange. Even so, he was in no position to complain. Such nourishment was keeping him alive, and the fact that on several occasions he had been unable to keep his meals down had made him feel ashamed of his ungrateful stomach, as well as being a setback to whatever chance he had of recovering from his illness.

Ysatel looked disappointed when he refused to eat any more, but knew better than to try to force food upon him. She left him – after wiping his face and saying a few words that he did not understand but whose tone was comforting – and Terrel lay still, fighting off the approach of nausea by concentrating on the things he could see and hear.

His world had shrunk to this one room. It was a dark place, with the only light coming from the doorway of the adjoining room during the day or from a sparingly used candle at dusk. The air smelled permanently of damp wood and earth, and it was cold most of the time now that winter had arrived. During the long night the hut's larger room was quite crowded, with several people sleeping there, but in the hours of daylight it was often quiet and empty – although someone usually came to check on him at regular intervals.

At that moment, as far as he could tell, Ysatel was the only other person there, and – judging by the odours of wood smoke and cooking that drifted in through the door – she was preparing a meal for some of the others. Terrel could not see her, but was able to listen to her movements; to the clank of a ladle against the sides of a metal cauldron and the crackle of the fire. At the same time he recognized the sound of running water coming from outside, something that was always there, a constant

backdrop to life in the village. In the distance he could
hear dogs barking and men's voices calling to one another
– and this brought other shadowy memories floating to
the surface of his mind.

Since his arrival Terrel had occasionally been carried
outside the hut, and his brief glimpses of the village had
revealed a squalid shantytown of ramshackle buildings,
clinging to the lowest slopes of the great black mountain.
Above the huts, the river that ran down from the intimidating peak split into many small branches – cascading
over the bare rocks as dark foam and dancing in hundreds
of small pools. The water was so full of silt that where it
was relatively still it appeared almost black. The river
seemed to be the centre of a good deal of activity, and
the houses were built mostly to either side of the extended
waterfall, though a few actually stood in between the
various streams. From his brief observations Terrel could
not understand what the villagers did, nor why they had
chosen to live in such an apparently inhospitable location.
It was a place of poverty, of dirt and danger, where life
evidently held few pleasures and no luxuries. The bare
room in which he lay was testament to that. And yet he
had been taken in and cared for. A foreigner, whose
appearance could hardly have been reassuring and who
could not even speak their language, had been rescued
and brought to their home. He had been fed, bathed –
and even clothed. At some unknown point Terrel's own
garments had been replaced by a simple shift of a coarse
grey material. His only other possessions – his boots and
Muzeni's clay pipe – lay beside the narrow pallet where
he now rested. He was at the mercy of strangers, helplessly reliant on their charity and compassion, and needing

their help for even the most basic tasks. It could have been humiliating, but for the most part Terrel simply felt grateful. He knew he must be a considerable burden to Ysatel and her family, and he couldn't work out why they were being so good to him. The contrast between their treatment of him – especially as they had seen the true nature of his eyes – and that of the people of his own homeland, most of whom had reacted with horror or enmity, was as mystifying as it was welcome.

The light outside the hut was beginning to fade now and, grateful for the fact that his stomach seemed to have settled, Terrel allowed himself to drift back into sleep.

Ysatel looked up from her cooking, and smiled fondly when she saw her husband walking towards her. She had been Kerin's wife for almost five years now, but his daily return to their home still had the power to raise in her a mixture of desire, pride and protectiveness that sometimes threatened to overwhelm her. He was an almost legendary figure among the inhabitants of Fenduca, a village 'elder' even though he was little more than forty years old, and Ysatel had been in love with him for as long as she could remember. She also knew that although he loved her dearly, she could never entirely overcome the memories of Aryel, his first wife and the mother of his sons. The fact that Aryel had been dead for twelve years had allowed Kerin's feelings of grief and guilt to fade from view, but they were still there, hidden deep. Ysatel knew she could never erase the past – nor would she want to – but she also knew that she brought Kerin great happiness.

Her pleasure at the approach of her husband was

diminished slightly when she recognized the man who walked stiffly at his side. Farazin Lanta was the village sky-watcher, their interpreter of dreams, and as such he was held in awe by many, and commanded the respect of his fellow elders. To her shame, Ysatel often found him both pompous and dull, and on this occasion she knew that his presence would mean another long and pointless discussion about the strange boy who now lay in their house, dreaming his even stranger dreams. His arrival in the village had caused much consternation, and the debate over whether he was a sharakan or a sorcerer – or whether any foreigner *could* be a sharakan – had raged for some time. Interest was waning now that he'd been there for almost a short month, and he had received few visitors during the last day or two. The exception was Farazin who, naturally enough, was the person most people looked to to solve the mystery and decide the boy's fate.

Ysatel rose to her feet to embrace Kerin. He smelled, as always, of the river, and he was cold. He kissed her and smiled wearily, then sat down to warm himself by the fire.

'Won't you join us, Farazin?' Ysatel offered. 'There's more than enough.'

'Thank you,' the sky-watcher replied, accepting the invitation as his due. He too sat down, wincing slightly as his old joints protested.

'Is there any change in the boy?' Kerin asked.

'He took a little more soup today,' Ysatel replied, as she went back to stirring the cauldron. 'And he's not been sick. But the fever's still in his eyes.'

Although the stranger had seemed to be on his way to recovery after he'd been brought to Fenduca, he had then suffered a relapse, and had been sliding in and out of consciousness ever since. It had seemed to Ysatel that the boy was suffering from more than just his physical ailments – although they were bad enough – and she suspected too that he felt lost and without hope. He often appeared happier and more animated when he was dreaming than when he was awake, but he'd occasionally had nightmares too. Some had obviously been terrifying, judging from the unearthly noises he made – noises that had awoken the entire household.

'His dreams have no way of release,' Farazin opined, 'so they turn inwards as fever.'

That seemed too simplistic an explanation to Ysatel, but she was not prepared to argue the point.

'He will be well eventually,' Kerin said. 'He's in good hands.' He smiled at his wife. 'Then we'll learn the truth.'

'Has he said anything else of interest?' Farazin asked.

Ysatel shook her head.

'Nothing I can make sense of.'

In the past, some of what the invalid had said had sounded like the wanderers' tongue, but as Farazin was the only villager reasonably fluent in that ancient language, the others had only been able to guess at occasional words. When the sky-watcher had tried speaking to the boy, using the archaic form of address, there had seemed to be a few sparks of recognition in his face, but neither had been able to make the other understand what they were saying.

'Is he sleeping now?'

Ysatel nodded.

'Then I will wait and see if he wakes up after we have eaten,' Farazin decided.

Ysatel turned to her husband, wanting to change the subject.

'Did you have any luck today?'

'A few pebbles,' he replied dismissively. 'Nothing of real interest.' It was his usual answer. Good days were increasingly rare now.

'Will the boys be home soon?'

'They're on their way.'

Even as he spoke, Ysatel caught sight of her stepsons. Aylen, apparently oblivious to the danger, was skipping over some wet boulders towards the path. He led a charmed life – his due-name of Chute had been earned during a childhood escapade, when he'd survived a fall into one of the most precipitous parts of the river – but his antics still left Ysatel breathless with worry sometimes. Olandis, as always, followed in more sedate fashion, a steady carthorse to his brother's unruly colt. The curious thing was that their mental characteristics were the opposite way round. Aylen was the brighter of the two, but his opinions were stronger and more cautious. For his part, Olandis often acted on instinct, using his heart rather than his brain, and Ysatel loved him all the more for it. The fact that it had been Olandis who had wanted to rescue the foreigner, and that it had been Aylen who had worked out a way to do it without breaking the dictates of moon-lore, was typical of the brothers' relationship. They were very different, but their skills and temperaments complemented each other – and they were inseparable.

The very fact that they had retrieved the boy from forbidden territory had been one of the things that had made the dispute about him so vehement. Some of the villagers thought he should have been left to fend for himself, to face the consequences of his foolish actions, but Kerin had steadfastly defended his sons' actions, arguing that to abandon anyone in such circumstances would have been an act of inhumanity. Nonetheless, as time dragged on and Terel – if that really was his name – failed to recover his health, doubts had begun to grow in his mind too. His faith in his wife's nursing abilities had not wavered, but he had begun to wonder if the boy was truly beyond help. However, he was not about to express such thoughts openly – especially when people like Cutter might get wind of his change of heart and start making trouble again.

'Will the Red Moon be full tonight?' Kerin asked, changing the subject himself this time. Ordinarily it would have been a statement rather than a question – like every other Maculian, Kerin was aware of and respected the movements of the heavens – but a few of Farazin's recent declarations had raised some doubts.

'It will,' the sky-watcher replied firmly. 'It is only the Dark Moon that's behaving oddly.'

'Why is that?' Ysatel asked. 'What do you think it means?'

'Observation and prayer will answer that in due course,' Farazin replied. His condescending tone made it clear that he thought that Ysatel – a mere woman – should not be concerned with such matters. She was about to respond, wishing that for once he could simply have said 'I don't know', when she caught the warning look from her husband and remained silent.

'So flags will be set at the shrine as usual?' Kerin said.

'At first light tomorrow,' Farazin confirmed. 'They are already prepared.'

'Did you include any pleas on behalf of the stranger?' Aylen asked. He had caught the tail end of the conversation as he joined the group. As he spoke he threw himself down by the fire, leaving Olandis to go into the house and store their tools.

'The Red Moon is not appropriate for healing,' Farazin said.

'You think love can't heal?' Ysatel asked before she could stop herself.

The sky-watcher gave her a measuring glance.

'In itself, no,' he said.

'Is he still asleep?' Aylen asked as his brother emerged from the cabin.

'Like a baby.'

'Not dreaming then?'

'Not as far as I can tell.'

'Let's eat,' Ysatel said, grateful to her stepsons for diverting attention from her provocative comment.

As she began ladling out the fish stew and passing the bowls around, she became aware of another man approaching and wondered, with a sinking heart, what Cutter might want. One thing was certain; with these extra guests there was little chance of a quiet and pleasant family meal.

Mitus Levien, known to the villagers as Cutter, was of average height, but his broad shoulders, thick neck and large hands gave the impression of size as well as strength. His face appeared to be made of slabs of granite, from which his close-set eyes glared out in a permanent scowl. The impression of menace was reinforced by the dog that loped at his side, a squat, ill-tempered beast called Scar.

The newcomer nodded to Kerin and Farazin in

greeting, all but ignoring Ysatel and the younger men, but he did not speak at first.

'Will you join us, Cutter?' Ysatel asked. The invitation was a formality. The community's survival depended upon a degree of cooperation, and sharing food when it was plentiful was an expected form of hospitality. However, Mitus prided himself on his independence – some said he thought himself above mere screenhandlers – and Ysatel did not think he would accept her offer.

'No,' he replied, as expected. 'Thank you.' The civil response sounded like an afterthought.

'Are you sure? There's—'

'You have enough visitors already,' Cutter said pointedly.

The ensuing silence dragged on.

'We've found nothing worthy of your services today,' Kerin said eventually, glancing at his sons for confirmation. 'A few pebbles, nothing more.'

Cutter nodded, absently patting the jewel-pouch that hung from a strap over his shoulder.

'Then I wish you better fortune tomorrow,' he said.

Scar had sat down at his master's feet, and neither man nor dog showed any sign of moving in spite of Kerin's hints.

'Have you news for us?' Farazin asked.

'The Nemenz girl's come down with a fever.'

'I will visit her.'

'Some people are saying she caught it from the foreigner,' Cutter added.

Ysatel wondered just who 'some people' were, but kept her own council and allowed her husband to answer.

'I doubt that,' Kerin commented mildly. 'He's hardly

been out of our cabin, and certainly nowhere near her house.'

'Contagion follows its own paths,' Cutter responded.

'Then why have none of *us* been affected?' Kerin countered. 'All such paths must begin here, so surely we are the more likely targets.'

'His fever comes from being too long without water,' Ysatel added, unable to stay quiet any longer. 'That can't be the case with Liliana, can it?' She had spoken in a reasonable tone, but Kerin could hear the anger beneath her words and reached out to put his hand over hers.

'Evil spreads in strange ways,' Cutter said, glaring at Ysatel, then turning his attention to Farazin. 'Don't you think we should bring the matter before a gathering?'

'Again?' Ysatel exclaimed, but fell silent at the warning pressure from Kerin's hand.

'I will examine the boy once more tonight,' the sky-watcher replied. 'I'll decide what is necessary then.'

Mitus seemed about to say something more, but evidently thought better of it. He turned abruptly and strode away, and Scar jumped up to follow his master.

'That man's an idiot,' Olandis remarked when Cutter was well out of earshot.

'Hardly that,' Kerin replied. 'I don't like him any more than you do, but at least he has the courage to say to our faces what others may be saying behind our backs.'

'But it's nonsense!' Ysatel cried.

'Of course. But not everyone is as observant or as clever as you, my love. And you know what this place is like for rumours.'

'And like it or not,' Aylen put in, 'Cutter's word carries a lot of weight with some people.'

'Don't worry, Ysy,' Olandis added, 'we won't let them do anything stupid.'

Kerin and his sons were the only ones Ysatel allowed to use the familiar shortened version of her name, and the boys did so often now, as a way of showing their affection for her. Between them, her three men – as she often thought of them – had managed to placate her a little, but the fifth member of the party saw no reason even to try.

'We don't want unrest,' Farazin muttered. 'Perhaps another gathering would clear the air.'

'You really think that's necessary?' Kerin asked, before his wife could say anything.

'Would you rather men like Cutter spread their ideas by stealth?'

Farazin had a point, and for the rest of the meal no one tried to dissuade him from the path he had chosen.

When they had all eaten their fill, the sky-watcher rose stiffly and went into the cabin. Ysatel wanted to follow, but knew better than to do so. He would want to examine the patient alone. She contented herself with leaning against Kerin, sharing his warmth as the fire burnt down to embers and his sons cleared up after the meal. The sound of Farazin's voice drifted softly from inside their home.

The stranger was sleeping and, although Farazin would never have admitted it to anyone, he was glad not to have to look into those peculiar eyes. The boy was breathing slowly and evenly, and gave no sign of dreaming. He was still painfully thin, but his earlier pallor was gone and his face no longer bore the lines of constant pain.

'Well, young man, there's not much you can tell me in that state, is there.'

In spite of his words, the sky-watcher made no move to wake the foreigner, unwilling to disturb his apparently peaceful rest.

'So what am I supposed to say to the gathering, eh?' Farazin went on quietly. 'You don't look much of a danger to anyone, but Mitus was right about one thing. Evil can spread in mysterious ways. So what is it that you are? A sick child? An outcast? Or a demon? The moons tell me nothing.'

The old man turned his eyes upwards, as if he could look through the roof to the stars above, and did not notice the stranger's eyelids flicker as he awoke.

'Are you a sharakan?' Farazin asked, speaking as much to himself as to the boy on the bed.

'Enda va'an sharakan?'

The words sounded indistinct to Terrel, so that at first he was unable to decide if they had been part of a dream or not. As he struggled towards wakefulness, he saw the outline of a figure standing over him, and recognized the stooped shoulders and the mane of grey hair. This was the one whose speech was sometimes different from the others. Terrel could not understand why this should be so, and what he heard still made no sense, but some of the old man's words seemed vaguely familiar – as if their meaning was just out of reach.

On this occasion, Terrel had no idea what he was talking about, but one of his rescuers had said something similar soon after they had pulled him from the lagoon, and it had been repeated several times since. It was frustrating that he had no way of answering what they clearly regarded as an important question. He wanted to try to communicate, but his voice would not come – and before he was able to attract the old man's attention, he turned and shuffled from the room, leaving Terrel alone with his thoughts once more.

In some ways his visitor reminded him of Shahan, and he wondered whether he might be a seer – and then he wondered if he would ever see the ghosts again. This was a dangerous line of thought, and he pushed it aside hurriedly and deliberately began to think about the other people he'd come to recognize during his enforced idleness.

There was Ysatel, of course. His two rescuers, Aylemirana and the other one. And an older man, who might be their father. He had seen several other faces too, but none of them often, so he'd had no chance to work out who they were or how they fitted into the household. Even with those people he'd seen frequently, he was often confused. As soon as he thought he'd begun to sort them out, he found they'd apparently been called by quite different names. In the end he had given up any attempt to learn their names – except for Ysatel, his most constant companion – and had decided to let fate decide what he learnt of the others.

He heard movement then as preparations for the night were made, but darkness was falling quickly and he recognized none of the shadowy figures. Giving up his fruitless attempts to get his voice to work, he allowed himself to slide back into the oblivion of sleep.

That night Terrel dreamt of Tindaya, where he had witnessed his own death and, for the first time, he laughed in response. What chance was there that he would ever be able to return to Vadanis, let alone to the sacred mountain? His exile meant that he would cheat fate.

He awoke the next morning to the sound of voices. That in itself was not unusual. He had often been aware of people around him, both inside his room and further away. Sometimes their conversations had sounded reasoned and respectful, while others had been fierce arguments – and this had often made him feel very uncomfortable because he wondered if he was the cause of the disagreements. However, this time there seemed to be a large number of people – many of whom were talking or shouting over each other – and it was clear, even without understanding a word that was being said, that tempers were running high.

Terrel was beginning to feel afraid when another sensation, one that came from deep inside his own being, banished all other considerations from his mind. The trembling impulse drove him to throw off his blanket and lurch from the pallet. It was the first time he had risen without help since his arrival, and the movement set his head spinning, but he was obstinately fixed upon his purpose, and desperation lent him strength. Staggering on uncertain legs, he made his way, unseeing, towards the light.

A sudden silence fell as he released his hold on the doorframe and stumbled out into the sunshine, and he looked up to see a great crowd of people all staring at him.

'There's going to be an earthquake!' he cried hoarsely, waving his arms. 'An earthquake!'

His audience seemed frozen as they stared back at him, a mixture of surprise and incomprehension in their eyes.

'Please, you've got to—'

The desperate certainty that had overridden Terrel's infirmity crumbled into dust then as his strength gave out altogether, and he fell to the ground in a heap. He was unconscious even as the first tremor hit.

CHAPTER FIVE

The impact of the earthquake was too sudden and too disorientating for the villagers to react with anything other than panic. Screams filled the air, and there were ominous noises from the earth itself as soil and rock shifted beneath their feet. Many people were thrown to the ground, unbalanced as much by shock as by the vibrations. Some looked up at the black mountain, afraid of an avalanche that might destroy the entire village, but although there were several landslides they were all relatively minor. Even so, the crashing of rock as it disintegrated and fell was terrifying, more immediately threatening than the growl that came from deep underground as Nydus shrugged and rearranged its surface once again. The river spat and boiled, with spouts of water leaping into the air at impossible angles. The wooden structures of the village's homes creaked and groaned, and a few of the huts began to sway violently as they were caught in the reverberations of the tremor, until their timbers distorted beyond endurance and collapsed or flew apart. Caught in the grip of forces they recognized well enough but had no hope of controlling, the people of Fenduca could only tremble and pray and wait for it to end. It seemed to them that, far away and pale in the morning sky, the Amber Moon was shaking too.

In all, the quake lasted only a few moments, but its repercussions were to last much longer. Even after the land had stopped moving, the river still ran erratically, with sudden surges flowing down from above for no apparent reason, and streams forging new courses.

Such tremors were common enough in most regions of Macul, but there was usually some warning. Almost all were triggered – or at least influenced – by lunar configurations, so the sky-watchers were able to predict when they were most likely to occur. In addition, the villagers in Fenduca kept a small number of wolf-fish in one of the rock pools, and observed them closely at regular intervals – especially when the moons were aligned unfavourably. For several hours before an earthquake, these fish became abnormally agitated, and when this happened the villagers took what precautions they could. Fenduca's position beneath the precipitous slopes of the mountain, and so close to the inherently unstable river bed, made it particularly vulnerable to the impact of tremors. Nevertheless, the villagers accepted the risks as an integral part of their way of life and, when they were given some idea of what was coming, they were accustomed to dealing with such disruptions. On this occasion, however, the onslaught had come out of the blue, leaving them unprepared and doubly disorientated.

In retrospect it was fortunate that most of Fenduca's

inhabitants had been part of the impromptu gathering outside the Mirana cabin. At that time of the morning many people would usually have been at work in the river, and the fact that they had been crowded together on what was a relatively stable part of the terrain had probably saved many lives. As it was, the number of casualties was still distressing. Two men, who had left the shrine as soon as the flag ceremony was over in order to claim the best spots in the river, were dead – one drowned, the other dashed against rocks by a sudden deluge of water. Another was missing, his body almost certainly buried beneath one of the landslides. In addition, four homes had been completely destroyed, two crushed by falling rock and two washed away by torrents of diverted water. Three of these homes had been unoccupied, but the fourth – belonging to the Nemenz family – was not. Liliana had been unable to attend the ritual at the Red Moon's shrine because of her fever, and her mother had stayed behind to nurse her. They had both been carried away and drowned when a natural dam higher up the mountain-side had given way, and Liliana's father had been badly injured during his desperate and hopeless attempts to save them. Solan now lay in a neighbour's hut, with both legs broken and one of his hands crushed beyond repair – tormented not only by his own injuries but also by the loss of his family. And he was far from the only one needing the ministrations of friends. Many others had been injured or made homeless by the quake. Although the tremor had been mild compared to others that Fenduca had endured, its timing had left the villagers shaken and afraid.

In the immediate aftermath of the upheaval, there had

been too much to do for any other considerations to be
taken into account. However, once the most pressing
needs had been seen to and a semblance of calm had
returned, the mood began to change.

Terrel's unexpected excursion had left him weak and
feverish, and he spent much of the day fading in and out
of consciousness, plagued by dream visions. When he
awoke he was back in his room, alone. He remembered
his premonition but nothing of the quake itself – and was
desperate to know whether his warning had been heeded.
However, beyond the self-evident fact that Ysatel's home
was still standing, he had no way of telling what had
happened – and as no one came to see him, he could not
even attempt to find out.

A mixture of memories and foreboding mingled with
nightmare images in his overburdened brain, but he
slowly managed to separate fact from fiction, and was
gradually able to think a little more clearly. Even though
he did not remember the tremor, he was sure that one
had taken place. Quite how he was able to make these
predictions had always been a mystery to him, but it had
happened too many times now for him to doubt his peculiar talent. The certainty simply arrived in his mind un-
bidden, transmitted as an internal trembling deep inside
him. He had learnt to trust his instincts, and had used
them to good effect in the past – and now he could only
hope that his efforts had been of some benefit to his new
companions.

Time passed, and still no one came to see him. Terrel
slept again – dreamlessly for once – and woke feeling
rested and refreshed. He was still alone, but a small thrill

of happiness lightened his usual misery. Physically, he felt better than he had done since he'd been cast adrift from Vadanis, and – for the first time in exile – he was able to entertain a little hope. It was as if being able to warn his hosts about the impending danger had awoken in him an inner strength he'd forgotten he possessed. That in turn was giving him a renewed sense of purpose, reinforcing his belief that it might still be good to be alive.

He almost forced himself to get up, but thought better of it, remembering his earlier collapse and deciding to wait until someone could help him. He lay back, hoping that Ysatel – or one of the others – would visit him soon, and in spite of fully intending to stay awake until they did, he fell asleep again.

'We've taken a viper into our midst!' Cutter declared.

'This is no viper,' Kerin retorted. 'Look at him!' He pointed to where Terrel sat on a blanket, watching the proceedings through half closed eyes, his whole body tense. The boy had still been asleep when, at Cutter's insistence, he had been carried out of the hut to face his accusers, but the noise of the arguments had woken him. He had glanced around, looking at the audience with a mixture of apprehension and uncertainty that had since changed to fear. Although he looked harmless enough, most of the villagers had glimpsed his eyes, and knew that there was something odd about him.

'How can he be a threat to anybody?' Kerin challenged.

Terrel was obviously still very weak. Even his good arm was thin and wasted, and his face was gaunt, with dark shadows beneath his eyes.

'Sorcery doesn't require physical strength,' Mitus countered.

The villagers' discussion had now been left to the two men whose views were most directly opposed to each other. The rest had either had their say already or were content to leave the debate to the two spokesmen.

The earlier meeting had been brought to a sudden halt by the stranger's unexpected and incomprehensible announcement, and by the turmoil caused by the earthquake, but it was inevitable that the arguments about him would be raised again at this later, formal gathering. Once again, at Farazin's decree, the inhabitants of Fenduca had come together outside Kerin's house, in order to discuss matters that concerned everybody – and which, after the events of the day, had taken on an increased urgency. Theoretically, only the elders were supposed to speak at such a gathering, with anyone else who wished to make their views known doing so through one of their representatives. In practice, Farazin had let everyone have their say. The two main protagonists now faced each other across the open space where the boy sat.

'This is a child,' Kerin stated. 'A sick child. Will taking revenge on a defenceless innocent reverse any of our losses?'

'How can you say he's innocent?' Cutter demanded. 'Ever since he arrived here it's been one thing after another. Our children have been exposed to alien fevers. There have been more accidents in the river. We've had nothing but poor finds in spite of the winter rains. And how can you deny what happened today?'

'That was an act of nature—'

'If it was a natural event, then why wasn't Farazin able to predict it?' Mitus cut in.

'The moons are not the only factor in—' the sky-watcher began, but Cutter was in full flow now, and overrode him easily.

'Who but a sorcerer could survive in the forbidden waters of Anador?' he asked. 'Who but a sorcerer would speak in such a barbarous tongue? And who but a sorcerer could conjure forth an earthquake to save himself from our vengeance, and kill the girl he had infected?'

'He conjured nothing,' Kerin insisted, but he could feel that the majority of the onlookers had begun to side with his opponent.

'You all saw him!' Cutter cried, appealing to the crowd. 'Waving his arms and yelling in that evil tongue. What else could he have been doing?'

'He could have been trying to warn us,' Ysatel said. That had been her belief right from the start, and it persisted – even though she could prove nothing and, even though on the face of it the idea seemed absurd.

'Ah, so he's a wolf-fish now, is he?' Cutter remarked scornfully, provoking laughter and a few cries of derision. 'If he knew the tremor was coming, then it proves he's a sorcerer – and makes it all the more likely that he was the cause of it too.' He seemed quite happy with this circular argument, and fell silent for the moment.

Knowing that she should not have spoken, Ysatel glanced at her husband, hoping that he would support her even so. Kerin would not look at her, but kept his gaze fixed upon Cutter, his expression grave. Neither man was willing to give ground, but no one else was prepared to enter the argument at this stage, and so the silence dragged on.

It was eventually broken by the subject of their debate himself.

The boy spoke quietly, in a rasping voice, and to an unbiased ear his tone would have seemed anything but threatening. In fact, to Ysatel it sounded more like a plea for understanding, but many of those present reacted with fear, seeming to think that he was casting another spell. The seeds of doubt sown by Cutter had taken root.

'Shut him up!' Mitus shouted. 'Or I'll get Scar to do it permanently.'

At the sound of his name, the dog rose from his haunches and growled, his small black eyes fixed upon the stranger. In response, two people moved forward into the arena. Ysatel went to kneel beside the boy, putting a finger to her lips to motion him to silence. He looked at her in bemusement, but obeyed. The second person was Olandis, who strode forward, shaking off his father's attempt to restrain him, and glared at Cutter.

'You would set a dog on a defenceless child?' he said accusingly, his rage and scorn obvious to all.

'He may not be so defenceless,' Cutter replied. 'And if Scar has to tear your throat out to get to his, then he'll do it.'

'Go ahead then, let him try,' Olandis said, drawing a knife from his belt.

The dog had taken a couple of paces forward, without any order being given. He snarled, baring predator's teeth, and switched his attention to his master's latest foe.

'You're no match for—' Cutter began, smiling nastily.

'Enough!' The sky-watcher's usually frail voice was raised to a roar of outrage that shocked everyone there into silence. 'This has gone far enough,' Farazin went on. 'There is no need for violence. We simply have to decide what should be done with the boy.'

'For myself,' Cutter responded immediately, 'I'd like to see him dead, but failing that, let him be cast back into the tainted waters he came from. He's not wanted here.'

There were mutterings of agreement from some of the onlookers, until Kerin looked around, shaming them into silence.

'Nothing need be done,' he said. 'The boy will stay with me. I'll take responsibility for him.'

'Then you take responsibility for the next disaster too!' Cutter declared. 'The next deaths!'

'They were no more his fault than yours,' Kerin responded.

'Enough!' Farazin admonished them again, then turned to look over the entire group. 'You've heard the options. Are you content to let the elders decide our course, or is it to be put to a vote of all the people?'

For a few moments no one spoke, then Kerin stepped forward to stand next to Olandis.

'I will accept neither,' he stated bluntly. 'I will not condone murder, regardless of who votes on it. If you won't allow the boy to stay, then I'll take him away. My family will leave Fenduca.'

Still kneeling beside her patient, Ysatel felt her heart swell. She was not aware that Aylen was now standing beside her until he put a gentle hand on her shoulder. They were together in this.

The resentful muttering that had been provoked by Kerin's first denial had changed character when he threatened to leave the village. He was the settlement's founder, the first man to have set foot on the black mountain after it had emerged from the depths of the planet, and the first to defend the rights of the people of Fenduca when

the upper slopes had been cordoned off. As such he was
a hero to many, a talismanic figure, and almost everyone
there would feel diminished by his absence. The fact that
he felt strongly enough to defy the elders and to make
such a threat, to condemn his own family to exile for the
sake of the foreigner, swayed many of those around him
– as he had hoped it would. Unfortunately, the only effect
upon Cutter was to make him even more belligerent.

'You would deny the elders, the rest of our village?'
he exclaimed. 'Such arrogance is beyond belief.'

'No vote has yet been taken,' Kerin pointed out calmly.

'There can be no vote!' Cutter shouted. 'You've seen
to that. Now there can be only justice.' Before anyone
could react, he hissed a command to his dog and pointed
to the stranger.

Scar leapt forward, his bared fangs and a low-throated
growl announcing his attack. Olandis, who had sheathed
his blade again when his father came up beside him, was
the only one close enough to get between the dog and his
prey, and he threw himself into the hound's path. The
two of them went down in a snarling heap as Ysatel
screamed. Scar's fearsome teeth ripped a long tear in
Olandis's forearm, and the dog easily broke from his
grasp. As the young man lay bleeding on the ground, Scar
bounded on, ready for his next victim. Ysatel tried to
shield the boy but was dragged away, protesting, by
Aylen, who knew his stepmother was no match for such
bestial fury. Everyone else was frozen in horror.

The stranger did not seem to understand the danger
he was in, for he made no move to defend himself, and
the outcome seemed inevitable. Scar pounced, landing
heavily on the boy's chest and shoving him to the ground.

Murderous jaws closed on his exposed neck as Cutter crowed in triumph, and many looked away, not wanting to witness the carnage.

It was a few moments before anyone realized what was happening – and when they did they were stunned into silent amazement. Far from tearing out the foreigner's throat, Scar was licking his face happily, while the boy himself was laughing, his expression one of pure joy.

CHAPTER SIX

If I'd known you'd crossed the moat, I'd've looked outside the palace sooner.

The words sounded silently in Terrel's head. As was often the case, Alyssa's initial statement was enigmatic to say the least, but he did not mind at all. Just hearing her voice was enough.

Alyssa! he exclaimed, laughing.

You taste odd, she remarked.

I thought I'd never see you again.

You're not exactly seeing me, are you? Just this brute I've borrowed.

You know what I mean.

The dog stopped licking Terrel's face then, and raised its head to look around. Its forepaws were still planted heavily on his chest.

What's going on?

I don't really know, Terrel replied.

For the past few moments he had been oblivious to

what was happening around him, knowing only that – against all the odds – Alyssa had found him again. Now, as he joined her in looking at the frozen scene, he tried to make what sense he could of it. When he had woken and found himself outside, once more the focus of attention of a large number of people, he'd thought at first that he'd returned to the same gathering. Then he had realized it was now late afternoon, not morning, and recalled his time alone in the hut. He'd remembered trying to warn them about the tremor and, glancing about him, had seen the signs of the destruction that had evidently followed. It was no wonder that the mood of the villagers seemed to be one of anger and dismay, but he hadn't been able to work out why some of their hostile feelings seemed to be directed towards him. Far from being grateful that he'd tried to raise the alarm, it seemed as if he were being blamed for something. Feeling disillusioned, Terrel had tried to explain, but his words had been met with only blank incomprehension – and some onlookers had even flinched, as though they were afraid of him.

Then there had been some sort of confrontation, and the dog had attacked one of Terrel's rescuers before turning its attention to the boy himself. He had been too stunned to be afraid, and then – miraculously – Alyssa had been standing over him, her special madness glinting in the dog's eyes.

He was about to try to explain all this to her when she turned away to face the large man who had been the most vociferous and antagonistic of all. He held a dagger in his hand now, and was bearing down upon Terrel with murderous intent in his eyes.

I don't like the look of him, Alyssa said quietly. She fixed the would-be attacker with her black gaze and growled.

The man came to a halt, his expression changing from one of fury to incredulity. He said something Terrel could not understand and Alyssa barked in response, moving forward a little and baring her fangs to make her intention even more plain.

This one I know about, she told Terrel. *For the rest you'd better tell me which are friends and which are foes.*

He's the only one you need worry about, he replied. *Keep him away and the rest will take care of itself.*

Cutter's disbelief was turning back to rage again. To be thwarted by his own dog was not only incredible, it was humiliating.

'What's got into you, Scar? Get out of my way.'

The creature's only reaction was to snarl again and edge forward slightly.

'Kill him!' Cutter repeated, pointing at the foreigner. 'Kill!'

The hound ignored the command and stood its ground.

When Cutter had drawn his knife and stepped into the arena, some of those nearby had made half-hearted attempts to restrain him. He had shrugged them aside, only to be faced with more determined opposition from his own dog. The onlookers made no further attempts to intervene, and watched the stand-off between Scar and his master in amazement.

'Then get away and let me do the job myself!' Cutter shouted, slicing the air with his dagger.

The hound did not move, but growled again, and

Cutter reluctantly took a step back, admitting defeat. The look on his face defied description.

'He's put a spell on the dog,' he declared abruptly. 'This is proof he's a sorcerer!'

'It's proof your dog has better sense than you do,' Ysatel retorted. 'He can see there's no harm in the boy.' She shrugged off Aylen's grasp and went to tend to Olandis, who was still sitting on the ground, clutching his wounded arm.

'Put your blade away, Mitus,' Farazin commanded. 'There's been enough bloodshed already.'

'This is madness!' Cutter yelled. 'The boy's a sorcerer. What other explanation is there for my own dog to turn against me?'

No one had an answer to that. Even Ysatel remained silent, looking up from her stepson to glance at the dog.

'Even if he is,' Farazin replied eventually, 'he's caused no harm here. All he has done is protect himself.'

'But the quake—'

'You've no proof that was anything to do with him,' Kerin interrupted. 'None at all.'

'Put your knife away,' Farazin repeated. 'Kerin, on behalf of the elders, I accept your offer of responsibility for the boy, for tonight at least. We will meet again in due course, but this gathering is over.'

Some of the crowd muttered at this, and Cutter looked as if he were going to voice his outrage, but eventually thought better of it. Sheathing his dagger, he turned and marched away, soon followed by most of the other villagers as they began to return to their own homes. The dog trotted back to sit peaceably beside the stranger, while Aylen joined Ysatel and helped his brother to his feet.

'We must bandage that,' Ysatel said. 'Aylen, put some water on to boil.' As she spoke, she glanced at her husband, with a small smile that said, 'Don't worry, he'll be all right.'

Kerin nodded gratefully, knowing that his son was in good hands, and went to speak to Farazin.

'Thank you,' he said quietly.

'You may not thank me if he really *is* a sorcerer,' the sky-watcher replied.

'I'll take my chances on that.'

'You know this isn't the end of the matter? Cutter's not going to let it rest now.'

'I know,' Kerin said heavily, 'but at least it gives us some time to consider.'

'Did you mean it? About leaving the village?'

'I don't say things I don't mean,' Kerin answered. 'But I hope it doesn't come to that.'

Farazin nodded.

'Go and tend to your son,' he said. 'We'll speak again in the morning.'

Dusk was closing in now, the sun hidden behind the bulk of the mountain's southern flank, and Kerin was only too happy to rejoin his family. Farazin shuffled away, taking the last of the curious onlookers with him.

'How is it?' Kerin asked.

'Not too bad,' Olandis replied, but his face was pale from shock and loss of blood. 'What happened to Scar?'

'I've no idea.'

'One moment he was a raging monster, the next he's like a friendly puppy,' Olandis said, glancing suspiciously at the dog. It seemed quite pleased with itself, and was watching what was happening around it with happy curiosity.

'I think Terel may have a way with animals,' Ysatel commented. 'Hold still while I wash your arm.'

A little while later, once Olandis's wound had been bandaged and he'd been helped inside to his bed, Ysatel and Aylen returned to bank down the fire.

'I've a bone to pick with you, young man,' she said.

'I only did what I had to,' Aylen replied, knowing what was coming.

'In future, please let me make my own decisions. I don't appreciate being dragged about like that.'

'I didn't want the boy to be harmed,' he said, 'but he's not worth sacrificing *you* for.'

He spoke so seriously that Ysatel had to turn away to stop him seeing the tears in her eyes.

'Besides,' Aylen added, 'how was I to know Scar was going to switch allegiance? Look at him. He doesn't look as though he'd harm a flea now.'

They glanced at the boy and the dog, who seemed to be absorbed in each other's company and quite at ease. Without realizing it, they both found themselves smiling at the sight.

'I wish we could talk to him,' Aylen remarked quietly. 'He must have some tales to tell.'

Ysatel nodded, but said nothing.

'Do you think Scar will let us near him?' Aylen asked.

'There's only one way to find out,' she replied.

These are friends?

Yes.

Terrel allowed himself to be lifted into Aylen's arms and carried towards the hut.

Stay with me, he said urgently, but he needn't have

worried. Alyssa was trotting behind the young man, watched closely by Ysatel. Once inside, both Kerin and Olandis eyed the hound narrowly.

Terrel was laid on his own pallet and Alyssa curled up next to him, provoking a comment from Aylemirana which made Ysatel laugh. After that they were left alone while the family gathered in the other room of their home. The sound of their discussion drifted through the doorway, but neither Terrel nor Alyssa could tell what they were saying and, in any case, they had more than enough to talk about themselves.

It's been so long, Terrel began. *I thought . . .* He shied away from completing the sentence.

It took me a long time to find you, Alyssa explained.

Do you still have the ring?

For answer, Alyssa bared her teeth and Terrel saw the 'ring' wrapped around one of the canine fangs. He had not thought to look for it before now, and laughed at the choice of hiding place. The ring was made of twine, a length of thread, and a strand of his own hair. It had begun as a joke between the two friends, but was now more precious than any jewel because it acted as a beacon, enabling Alyssa to find Terrel wherever he was. By a process that Terrel had given up hope of ever under-standing, the ring left Alyssa's own finger and transferred itself to whichever animal she chose to 'borrow' when her spirit went wandering.

Then why couldn't you find me?

All that magic.

Terrel was about to ask her what she meant, but then the answer came to him.

You mean the ocean?

Alyssa had always regarded water with a certain amount of dread. She had never been able – or willing – to explain why, but their adventures on Vadanis just before Terrel's exile had reinforced her belief. The elemental had feared water too, regarding it as a magical substance.

The sea, Alyssa confirmed. *The moat. I never thought you'd be* outside *the palace.*

Given her phobia, it was not hard to explain her long delay in finding him. He was *overseas*, after all, divided from her by a vast, moving bulk of water. She would have found it hard to believe at first – and hard to deal with later. The fact that she was there at all was testament to her loyalty and determination.

I looked and looked, in every room, she went on, *but you weren't there, so I found another window.*

Terrel was used to Alyssa's occasionally oblique way of expressing herself, and knew what she meant – that having determined he was not on Vadanis or any of the other Floating Islands, she had gone on to look further afield.

That's when I felt a faint echo of you, she added.

I've been ill, Terrel said, wondering if the weakness of his own spirit and his lack of faith might have hindered her search.

I know. I can smell it on you. Taste it too.

Really?

Being a dog has some advantages. You are *recovering though, aren't you?*

I think so. Now that you're here, I'm sure I will. It seemed to him that the timing of her arrival could not have been a mere coincidence. *I'm glad you arrived when you did.*

I think I must've known you were in danger, she said thoughtfully. *As it was I was nearly too late.* She shuddered at the idea. *This hound would've torn you to pieces.*

Why did you bite that man? Terrel asked. *He's one of my friends.*

That wasn't me, really, she replied. *I'd only just arrived, and it took me a few moments to get control of his instincts. Once I was used to him, it was easy enough. Dogs are simple compared to horses or cats.* She spoke from hard-won experience.

You only just made it in time, Terrel said, grimacing at the thought.

But I was *in time*, she replied, sounding smug now.

You saved my life.

You're not ready to be a ghost yet, she told him. *Neither of us is.*

Terrel thought about that for a while, his spirits recovering, until he was able to grin at another memory.

Did you see the look on his owner's face when you turned on him? he asked eventually.

Serves him right, Alyssa commented. *The problem is I'm going to have to leave this beast sooner or later, and then he's probably going to revert to type. You won't want to be around when he does.*

Terrel hadn't thought of that, and the prospect dismayed him.

You don't have to go yet though, do you?

I'm fine for a while, she assured him. *As I said, dogs are simple enough. I'll stay as long as I can, then get him well away before I go.*

Terrel recalled the last time Alyssa had been forced to stay in one particular creature for a long time. The stonechat's mind had, if anything, been even simpler than the hound's – but even so, the prolonged confinement within one frame had led to problems for Alyssa, both mental and physical. She needed to return to her own body to 'rest', and anything that prevented her from doing so only exaggerated the oddities of her own mind. Alyssa was one of the inmates of Havenmoon who – at least by the standards of the outside world – really *was* mad.

Your own body . . . Terrel asked hesitantly. *It's . . .*

Still at the haven, she replied. *Still sleeping. I've come to no harm, Terrel. I told you before, I'm being protected.*

He had not seen Alyssa in her own form since he'd fled Havenmoon, leaving her comatose in a dungeon cell beneath the house that had been his home for the first fourteen years of his life. And he knew that if he *did* see her now, it would mean that she was dead. This thought was too appalling to contemplate, so he took comfort – as always – in her varying presence and in her voice. It renewed his determination to return to Vadanis so that they could be reunited in both body and spirit. He was ashamed of his earlier pessimism now.

I will come back for you, he vowed.

I know. And I'll wait for you. But you have other—

She broke off then, and half rose to her feet as the candlelight from the adjoining room flickered and changed. A figure appeared in the doorway.

It's Ysatel, Terrel reassured her, and the dog sank back down again.

Ysatel set a dish of water and a bone next to the hound, then went out again, only to return a few moments later with a bowl of soup. She began to feed her patient, but Terrel surprised her by reaching out and taking the spoon, and beginning to ladle broth into his own mouth. Ysatel smiled, and said something that was evidently intended to be encouraging. Terrel's movements were shaky, but grew more certain as he went on. By the time he'd emptied the bowl, Alyssa had lapped up the water and was gnawing contentedly on the bone.

So there's kindness even among barbarians, she remarked as Ysatel carried the empty dishes away.

They've been very good to me, Terrel said. *Ysatel and her family, I mean.*

Perhaps land doesn't have to move.

It ought to, but . . . Terrel shrugged. He was being forced to reconsider many of his beliefs.

You should rest, Alyssa told him.

But Terrel did not feel like sleeping. He had never felt less like sleeping.

Are the others with you? he asked.

They're close, she answered warily, *but—*

She fell silent as a faint glimmer appeared in a corner of the room. Terrel was delighted when this resolved itself into the spectral form of Elam, his boyhood friend. The ghost looked around, appraising his new location.

At least you've got a roof over your head this time, he remarked.

CHAPTER SEVEN

There ought to have been so much to say, but for a few moments Terrel found himself speechless. He had not seen his friend – or rather his friend's ghost – for what seemed like a very long time. Even before his enforced exile they'd been unable to meet, because none of the ghosts had been able to come near Betancuria. That in itself was one of the mysteries none of them could fathom, and it had meant that Terrel's sense of isolation had begun even before his long and lonely journey on the raft. But now, with Elam's reappearance, his typically sardonic comment and apparently offhand attitude, it seemed that nothing had changed – and there was nothing to be said. The three of them were together again – and that was all that mattered.

When I said we'd have some adventures, Elam remarked eventually, *I didn't expect you to go* this *far.*

I didn't exactly have much choice in the matter, Terrel replied, with a slight grin.

I'm not sure which of us was more careless, Elam added. *Me for getting killed, or you for getting chucked in the sea.*

Terrel was about to respond that neither had been a matter of carelessness, but the memory of his friend's murder stilled his tongue. The fact that he had been – at least in part – responsible for Elam's fatal confrontation with Havenmoon's warden still distressed him.

You survived, at least, Elam went on.

Only just.

So I see. Where is this place?

Somewhere in Macul. That's all I know.

It feels wrong, doesn't it, Elam commented.

What do you mean?

Not moving. Can you imagine? *This land's always been here, always fixed in the same place.* Elam shuddered theatrically.

I don't feel that way. At least not any more.

But you're among barbarians. You're lucky to be alive.

I know, Terrel admitted, though he was beginning to feel irritated by his friend's attitude. *But if it hadn't been for the people here, I'd have died. They—*

They're probably just waiting to fatten you up before they eat you.

You don't know what you're talking about.

Most barbarians are cannibals, Elam persisted. *Everyone knows that.*

This was the sort of bigoted remark that Terrel, like all the inhabitants of Vadanis, would have believed – without thinking – until recently. Now it made him angry.

That's rubbish!

Elam was obviously startled by his friend's vehemence.

All right, there's no need to get so worked up. I thought—

Nobody thinks. That's the problem, Terrel cut in.

I'm sorry. Elam sounded genuinely contrite, and Terrel regretted having been so harsh. Not so long ago, he would have believed everything the other boy did.

It's just that the people here have been very good to me, he explained. *They saved my life when I was about ready to give up, and they've looked after me ever since – at some cost to themselves. I've been treated better by these* barbarians *than by most people at home.*

Have you ever wondered why land not moving should be a bad thing? Alyssa asked. She had been listening to their exchange, and had grown increasingly uncomfortable as the argument developed. *Who says it* ought *to move?*

Neither of her companions answered. It was simply one of those basic beliefs that everyone on the Floating Islands took for granted. Questioning such things would never have occurred to the friends if they hadn't been forced to leave their homeland.

If the tunnel has twists and turns, Alyssa added, *you may not be able to see light at the end of it.*

Even as a dog she still says the most bizarre things, Elam remarked, grateful for the diversion.

At least I don't have to sing this time, Alyssa commented incongruously.

Elam looked nonplussed, but Terrel laughed, recalling Alyssa's bravura performance as a singing cat in the tavern on Vadanis.

Just be thankful you weren't there, he told his friend. *If this creature's howl is as painful on the ears as her cat's yowling was, then you'd be better off keeping your distance.*

I'll take your word for it, Elam said.

They were silent for a while. Although the atmosphere

had been restored to one of good humour, there was still a little tension between the two boys. They were not used to having to deal with such an awkward situation.

Do you think you'll be able to get back home? Elam asked eventually, his tone uncharacteristically serious.

Of course I will, Terrel stated emphatically, *but right now I don't see how. The Empire must be miles away, and getting further all the time.* He had not considered the practical difficulties of fulfilling his promise before that moment. It suddenly seemed like a daunting task.

They'll come closer again, though, won't they? Elam asked doubtfully.

I suppose so. But that might not be for a year or so, Terrel replied, remembering the charts that had shown the islands' complex course within the vast expanse of the Movaghassi Ocean. The reality of his situation was beginning to sink in even as he spoke. Until this point his concerns had simply been about surviving from one day to the next. He had not dared wonder about the future; it would have seemed like tempting fate. Now he'd been forcibly reminded of the extent of the disaster that had befallen him. A whole year?

Even then, you'd have to find a boat willing to make the voyage, Elam said, adding to Terrel's growing sense of unease. *Vadanis doesn't get many visitors from Macul – or anywhere else for that matter.*

The truth was that Vadanis didn't get *any* foreign visitors. Nor would the inhabitants have wanted any. They were more than happy with their isolation.

I'll deal with that when the time comes, Terrel said, not wanting to dwell on such extra difficulties. *I've got to get my strength back first, before I can think of going anywhere.*

Elam nodded, sensing his friend's mood and deciding not to pursue the point.

Is everything all right on Vadanis? Terrel asked. *I mean, are the islands back on course?*

Not yet, Elam replied, *but they will be soon. And the rotation's slowing down. If it weren't for the fact that the Dark Moon still isn't doing what it's supposed to, everyone would be happy. Even Betancuria's getting back to normal now that the central section of the mines has been sealed off.*

So the Ancient's kept its side of the bargain?

So far, Elam confirmed. *Thanks to you. Muzeni and Shahan were really pleased with what you did.*

It wasn't just me, Terrel said, glancing at Alyssa.

Well, I suppose my advice did help a bit, Elam said, grinning.

'*Maybe not all rivers run downhill,*' Terrel quoted, remembering. *What made you send that message?*

I'm not sure. It was just something I felt needed saying at the time. I'd've loved to have been there to see the water flowing uphill!

That was the elemental's doing, not mine.

But you gave it the idea. Alyssa told us all about it. Of course, the seers are taking the credit. Apart from— He broke off abruptly, and Terrel only caught a diminishing echo of the thought that was to have followed.

Elam? Alyssa said, a warning note in her voice.

One of your barbarian friends is coming, Elam said, sounding unaccountably relieved, and Terrel, who had been about to ask his friend what he'd stopped himself from saying, was distracted by the appearance of Ysatel in the connecting doorway. She was holding a candle, one hand cupped around the flame to protect it from draughts.

For a moment, Terrel expected her to be terrified by Elam's ghost, but it was soon obvious that the other boy was completely invisible to her. She smiled at Terrel, and said something quietly to him. He wanted to respond, but knew she wouldn't understand anything he said, so remained silent – though he returned her smile. Apparently satisfied, Ysatel turned and went back to her family, leaving her patient in near darkness again.

I'm glad I didn't see you when you were looking bad, Elam remarked.

What do you mean?

She told you you were looking much better than before.

You understood what she said? Terrel exclaimed in astonishment.

More or less. I got the sense of it, anyway. You could too if you weren't so pure and principled.

What do you mean?

She's got to think *something before she says it.* Elam pointed out. *So why don't you use psinoma? Look inside her head.*

But that's—

No, it's not, Elam cut in, anticipating his friend's objection. *She's trying to say something to you. How can that be private? She* wants *you to know what she's thinking.*

This argument had little effect on Terrel. All his instincts told him that it would be wrong, and he remembered Alyssa telling him that all magic exacts a price. What he had to do was decide whether, on this occasion, it was a price worth paying.

I don't think I can, he said.

That's what you said to Babak, Elam countered. *But you were able to use the glamour, weren't you? And you talk to us using psinoma all the time now. Why not with her?*

It's not the same. Terrel recalled a similar argument with Babak, his tutor in such things, about using psinoma – 'invisible words' – to transfer thoughts directly between minds. His objection had been to the fact that, if you had sufficient talent, it was possible to use the technique without the other person even being aware of what was happening – and Terrel had believed this to be both wrong and dangerous. On the other hand, he longed to be able to talk to Ysatel and the other villagers, and so – for the moment – he set aside the moral arguments and concentrated on practical issues.

But when I talk to you, we're using the same language, he pointed out. *Their words aren't the same.*

You got on all right with the elemental, Elam said. *What language did it use?*

Terrel had to think about this.

That wasn't like an ordinary conversation, he replied eventually. *It was more like simply knowing what—*

Well, this is just an extension of that, Elam interrupted. *It may not be perfect, but you'll get by. And if you're not too squeamish about it, you'll soon get to learn their language. Then you can be a proper gentleman and talk to them out loud.*

His friend's mildly sarcastic tone needled Terrel, but he did not respond. He was considering the fact that Ysatel had sometimes seemed to know what he was thinking – and that perhaps he could use the connection in the same way. Although it still seemed like prying, being able to communicate with his hosts would make his situation so much easier.

Do you think I should try this, Alyssa?

The dog, who had apparently fallen asleep soon after Ysatel's visit, opened one eye and looked at him solemnly.

You're the only one who can choose which doors to open, she said. *And which to go through. If you have motive and means, and one is good and one is bad, what does that make the action?*

Moons! Elam hissed in exasperation. *Stop talking in riddles. I'm trying to help.*

Terrel is good at solving riddles, she responded calmly. *Let him decide for himself.*

Call her, Elam urged. *Call Ysatel in here and try it.*

Not yet, Terrel said. *I have to think about this.*

The ghost threw up transparent hands in frustration.

Have it your own way, he muttered. *I suppose you're too principled to want me to tell you what else I've overheard.*

Like what?

They think you're a sorcerer. Even your friends are suspicious.

Why would they think that?

Well, first of all you've tamed this lovely hound – his name's Scar, by the way – and no one, except somebody called Cutter, has been able to do that before. Of course, that was nothing to do with you, really, but they don't know that, do they? How could they? I don't suppose they have too many sleepers round here.

That's hardly enough to make me a sorcerer, Terrel said, still bewildered.

Then there's your eyes, of course, Elam went on, *and the fact that you speak a different language. And they're puzzled by the way you got here. I don't understand that bit. But the main thing is that some of them think you caused an earthquake.*

Caused? Terrel exclaimed in horror. *How could – I was trying to* warn *them.*

Just knowing it was coming was a kind of magic, Elam said. *Not exactly a common talent, is it?*

The arguments that had raged about Terrel at the gatherings, and the hostility he had felt, made sense to him now. What was more, such understanding might help him try to put things right – if only he could learn to talk to the villagers. Then he could convince them that he meant no harm, that he had wanted to help them. A good end, it seemed, might justify bad means.

He was about to call out to Ysatel, but realized that all was now quiet in the next room, and decided to leave his first attempts till the morning. She would not thank him for disturbing her rest.

I think you should try to talk to them, don't you? Elam said, echoing Terrel's thoughts. *Or this could get very complicated.*

You mean it isn't already?

Point taken.

When are Shahan and Muzeni going to come and see me?

I don't know. I normally have to tag along with them, listening to their endless arguments – but they've got a lot to do at the moment, which is why I was able to slip away and follow Alyssa.

I'm glad you did, Terrel said. *It's good to see you. What are they up to?*

Elam hesitated before he answered, and the dog gave a sort of snuffling growl.

Oh, the usual stuff, Elam answered with elaborate nonchalance. *You know, poring over ancient books.*

The Code?

Elam shrugged non-existent shoulders.

Probably.

I bet they're annoyed that the seers are taking all the credit for averting disaster, Terrel probed gently.

Not all *the credit. Jax is the one who's being treated like a hero.*

Jax? The Emperor's son?

The prince has now been officially hailed as the Guardian.

But I thought—

The dog growled in earnest this time, and for a moment Terrel wondered if Alyssa had gone and it was Scar who was curled up next to him. But then he realized that she wouldn't leave without any warning, and told himself not to be so silly.

What's the matter? he asked.

You're walking into a dangerous room, she replied, but he had the feeling that she was talking to Elam, not to him.

Don't you think— Elam began.

That's not for us to decide, Alyssa declared, overriding him sharply.

What's going on? Terrel asked.

Elam looked away, his evasiveness quite out of character.

I'm not supposed . . . he muttered. *I've said too much already.*

Fragments of memory stirred in Terrel's mind. It had been the enchanter – the malevolent presence who had plagued his dreams – who was supposed to have become a hero. The enchanter, whom he had glimpsed only once from a distance, but whose taunting voice was so familiar, had been his go-between, allowing Terrel to make a bargain between the Seers' Council and the elemental. And it was the enchanter who had signed the mocking letter that had sent Terrel into exile, a letter that had ended, 'Farewell, brother'. And Terrel's recurring nightmare, the thunderous ocean of red pain, had been an echo of a time before he had been born, when he had been blind and hidden – but not alone.

But now it seemed that Prince Jax was the hero. Did that mean he was the enchanter? If he was, then that meant . . . Terrel's mind balked at the logical conclusion. No, it wasn't possible. And yet . . .

He came out of his reverie to see Elam's spectral image flicker.

Don't go! Don't! It was half demand, half despairing plea.

It's not always my choice, you know, Elam replied plaintively – and then he was gone, vanished into his own world, around the corner that his friend could never turn.

Elam! Come back! Terrel gasped, though he knew it was hopeless. *Where are the others? I have to talk to them.*

There was no response and, angry now as well as confused, Terrel turned to Alyssa, his last hope.

The dog appeared to be sound asleep, and could not be roused. If Alyssa was still inhabiting Cutter's hound, she was either deeply unconscious or pretending to be so. Either way, Terrel knew he'd get no answer to his questions now.

What was worse, he believed that she'd had something to do with Elam's importunate departure. In some things, it seemed, he could not even trust his closest friends.

CHAPTER EIGHT

When Terrel woke the next morning, he knew immediately from the quiet stillness around him that he was alone in the hut. Ysatel and her family had gone and so – to his dismay – had Alyssa. He had no idea at what point the dog had left, but the fact that Alyssa had felt it necessary to do so by stealth made his heart sink. On reflection, he found that he was not really surprised that she had gone, only disappointed – and another layer of regret was added to the sense of betrayal he'd felt after Elam's departure. He had often thought that Muzeni and Shahan – two seers from different centuries who had formed a ghostly alliance – might be hiding things from him, but discovering that both Alyssa and Elam were also part of the conspiracy made him feel both hurt and dejected.

It had taken Terrel a long time to get to sleep. This was not only because he'd been listening in the darkness for any sign that the dog might be stirring, but also because of the extraordinary number of new ideas and suspicions that were swirling about inside his head. And, if he was honest, he had also been afraid of what his dreams might bring. Eventually, however, exhaustion had overcome both frustration and fear, and the next thing he'd been aware of was the empty silence of a new day.

The only small mercy was that he remembered nothing of his dreams, but that still left him with more than enough to think about. Pushing aside his wilder speculations, he told himself that he would just have to wait until Alyssa and the ghosts returned. He was determined that the next time he saw Muzeni and Shahan he would not let *them* evade his questions. He would get some answers – or they could forget about any co-operation from him. A small, treacherous voice at the back of his mind whispered that getting answers out of the seers was sometimes like drawing blood from a stone, but that did not affect his resolve. The only problem was that he had no idea when he would get the chance to try. Alyssa might still be occupying Scar's body and so be able to return at any moment. On the other hand, she might have been forced to leave, and thus could come back in another shape altogether. In the meantime, all he could do was wait.

His brooding was cut short by a thin squealing noise coming from outside the hut. It was a sound he recognized and he sat up, peering into the other room to the outer door, hoping to see the new arrival. Alyssa had once appeared to him as a piglet – and Terrel was hoping for a repeat performance now. But no animal appeared, and he was about to lie down again – telling himself that he was getting excited over nothing – when he caught the sound of voices. One of them belonged to Ysatel and, alert once more, Terrel began to listen.

'Is Kerin here?' Chiva asked nervously.

'No. He's at the elders' meeting.'

'So's Azian. I wouldn't be here otherwise.'

Ysatel eyed the tiny piglet struggling feebly in her visitor's arms, and wondered why Chiva should want to hide whatever she was doing from her own husband.

'Why *are* you here?'

'You won't tell Azian I came, will you? He thinks I'm being silly.'

'And are you?'

'I don't think so,' Chiva declared, with a touch of defiance. 'We all saw what the stranger did with Scar. If he could do that . . .' Her voice trailed away.

'Your piglet doesn't look as if it's going to attack anyone,' Ysatel commented. Rather the reverse, she thought to herself. It was a puny, sickly-looking creature.

'Oh, he won't,' Chiva assured her earnestly. 'The sow won't let him suckle, even though there are only four others in the litter, and he won't take any other food. If he doesn't eat soon he'll die.'

Ysatel nodded, knowing that every animal – even a runt – was valuable to its owners. It was more than likely that others in the litter were promised in payment of debts, and with so few piglets having been born this time, the survival of even the weakest was vital.

'And you think the foreigner might be able to help?'

'Perhaps,' Chiva replied, sounding defensive now. 'I've heard it said that some sharaken have a way with animals. If he could just . . . Azian thinks it's a waste of time.'

'Well, men don't know everything, do they,' Ysatel commented wryly. 'Let's go and see what happens.'

The older woman smiled gratefully, and followed her neighbour into the hut.

Terrel was waiting when the two women came into his room. He had not caught all of what had been said, but the word 'sharaken' had jumped out at him. His suspicion that the two women had been talking about a piglet proved correct when he saw the animal in the stranger's arms. Ysatel said something then and, although he did not understand the words as such, he caught the gist of what she meant. He was overjoyed by the realization that the psinoma must be working as Elam had said it would, and – for the moment – the fact that her exact meaning made little sense to him did not matter. However, when Ysatel took the piglet from her companion's arms and placed it gently on the floor beside Terrel's pallet, the air of anticipation concentrated his thoughts.

The tiny, wrinkled creature was unsteady on its feet, and seemed to dislike being the centre of attention. Its eyes were dull, and when its legs gave way and it slumped to the ground, Terrel wondered whether it was close to dying. He was glad now that the dog had gone. The hound's mere presence might have been enough to frighten the piglet to death. As it was, Terrel felt no connection with it – he had known the instant he saw the animal that it was not Alyssa – and he was at a loss to know what he should do. Ysatel had asked him to heal the creature, but how was he supposed to do that? He didn't even know what was wrong with it. Even if he did, he was no miracle worker.

For the want of anything better to do, he leant forward and touched a finger to the piglet's snout. Its skin was surprisingly cool and rough and, in that instant, Terrel experienced a spasm, not of pain, but of an absolute weariness that – for once – was not his own. He fought against it instinctively, knowing that it was wrong. He was no longer aware of his surroundings, and within his waking dream a memory stirred – of a newborn calf, that had been left for dead, tottering to its mother on wobbly legs. He had done that – though he still didn't know how – and the calf had been in an even worse state than the piglet. Perhaps if . . .

Beneath his hand he felt the animal stir and sensed, rather than heard, the gasps of the watching women. A few moments later, Terrel sat back, close to exhaustion but feeling oddly content. As he did so, he saw that the small creature was trotting around the room, squealing and snuffling inquisitively.

Ysatel had left the room, but returned quickly with a bowl full of scraps. The piglet went to this as soon as she set it down, and began to eat enthusiastically. Ysatel said something that was full of both wonder and satisfaction, and the older woman clapped her hands and laughed.

Knowing that he must have done something right, Terrel lay back down on his bed and fell asleep smiling.

'Farazin managed to keep things under control,' Kerin reported, 'but feelings were running pretty high on both sides.'

'Cutter?' Ysatel asked.

'Actually, he didn't say much. He was more subdued

than I'd expected. Probably still humiliated over what happened with Scar.'

'You know the dog's gone?' Neither Ysatel nor any of the others had seen Scar's departure.

'Yes. There's been no sign of him, apparently. At least it means Cutter won't show up here and try to reclaim him.'

'I don't think he would anyway. He wouldn't want to risk being embarrassed again. So do you think he's changed his mind about the boy?'

'I doubt it. He's probably just biding his time. He's not a man to forgive and forget, so I'd wager he's planning something. He knew he'd have been outvoted today if he suggested anything too outrageous, so he just kept it to himself.' Kerin had been aware of Cutter muttering darkly during the meeting of the elders, but both he and Farazin had chosen to ignore it, hoping that common sense would prevail.

'You think he'd take matters into his own hands?' Ysatel asked. 'Defy the elders?'

'Maybe. I threatened to, didn't I?'

'But you didn't have to in the end.'

'No. Farazin saw to that.'

'And now it's all settled.'

'For the time being, at least,' Kerin conceded. 'The decision was clearly going our way as it was, but after Chiva's intervention there was never any doubt. Farazin was outraged, of course, and Azian was embarrassed, but she was going to have her say whatever we did.'

'Good for her,' Ysatel commented. 'She can be a silly old dear, but her heart's in the right place.'

'And what happened with their pig *was* quite

persuasive,' Kerin went on. 'After that it was obvious Terel was going to be allowed to stay. Farazin didn't even bother to put it to a vote.'

'So all we've got to worry about now is Cutter.'

'He's not to be underestimated,' Kerin agreed.

They both knew that Cutter wielded considerable influence in Fenduca. Almost everyone there was dependent on him to some extent. He was the one who oiled the wheels of trade, providing services of safe-keeping, money-lending and – most importantly – of bargain-sealing. Whenever merchants came to the village, it was Mitus they dealt with. In that way, the visitors were unable to pit one prospector against another and drive down prices. Everyone received a fair share of the proceeds – and Mitus, of course, took his cut. Even though Scar's apparent defection may have dented his reputation a little, he still commanded respect – as well as a certain amount of fear.

'He's not stupid, mind you,' Kerin went on. 'He won't try anything unless he's sure of some support. When the news of Lereth and Zolen's finds this afternoon gets around, people will be starting to think our luck's changed.'

'And Terel will be safe.'

'More than that. He'll be in demand. Every time an animal gets sick, at least.'

'It was amazing,' Ysatel told her husband. 'He seemed to know exactly what was needed, and the change in the piglet was incredible.'

'Is he still asleep?'

'He was the last time I looked. Whatever he did, it took a lot out of him.'

'Restocking his store of dreams?'

'Maybe, but I've never heard of a sharakan trading in that way before.'

'More's the pity,' Kerin declared. 'Practical help is often a lot more use than mystical guidance.'

'You'd better not let Farazin hear you say things like that,' Ysatel warned her husband. 'Sky-watchers can be touchy.'

Scar returned to his master that evening. The dog seemed to be back to normal – if a bit subdued and somewhat footsore – but although he resumed his guard duties for Cutter with his usual fervour, there was one noticeable difference in the hound's behaviour. As Cutter found out the next day, Scar became nervous and agitated whenever he was forced to go anywhere near the Mirana house, and if left to his own devices would not approach the place at all.

The news of the piglet's recovery soon spread throughout the village, and in most people's minds it was yet more evidence that the foreigner was able to exert a supernatural influence over animals. Opinion was still divided over whether this was a good thing or not, but now that Fenduca seemed – if anything – to be under a benign spell rather than a curse, most were prepared to give the boy the benefit of the doubt. For once Cutter kept his opinions to himself, and went about his business as though nothing had happened.

Over the next few days, Ysatel noticed several changes in her patient. He was eating much better than before, and visibly recovering some of his health and strength.

The boy also appeared to be particularly attentive whenever she was with him. He hung on her every word, often seeming to repeat them silently, as if trying them out for himself. He would sometimes try to repeat them out loud, and she encouraged him in this, teaching him simple vocabulary by pointing to things around him and suiting some actions to her words. At the same time, she occasionally had the eerie feeling that he knew what she was thinking, that he could anticipate what she was going to do even before she was aware of it herself. On one occasion he drained a cup of water and held it out to her just as she had been about to ask whether he wanted any more to drink. And they had been sitting outside one day – something he liked to do as often as possible now – when he warned her against picking up a metal bowl that had been placed too close to the fire, and which would have burnt her fingers. Each time, Ysatel told herself that it was just his intuition at work, but she was not always convinced by her own arguments. Even so, she began to enjoy the boy's company, taking pleasure in his improving health, and hoping that she would soon learn more about him.

There were, however, some rather more disturbing aspects of the stranger's behaviour that left her feeling puzzled. The first and most obvious of these was the disruption of his sleep – and sometimes her family's – by his nightmares. He often cried out, apparently in distress, and yet when she went to see what was wrong, he was sound asleep. She would watch him in the candlelight as he mumbled and twitched, wondering whether she should wake him, without ever being able to make up her mind to act. Eventually he'd grow quiet again and she would go back to her husband, unnerved by the thought of the visions the foreigner might be seeing.

A second, more subtle pattern emerged when he was awake. Whenever anyone approached, he looked up expectantly – hope flaring in his strange eyes – only to look disappointed when he saw who it was. It was as if he were expecting someone who never came. And the most curious thing of all was that this reaction could even be prompted by the appearance of an animal, or a bird. Ysatel soon gave up trying to interpret such behaviour, deciding to concentrate on practical matters rather than mysteries, but it bothered her nonetheless.

The midwinter sun was a pale orange disc behind a high layer of cloud. Even at midday it hung low in the sky, and its muffled rays provided little heat, but Ysatel was feeling quite warm. She had just returned home with a heavy bundle of firewood, and first the exercise and then the residual glow of the embers kept her from feeling cold. It would not be so for her men, she knew. Searching for finds in the river was cold work even in summer, and by the time they'd finished for the day, they'd all be chilled to the bone – and in sore need not only of the fire she was building but of hot food too. She was about to go inside to inspect her stores and decide what to cook, when Terel emerged from the doorway, lurching on his deformed foot and with a panic-stricken expression on his face.

'What is it? What's the matter?'

The boy's hands fluttered like demented birds, and he said something she could not follow, but he was clearly very agitated.

'I don't know what you mean,' she said, moving closer.

'Shak!' he cried. 'Shak!'

Abruptly he knelt on the ground and placed his good hand, palm down, on the dirt. Then he shook convulsively so that his fingers jumped and quivered.

'Shak,' he repeated. 'Soon. Come.'

'Shake?'

The boy nodded wildly, pointing to the ground.

'Shake! Soon.'

As soon as she realized what he was trying to tell her, Ysatel wasted no time. She turned and ran towards the river, shouting as she went.

'Get out of the river! There's an earthquake coming! Quick! Get out of the river!'

The men within earshot stopped what they were doing and looked at her, hesitating. But such was the force of conviction in her voice as she repeated her cry that several of them were soon scrambling towards the banks, shouting to others further away to do the same. Few thought to wonder that the warning had come from Ysatel, whose home was a long way from the wolf-fish pool. She was obviously in earnest, and only a fool ignored such an alarm.

When the tremor came, it was quite strong, but lasted only a few moments and did less damage than the previous one. Thanks to Ysatel, all those working in the river escaped the surges of water and the associated rockfalls. When the villagers learnt that she had been able to warn them because of the foreigner's premonition, their conviction that the stranger must be a sharakan – and not a sorcerer – was confirmed.

CHAPTER NINE

Terrel stared down into the fish-pool, watching the peculiar creatures whose placid movements were causing the surface of the water to ripple gently. He had never seen a wolf and had only a vague idea of what they looked like, and so he could not tell how these fish had come by their name. The strange tendrils that sprouted from the top and sides of their heads looked to him like the whiskers of a cat or the spindly legs of a spider.

'Do they sense the tremors coming through their feelers?'

'No one knows how they do it,' Ysatel replied.

What can I possibly have in common with them? Terrel wondered. What makes us both able to predict earthquakes? But these were questions he could not even hope to answer.

'They seem quiet enough,' he said.

'They are. When the fish are like this, there's nothing to worry about,' Ysatel told him. 'But we'll be keeping a close eye on them for the next few days. Farazin says there could be another quake soon.'

Terrel nodded, and looked up to where the White Moon hung like a pale disc in the eastern sky. It would be full the next day, and the day after that the Red Moon would also reach the point of its maximum influence. The combined effect was likely to be quite powerful. Then again, Farazin's predictions had not always proved accurate. In fact, the old man had told Terrel that the earthquake he'd successfully warned Ysatel about should actually have happened two or three days later than it had – when the Amber and White Moons had been full within a few hours of each other. Not even the sky-watcher knew why it had come so early, and at the time no one had thought to check on the wolf-fish to see whether they had also been fooled.

'What happens to the fish when there's a quake coming?' Terrel asked.

'They get agitated,' Ysatel told him, 'and swim much faster than usual. Sometimes they jump clean out of the water. And they wave their feelers about as if something's driving them mad.'

Terrel tried to relate this description to the internal trembling that he experienced, but couldn't see much connection. His certainty arrived *inside* him unannounced, not through any of his external senses. And he knew that Kerin's own experiences – his *jasper feet* – could only tell him about something that was already happening.

'How much warning do they give you?'

'Two or three hours, sometimes longer if it's a bad one.'

That was much more than Terrel could manage. He

usually only had a few moments to raise the alarm before a tremor struck.

'I wish I could talk to them,' he murmured to himself.

'Maybe you can,' Ysatel said, smiling. 'You seem to have done all right with the other animals.'

Terrel laughed, thinking that he had indeed conversed with some very strange creatures – including some Ysatel did not know about – but he was still convinced that the wolf-fish were beyond his understanding.

'I think they'd just run away if I tried to touch them,' he said.

'Or bite your fingers off,' she warned. 'They can be quite nasty when they're hungry.'

'In that case,' Terrel decided, 'I'm not even going to try.'

'Do you want to go back?'

The pool was on the opposite side of the river from their hut, and this was the furthest Terrel had ventured from his bed so far. Even though he'd recovered much of his strength, the trek had been an arduous scramble over rocks that were often slippery or sharp-edged. But curiosity overcame the weariness he felt.

'Not yet.'

Terrel had been in Fenduca for almost two median months now, and although he could recall little of the first half of that time, he had become progressively more active and inquisitive since the second tremor. He had seen a great deal for himself, but the key to his newly acquired knowledge was his ability to speak the villagers' language. Ysatel had been his tutor, both willingly and – to Terrel's slight shame – sometimes unknowingly. Following Elam's advice, he had first employed the psinoma to help him understand what she was saying, and had then tried to express himself to her in words – spoken aloud whenever possible, but implanted silently when that failed. Progress had been halting at first, but soon – much to his surprise and relief – phrases began to make sense on their own, without the need to pry into her thoughts. After a while he had begun to understand what other people were saying too. However, even though he was reasonably fluent now, Ysatel remained the person he was most comfortable with. They had come to regard each other as friends rather than just nurse and patient.

For her part, Ysatel found the fact that Terrel had progressed from near incoherence to fluency in little more than a month quite amazing. She had helped him as much as she could, patiently correcting his mistakes and nudging his memory when he stumbled over a difficult pronunciation or the construction of a sentence, but the boy seemed to have an uncanny knack of picking things up – including words she was reasonably sure he had never actually heard. He still faltered sometimes, and made mistakes, but those occasions were becoming increasingly rare. He was constantly hungry for knowledge, and asked questions about everything he saw. She had known Aylen since he was seven, and not even he had been able to match the foreigner's childlike curiosity.

'Can we sit and talk?' he asked now, his accent making even the simple words sound exotic.

'For a little while,' she replied, glancing up at the position of the sun.

They settled themselves on a ledge of rock, from where they could look out over the pool and the river beyond.

'Farazin said that the quakes were the result of the

land moving,' Terrel began, 'but Macul *doesn't* move, does it?'

'Not in the same way as Vadanis.' One of the few things Ysatel had been able to learn about his life – he still evaded some of her questions – was that he had lived on the Cursed Islands, or the Floating Islands as he called them. Even after he'd been accepted into Fenduca's community, *that* piece of information had caused some trepidation among the villagers, but Ysatel was used to the idea by now.

'But our lands do move,' she went on. 'Just not as fast. You should really talk to Farazin about this, not me. I only know what I've picked up from him.'

'I'd rather talk to you.'

Ysatel glanced away, not wanting him to see how much his comment pleased her.

'Tell me what you can,' he urged.

'All right,' she said, pausing to collect her thoughts. 'There are various forces that work on the land. The pull of the moons is one, of course, but there are others, underground. I don't know why. These forces build up as they push against each other, until something gives way and part of the land moves.'

'And that's what causes the tremors?'

'I think so.'

'It sounds dangerous,' he commented. 'When the moons pull on Vadanis, the islands just change course.' He had never heard the process described in those terms before, but now it seemed quite apt. 'It's much better that way.'

It didn't sound better at all to Ysatel, but she chose not to say so.

'It can be dangerous sometimes,' she admitted, 'but most of the time it's not even noticeable.' There hadn't been any tremors since the one Terrel had foreseen. 'We manage well enough.'

Terrel glanced at her, wondering whether he was being teased, but Ysatel's expression remained neutral. She was watching some men at work in the river, sifting through the silt for the small gemstones and nuggets that were the sole reason for Fenduca's very existence.

'I still can't believe the same forces produced *that*,' Terrel said, glancing up at the towering mass of the black mountain.

'Farazin says that maybe all mountains are built that way,' she replied, 'but most take hundreds or thousands of years. The astonishing thing is this one only took a few months.'

'Astonishing hardly covers it.' That anything so vast could just have grown out of the earth was unbelievable, but Terrel had heard Kerin describe what he had seen with his own eyes, and was certain that he had been telling the truth. The wonder was that the prospector had survived to tell the tale.

'There's nothing else like it in all the jasper forest,' Ysatel said, sounding almost proud. The jasper forest was the fanciful name given to the region of stone and water in which the villagers and other wandering prospectors spent their lives.

'Have you been up there?'

Ysatel shook her head.

'Only a few people had the chance before the soldiers arrived. By the time I got here the fences were already up, and I had no choice but to stay in Fenduca.' There was no regret in her voice. The village was a harsh and sometimes violent place, but it was where she had met Kerin.

'How long have you been here?' he asked.

'Ten years.'

Terrel was silent for a while, then he turned to look at her.

'Kerin's a lot older than you, isn't he?'

Unaccountably, Ysatel found herself blushing. She laughed to cover her embarrassment, wondering why the boy's guileless comment should have affected her.

'I suppose so. That sort of thing doesn't matter much when you love someone.'

Terrel nodded solemnly, apparently considering this idea. Something in his strange eyes spoke of hidden pain, and Ysatel wished that he could trust her enough to tell her his secrets. But he remained silent, and in the end she found herself volunteering some secrets of her own.

'I sometimes wonder why I haven't been able to have a baby,' she said quietly. 'I think Kerin would've liked to have had a daughter – but if it's not happened by now, it's not likely to, is it?' And in any case, she added to herself, there's nothing I can do about it.

Terrel had begun to look distinctly uncomfortable at this turn in the conversation, but Ysatel didn't notice. She was talking to herself as much as to him now, releasing something she had kept bottled up for a long time.

'Mind you, giving birth isn't something to be taken lightly. Lots of women die that way.' She hesitated, wondering whether to go on, then took the plunge. 'That's what happened to Aryel. The baby was a girl, but she only outlived her mother by a few days. Kerin never saw her. He should have been at home, but he was away longer than expected. Up there.' She nodded towards the mountain. 'He's never forgiven himself.'

Terrel had been aware that Ysatel was not the mother of Kerin's sons, but this was the first time he'd heard any of the family history. He didn't know what to say.

'The boys grew up without a mother,' she went on. 'It's a wonder they're not wilder than they are.'

'They had you,' Terrel said.

'Only for the last five years. Before that Kerin had to do it all himself.'

'But you're a real family.' His accent often made words sound strange, but this time his voice seemed to be choked with emotion.

'Yes, we are,' she said firmly, pulling herself together. 'I'm sorry, Terrel. I never meant—'

'I never had a family,' he blurted out, interrupting her apology. 'My parents abandoned me when I was a baby. I don't even know who they are.' Having been reluctant to reveal much about his past, he wasn't sure why he felt compelled to make this confession now.

'You poor thing.' She glanced at him, thinking that such words of sympathy were of little worth. Not only had he been forced to endure his physical disabilities and, more recently, his exile from his homeland, but now it seemed that he had never known anything but hardship and loneliness.

Terrel shrugged, and her heart went out to the boy as he tried to appear nonchalant. He shivered, and Ysatel glanced quickly at the wolf-fish, fearing that he might be anticipating another tremor. But the fish were still moving calmly within their self-contained realm, and she realized that Terrel was simply getting cold.

'Come on,' she said briskly. 'We'd better get back and light the fire for dinner.'

As they got up she put an arm round Terrel's shoulders and gave him a hug. When he looked at her in surprise, Ysatel smiled.

'You're part of our family now,' she told him.

CHAPTER TEN

The past month had been a hectic period of discovery for Terrel, as well as a time of fluctuating emotions. As his health improved and he was able to move about more freely, he had come to know more of the people of Fenduca and of their way of life. Now that he could talk to the villagers, he had been accepted by most of them – although some were still wary of him. A few even seemed to be in awe of his arcane talents, and the resentment that had accompanied his arrival had now largely disappeared. Even Cutter, who had more reason than most to dislike the foreigner, seemed prepared to tolerate his presence.

For his part, Terrel had come to appreciate and admire the spirit of defiance and obstinacy that kept the villagers in what was a dirty and dangerous place, where mere survival was hard enough and deprivation was commonplace. The fact that they had been able not only to endure but also to build a complex, genuine community – even if it was fractious and sometimes violent – was a testament to their willpower and vitality. There were few among them who had not been touched by tragedy, but amid the dust and mud of Fenduca there was often time enough to celebrate as well. Whether this was occasioned by an unusually good find, a marriage, the birth of a healthy child, or simply the full of one of the moons, mattered little. In the end, they were all celebrations of life itself.

Even so, there were more reasons for sadness than for joy, and none of the villagers led a comfortable life. Even Kerin and his family, who were better off than most, were often cold and hungry, and Terrel was acutely aware that he was a burden upon their meagre resources. None of them ever complained about the cost of their continued hospitality, but Terrel wished he could contribute more to the household. His only opportunities to do so had been when the villagers brought their animals to see him.

Following his success with Chiva's piglet – and his earlier 'taming' of Scar – the boy had gained the reputation of having a 'healing way with beasts'. He had tried to explain that he had no such skills, no magic, but people insisted on consulting him anyway. At first Ysatel had to help him understand what was wanted, but eventually he'd been able to talk directly to the visitors and – much to his own amazement – had met with some success in relieving the ailments of several domestic animals. He still had no idea how this was possible. Everything he did was governed purely by instinct and, although he could generally feel some sort of connection with the creature, what happened after that was as much a mystery to him as it was to everyone else. The closest he could come to an explanation was that, perhaps, at some subconscious level, he persuaded his patients to heal themselves. However, when this happened, the owners were not interested in the whys and wherefores. Their response – following Chiva's example – was to return with a small present of food or other goods in payment. Actual coinage was rare in Fenduca, but many other things could be used as money, and the village had a complicated bartering system. At first Terrel had felt awkward about accepting such gifts, but his doubts had soon been overcome by practical considerations. Naturally enough, he passed all such rewards to Ysatel, but they were not nearly enough to repay her family for all they had done for him. Nevertheless, his exploits – which often left him exhausted and in pain – did more than anything else to confirm his place in the household, and in the village as a whole.

There had only been one occasion when Terrel had not been able to help his visitor. This was when a little boy had come to the hut, hesitated in the doorway, and then been beckoned inside by Ysatel. He was carrying a small green snake which he placed carefully on the floor, before prodding it gently with a finger and looking up at Terrel expectantly. Even before picking it up, Terrel knew that the creature was dead, and he wondered what he should say to the child. The snake's scales were smooth and cool, but its eyes were filmed and its jaw hung slackly open.

'I can't help,' he began hesitantly. 'It's—'

'We don't have enough dreams for this trade, Davi,' Ysatel cut in, her voice firm but gentle. 'There are some things even a sharakan can't do.'

The boy nodded solemnly, held out his hands for the snake and, when Terrel returned it to him, went away again – all without uttering a single word. Terrel never discovered whether the creature had been Davi's pet or if he'd simply found its dead body somewhere, but he could not help remembering the look of disappointment in the boy's eyes, and he wished that he really were a sharakan. At least then he would have known how to explain his failure.

Even as he became reasonably proficient in the language of Macul, the word 'sharakan' had remained an enigma. In conversations with Ysatel, Farazin and others, the nearest Terrel had come to understanding was its literal translation of 'dream-trader' – but what exactly that *meant* was still an elusive concept. His hosts tried to make it clearer for him, but with only limited success. There was power involved, a kind of magic, and a sharakan could obtain guidance from the moons and stars – which made Terrel think of the obvious comparison with the seers of his homeland – but no one could actually tell him what these men *did*.

Conversations like this were bound to make him think of Alyssa and her ability to 'see' other people's dreams. Such an attribute might be useful in Macul. However, thoughts of Alyssa inevitably led to other reminders of the world he had been forced to leave behind, of all the things he had lost.

The one thing that consistently spoiled Terrel's peace of mind, during a month in which he made generally positive progress, was the fact that there was still no sign of Alyssa or her retinue of ghosts. Their abandonment of him seemed particularly cruel, given his uncertain circumstances and the unanswered questions they had left him with – and even though he knew they were not always masters of their own fates, he could not believe that their long absence was anything other than deliberate. He was reasonably certain that Muzeni and Shahan were capable of such callousness if it suited their purpose, but the bonds between him and Alyssa and Elam had been forged out of friendship and love, and he simply couldn't understand why they did not return.

Although he fought against these feelings of hurt and betrayal, he didn't always succeed. In his more charitable moods he invented any number of credible reasons for their not coming back to him, but by the time a long month had passed he was beginning to run out of excuses. More than once, recalling the timing of Alyssa's previous visit, he wondered whether he should try and get himself into another potentially lethal situation, so that she'd recognize his peril and have to return to save him again. Fortunately, common sense prevailed, and he had done no such thing.

'Zolen got back from Tcfir today,' Aylen reported. 'The water level's still rising. Unless something changes, it'll go the way of the other settlements in the valley.'

'It's the same everywhere,' Ysatel said. 'Why should the soldiers care that their debris is turning more and more of the province into swampland? It's not their homes being drowned.'

'Uncertainty over the moon-lore isn't helping,' Olandis added. 'No one seems to be sure what they can and can't do.'

'Is that because of the Dark Moon?' Terrel asked. He rarely joined in any family discussions, preferring to listen to the others, but on this occasion he couldn't help himself. The Dark Moon's anomalous behaviour had caused much confusion on Vadanis too – and he'd already heard Aylen and Olandis complaining that the local tides were becoming unpredictable.

'It is,' Kerin confirmed. 'At least in part.'

'Tell him the other part,' Olandis prompted.

'The sky-watchers haven't been able to keep up with what's happening. As well as the Dark Moon's cycle speeding up, the waste from the mines has dammed several waterways, so lakes are getting larger and rivers are changing course. No one could have foreseen such things.'

'Not even the sharaken?' Olandis said, a challenging look in his eyes. 'They're the ones who *make* the moon-lore, after all. Why haven't they told the sky-watchers what to do?'

'Such things take time,' Kerin replied. 'You forget where they live.'

'Tefir hasn't *got* much time,' his son pointed out.

'Where do the sharaken live?' Terrel asked. As always, any hint of a disagreement among the family made him feel uncomfortable, and he sought to distract them.

'In the interior,' Aylen replied. 'In mystic palaces atop the distant mountains.' He spoke in a deliberately dreamy yet portentous voice.

'You shouldn't speak so disrespectfully of our guides,' Kerin admonished his sons, 'especially as there is a guest at our meal.' He was trying to sound stern and disapproving, but Terrel could not help feeling that his heart was not in the argument.

'Sorry,' Aylen said, grinning.

'Terrel has a right to know what they're like,' Olandis

said. 'What they do – or don't do – affects him now as well as us.'

'Have you ever seen their palaces, Aylen?' Terrel asked. For a long time he had thought of the younger brother as Aylemirana, but he understood their system of names now – although he was still not sure why they each needed two or three. Where he came from you only needed one. It was a trivial difference between the two lands, but it still took some getting used to.

'Me?' Aylen said, looking surprised. 'No. Gate's the only one of us who's done much travelling, and I doubt even he's been that far.'

Everyone looked at Kerin, but he just shook his head, frowning slightly.

'Does anyone want more soup?' Ysatel asked, signalling the end of that conversation for the time being.

Everyone except Terrel accepted a second helping. Although he was immensely grateful for everything he received, he often found the food unappetising, and the broth that night had been unusually thin and tasteless. Even his memories of the frugal fare at Havenmoon seemed luxurious by comparison. None of the others made any comment about the meal, but Ysatel was obviously dissatisfied with her efforts.

'Do you think you'll be able to go fishing again soon?' she asked hopefully.

Kerin's sons deferred to their father in such matters, and so it was he who answered.

'Maybe. We'll see how we do in the river tomorrow.'

'Could I go?' Terrel asked.

An awkward silence followed his suggestion, and he began to wish he hadn't spoken. He was constantly hoping to find ways to contribute to the family's wellbeing, but on further reflection he could see that it was not a practical idea.

'He could probably charm them onto his hooks,' Aylen remarked, trying to make light of the situation.

'I doubt if you could handle a canoe,' Kerin said more soberly.

'Perhaps Terrel could come with one of us,' Olandis suggested. 'That way we'd only lose one screenhandler.'

'We'll see,' his father said, and the subject was closed.

Ysatel normally cleared away once they had finished eating, and then the family made their preparations for the night. However, this particular evening was unusually mild, and because the daylight was now lasting a little longer, they decided to stay round the fire for a while. Aylen teased his brother about the attentions he'd been receiving from one of the village girls, Ysatel checked the progress of the wound on Olandis's arm, and Kerin reminded them to think about what they should put on their prayer-flag for the forthcoming moon-days. Then Aylen raised a more contentious subject.

'There's a rumour going round that the soldiers are thinking of moving the fences lower down the slope.'

'What for?' Ysatel exclaimed. 'Haven't they taken enough already?'

Terrel had been told the history of the black mountain. The fact that it had been claimed by Macul's king, almost as soon as he had learnt that its dark rock contained almost unlimited supplies of precious stones and minerals, was the central injustice of Fenduca's existence. The soldiers who had driven off the prospectors and built defences to keep them out had, in effect, stolen those treasures – which were normally only found deep underground – from the very people who had discovered them. Terrel now knew that he was not the only one whom fate had cheated.

'Nothing's ever going to be enough for Ekuban,' Olandis commented bitterly.

'Does Vadanis have a king?' Aylen asked.

The question took Terrel by surprise. His hosts had recognized his reluctance to discuss his homeland, and their curiosity had been muted of late. When he'd first been able to talk to them, they had been full of questions – Does everyone on Vadanis have eyes like yours? Can you feel the ground moving all the time? Why did you leave? – but now they rarely bothered, knowing his answers would be evasive.

'We . . . we have an emperor.'

Aylen smiled, evidently amused by the idea that a small group of islands – whose total area was only a tiny fraction of that of Macul – should consider itself an *empire*.

'And does he exploit his people as Ekuban does?'

'I . . . wouldn't know about that.'

'Leave the boy alone, Chute,' Kerin said. 'What's he going to know of emperors or kings?'

What indeed? Terrel thought, the spectres raised by his conversation with Elam returning to haunt him.

'There's another rumour, that the soldiers are going to be looking for more volunteers soon,' Aylen said. 'Think they'll get any?'

'Only the most desperate,' his father replied. 'As usual.'

Inside the military boundaries, the upper part of the mountain was being dismantled piece by piece so that its riches could be sent to the royal court. Such an enormous enterprise naturally required vast amounts of manpower, and the king's contractors employed hundreds of miners in conditions that amounted to little more than slave labour. Even so, such employment was often sought by those who had had enough of the uncertainty and almost hopeless grind of life in Fenduca. Terrel had learnt that the village's name, translated literally, meant Lower-down, and this was apt in both a literal and a metaphorical sense.

'If our luck doesn't change soon,' Olandis said, '*we* might be getting desperate.'

'Don't say that!' Ysatel gasped. 'Not even in jest.'

'I wasn't joking,' he responded grimly. 'We've found nothing worthwhile for days. Maybe I *should* go up there.'

'Don't be daft,' Aylen told him.

'What's daft about it? At least I'd get a regular wage.'

'You'd get a pittance!'

'And I could use it to help you,' Olandis went on. 'At the very least, you'd have one less mouth to feed.'

'Such a thing would help none of us,' Ysatel declared. She was white-faced with shock – horrified by the fact that Olandis might even be considering such a venture – and glanced at her husband for support.

'You're a fool if you think it would do any good,' Kerin stated, stony-faced. 'But you'll have to make up your own mind, as always.' With that he stood up, signalling that the discussion was at an end.

The hut was very quiet that night, and Terrel felt the tension more than any of them. Living there had given him his first intimation that a family unit could work, even in poverty-stricken circumstances, and the argument had allowed him to see that – even within such a close group – there could be cracks in the foundations of love and mutual respect. Olandis's anger and Ysatel's dismay had affected the boy deeply, and the comment about 'one less mouth to feed' had made him feel dreadfully guilty.

Terrel's nightmares had receded during the last month, as he had grown accustomed to his new life, but now – with all his doubts and fears crowding back – he was reluctant to commit himself to sleep. When he finally managed to do so, his anxiety proved to be justified.

The mocking voice of the enchanter haunted his dreams, bringing with it pain and a redoubled sense of loss, until a sword flashed down, glinting in the starlight – and Terrel was plunged into an endless, swirling darkness.

CHAPTER ELEVEN

Most of the villagers hung back from the initial confrontation, intimidated by the soldiers' polished steel and impassive stares. Only Farazin and Kerin went forward, and even they were forced to halt below the ledge where the janizar stood, so that they had to talk with him from a literally inferior position. Although Yahn's expression of open contempt did not change, he was aware of the identity of the two men. He was obliged to treat the skywatcher with at least the pretence of respect, and he knew that Kerin – unlike most of the scum ranged below him on the mountainside – was a man to be reckoned with. Yahn had not risen to his present rank of janizar, which brought with it the command of over two hundred men, without realizing that information was a valuable weapon. While the inhabitants of Fenduca were not his enemies in a technical sense, he thought of them as the opposing force in the continuing battle for the mountain, and treated them accordingly. In truth it was a one-sided battle, but that only made him all the more determined that his victory would be complete.

'There is something you wish to discuss with us, Janizar?' Farazin asked.

'No discussion is necessary,' Yahn announced, his voice carrying easily to the gathering below. 'I come to inform you of three things. The first of these is self-evident.'

Without turning round he signalled to one of his deputies, and there was movement at the recently opened gate in the fence behind him. A dishevelled group of men shuffled forward, several of them limping. A few had to be supported by their fellows, while others had arms in rough slings or were covered in grimy, blood-stained bandages. One man had a cloth wrapped around his head, covering his eyes, and was being led by one of his companions. All their faces were drawn with pain and despair.

'We have no more need of these workers,' Yahn stated. 'Do with them as you will.'

As he spoke, one of the pitiful band stumbled and fell, only to be prodded to his feet by a guard's spear.

'If you treat them like this,' Kerin said, 'no one will be willing to work for you.' Although he spoke quietly, those who knew him could hear the suppressed rage in his voice.

'I don't think that's likely,' the janizar replied patronizingly. 'To my mind it should be an incentive for the miners to take greater care of themselves, and remain fit for work. Accidents are a sign of incompetence. Am I supposed to pay the king's wages to men who can no longer carry out their duties?'

Kerin did not respond, knowing it would be pointless.

The discarded miners continued down the slope, towards an uncertain welcome from the villagers. Most of them were strangers, but two were former inhabitants of Fenduca who had been desperate enough to accept the king's wages – something many of those they'd left behind had regarded as a betrayal. Now they would not be able to support themselves, and knew they were unlikely to find much pity or charity among those who had few resources to spare.

'Let's see if you treat them any better than I would,' Yahn said, a malicious grin on his face.

'What else?' Farazin asked.

'The perimeter fence is to be moved,' the janizar replied. 'The section of the river above a line drawn from the base of Leaven Scree to the point of Raven's Crag is now to be considered part of the military compound.'

There were some groans from the crowd at this, not least because the area described included the Demon's Cauldron, a deep pool in which silt and other debris collected. Several good finds had been made there recently by those willing to risk diving within the swirling waters, and it was obvious that this was the main reason for the change in the boundary.

'What right have you to do this?' a voice cried out. 'Why—'

'What right?' Yahn roared. 'The right of law! The word of King Ekuban himself. Would you challenge that? You are scavengers, feeding off the crumbs from my table. It is you who have no rights. You're lucky I let you stay here at all. A less charitable man would've got rid of you long ago. This mountain is mine! And I will take *all* of it if necessary.'

His tirade silenced the onlookers' protests. The janizar looked around, challenging any of them to make so much as a sound, but their token resistance was over. At one point Yahn saw a face he did not recognize – a crippled boy whose eyes looked odd and whose pale face was frozen in shock. One more hopeless misfit, he thought dismissively and passed on, his gaze finally coming to rest on Kerin. Even he had nothing to say.

'It has been noted that two of your *dwellings* . . .' Yahn pronounced the word as if he thought the villagers' homes hardly deserved such a name, '. . . are in the prohibited zone. You have until sunrise tomorrow to remove your belongings and any other material. The rest of the area is out of bounds as of this moment, and the removal of *anything* else will be considered theft of royal property. You all know the punishment for such a crime.'

He paused to let that point sink in. As expected, no further objections were voiced aloud.

Yahn knew all about the Demon's Cauldron. He had been furious when he'd discovered that several significant finds had been made there, because it meant that his own miners' checks and filters higher up the river were not working properly. But he was calm now, knowing that whatever treasures lay within its turbulent depths would come back to him. He'd have the entire thing drained if necessary.

The fact that the value of the produce from the mining operation had increased every year since he'd been given command of the black mountain garrison was a source of great pride to the janizar. At the time he'd seen the appointment as a double-edged sword, but his subsequent success had made him more ambitious than at any time

in his career. He was determined that when he eventually returned to court it would be to a hero's welcome,
and for that he knew he had to keep up the flow of riches
for some time to come. Last year's tally, compiled from
the meticulous records of each heavily guarded convoy
sent to Talazoria, Macul's royal capital, was only slightly
up on the year before, and well below the self-imposed
quota Yahn had desired. In the early days the mining had
been easy – little more than a matter of picking up various
valuable stones and ores from the ground. Now the
process involved much more intensive labour and, while
he and the engineers who organized the actual excavations
had made sure that their operation was more efficient
than ever before, there was a chance that output might
begin to fall soon. Yahn was determined to do everything
in his power to prevent that happening.

'Finally,' he went on, 'I can offer employment, at the
usual terms, to any able-bodied men who want it. This
gate will remain open until dusk, and my deputies will
process any volunteers.'

Some of those in the crowd had evidently been
expecting this announcement and, amid dark mutterings
and the exchange of a few poisonous glances, three men
walked forward after only a slight hesitation.

'So much for your theory, Kerin,' the janizar remarked
with a smile.

For the rest of that afternoon the people of Fenduca made
the best of the new situation. Some of the villagers helped
the two families who were being forced to move, carrying
their meagre possessions to new locations, and salvaging
as much of the material of the huts as they could. Others

made arrangements for the injured miners. Even though they were not exactly welcome additions to the population, they would not be allowed to starve if it could be helped. At the same time, several more men collected their belongings and made their way, shame or defiance on their faces, towards the soldiers' domain.

Terrel, who had been appalled both by the janizar's callous actions and by the villagers' meek acceptance of them, spent much of the time with Ysatel. The lines of her face were drawn tight, concealing emotions he could not begin to fathom, and when he expressed his disbelief at the injustices of the day, he was taken aback by her exasperated response.

'That's just the way it is, Terrel,' she snapped.

'But—' He had never seen Ysatel so angry before.

'Who are we to argue?' she went on. 'The janizar was right. We *are* living on their scraps – and there are going to be fewer than ever now. Yet we stay on, hoping for a miracle that never comes. And why? Because we're obsessed. We all think that one day – perhaps tomorrow – we'll find that perfect stone or a nugget big enough to make our fortune, something that would allow us to leave here on our own terms. It'll never happen, of course. The only way we'll leave here will be when Yahn decides to drive us away altogether.'

Terrel had stood, paralyzed by shock as her bitterness spewed out, unable to think of any response. There was something hard in Ysatel's voice, something compressed. Her eyes were dry, as if she was beyond tears, but Terrel knew that her feelings were coming close to crushing her heart, her spirit. And that was a prospect he could not bear.

'Why don't you—' he began hesitantly.

'Talk to Kerin?' she said, completing his question for him. 'What good would that do? He's more obsessed than the rest of us. This is *his* mountain, remember? It'll be the death of him. And me too, I shouldn't wonder.'

She *was* crying now, her hard-won control deserting her. When Terrel hesitantly reached out a hand towards her, she took it gratefully. He put his good arm around her shoulders, and held her until her weeping slowly subsided.

At last she drew back, wiped her face with her sleeve, and gave him a wan smile.

'I'm sorry, Terrel.'

'What for?'

'These aren't your problems,' she told him. 'At least you know where you want to go when you leave here.'

During the night, one of Fenduca's problems partially solved itself – although in a way that gave no one any pleasure. Two of the ex-miners died of their injuries, and several others – those whose legs were not too badly damaged – left of their own accord to try their fortunes elsewhere. Of the three men that remained, two were permanently crippled and were not likely to live much longer, and the third – the one who had been blinded – was wandering in a dream-world of his own, refusing to even touch the food he was offered. He talked aloud much of the time, addressing an invisible audience, but he made little sense, and did not respond if anyone spoke to him.

Terrel spent part of the next morning listening to the man's ramblings, which resembled his own feverish delirium – but with one terrible difference. When this nightmare ended, its victim would wake to the horror of a world he could not see. Terrel was about to turn away, knowing that there was nothing he could do, when the man said something that made him hesitate.

'Why is the palace so dark? All the rooms. All the rooms. Dark.'

Anyone else hearing this would have dismissed it as mere nonsense – the miner had obviously never been inside a real palace in his life – but to Terrel it sounded so much like something Alyssa might have said that he was immediately intrigued. He waited, listening with renewed interest, but the man was silent for a while, and when he did speak again his words meant nothing.

For a few moments Terrel had wondered if, rather than taking the form of an animal, Alyssa had tried to take a human body, choosing one whose apparent madness matched her own. But the more he thought about this, the more ludicrous the idea seemed. It had been a co-incidence, nothing more.

CHAPTER TWELVE

'Ready?' Olandis asked.

'I think so.' Terrel looked down at himself, realizing for the first time that he had grown taller since leaving Havenmoon. His clothes, made up of some of his old things and others that Ysatel had altered to fit him, felt strange, and his boots were beginning to feel tight. He would need new ones soon, but he had no idea where to get them from.

'You'll do,' Ysatel said approvingly, then turned to Olandis. 'Have you got everything?'

'Yes.'

'You'd better be off then.' She was trying to sound bright and cheerful, but her underlying anxiety was obvious.

'Don't worry, Ysy,' Olandis said, kissing his step-mother's cheek. 'We'll be back before you know it. And Terrel's going to be fine, aren't you?'

Terrel nodded.

'We're going to catch *lots* of fish,' he declared.

'That's the spirit,' Olandis said, laughing as he hoisted his pack and settled the straps on his shoulders.

However, before Terrel could lift his own, much smaller bag, a voice sounded from outside the hut.

'Ysatel, are you there? Is the boy there?'

Ysatel went to the door, followed by the others, to discover a young woman standing outside, a heavily wrapped bundle in her arms.

'Hello, Tisa. Do you want me for something?'

Whatever impulse had brought Tisa there seemed to have deserted her now, and she opened and closed her mouth several times before answering.

'Him,' she said, nodding at Terrel. 'I thought—' The bundle coughed, then began to wail and the woman fell silent, looking down at her baby.

'You thought?' Ysatel prompted eventually.

'It's little Jessett. She can't seem to lose this fever. I've tried everything I know.' Tisa glanced up, her eyes bright with tears. 'I thought he might help her.'

'Terrel?'

Their visitor nodded eagerly.

'He helped all those animals.'

Ysatel glanced at the boy, and saw the horrified expression on his face.

'Do you want to try?'

Terrel said nothing, his reluctance clear. It was one thing to try to restore the health of an animal, but a child was something altogether different. He did not feel ready for such a responsibility, and wished the woman would go away.

'Please . . . Terrel.' Tisa evidently had to force herself

to use his name, and he realized how much courage it must have taken for her to come this far.

'I probably won't be able to help,' he said.

'I know that.' Hope sprang into Tisa's eyes nonetheless. 'But could you try? I'd be very grateful.'

'All right.'

'Come inside,' Ysatel said.

Terrel sat on one of the pallets, and Tisa gently laid the baby on his lap so that he could cradle her in his good arm. Like most boys of his age, Terrel found infants both embarrassing and disgusting. All he could see of Jessett was her face and the top of her head, but she smelt revolting. She was still wailing, but faintly now – as if she was too weak to make much of an effort – and she coughed intermittently. Her eyes were screwed tightly shut, and beneath the wispy strands of hair, her scalp was mottled. Her face was red too, her lips almost purple, and heat radiated from her skin.

'She's too hot,' he muttered, wondering why her mother hadn't had the common sense to see that for herself. He tried to loosen the baby's clothing but his right hand was too clumsy, and he had to let Ysatel do it for him. The sweet, sickly smell grew more powerful.

Uncomfortably aware of his expectant audience, Terrel hesitated, then made himself act. Using his right hand, he laid the tips of his crooked fingers on the baby's forehead. Hoping that some hidden instinct would take over, as it had done with the animals, he tried to relax and waited to fall into a waking dream – but he remained alert and aware of his surroundings. He felt a wave of heat flow through his body, but that could just have been because he now felt utterly foolish. The baby stopped crying. Flashes of pain that seemed to come from all Terrel's bones in turn made him wince, and this was followed by an unexpected sense of peace, but all the changes were inside him. He felt sure he hadn't affected the outside world. Jessett began coughing again, then wailed even louder than before. Her illness was still discolouring her skin, and when she opened her eyes the fever still burned in their depths.

Terrel looked up, sensing the disappointment all around him.

'I'm sorry.'

Tisa nodded briefly.

'Thank you for trying,' she whispered, then all but snatched up the baby and fled from the hut, so anxious was she to be gone. Terrel thought that she was probably wishing now that she had never come. His failure, even though he had really expected nothing else, made him feel wretched.

'Are you all right?' Ysatel asked.

'Yes.' The fact that he wasn't tired was further evidence that he had not achieved anything.

'Let's go fishing then,' Olandis said.

The first part of their journey was on foot, because the upper stretch of the river was too shallow and rough to take even the smallest craft. Terrel was aware that he was slowing Olandis down, and was glad when – after an arduous trek – they reached the place where the canoes were hidden in thick undergrowth. They were to take only one boat – Terrel wouldn't be able to handle one on his own – so the packing away of their stores while still leaving enough space for themselves and the fish they hoped to catch was an exacting task. When all was ready, Terrel clambered into the canoe, then Olandis pushed it out into the river and jumped in himself. Being on water again brought back some unpleasant memories, but under Olandis's guidance the boy soon felt secure enough.

At first they moved swiftly, pushed along by a strong current. Terrel began to feel nauseous and unaccountably weary, but by the time they reached the main river, where the water moved more sluggishly, he felt better and was able to join Olandis in wielding one of the short oars. He found he could only paddle effectively on the left side, and so did not try to do anything else. His partner took care of the steering, switching his own oar from side to side to balance out Terrel's efforts. They had little time or breath for talking until, soon after midday, they reached a spot where Olandis thought there might be some fish. After showing Terrel how to bait the hooks and trail the lines from the stern of the boat without getting them tangled, as well as testing the tension of the lines with his fingers, Olandis began to move the canoe slowly back and forth across the wide expanse of calm water. After their earlier frenetic activity, the whole process seemed remarkably peaceful.

'What should I do?' Terrel asked.

'Nothing. Just let me know when you get a bite. The silvertails run in shoals here, so if we get one we should get a lot more.'

They drifted on for a while, each lost in his own thoughts.

'Anything?' Olandis asked, as they completed another crossing and he began to turn the boat around.

Terrel shook his head.

'I don't suppose you can *make* them appear?' Olandis said with a grin.

'Charm them, you mean,' Terrel replied, recalling Aylen's comment. 'No. I need to touch a creature to make any sort of connection with it, and even then I don't actually know what I'm doing. And fish are just too strange anyway.'

'All right. One more traverse, then we'll try somewhere else.' Olandis began to paddle steadily again. 'Was there no connection with the baby at all?'

The question took Terrel by surprise, and it was a few moments before he answered.

'No, not really,' he said, peering down into the sun-sparkled water.

'Pity. We could do with a healer right now.'

'It's not something I can control,' Terrel confessed. Being reminded of his failure had made him feel defensive.

'You did your best. That's all anyone can ask. Dreams have their own ways.'

Terrel was about to ask what Olandis meant when he was distracted by a flash of silver beneath the boat. Moments later he felt a tug on one of the lines, quickly followed by a similar pull on the other.

'We've got a bite! Lots of them!'

'Great. Just hang on. I'll come and help.' Olandis stowed his paddle, moved carefully to Terrel's side, and felt the tension in the lines for himself. 'This one first,' he decided.

The bottom of the canoe was soon covered with a mass of silver-scaled fish, their tails flapping and their mouths uselessly open to the air. Terrel had felt nothing when he touched them, but nonetheless he experienced a small measure of disquiet as he watched them die. Olandis, on the other hand, was jubilant, having landed as good a catch as he could have hoped for at the first attempt. He threw the lines back in as soon as they were free, without even bothering with bait, and was rewarded by a second, albeit smaller batch. In all, they now had over two dozen sizeable fish.

'Not a bad start,' he commented. 'At this rate we'll be able to get back to Fenduca tomorrow.'

As it turned out, his optimism was misplaced. They caught nothing more that day, and by the time they came to make camp, frustration had soured their mood. As Olandis set about the messy task of gutting the fish, Terrel did what he could to be of use, tending the fire and preparing food from their supplies.

When darkness fell and they'd completed their appointed tasks, Olandis began to cheer up a little and seemed more inclined to talk. Even so, Terrel was nervous about raising the subject that had been on his mind for the last three days – ever since Janizar Yahn had made his announcement – fearing that it would spoil the mood again. In the end, Olandis did it for him.

'I suppose the new fence'll be finished by now,' he remarked. 'It's a shame there wasn't another quake while they were building it.'

The time of greatest danger, according to Farazin's calculations, had passed two days ago, and there had not been the slightest tremor.

'Are the soldiers always so brutal?' Terrel asked.

'That was nothing,' Olandis told him. 'I've seen much worse. With a king like Ekuban, what else can you expect?'

'Is he so bad?'

'He's a tyrant. He stays in power because he controls everything – wealth, food supplies, trade – and he has the army to enforce his laws. The gentry all lounge about in their jewelled palaces, while the rest of us have barely enough to eat. They say the floor of Ekuban's bedroom is made of solid gold, and that every chair he sits on has to be decorated with at least ten large gemstones. Any such stone would be a fortune for one of us. Riches are the only way to win a decent life, it seems, which is why places like Fenduca exist. The only alternative is to join the army and become one of the oppressors. Only someone who has no conscience would do that, so it's not surprising most soldiers are bastards.'

'It doesn't seem fair,' Terrel said.

Olandis laughed.

'Of course it's not fair!'

'Don't the sharaken have any say in the running of the country?'

'They don't concern themselves with matters of the world,' Olandis explained. 'As Farazin keeps telling us, they are "of the spirit". Why should they help the likes of us?'

'Has anyone ever asked them to?'

Olandis looked shocked, then grinned.

'I keep forgetting you're a foreigner,' he said. 'Look. The sharaken aren't like us. True, they're above the king's laws, but they live in a different world of dreams and magic.'

'But they must use the magic for *something*,' Terrel persisted.

'Why? I don't suppose they're even aware of what goes

on outside their rarefied domain, and probably wouldn't care even if they did.'

'On Vadanis, the seers advise the Emperor about everything.'

'Well, it's different here. And it's not really your problem, is it? I thought you were going back to your islands as soon as you get the chance.'

'I am,' Terrel conceded. He had not forgotten his promise to Alyssa.

'Who's Alyssa?'

For a few moments Terrel was too stunned to reply.

'A friend,' he said eventually. 'How do you know about her?'

'You still talk in your sleep sometimes. In your own language, of course, so we can't tell what you're saying, but her name seems to crop up quite often. Is it her you're going back to?'

'Yes.'

'You're a bit young to be in love, aren't you?'

Terrel was too flustered to respond.

'I'm only teasing,' Olandis assured him. 'You're lucky. I wish I could find someone worth going halfway round the world for.'

'I thought there was a girl in the village?'

'You shouldn't pay much attention to what Aylen says. Even if Elyce loves me I don't feel the same for her, and that's no good, is it?'

There was a short, thoughtful pause.

'Ysatel would follow your father round the world,' Terrel said quietly.

'I know. In a sense she already has. The sad thing is I'm not sure he'd follow her.'

'Do you miss your mother?'

'Every day,' Olandis replied, then realized who he was talking to. 'But I'm not complaining. At least I got to know her for a while. And we both love Ysy a lot. Aylen even more than me, I think.'

They were silent for a while, and then Terrel returned to an earlier topic.

'Did you mean it when you said you might join the miners?'

'Not really. I've thought about it sometimes, but there'd only be one reason good enough to actually make me do it.'

'What's that?'

'If I thought there was a chance of getting the miners to throw the soldiers out and claim the mountain for ourselves,' Olandis replied.

Two days later, when they arrived back in Fenduca, Olandis and Terrel were greeted by Ysatel before they had even reached the hut. She was smiling broadly, and it was clear that she had more than the welcome arrival of food on her mind.

'I hoped you'd be back today.'

'Missed us, did you?' her stepson said, grinning.

'Of course, but it's Terrel everyone's waiting for.'

'Why?' Terrel was puzzled, and rather alarmed.

'Little Jessett recovered from her fever the day you left,' Ysatel replied. 'Only a few hours after you saw her.'

'But I—'

'It doesn't matter,' she went on. 'Tisa's been telling everyone you saved her baby's life. You're a hero now, whether you like it or not.'

CHAPTER THIRTEEN

The next few days were hectic. No one believed Terrel's claim that Jessett's recovery must have happened naturally, that the only possible thing he had done was to suggest loosening her clothing to allow her skin to cool. It was pointed out that the baby's return to health had been remarkably rapid given how long she had been suffering, and Terrel's belief that this was just a coincidence was dismissed as false modesty. Even Ysatel, with whom he tried to discuss the matter sensibly, told him that he 'couldn't argue with results'.

After that, his attitude changed. He was more or less obliged to try to help others, and it would have been churlish to refuse, so he made the best of it – hoping for guidance, but not really expecting any. He was afraid that his true lack of ability would soon become apparent, and he dreaded the moment when the truth would dash the villagers' hopes – hopes that had been raised to unrealistic heights.

His only consolation came from remembering something Babak had said, when talking about the efficacy of the potions he sold. 'If my patients *believe* they're going to get well, then they do. The human mind is a wonderful physician.' The self-styled apothecary had made a living out of that philosophy, and now Terrel had to try to do the same. The least he could do was give the villagers a chance to heal themselves. However, that still did not make him feel any less of a fraud when he held someone's hand or touched their forehead, but he persevered, hoping to do more good than harm. He soon found that the actual process – the contact between him and his patients – became an end in itself. Terrel had been in pain his whole life, from a time even before he was born, and he could not only recognize it in others but could also trace its patterns. He *understood*.

There were no instant reactions, as there had been with the animals, and – just as with Jessett – Terrel did not fall into an obvious waking dream, but he nevertheless felt that some sort of connection was being made whenever he tried to help someone. He wondered whether this might be an unconscious extension of the psinoma, but made no deliberate attempt to pry into his patients' minds. Instead he simply spent some time with them, talking if that seemed appropriate, and offering a few practical suggestions – things that to him were just a matter of common sense. Everyone was grateful for his efforts, and he could only wait until disillusionment set in.

It never did. In each case, sometimes within a few hours but more often within a day or two, there was at least some improvement in the patient's condition. No one understood less about what was actually happening than Terrel himself, but his successes were too consistent for it just to be a coincidence. He ceased to question what was happening and simply accepted it, thinking that perhaps his own faith might actually be making whatever he was doing even more effective. There were times when he tried to analyze his actions, but the failure of such attempts was more than offset by the satisfaction he gained from helping people – and, as before, by the gifts he received in return, which allowed him to repay Ysatel and her family for their kindness.

Terrel had no knowledge of the internal workings of the human body – in fact just thinking about it made him feel squeamish – but it seemed that he was more successful in dealing with the effects of illness or injury, rather than with the underlying cause. He could cool a fever without ever identifying the infection from which it sprang. He could stem the blood flow from a wound without being able to close the gash itself. He could not mend a broken bone, but seemed able to alleviate the pain associated with it. Whether a fracture healed properly or not depended on several other factors – the seriousness of the injury, how it had been splinted, the physical strength of the patient – but there were those who claimed that Terrel's intervention speeded up the process no matter what the circumstances were. That, in fact, was the most extraordinary aspect of the whole thing. Once relieved of some of the discomfort of their ailment, most of his patients improved of their own accord within a relatively short space of time. Terrel believed that they were healing themselves – they *thought* they were getting better, so they did – and this idea was backed up by the fact that many of his most obvious

successes came with small children. Their faith in him
was the simplest and the strongest – they were used to
believing what grown-ups told them – and even though
Terrel was still quite young himself, they regarded him
with awe. Once they overcame their instinctive distrust
of his strange appearance, they hung on his every word.
Their developing minds held powers he could only guess
at, but each child he treated got better again. And that,
in turn, enhanced his reputation with the adults. Of
course – as Ysatel pointed out when he tried to discuss
his theory with her – this didn't explain Jessett's
recovery. She had been too young to understand what
was going on. Terrel had no answer to that, but was
simply glad that he had been able to help.

There were exceptions, of course – primarily the three
men who now lay in the communal hut that was used as
an infirmary for those who had no homes to go to. These
unfortunates were tended intermittently by some of the
village women, and no one believed that they would live
for long. Two of them were discarded miners – the third
had died while Terrel and Olandis were away fishing –
and the other was Solan, the man who had lost not only
his health but also his wife and daughter in the first earthquake. He had been languishing there for more than a
long month, surviving much longer than anyone had
expected.

Terrel didn't hold out much hope for the three men
and, even though this seemed callous, he spent little time
with them, concentrating instead on cases that would
derive a more immediate benefit from his putative talent.
However, as the days passed and the demands on his time
grew less, he found himself visiting the hut more often,

hoping if not for a cure then at least to ease their suffering a little.

Ysatel went with him whenever she could, aware that Terrel was still not back to full health himself. He protested that he was doing nothing strenuous, but she could see the weariness in his face, and guessed that becoming a healer and working for as many hours as he was able had stretched the boy's resources to the limit. He had had a few dizzy spells – which could possibly have been a delayed reaction to his efforts to help others – and Ysatel was determined that he should not wear himself out completely. She admired his compassion and selflessness, but knew that he would have to learn to pace himself. As a result she accompanied him to the infirmary to make sure he did not stay too long.

Solan's plight was pitiful. He had been a strong man, not big but wiry and agile, but now he was wasting away, his life all but destroyed by the rockfall. When he was awake he was in constant agony, pain that Terrel's ministrations had only been able to dull, but things were even worse when he was asleep. Then he relived his hopeless attempts to rescue his loved ones, crying out and driving himself into a frenzy that only made his physical torment more excruciating. Terrel sensed the echo of his distress – of both body and mind – whenever he held the man's good hand in his own, and it was on one such occasion that he felt, with a certainty he did not question, that Solan was going to die soon.

He also knew that if the man died in his present state, then his torment would live on in the next world, his spirit lost in an endless cycle of misery. Terrel remembered the anguished face of Kativa, whose ghost had been imprisoned by grief for two hundred years. He had been responsible for her being able to move on at last, and that memory gave him the incentive and the strength to act now.

'It wasn't your fault, Solan,' he said softly, as the invalid groaned in his sleep.

Ysatel, watching with some concern from her position by the doorway, was about to say that the injured man wouldn't be able to hear anything, but then Solan grew quieter and his sudden repose stilled her tongue.

'It wasn't your fault,' Terrel repeated forcefully. 'You have to listen to me, Solan. You did all you could. It's just something that happened.'

He paused then, and although his patient still seemed to be asleep, his face was more peaceful and his breathing had grown steadier. Ysatel found that she was holding her own breath.

'They know you tried,' Terrel went on. 'You have no need of forgiveness, from them, from yourself, from anyone. The dream can be changed.'

There was another pause, briefer this time.

'I don't know why you didn't die too,' Terrel said, as if answering an unspoken question. 'Who can know such things? But that wasn't your fault either. You have to believe me, Solan. This is the most important thing you'll ever do, but you don't have much time. None of this was your fault.'

Terrel's voice had been rising, his tone becoming more urgent, but then he felt the pressure of his own grip being returned by his patient's fingers for the first and last time, and he fell silent, hoping. Solan's face changed again. It was not a smile; that would have been too much to ask. But the pain was gone at last.

'You can go to them now,' Terrel said quietly.

The air in the hut became very still.

'He's dead,' Terrel said a moment later, releasing the lifeless hand.

'Did he . . . ?' Ysatel's voice failed her.

'He understood, I think. In the end.'

'You're . . . you're a good man, Terrel,' Ysatel whispered.

He turned round to look at her, and was astonished to see that she was crying. It was the first time anyone had referred to him as a man, rather than a boy, and he didn't know how to react to that – or to her tears.

The next day, Terrel headed straight from Solan's burial to the infirmary hut. When she realized where he was going, Ysatel ran after him and took his arm.

'You've done enough for now,' she told him. 'Why don't you get some rest? You were talking in your sleep again last night.'

Terrel had no memory of any dreams, but knew that she wouldn't lie to him.

'I'm not tired.' The stoop of his shoulders and the drawn look on his face told another story, but Ysatel knew she had little chance of getting him to admit it.

'I'll come with you, then.'

'And make sure I don't stay too long?'

'Exactly,' she admitted. 'Someone has to look after you.'

They began walking again.

'I feel responsible,' he said.

'I know you do, but—'

'I should save my energy for people who really matter?'

Ysatel had been thinking the same thing, but hearing it put so bluntly made her feel ashamed of herself.

'They don't have anyone else,' Terrel added. 'I was like that before Aylen and Olandis found me. I'm only alive because they thought I mattered.'

'And they were right,' she said.

'One of the miners is going to die soon, but Talker won't unless we let him. Apart from his eyes there's nothing physically wrong with him.' They had taken to calling the blind man Talker because that was what he liked to do. Nobody knew his real name.

'But his mind has gone,' Ysatel said. While he was the only one of the infirmary inmates who ever spoke much, what he said was usually gibberish. Terrel's efforts had helped him to begin eating and drinking again, but nothing more. His eyes, when they were uncovered, looked normal but it was clear from his reactions – or lack of them – that he was completely blind. The villagers assumed that this was what had driven him mad.

'Not gone,' Terrel corrected her. 'Different.' The miner's ramblings had reminded him of some of Alyssa's more bizarre comments. 'What he says might make perfect sense to him.'

They had reached the hut by now, and were surprised by what they saw when they looked inside. Talker had left his own pallet, and was kneeling beside the other patient. He was holding the dying man's hand, just as Terrel had done on earlier visits, and the expression on his face was serene.

'What's he doing?'

'I don't know. I'd've said he was copying me, but he can't have seen what I did.'

At the sound of their voices Talker turned his head, his sightless eyes staring past them.

'Flying,' he said clearly. 'No pain now.' He patted the limp hand within his grasp.

Terrel and Ysatel went forward and found, as they had expected, that the injured miner was indeed no longer in any pain. He was dead, but his passing had apparently been peaceful enough. And he had not been alone.

'Did you help him?' Terrel asked.

'All wings come from the sky,' Talker said doubtfully. 'Touch me, touch you.' He turned back to the prone figure. 'Touch him.'

'You were trying to help him, weren't you?' Terrel persisted. 'To make it easier for him?'

Talker turned his blank eyes towards Terrel.

'There's a star inside you,' he stated in a tone devoid of any surprise. 'A shining star.'

Terrel was astonished by this comment, but had no chance to respond because the blind man suddenly fell into a dead faint and collapsed on to the floor. It took all Ysatel's and Terrel's strength to lift him onto his own pallet.

'You think he might be a healer too?' she asked breathlessly.

'Maybe.'

'What was all that about a star?'

'Nothing,' Terrel lied. 'Just more of his nonsense.'

Talker remained unconscious for the rest of that day and all the following night. After conducting the second burial rite in two days, Farazin accompanied Terrel to the infirmary hut to inspect the last remaining patient.

The blind man lay quite still, his breathing barely noticeable.

'Is he dead?' Farazin asked.

'No, but this isn't an ordinary sleep. I'm beginning to wonder if he'll ever wake up.'

'Perhaps that's for the best.'

Something in the old man's tone made Terrel look up curiously.

'Why did you say that? Have you seen anything like this before?'

Farazin hesitated before answering.

'Come with me,' he said eventually.

Terrel followed the sky-watcher outside, and fell into step beside him as they went down the slope to Farazin's own hut. He waited as the old man went inside – emerging a few moments later with an oil lamp – and then they headed west, out of the village.

'Where are we going?'

'You'll see soon enough. It's not far.'

'Then why do we need the lamp?' There were still several hours of daylight left.

'All in good time.'

After that Terrel kept his questions to himself, and concentrated on keeping his footing on the rough path. A quarter of an hour later they climbed over a ridge, and came to the entrance of a cave.

'Have you ever been underground before?'

'Yes.'

'Good. Some people find it hard to deal with,' Farazin remarked as he lit the lamp.

The cave proved to be the start of a long, winding tunnel that led into the heart of the hill. Daylight was soon a distant memory, and without the lamp they would have been plunged into utter darkness, but the stone underfoot was reasonably smooth, as if many people had walked this way before. Terrel was given no clue as to where they were going, and knew better than to ask.

Eventually the passage widened out into a large cavern that was full of extraordinary rock formations. Terrel had no time to admire these stalagmites, however, because his attention was drawn instantly to three human figures who lay on roughly-hewn stone slabs near the centre of the cave.

'They're alive,' Farazin explained as he and the boy moved closer, 'but they haven't moved for more than ten years.'

The old man evidently expected Terrel to be astonished by this revelation, but the boy merely nodded, staring at the trio – two men and one woman, all between twenty and thirty years of age.

'Do you call them sleepers?' he asked.

'Yes. But only a few of us know about them.'

'Why do they have to be kept secret?'

'We don't want to frighten people.'

'Then why bring *me* here?'

'I thought maybe . . . maybe you could heal them, somehow. Help them to wake up.'

Terrel sensed that such a task would be quite beyond him, but he knew that Farazin wouldn't accept this until he tried. He was nervous as he went forward and touched the hand of one of the men. The sleeper's skin was cool, not completely lifeless, but Terrel sensed no connection to the man at all. His thoughts flew back to Alyssa, who lay in the basement of Havenmoon in a similar suspended state. He had fondly imagined returning to her side, rousing her and taking her into his arms. Now he was plagued by the fear that when he did find her again she might still not be able to wake up. The hideousness of that thought made him close his eyes.

Quickly, without any hope, he tried to reach the other two, then turned back to Farazin and shook his head in answer to the sky-watcher's unspoken question. The old man nodded and gave a slight shrug, betraying resignation rather than any real disappointment.

'Tell me about them,' Terrel said. 'What happened?'

'They were among the first to explore the black mountain – before the military took over, that is – but something happened up there. No one has any idea what. They all fell into a deep sleep, and nobody could wake them. They weren't dead, but . . . well, you've seen them. They haven't had anything to eat or drink for all those years, but they haven't wasted away, and only seem to have aged a little bit. It's incredible.'

'Their spirits are wandering,' Terrel said quietly.

Farazin glanced at the boy in surprise, but Terrel did not explain.

'There were others on the mountain at the time, of course,' the sky-watcher went on. 'Including Kerin. But as far as we know no one else was affected. Kerin still wonders why they fell asleep and he didn't.'

'And now you think the same thing's happened to Talker?'

'*Something* happened to him up on the mountain,' Farazin pointed out, 'and you said yourself it's not a normal sleep.'

'I don't think it's the same thing,' Terrel said, but was

saved from having to justify this opinion when a strange sound came from the tunnel – a kind of whirring noise, which grew louder as they listened.

'What's—'

'Wings,' Terrel said, and moments later a pale grey dove flew into the cavern, its feathers glinting as it emerged into the lamplight.

'Great moons!' Farazin breathed. 'How did it—'

He did not finish the question, but fell silent in amazement as the bird swooped across the cave and alighted, with a last frantic flutter of its wings, on Terrel's outstretched hand.

About time too, Alyssa declared.

What do you mean? Where have you been? Terrel responded. *Why did you leave me alone for so long?* His heart had leapt as soon as the dove appeared, and he had not needed to see the 'ring' around one of its legs to know it was Alyssa, but her brusque greeting had confused him.

Hasn't it ever occurred to you that what you *do might have some bearing on what* we're *able to do?* she asked.

CHAPTER FOURTEEN

Because their bones lie easily here, Alyssa said.

What? Terrel was in no mood for starting a conversation in the middle.

That's why you chose this place, she explained.

Terrel looked around at the glade. It was a small circular dip, surrounded by bare, stunted trees. Alyssa's dove was perched on one of the pale grey rocks that poked up through the bracken and coarse grass.

I didn't choose it. It had simply been the first place they'd come to where they could be alone, out of sight of the path or the village.

Alyssa decided not to argue with him, just as she had refused to explain her comment about Terrel's actions dictating when she and the ghosts were able to visit him. He had asked her what she meant, but her answers had been typically obtuse – and with Farazin there in the cave as well, Terrel had become flustered. The sky-watcher had naturally been unaware that Terrel was talking to the bird, and had been asking questions of his own. Holding two conversations at once had proved impossible, but Terrel could not think how to get away from Farazin, and had been obliged to stay with the sky-watcher until they were in the open air again.

The dove had ridden on Terrel's shoulder as they made their way along the dark passages, her claws adjusting their grip whenever he stumbled. Farazin had clearly been intrigued by the bird's presence, but the boy had offered no explanation – beyond saying that it must have become lost in the caves and was allowing him to help it because of his natural affinity with animals.

Once they reached the entrance to the outside world, Alyssa had flown off, coming to rest a short distance away, and Terrel had told Farazin that he needed to be alone to think for a while. The old man had looked disappointed but had accepted the decision, returning to Fenduca alone while Terrel headed along the ridge and entered the nearby woodlands. He had stopped in the glade – which Alyssa seemed to think was an ancient burial site – simply because it offered a place to rest in some privacy. He sat down on one of the boulders.

Are the ghosts here?

Oh no, they passed on a long time ago.

For almost the first time he could remember, Terrel felt genuinely angry with Alyssa.

Stop playing games. You know what I mean.

His obvious annoyance seemed to startle her, and she ruffled her neck feathers.

They'll be here soon, she said meekly.

Good. He was already regretting his harsh words. *I'm glad you're here.*

So am I.

What had prompted her to appear now? Terrel wondered, but didn't bother trying to ask again. He hadn't been aware of being in any danger. Could it be that Alyssa arrived – with the ghosts, if necessary – simply because he was in need of their help? And if so, what did that imply? Had he unknowingly sent her some kind of signal? Or had he merely taken another step down an unknown road – a road on which there were only certain points where the others could come to him? If that was true, he wondered where the journey was leading, and why he was the one who was travelling there.

He dismissed all these questions for the time being as his thoughts returned to Alyssa's last visit and, more specifically, to the conversation with Elam that had ended so abruptly.

Who am I, Alyssa? he asked quietly. *Who am I?*

Yourself, she answered. *Isn't that enough?*

No. Not any more.

They were silent for a while, looking at each other.

What difference will it make? Alyssa asked eventually.

I'll know the truth, he said.

It's just words. Nothing really changes.

Words are important.

You taught me that, she agreed. *But they can lie too. I learnt that for myself.*

That's why I want the truth.

Whose truth?

Terrel was about to ask what she meant – surely the truth belonged to everyone – but he was distracted by the arrival of the ghosts. He had never before met with them in the open in broad daylight, and his first reaction was surprise at how pale and translucent they appeared in the sunshine. Muzeni, whose image always seemed to be less sharply defined than the others, was especially faint. Even the colours of his outlandish clothes seemed faded to mere shadows as he glanced around and settled himself on one of the stones. Shahan remained standing, a concerned expression on his lined, angular face.

Terrel looked round for the last of the trio, but there was no sign of his friend.

Where's Elam?

Different corner, Alyssa said.

I think he was bored with us, Muzeni added wearily. *Can't blame him, really.*

Perhaps if you weren't so argumentative, Shahan remarked, looking down his great beak of a nose, *he wouldn't feel that way.*

It takes two to argue, the heretic pointed out. *If you— Be quiet!*

The seers both looked at Terrel in surprise.

I have some questions for you, he went on, before they had a chance to respond, *and I haven't got time for your bickering. I want some straight answers, or you can forget about me ever listening to you again. Understand?*

There's no need to— Muzeni began.

Yes, there is! Terrel snapped. *I've had a long time on my own to think since I left Vadanis, and I've worked a few things out. All you have to do is tell me if I'm right.*

The ghosts exchanged glances.

We owe you that much, Shahan conceded soberly.

Thank you, Terrel replied, his sarcastic tone masking his relief. *I have a brother, don't I? A twin brother.*

Yes.

He did this to me, didn't he? Terrel gestured towards his twisted limbs. *Before we were born.*

The surprise on the faces of both men seemed genuine, and neither of them answered.

I never saw it properly, Alyssa said. *It was part of you.*

Terrel knew she was referring to his recurring nightmare, the hate-filled dream that had at last begun to make sense. The thunder in the red ocean had been his mother's heartbeat, the pain the result of his battle with the enchanter – the battle that had begun even in the womb.

And he's been my enemy ever since, Terrel went on. *Do you know why?*

This time nobody answered him.

He's an enchanter. Did you realize that? He invaded my dreams, and he can control people. He's already been responsible for three deaths, maybe more for all I know. Mirival, a girl called Mela who was carrying his child, and . . . He broke off to look at Shahan, and realized that the ghost already knew what was coming. *And you, Shahan. He tried to kill me too, at Betancuria, and when that failed he made sure I was forced into exile. He actually sent me a letter gloating about it. At first I thought he was just mocking me when he signed it 'Farewell, brother', but it was true. And now, after all that, he's become a hero.*

We know who the real hero was, Alyssa said. *No one else could've done what you did.*

Terrel waved that aside, recalling all the other clues that had finally led him to believe the unbelievable.

My brother is Prince Jax, isn't he? he said, and waited.

For a few heartbeats only the wind disturbed the silence in the glade, rustling the fallen leaves and bracken. Even the birdsong had stopped, as if the whole world was holding its breath. Terrel told himself that he was ready for the answer, that he had prepared himself for what he was convinced must come, but when Shahan's voice finally sounded in his head, he was still shocked.

Yes, Jax is your twin. You are the son of Emperor Dheran and the Seventh Empress.

So I'm a prince of the Floating Islands? Terrel heard himself utter the absurd words as if in a trance.

Technically, yes, Shahan replied. *But as Adina rejected you at the time of your birth, and only a few people know of your existence, it's a moot point.*

For the first time in his life Terrel knew who his parents were – the parents who had abandoned him to life in a madhouse. The mixture of curiosity and resentment that had made him wonder about his family so often in the past was replaced now by a new combination of emotions – incredulity, anger, and – to his surprise – a deep sadness.

She rejected me because of this, he said, holding up his clawed hand. *And these.* He motioned towards his eyes.

Shahan nodded.

She was in great pain, and your arrival had been an enormous shock. Everyone knew her child was to be born that night, but no one had foreseen twins.

That's no excuse for what she did, Alyssa said fiercely.

I agree, Shahan said. *But the real tragedy was that all of those present, myself included, allowed her to prevail. It's something I lived to regret.*

But you came to find me.

Eventually, yes, when it was clear that the current interpretation of the Tindaya Code was failing.

And Jax had you killed because of it.

I know nothing of that, Shahan replied, but his tone indicated that he had every reason to believe Terrel was telling the truth.

Why didn't you let me know about this before? You once told me I'd been robbed of my birthright. You could have said something then.

It was complicated, Muzeni said, speaking for the first time since the discussion had begun. *By the time we realized you might be important, a great deal had changed. The Dark Moon had thrown everything into confusion and, as if that weren't enough, the various reinterpretations of the Code seemed to be at odds with one another. The only thing that remained certain was that it predicts a series of events between one four-moon conjunction and the next. You and Jax were born on the night of one such confluence, the first in seventy-five years, but now no one knows when the next one will be. Both your destinies should have been part of the oracles, but so much else was changing, and you already had such a lot to contend with. To put it bluntly, we weren't sure of you.*

Which is why you tested me! Terrel realized. *With Kativa.*

That's right, Shahan admitted. *It was the best we could do at the time.*

And that gave us confidence that you could go on to a greater task at Betancuria, Muzeni added.

You have to admit that was a good thing, Shahan said defensively. *You did save Vadanis, after all.*

But Jax took all the credit, Alyssa pointed out. *He's the one the seers are calling the Guardian.*

As things turned out, yes, Muzeni conceded, *but the main thing is that the islands are safe.*

And I ended up here, Terrel concluded.

Where you also seem to be doing some good, Shahan commented approvingly.

So what now? Is my destiny still part of the oracles?

Undoubtedly, Muzeni replied. *But your path may not be yours to choose.*

So who does *choose?* Terrel asked angrily. *You?*

The Code is—

Wait a moment! Terrel cut in. *You knew, didn't you? You knew I was going to be exiled!*

We thought it was a possibility, Muzeni admitted.

And you didn't do anything about it?

There was nothing we could *do*, Shahan protested.

We were aware that you might have to leave Vadanis, Muzeni added, *but we didn't know it would be against your will.*

You thought I'd choose *to leave?* Terrel asked incredulously.

The Code speaks of landscapes that simply don't exist on the islands, Shahan answered. *Which meant—*

Well, I've seen them now, Terrel snapped, thinking of the strange rock formations, the black mountain, and the swamps and rivers of Macul. *So I can go home.*

He glared defiantly at the two ghosts, but they made no comment.

When will the islands next be at their closest point to the coast here?

That's difficult to say, Shahan replied. *The council's working on the details of the new course. It won't be for some time, though. The Dark Moon's still accelerating and—*

Well, when they get there, I'm going home, Terrel declared.

You'd be a fugitive in your own land.

I don't care. I've sworn to get back.

It may not be possible, Terrel.

Really? Why should I believe anything you say? All you've done is lie to me.

Not lied, Shahan said. *There were some things we thought it wisest to withold from you.*

So now *what have you decided not to tell me?*

The Code is ambiguous, Muzeni replied. *It will probably remain so until all the prophecies have played themselves out. Anything we could tell you now would just be speculation.*

You're hiding behind words, Terrel claimed. *You've* always *known more than you're willing to admit. You used me, and you used my friends too. They'd never have let me be sent into exile if they'd known.*

Maybe not, Shahan conceded, *but Elam and Alyssa knew what was at stake, just as you did.*

But that's over now. The islands are safe!

For now.

What do you mean? I kept my bargain. I kept it!

Muzeni and Shahan glanced at each other, and Terrel was about to accuse them of keeping something from him again, when he was distracted by the sound of another human voice.

'There you are, Terrel. Farazin told me I'd find you out here somewhere.'

It was Kerin. He strode into the clearing, carrying a small hunting bow. Terrel saw him look at the dove, and reacted in horror.

'Don't shoot!' he cried aloud, while at the same time silently urging Alyssa to leave.

The bird flew off and, to Terrel's relief, Kerin made no move to take one of his arrows from the quiver slung over his shoulder.

'Not much meat on that,' the hunter remarked, as he watched the dove's flight. 'But you can't get sentimental about all animals, you know. We have to eat.'

'I know.' Terrel's moment of panic was over. The bird was just a bird once more. Alyssa had gone, and – as a result – the ghosts had vanished too. Kerin had given no sign of having known they were there, but it still made it easier for Terrel to concentrate – in as much as he could concentrate on anything after all the recent revelations.

'Are you all right?' Kerin asked. 'You look a bit upset.'

CHAPTER FIFTEEN

'Those sleepers are strange, aren't they?' Kerin said, mistaking the reason for his companion's preoccupation.

'Yes, they are,' Terrel replied.

They were walking slowly back towards the village.

'And now it seems we've got another one.'

Terrel did not bother to contradict him, even though he was reasonably sure that Talker's condition was not the same as the group in the cave. In spite of everything else that was on his mind, he had just remembered that Alyssa's coma was somehow connected to the elemental in the mines at Betancuria. Was it possible that the creature's influence could have stretched this far? And then something else occurred to him. Could the elemental have been responsible for the phenomenal growth of the black mountain? Terrel rejected this idea almost as soon as he thought of it. The mountain had appeared more than a decade ago, and the elemental had not been noticed in Betancuria until last year. Not only that, but the distances involved must be too great even for a creature of such extraordinary powers.

'Don't you think so?' Kerin asked.

'What?' Terrel realized that he hadn't heard what the villager had said. 'I'm sorry, I was miles away. What were you saying?'

'I was just wondering if you believed in ghosts.'

Terrel tried to hide his nervous confusion by laughing, even as he wondered whether Kerin had seen something in the glade after all.

'It's just that some of the kids in the village won't go near that place,' the prospector explained. 'They think it's haunted.'

'Really?'

'Amazing the imagination they have at that age, isn't it?'

'Yes, it is.'

'It's a shame we have to grow out of it, eh?'

An hour or so before dawn, when the rest of her family was still asleep, Ysatel was roused by a rustling sound coming from the second room. She got up carefully, and went over to the connecting doorway. There was just enough light filtering in from the Amber Moon – which at two-thirds full was the brightest of the moons that night – for her to see that Terrel was sitting up in bed, and appeared to be fully alert. The soft illumination made his eyes shine like jewels.

'Are you all right?' she whispered.

He nodded, but did not look at her, and seemed to be preoccupied with something. He closed his eyes, and a moment later Ysatel had the feeling that the boy wanted

to be left alone so that he could dream. She smiled, understanding, and went back to her husband.

You can open your eyes now, Elam told him, sounding
amused. *Or are you going to pretend to dream all the time
we're here?*

Terrel ignored him.

She's very obliging, isn't she? Elam remarked. *All you
have to do is think it, and she does what she's told.*

Don't you ever *mock her!* Terrel snapped, glaring at his
friend.

*All right, all right. There's no need to set my tongue on
fire.*

Are dreams so important here? Shahan asked.

*Yes. The sharaken – which I think might be Macul's
equivalent of the seers – are called dream-traders. I don't
understand it all, but people here regard them as a source of
magic and power.*

The ghosts – all three of them this time – had arrived
shortly after Alyssa, in the guise of a mouse, had burrowed
her way to Terrel's bedside. In the near darkness their
shapes were much brighter and clearer, but Ysatel obviously hadn't seen anything. Their spectral light did not
even cast any shadows.

Have you calmed down since this afternoon? Muzeni
asked. The long-dead heretic seemed genuinely concerned, and the patronizing tone he often employed was
noticeable by its absence.

I'm not sure, Terrel replied grudgingly.

Well, have you forgiven us, at least? Shahan enquired.

I don't know if I'll ever do that.

Oh, come now, Muzeni began.

He's twisting your beards, Elam told them. Then, seeing their baffled expressions, he added, *He's getting his own back. Teasing you.*

Don't bet on it, Terrel said. *What they did was close to unforgivable. If you didn't have such a big mouth, I might never have known.*

Me? Elam spluttered. *A big – How can you say that?*

You'd have worked it out for yourself sooner or later, Alyssa said.

Probably later, Elam added, *knowing how slowly your brain works.*

The old men had been following this exchange with some puzzlement, but when they noticed that Terrel and Elam were both grinning now, they began to look more hopeful. No one could tell what the mouse was thinking, but then that was often the case with Alyssa anyway.

I'm still going back to Vadanis the first chance I get, Terrel said, becoming serious again. *Nothing you can say is going to change that.*

You must do what you think is best, Shahan said.

But?

No one ventured a response.

You said before that it might not be possible, Terrel pointed out. *Don't you think you owe it to me to explain that?*

Your role in what happens won't be completed until the next four-moon conjunction, Muzeni told him. *Until then, there's no telling—*

And when will that be? Terrel interrupted.

The latest estimate is forty-six years from now, Shahan replied.

Forty-six years! Are you insane? *I'll be an old man by then.*

But if the Dark Moon keeps changing orbit, the seer added, *it could be earlier.*

Oh, that's all right then, Terrel muttered sarcastically. *It's already fifteen years ahead of schedule.*

I don't care. This is all meaningless. I've done my part. I kept my side of the bargain with the elemental, the islands aren't going to collide with the mainland – and that's enough. I'm going home. I don't care if I'm a prince. Alyssa's right, I'm still myself. That's all that matters.

It's because of who you are that you've come this far, Muzeni said. *Titles don't mean anything on their own.*

We can agree on that, at least, Terrel replied. *Jax is welcome to be the Guardian. Let him be the hero from now on.*

You think he can? Shahan asked.

His pointed question silenced Terrel for a time, but did not alter his resolve.

Rather him than me, he said defiantly.

Let's forget about the future for a while, shall we? Elam suggested. *And concentrate on the present. Why are we here now?*

Terrel pulled a face, but realized that the argument was going nowhere, and decided he should make the most of his time with the ghosts.

This is a strange place, Elam added. *So I suppose it's not surprising you fitted in so easily.*

They're good people, Terrel replied. *Most of them, anyway. They've treated me very well.*

They obviously recognized your regal importance.

Very funny. Terrel still met with a blank wall of

disbelief whenever he thought about his blood family. Intellectually, he had accepted it as the truth; emotionally, the idea seemed utterly absurd.

It's because they knew he was a healer, Alyssa claimed.

How could they know that when I didn't even realize it myself? Terrel asked. *I'm still not sure it's really true.*

But it works, doesn't it?

Yes, but I don't understand how.

Tell us about it, Shahan suggested.

As Terrel did his best to describe the workings of his mysterious talent, he wondered how Alyssa already seemed to know all about it. There had been no time to discuss his recent exploits in Fenduca, but nothing he'd said appeared to come as any surprise to her. The others were duly impressed by what he'd achieved, and in listing his various accomplishments he began to feel the stirrings of pride.

You've always been like that with animals, Alyssa said when he'd finished. *This is just an extension of that.*

Terrel glanced down at the mouse and wondered if, when she borrowed the various creatures' bodies, Alyssa retained enough of their instincts and awareness to recognize his ability.

I think that's the only reason I was able to survive in Betancuria, she went on.

That came as a surprise to Terrel. He had not been aware of helping her while they'd been in the mining district. Although the stonechat had slept next to his skin often enough, the protection he'd offered had simply been physical. If any healing had taken place, it had been completely unconscious.

You say that what you do is instinctive? Muzeni asked.

In the sense that I do anything, yes.

I suspect, therefore, the heretic said, in the slightly pompous tone he often adopted when expounding one of his theories, *that these instincts became ingrained before you were born. If you're right, and you suffered your injuries at the hands of your twin brother, it's possible that in defending yourself from something even worse, you may have developed means of protecting the core of your wellbeing and of blunting the effects of pain. And now you've found a way of passing on this knowledge to others.*

The phrase 'something even worse' triggered a memory of something the enchanter had said to Terrel – *Perhaps I should have crushed your skull instead of just an arm and a leg* – and he shuddered at the thought of what might have been.

That hypothesis may bear some examination, Shahan said thoughtfully, *but it doesn't explain the time delay with human patients, compared to the instantaneous response of the animals.*

Elam glanced at Terrel and rolled his eyes, but it was Alyssa who cut short the erudite debate that might have followed.

Human beings have to convince themselves and their own bodies, she remarked. *Animals just know – and do it.*

As you are in a unique position to know, my dear, Muzeni commented.

Actually, I've got another idea, she went on, ignoring the interruption. *I think it's nature's way of compensating Terrel for his physical afflictions. He's lived with pain his whole life, and so he knows how to deal with suffering.*

You never stopped my knees aching, Elam complained, pretending to be affronted.

I didn't know I could.

He did *help you at the observatory, though*, Alyssa said. *That time you fell through the roof. Terrel stopped the bleeding and made your headache better. If it hadn't been for him, you might have died then and there.*

The others were silent, their thoughts moving from that fateful night to the time when Elam *had* died, only a few days later. There had been nothing Terrel could have done about that. It was a sober reminder – like the deaths of Solan and the two miners – that no matter what powers Terrel possessed, their scope had limits.

Tell us more about this Talker, Muzeni requested.

He's still unconscious, as far as I know.

But you don't think he's another sleeper?

No. It feels different.

His spirit is trapped, not wandering, Alyssa confirmed.

Do you really think he saw the star inside me? Terrel asked. *The only time I was able to see the amulet was when I was inside the elemental.*

Perhaps he's found another way of seeing, Alyssa suggested, *now that his eyes don't work.*

It would be interesting to talk to him when he finally wakes up, Shahan commented.

If you can make any sense of what he says, Terrel remarked.

So he's got something in common with Alyssa, then? Elam said, grinning. *She—*

There's someone coming, Alyssa warned.

The half-light that precedes dawn was creeping into the hut and as Terrel looked up, a small figure appeared, silhouetted in the outer doorway. It hesitated there, then came on, tiptoeing over to the second room.

'Hello, Davi,' Terrel said, recognizing the child who had brought him the snake. 'What are you doing here?'

'Have you seen my mouse?' Davi asked. He was obviously very nervous.

It's all right. Alyssa's words sounded silently inside Terrel's head. *I have to go now anyway. You can give the mouse back.*

Terrel nodded, reached down and scooped up the small creature in his good hand. As he watched, the ring around its neck dissolved into thin air – something that he'd seen before, but which still made him feel very strange. He wished that Alyssa and the ghosts could have stayed, but he knew better than to argue.

'Here you are,' he said to the boy, holding the mouse gently in his outstretched hand.

'I thought she'd come to you,' Davi said, stepping forward to reclaim his pet. He took it, stroking her fur carefully, then blinked and glanced around the room.

'Where have your friends gone?' he asked.

CHAPTER SIXTEEN

'When do you think he'll get here?'

'I'm not sure. Possibly about a short month from now,' Farazin replied. 'Not that anyone's actually sure what a short month is any more.'

Terrel nodded, appreciating the sky-watcher's problem. The fact that you could not see the Dark Moon, that it looked the same whether it was full or new, made any observations extremely difficult. The moon was totally invisible during the day, and the only way its progress could be measured at night was by watching as it moved in front of distant stars or, – on much rarer occasions – when it eclipsed the other moons or the sun. What was more, Farazin had none of the optical instruments that the seers of Vadanis had devised to aid their astronomical calculations.

'I was taught that it's impossible for the Dark Moon's orbit to change,' the old man complained. 'And yet it has. It doesn't make any sense.'

'It's got bigger too,' Terrel said.

Farazin looked at him, obviously wondering whether he should take this second impossibility at face value. His confusion was painful to watch, and Terrel wished he hadn't spoken.

'At least that's what the seers on the islands think,' he added, by way of explanation.

'I wouldn't know about that,' Farazin responded gruffly.

The two of them were sitting just inside the doorway of the sky-watcher's home, watching rainwater cascading off the eaves and running in small rivulets down the path outside.

'Perhaps the sharakan will be able to tell you what's happening,' Terrel suggested hopefully.

Ever since a traveller had brought the news that one of the dream-traders was visiting a nearby village, and was apparently planning to come on to Fenduca in due course, Terrel's mind had been full of questions. But no one in the village had been either willing or able to answer them.

'Perhaps,' Farazin said. 'But he's just as likely to keep any information to himself. They're a law unto themselves.'

'You don't seem very keen on the idea of his coming.'

'I'm not. I prefer messages being passed on to me in the usual way. Having one of the sharaken here can mean trouble.'

'They've been to Fenduca before, then?'

'Yes, but the last one came over six years ago.'

'What did he want?'

'No one ever found out,' Farazin replied, then looked

down at the chart laid out on his lap. 'Let me see. The White Moon is new, the Amber will be full tomorrow, and the Red is at one quarter and waning. And I *think* the Dark Moon is full now. That means . . .' He fell silent, obviously lost in thought.

Terrel didn't like to interrupt, even though there was a lot he wanted to ask about the sharakan's visit. He had the distinct impression that this was something Farazin no longer wished to discuss – which was confirmed when the sky-watcher came to the end of his mental calculations, muttered something to himself, then looked at Terrel and made a very obvious effort to change the subject.

'How's Talker today?'

'Not too bad. Do you want to come and see him?'

The miner had been unconscious for almost three days, but had then woken apparently none the worse for wear. Terrel was glad that the blind man had proved not to be another sleeper.

'No. I'll leave him to you,' Farazin said. 'Is he still talking in riddles?'

'Yes.' No one except Terrel paid much attention to anything Talker said. Even he could make little sense of the disjointed ramblings, but the occasional reminders of Alyssa's speech patterns had kept the boy interested. He had tried to question Talker about the star he claimed to have seen, but had been unable to get a sensible answer.

'Do you really think he could be a healer?' Farazin asked, his own doubts obvious.

'Yes, I do.' Terrel had tried to involve his 'apprentice' when he'd been asked to visit a sick child the previous day, but the girl's parents had objected – and

Terrel had given way rather than cause any distress. That evening Talker had seemed dejected, his usual flow of nonsensical chatter reduced to occasional short utterances. Terrel had spent some time with him, hoping his presence would be a comfort, and realizing in the process that Talker was probably lonely. He was the last patient left in the infirmary, and his blindness not only isolated him but also prevented him from leaving the hut on his own, so he had to rely on visitors for any sort of human contact.

'I just hope someone will give him a chance,' Terrel added.

'You can't blame people for being wary of him,' Farazin said.

'Because he's mad, you mean?'

'And blind. He can't even see what he's doing.'

'That doesn't matter. Touch is more important than sight. He may *look* odd, but I don't exactly look normal and people accept me.'

'They do now,' the sky-watcher conceded. 'But some people had reservations about you before you proved yourself.'

Terrel couldn't deny the truth of that, though the injustice still rankled.

'How is Talker supposed to prove himself unless he's given the opportunity to try?'

Farazin shrugged, then began to study his chart once more. Although something about the possible source of Talker's healing had just occurred to Terrel, he said nothing – but he wished that Alyssa was there to discuss it with him.

It had been three days since he'd seen her and the

ghosts, and he wondered when they'd return. He hoped it would be soon. During those three days it had rained almost continuously, and the level of the river had risen appreciably so that in places it was now a raging torrent. Although this hadn't caused any serious accidents so far, Terrel had the feeling that it was only a matter of time before his talents might be called upon again. The villagers had been forced to cut back on their prospecting, and this – combined with the loss of the Demon's Cauldron – made it a difficult time for many. As frustrations grew, it became more and more likely that someone would do something foolish.

During the last few hours the deluge had eased a little, and there had even been a few glimpses of blue sky amongst the previously uniform grey of the clouds. But now a new squall blew across the village, bringing with it a fresh downpour that lashed the mountainside and churned up the surface of even the more placid sections of the river.

'Does it often rain as much as this?' Terrel asked. Although the winter had apparently been relatively mild, he was used to a different climate, one that was ruled by the ocean – and where the islands were *in* the ocean. The wind and rain of the mountains of Macul seemed unusually violent to him. The only thing worse on Vadanis had been the tornadoes – and they had not been natural phenomena.

'Sometimes,' Farazin replied indifferently, rolling up his chart to protect it from a few drops blown in by the swirling wind. 'At least with all this cloud about no one can tell when I get the cycles of the moons wrong.'

*

When the rain finally stopped, Terrel walked up the hill to the infirmary and found that Talker had a visitor. Sitting next to him, apparently quite at ease in the company of a madman, was Davi. Terrel was delighted by this development, and was about to greet them when Davi glanced up and held a finger to his lips. Talker was holding something in his cupped hands. The ex-miner's fingers were dirty and calloused, but he moved them with a certain grace, and was now evidently treating whatever lay on his palms with great care. There was an expression of delight on his face.

'Ri-deep.'

Talker reacted by echoing the croak exactly, and then he laughed. His mimicry had been so precise that had Terrel not seen his lips move, he would have looked around for a second frog.

'Ri-deep.' The real frog, which Terrel could now see in the blind man's hands, seemed similarly impressed.

The croaking conversation went on for some time, reducing all three humans to laughter, before Terrel made himself interrupt.

'Is this one of your pets?' he asked the little boy.

'Not really. I just found her in the river and thought Talker might like to see . . . to meet her.'

'That was kind of you. Do you like the frog, Talker?'

'Ri-deep,' the miner replied, grinning broadly. 'Feet of fish and wings of mouse.'

'I think that means yes,' Davi said.

'I think you're right,' Terrel agreed.

'Many floating dreams in their bubbles,' Talker said, nodding. 'Many.'

'Frogspawn,' Davi translated. 'She's pregnant.'

Such an explanation would never have occurred to Terrel, but he could see how it might make sense.

'Can you always tell what he's talking about?'

'Not always,' Davi replied solemnly. 'You have to listen sideways.'

That, Terrel thought, made as much sense as anything. Davi could not be much more than five years old, but he was a remarkable child in many ways. His friendship with Talker was only the latest indication of this. Apart from his unusual affinity with all living creatures, he had also taken the presence of the ghosts – and their sudden disappearance – in his small stride. At the time Terrel had not been sure what to tell him, but had decided in the end to stick to the truth. Davi had simply nodded, and commented that these ghosts 'weren't like the ones in the glade'. According to him, Elam and the seers had been 'proper people', whereas the others were just shapes. He had also agreed, without demur, that the ghosts' visit would remain their secret. Davi had asked whether they would come back and, if they did, whether he could meet them properly, but after that he had not mentioned the subject again.

For his part, Terrel had wondered how the little boy could have seen around that particular spectral corner, when neither Ysatel nor Kerin had been able to do so. Was it simply that his young mind was more amenable to 'impossible' sights? Perhaps he had some special talent that was unique to him.

'Can you teach me to listen sideways?' Terrel asked now.

Davi cocked his head to one side – in a gesture that reminded Terrel of Alyssa – and frowned.

'I'm not sure,' he said.

'Jewels burning,' Talker announced, turning his blind eyes towards Terrel. 'Five shadows, one flame. Wings within wings.'

Terrel looked at Davi expectantly, wondering whether this might be an obscure reference to the amulet from Tindaya, but the young boy just shrugged, evidently at a loss.

'I don't know what he means,' he said.

Talker twisted round, offering the frog back to Davi. 'Jump legs deeper round.'

Davi accepted the creature, cradling it in his much smaller hands.

'I'll take her back to the river.'

For the first time a touch of uncertainty entered Talker's expression. A moment later, he was looking distinctly anxious.

'Mountain blood dreams,' he mumbled, then pushed himself to his feet.

The others got up too, steadying the blind man as he swayed a little. Terrel was about to ask what the matter was, but then the question became irrelevant. A distant rumbling noise made his blood run cold. He knew immediately that this was no ordinary earthquake – there had been no internal trembling to warn him – but the ground was shaking nonetheless.

Terrel left the others and ran out of the hut as fast as he was able, then turned to look up at the source of the noise. What he saw was worse than anything his imagination had already conjured up.

High above them, on the far side of the river, a great wall of black mud was sliding down the mountainside, swallowing everything in its path.

CHAPTER SEVENTEEN

There was nothing Terrel – or anyone else – could do. There hadn't been any warning, and the speed and power of the avalanche was so great that there was no question of trying to go to the aid of those directly in its path. The onlookers could only watch helplessly as the churning deluge rolled on. Within moments the entire eastern side of the village was engulfed and the only thing that saved the rest was the river bed itself, which contained the edge of the gigantic mudslide. As it was, the sudden impact created miniature tidal waves, set off explosions of foam and dirt, and diverted the river into a hundred new streams. All of these caused some danger, but the damage was negligible compared to the devastation on the far bank.

In less time than it took Terrel to catch his breath after his dash from the hut, the shape of the mountainside had changed beyond recognition, and half of Fenduca was gone for ever.

*

In the days that followed, all those who were physically able to do so were kept fully occupied by their rescue attempts. It was backbreaking work, hampered by further falls of rain and the constant fear of another avalanche, and for the most part their efforts went unrewarded. Although a few bodies were recovered, no one was found alive, and most of those who were missing were eventually presumed to have died.

It was much the same story with the village's property. Everything in the path of the mud had either been swept away, smashed to pieces or buried so deep that it was now permanently out of reach.

The only solace for those coping with the disaster was that it could have been much worse. If the mudslide had happened in the evening, or at night – rather than in the middle of the day – many more people would have been at home in their huts, and the death toll would have been even higher. However, those from the eastern side had survived with nothing more than the clothes they stood up in, and many of the homes on the relatively unscathed west bank were now overcrowded with homeless refugees.

A lot of people had been injured either in the mudslide or during the salvage work that followed, and Terrel was kept very busy, every waking hour filled with the need to ease some sufferer's pain, until he was close to exhaustion himself. His dizzy spells began to happen more often, but he dismissed Ysatel's concerned pleas that he get more rest, knowing that his healing talent was one of the few things that gave the villagers some comfort.

He was helped in his efforts by several of the women and even some of their children, but also – most surprisingly – by Talker. Terrel had encouraged the blind man to try to help when it became clear that all possible avenues ought to be explored, and – in spite of some initial suspicion on the part of the patients and other villagers – Talker met with increasing success. Davi had become his 'eyes', leading the blind man to anyone who needed him, and sometimes translating the miner's peculiar utterances into something the others could understand. Terrel was naturally delighted by this development, partly because it took some of the pressure off him, and partly because it gave Talker a new purpose in life. Before many days had passed, the ex-miner had been accepted into the community in a way that would never have been possible under any other circumstances, and he seemed much happier in himself. But he paid a price for his successes, in the form of periodic blackouts. Although none of these lasted as long as his earlier spell of unconsciousness, they nonetheless caused some anxiety. However, Talker himself seemed to take them in his stride, often waking and going straight back to work as if nothing had happened.

Most people assumed that he had learnt his burgeoning skills from Terrel, but the boy knew this was far from being the whole story. Even if he had prompted their use, Talker must have had some innate abilities of his own, and Terrel wondered whether his sudden blindness might also have been a factor in their emergence. Was it possible that his healing was in some way compensation for his handicap, just as Alyssa thought his own talent might have stemmed from his injured limbs? Either way, Terrel was simply grateful for the extra help.

Terrel lost track of how many people he helped to heal themselves during the aftermath of the disaster, but he was in little doubt as to which encounter had been the most memorable. Cutter had sustained only minor injuries in the mudslide, but he had lost his home and most of his possessions. Fortunately for him – and for several prospectors – his jewel pouch had been strung around his neck as usual when the catastrophe had happened, but he'd spent more time and effort than was sensible in trying to recover his other belongings. As a result some of his wounds had become infected and this, combined with his exhaustion, had left him vulnerable to illness. When Terrel had come to see him, the fever had taken hold and Cutter's eyes were wild, obviously seeing visions from the nightmare world he now inhabited. Although he seemed unaware of his surroundings, he had reacted to Terrel's presence – snarling angrily and waving hands made feeble by disease. Terrel ignored his evident animosity and tried to calm him, hoping that this would be the first step in Cutter's recovery. Eventually, overcome by his own weakness, Mitus had allowed Terrel to touch him, and soon after that had fallen asleep.

He slept all night and all the next day, waking only when Terrel returned the following evening to check on his progress. The rest had clearly done him some good; the fever had begun to abate and his eyes, while still wary, were no longer full of dreams. He said nothing, answering Terrel's questions with either a nod or a shake of his head, but he allowed the healer to take his hand again. For the first time with a human patient, Terrel found himself falling into a different realm, 'seeing' beyond himself to a landscape of sensation and mystery. Although it lasted only a few moments, it was enough for him to be certain that Cutter was on his way to a full recovery – and from the frightened look of wonder on his face, it seemed that Mitus had felt something too. No words were exchanged, but by then none was needed.

Adversity brought the people of Fenduca closer together, reinforcing their need for cooperation. After the initial necessities had been taken care of, the village elders asked various families and individuals to undertake specific tasks for the benefit of all. Some turned their attention to building new shelters on the untouched ground of the western side. The far bank of the river was still shifting, treacherous terrain, where each day brought fresh mud-slides, so nothing was possible there – and with the in-firmary full to overflowing and every available hut filled to capacity, the need for extra sleeping space was urgent. Others were asked to collect food – either by hunting, fishing or gathering early spring crops – and to distribute it to everyone in need. Firewood was urgently required too, and a number of the older children were sent to forage in the nearby woods. A group of men were instructed to return to their prospecting, on the understanding that any proceeds from their finds would be divided among those who were unable to return to work yet. In this way, Fenduca was able to continue trading with the outside world, albeit on a much reduced scale, and could acquire more of the things they needed to rebuild the life of their village. There was some grumbling about the division of labour, but for the most part the system worked well, and a semblance of normality began to return.

'Farazin's called a gathering for tomorrow morning,' Kerin said.

'I know,' Olandis replied.

'Lereth told us on the way up here,' Aylen added.

The brothers had just returned from their latest fishing trip and, for the first time in ages, the family was able to sit round the fire together for their evening meal. The weather had relented at last, and the day had been sunny, with the promise of spring in the mild air.

'Do you know what he wants to discuss?' Ysatel asked.

'I think he wants to decide how soon we should go back to normal,' Kerin replied. 'The sharing's worked, up to a point, but it's not a long-term solution. There's always some who think they're getting nothing but the tail-bones of the fish.'

'But that's always been true!' Ysatel exclaimed. 'What about those families who haven't got anyone left to earn an *ordinary* living? What about the orphans, or the people still in the infirmary?'

'No one's suggesting we abandon them,' Kerin said calmly, 'but can you imagine what would happen if one of the prospectors made a really big find, the sort of thing that would transform their life? Should he still be expected to share it with everyone else?'

'There's only been a few allowed to work,' Olandis pointed out. 'Most of us haven't had the *chance* of a big find.'

'I know that,' his father responded, 'but this sort of problem will arise sooner or later. In the end, people will have to learn to stand on their own two feet again.'

'Even if they don't *have* two feet?' Ysatel asked indignantly. Both she and Terrel had tended people who were unlikely to be able to walk again.

'We'll do what we can for those who can't help

themselves,' Kerin told her, 'but am I supposed to put their welfare before that of my wife and children?'

Ysatel looked as though she was about to say something more, but evidently thought better of it.

'Nothing's decided yet,' Kerin went on. 'We'll see what the feeling is at tomorrow's gathering. The elders are going to want your advice, Terrel.'

'Me? I'm not even—'

'You're one of us now,' Aylen said, anticipating Terrel's reaction. 'You've proved that many times over.'

'And if we're ever to return to normal,' Kerin added, nodding his agreement, 'we need to know how the health of the village is likely to progress. Who else should we ask about that?'

Although Terrel was now at ease with most of the villagers when he met them individually, the thought of addressing the entire gathering made him feel very nervous.

'All right,' he said quietly.

'Is the food ready yet?' Aylen asked. 'I'm starving.'

'Nearly,' Ysatel told him. 'We'll eat as soon as the others get here.'

'They're on their way,' Olandis said, pointing.

Everyone looked round to see Talker and Davi walking down the path, hand in hand. The contrast between their first expeditions, when Talker had moved slowly and carefully, testing each cautious step, to their present almost carefree progress, was extraordinary. The two had been constant companions for several days now, and Talker obviously had complete faith in his young guide. They both shared Terrel's tiny room at night – Talker because he had nowhere else to go, and Davi because he wanted to stay with his charge.

As usual, the two friends were talking as they strode along. Davi was the only one who could make any sense of what the blind man said, and it never seemed to bother him that Talker almost never responded directly to anything he said. It made for some very peculiar conversations, but somehow the partnership worked.

'They're an odd couple, aren't they?' Aylen remarked.

'Davi's always been a bright lad, and good with animals,' Ysatel commented thoughtfully, 'so it's no wonder he took to Terrel, but I wonder what he sees in Talker.'

'Another healer?' Kerin suggested.

'Talker's certainly the biggest pet Davi's ever had – so far,' Olandis said, grinning in spite of his stepmother's disapproving glance.

'They're both remarkable,' Terrel stated seriously. 'I don't know which of them I admire the most.'

The discussion was cut short then, because the strange pair were now within earshot. Greetings were exchanged as the newcomers took their places next to the fire, and then Ysatel began passing round the bowls. She had to move across and take Talker's hand in her own to guide him, and as she did so the ex-miner smiled.

'Warm wings,' he commented.

'Why thank you, kind sir,' she replied, smiling herself.

'Swimming one, bubble-like.' He seemed very pleased about something. 'Echo dreams.'

Ysatel glanced at Davi, hoping for some enlightenment, but the boy spread his hands to show that he didn't understand either. Terrel was the only one who noticed that Davi's face had coloured a little, and wondered if the child was embarrassed about something. However, he soon forgot about it as the meal progressed and the conversation moved on to other matters.

The formal gathering gave the villagers their first opportunity to discuss exactly what had happened, and to plan for the future. It was obvious that the mudslide had been composed of vast amounts of material discarded from the mining operations above, but there were various theories as to why the slide should have happened when it did. The most commonly accepted argument was that several days of heavy rain had simply made the debris unstable, but not everyone was convinced that this was the whole story.

'Yes, it's true,' Farazin admitted in answer to someone's question. 'Two moons *were* close to being full that day, but I doubt if that could have been responsible for the accident.'

'When's the next such alignment?' Zolen asked.

'Eleven or twelve days from now. The Amber and Red Moons will be full then, within a few hours of each other. We must be vigilant, as always. But an avalanche is not an earthquake. The moons only affect the land as a whole. They don't affect small parts of a single mountain.'

'But if that small part had already been made vulnerable by the rains,' Zolen persisted, 'then isn't it possible that the moons' influence might have tipped the balance?'

'I suppose so,' Farazin conceded.

'You realize we have no means of getting any advance warning of a tremor now?' Lereth asked. The avalanche had overwhelmed the wolf-fish pool, and the fish were either dead or had been swept away. Most people were aware of this, but it had seemed of little consequence compared to all the other problems they were facing.

'We can catch more wolf-fish if we need to,' Kerin said. 'We'll just have to find a suitable pool for them.'

Everyone knew Kerin's sons were the best fishermen in the village, and – even though capturing wolf-fish was a difficult task – no one doubted that they could do as their father suggested.

'There's nowhere suitable at the moment,' Zolen said. He was one of the few prospectors who had been working in the river again, exploring its new contours. 'But it shouldn't be too difficult to construct a pool if need be.'

'Why should we worry about the fish?' one of the younger men asked. 'We have Farazin's calculations to rely on, and if that fails, we have Terrel.'

'I can only give you a few moments' warning,' Terrel said, still feeling uncomfortable with so many eyes upon him. 'The fish gave you much longer than that.'

'And the phases of the moons are not an infallible guide to danger, as we've seen,' the sky-watcher added.

'So we *should* replace the fish,' Kerin concluded.

'Aren't we forgetting something?' one of the other elders asked. 'The mudslide wasn't the result of an earthquake. There was no warning this time, from any source. Who's to say there will be next time?'

'We don't know if that's true,' Farazin objected. The lookout posted to watch the fish-pool had been one of those to die, so there was no way of knowing whether the creatures had reacted.

'Why didn't you see it coming, Terrel?' Zolen asked.

Taken aback by the faintly accusatory nature of the question, the boy could only shake his head, suddenly tongue-tied. But then Cutter – of all people – came to his rescue.

'Leave the boy alone,' he growled. 'He's done more for this village in the last month than most of you'll do in a lifetime. Just be thankful for his talents, and accept that they have their own limitations.'

His outburst shamed any doubters, and even though Terrel felt uncomfortable at being the centre of attention, he was both surprised and pleased that his former enemy had spoken up for him.

'I can't believe you're all still talking as if the mudslide was an accident,' another young man declared suddenly. 'Isn't it obvious? The whole thing was deliberate, simply the most convenient way for the miners to dispose of their waste.'

After this statement, the gathering fragmented into many separate arguments, and it was some time before Farazin was able to quieten things down again.

'You've no proof of this, Cardos,' the sky-watcher said when he was finally able to make himself heard. 'I don't believe—'

'You all heard what Yahn said!' the young man cut in. 'He'll drive us away if he wants to, and he's obviously found the perfect way to do it.'

'If Yahn wanted to kill us, he could have done so long before now,' Kerin said.

'Why risk a fight?' Cardos retorted. 'This way, he gets rid of his rubbish and flattens our homes at the same time. Two birds with one stone. If the slide had been a few paces further to the west, there might not have been anything left of Fenduca at all! If you really want warning of when it's going to happen again, we need someone up there.' He thrust out a finger, pointing towards the army camp.

'Are you volunteering?' Cutter asked mildly.

Cardos did not answer.

'He could be right,' Zolen said. 'Some of the soldiers were laughing when they saw what had happened down here. But if it's true, I don't see what we can do about it.'

There was some further argument then, but nothing was resolved, and when Cardos realized that most people either wouldn't or couldn't take his theory seriously, he fell silent. The discussion then moved on to the villagers' plans for the future, and the progress of their rebuilding work.

'The east bank's hopeless while it's this wet,' Lereth reported. 'Maybe when it dries out over the summer it'll become solid enough, but until then we can't trust it. The mud's there to stay, and we're all going to be stuck over here.'

'The river's only carrying away a fraction of the silt,' Zolen confirmed. 'We have to assume its course has been permanently altered.'

That brought the discussion round to the possible resumption of normal prospecting. As Kerin had predicted, several people argued that the communal working that had served them so well recently was redundant now, while others felt more time was needed before the usual free-for-all could begin again in the altered river-bed. No firm conclusions were reached, but before the gathering broke up Farazin promised that the elders would debate the matter further and let everyone have their decision as soon as possible.

Two days later, everyone who wanted to returned to the river with their screens, and the struggle began in earnest once more.

In the evening, Terrel joined Olandis and Aylen as they trudged wearily back to the hut. The brothers had had little luck, and were further dispirited to find no meal waiting for them when they got home. They were even more puzzled when their father and Ysatel emerged from the hut to greet them, hand in hand. Kerin rarely made affectionate gestures in public, but on this occasion he looked enormously happy.

'What's going on?' Aylen asked.

'Ysatel has something to tell you,' his father replied.

As he looked at her, Terrel found that he knew what she was going to say even before she opened her mouth, and his heart gave a leap of joy.

'I'm going to have a baby,' Ysatel said.

CHAPTER EIGHTEEN

'Don't ever let him cook again, Ysy,' Aylen pleaded. 'I'd forgotten how bad he is.'

The meal – although late and tasting rather unusual – had been one of their most enjoyable for a long time. Although Ysatel's news had come as an enormous surprise, Kerin's joy was so obvious that once the brothers had overcome their initial shock, they had been delighted by the prospect of a new addition to the family.

'Don't worry,' Ysatel told her stepson. 'Your father will soon get fed up with making all this fuss, and then I'll take over again.'

'It wasn't that bad,' Kerin protested.

He had been insistent that Ysatel get some rest, and once she had realized he wasn't going to accept any of her arguments – that she was pregnant, not ill – she had simply let him get on with it.

'Besides,' Kerin went on, 'nobody's allowed to complain about anything tonight. This is a time for celebration, isn't it, my love?' He put an arm around his wife, and she sank gratefully into his embrace.

'I was too frightened to talk about it at first,' she told them quietly. 'I've known for a while, I think, but I didn't want to say anything until I was sure.'

'And now you are,' Olandis said.

'Yes.' Her smile held secrets the others could only guess at.

'It's amazing,' Kerin said. 'After all this time. I'd just about given up hope.'

'Me too. I used to put messages on our prayer-flags,' Ysatel told her husband.

'I know.'

'You weren't supposed to know,' she said, shame-faced.

'But you stopped a long time ago,' Kerin commented quietly.

'I'd given up. Anyway, we have something better now.'

'What?' Olandis asked.

'Terrel.'

The young boy almost choked on the last of his soup, then met Ysatel's gaze.

'I'm pregnant because you're here,' she told him.

'You'd better not repeat that in the village,' Aylen remarked. 'You can imagine what the gossipmongers would say!'

Ysatel picked up a wooden spoon and threw it at her stepson, but they were all laughing now – except Terrel, who was blushing furiously.

'What do . . . do you mean?' he stammered. 'I haven't done anything.'

'You're a healer, Terrel,' she replied, 'and you were even before you knew it. There was something wrong with me – not with Kerin, or he couldn't have produced these two great lumps – and you must have helped put it right. And this is the result.' She patted her stomach.

'But—' His denial caught in his throat. Could it really be a coincidence, *another* coincidence? He had been aware that she wanted very much to have Kerin's child; he had seen the way she looked at Jessett when the baby had been brought to him for healing, and he remembered the confession she'd made beside the fish-pool. Had he known of the problem subconsciously? And sought to solve it? The idea seemed incredible, but then so had many other things he had seen and done recently. His healing *was* all subconscious, in a way. And he had touched Ysatel many times – ironically most often during his early days in Fenduca, when *she* had been tending to *him* – so it was just possible that the contact had allowed his instincts to take over. Even so . . .

'Don't worry,' Aylen advised Terrel, on seeing his worried look. 'Lots of women go mad when they're pregnant.'

'You're speaking from experience, I presume?' Ysatel enquired mischievously.

'If you are, my lad,' Kerin added, 'I want details.'

'It's common knowledge,' Aylen laughed, refusing to let their teasing get the better of him.

For a moment, Terrel's imagination took him back to the scene of his own birth, to his own mother, maddened by pain and shock . . .

'You look as if you've just seen a ghost,' Olandis commented.

'What's the matter, Terrel?' Ysatel asked quickly. 'I'm sorry, I haven't embarrassed you, have I?'

'No,' he lied, wishing it were that simple. 'I'm fine.' He smiled as best he could.

Although Ysatel did not seem convinced, the others took his answer at face value.

'Well, I don't care about any of the whys and where-fores,' Kerin said, kissing his wife's hand. 'I'm just glad it happened.'

'Do you think it'll be a boy or a girl?' Olandis asked.

'How's she supposed to know that?' Aylen said.

'It's a girl.'

They all looked at Ysatel in astonishment, and she burst out laughing again.

'You look like a shoal of ironfish.'

'How—' Kerin began.

'Talker knows, doesn't he?' Terrel exclaimed.

Ysatel stopped giggling and nodded.

'Davi told me he saw the baby when he touched my hand at the meal a few nights back,' she said. 'He wasn't sure at the time – and I think the poor child was too embarrassed to say anything in front of everyone else – but I ran into them again today. Talker held my hand and said some more of his nonsense, but Davi knew what he meant.'

'Just like the frog,' Terrel declared.

'What are you talking about?' Olandis said, completely bewildered. 'What frog?'

'It doesn't matter.'

'Are you sure Davi's got it right?' Kerin asked anxiously. 'Talker never seems to make much sense to me.'

'I trust them,' Ysatel told him. 'I was already pretty sure, but I hadn't said anything to anyone. So how could they know? What Davi said came out of the blue, but it just confirmed what I'd felt. And if Talker thinks it's going to be a girl, I'm not going to argue.'

'Then neither will I, my love,' Kerin said, his eyes shining.

The next day, the newly-established routines of the village were disrupted again, this time by an unexpected visitor. After the turmoil caused by the mudslide, most people had forgotten that a sharakan was supposed to be coming to Fenduca.

Word that he was on his way reached the village some time before the man himself, and when he finally rode into the settlement in the late morning, most of the community was waiting to greet him. Many called out, asking the sharakan for blessings or thanking him for coming to their home, but he did not respond. He was wearing a long cloak, with a large hood that fell forward so that no one could see his face, and as he did not speak nobody could be sure whether their welcome met with his approval. The sharakan was accompanied by an acolyte – a young man who rode on a donkey behind his master. Because he was bare-headed, they could see his face – but he seemed indifferent and even rather bored as he nodded coolly to those they passed. He too remained silent.

It was Farazin's duty to provide hospitality for the newcomers, and he had hurriedly thrown everyone out of his home so that the sharakan and his companion would have relatively spacious accommodations. But he had been caught unawares by their arrival, and there had barely been time to make the hut ready before the visitors brought their mounts to a halt in front of his cabin.

Farazin bowed as they dismounted.

'My home is your home,' he said in formal greeting.

The sharakan did not react, but simply swept past his host and entered the hut, leaving his acolyte to attend to details.

'The Collector will rest after his journey,' the young man announced. 'He will require food in one hour. Once he has eaten, a full gathering of the village will take place here.'

'Of course,' Farazin replied. 'I'll arrange it.'

The acolyte nodded, taking this for granted.

'In the meantime, I shall see to the stabling of our mounts. I trust you have a suitable place nearby.'

After a moment's hesitation, Farazin suggested that one of the half-built huts – one that was not yet occupied – might be used, and on being led to it the acolyte decided that it 'would have to do'. After unsaddling and rubbing down the beasts – he evidently did not trust any of the villagers to do this for him – he returned to the elder's hut and joined his master to await their midday meal.

The gathering that afternoon was unlike any Terrel had witnessed before. It was mostly a silent affair, with the villagers looking on as the acolyte instructed various individuals to come forward. Terrel had expected the sharakan to emerge without his cloak, and was looking forward to seeing the face of one of Macul's renowned mystics – but the man remained hooded so that his face could not be seen by any of the onlookers. And because he did not speak directly to any of the villagers, communicating instead only via his assistant, no one heard his voice either.

'It has come to the attention of the Collector that there is one here who shows a talent for healing,' the acolyte stated, after various of the elders had paid their respects.

'Actually there are two,' Farazin said.

'Bring them forward.'

Farazin beckoned to Terrel, then looked round to see where Talker was. As Terrel stepped into the circle of villagers, he began to feel rather nervous. He was not surprised that rumours concerning his exploits had spread beyond Fenduca – it was even possible that the soldiers had come to know of his gift and had reported it further afield – but he was not at all happy about being brought to the attention of the sharaken. He had asked Kerin why the visitor was called 'the Collector', but he had not known, and at the time Farazin had been too busy to bother with such questions. Now the title had taken on a faintly menacing air.

'This is Terrel,' the sky-watcher said.

The boy found himself looking into the impenetrable darkness beneath the hood, searching for a glimpse of the sharakan's eyes, for some spark of life – but could see nothing.

A delicate hand emerged slowly from within the folds of the cloak.

'Take the Collector's hand,' the acolyte instructed.

Terrel reluctantly did as he was told. The sharakan's skin was cool and dry, his grip firm but gentle. Beyond that Terrel felt nothing, no connection, no sense of illness or wellbeing. The man – like his face – was a void, invisible. It was a relief when the contact ended.

'Where do you come from, Terrel?' the acolyte asked.

The boy glanced at Farazin before replying, but on receiving the sky-watcher's nod, he spoke up in as steady a voice as he could manage.

'I come from Vadanis, in the Floating Islands.'

Terrel was surprised when this information evoked no reaction from either of the two visitors.

'You may go,' the sharakan's assistant said a moment later.

Is that it? Terrel wondered. He turned away, not sure whether to feel relieved or insulted, and saw Talker edging forward, holding the arm of one of the village women. As Terrel stepped back, he glanced around, wondering where Davi was, but the boy was nowhere to be seen.

The brief touching of hands was repeated with Talker, but on this occasion the acolyte asked no questions and simply waved him away. Then he leaned close, to consult with his master.

'There are others—' Farazin began.

'Where is the boy who is the blind man's usual guide?' the acolyte asked abruptly.

'I'm not sure,' the sky-watcher replied, looking round as Terrel had done. 'He should be here.' Spotting the boy's parents, he went over to speak to them, then came back to report. 'He's missing, I'm afraid. His parents haven't seen him since midday.'

'No matter.' The acolyte clearly saw no need to explain why the sharakan might have wanted to see the child.

'There are others . . .' Farazin repeated nervously, as several more villagers inched forward.

Watching, Terrel wondered why they were so eager. He couldn't understand the hope on their faces.

'There is no one else here of interest,' the acolyte declared, and a communal sigh escaped from the lips of the gathering.

'This gathering is over,' the acolyte announced, then turned and followed his master back to their lodgings.

The two visitors spent the afternoon ensconced in Farazin's hut, allowing only the sky-watcher himself to join them. The rest of the villagers accepted their dismissal meekly and, for want of anything better to do, returned to their daily tasks. Terrel spent his time at the infirmary, until his own weariness got the better of him and he went back to the Miranas' hut. He had been brooding ever since the gathering, and wanted to discuss it with someone he trusted. He had hoped that Ysatel would be there alone, but Kerin was with his wife, displaying his new-found overprotectiveness.

'You'll drive me crazy if you keep on fussing like this,' Terrel heard her say as he drew closer. 'And we'll never get anything done.'

'I know what's important,' Kerin responded, unabashed.

'Hello, Terrel,' she said, on seeing the boy. 'Talk some sense into him, will you?'

'Terrel's going to look after you all the time, just as I am,' Kerin claimed. 'Having a healer in the family is a wonderful thing.'

Terrel found himself teeming with conflicting emotions.

The fact that Kerin now included him as a member of the family touched him deeply, but he did not want to commit himself to having to stay in Fenduca for another eight or nine months in case he missed the opportunity of getting back to his homeland. He tried not to let any of this show on his face, and Kerin gave no sign of having noticed his confusion.

'Come and check on her now, will you?' he asked.

'Gate!' Ysatel exclaimed. 'Stop pestering the boy. And stop pestering me!'

'Please, Terrel,' Kerin persisted.

'Moons! Just do it, Terrel. It may be the only way to shut him up.'

Terrel went to them and took her hand. Although he felt rather embarrassed, that changed in an instant. In contrast to his contact with the sharakan, this felt immediate and welcoming, and he was enveloped by a waking dream of warmth and peace. The sensation was so powerful that his senses reeled and he almost fell, but Kerin caught his arm and steadied him. The dream held echoes; a small dream within another. Terrel smiled, thinking that this was how it *should* have been.

'Is she all right?' Kerin asked anxiously. 'Are they both all right?'

'Of course I'm all right,' Ysatel responded testily.

'All is well,' Terrel confirmed, releasing her hand and stepping back.

'Good.'

The boy had begun to feel very dizzy. He sat down on the ground with a bump, then keeled over.

'Now look what you've done,' Ysatel complained. 'He's worn out.'

'I only—'

Terrel heard nothing more of their conversation. He was unconscious.

When he awoke he had been covered with a blanket, and the fire was glowing brightly as evening drew in. Kerin and Ysatel were busy preparing food together, but none of the others had arrived yet. It took Terrel a few moments to clear his head, but then he sat up and stretched.

'He's awake.'

'Are you all right, Terrel?' Ysatel asked. 'Would you like some water?'

He shook his head.

'So, what did you think of the sharakan?' Kerin asked, saving the boy from having to raise the subject himself. 'You should be honoured that he wanted to meet you.'

Terrel did not feel remotely honoured.

'It was one of the strangest experiences of my life,' he said hoarsely.

Kerin was obviously taken aback by this response, but Ysatel smiled slightly.

'Are they all like that? So aloof and arrogant?' Terrel had formed a low opinion of the sharakan, and saw no point in hiding his feelings. Although he did not know whether the sharakan was typical of the rest of his kind, the boy hoped that they would not all behave so unpleasantly.

'I don't think—' Kerin began, but was interrupted by his wife's laughter.

'I told you he wouldn't be fooled,' she said. 'That's *exactly* how he behaved. Aloof and arrogant.'

'What good did he do?' Terrel asked, emboldened by Ysatel's agreement. 'I thought he'd answer questions, give us some guidance, anything that might help.'

'Sharaken are not practical men,' Kerin explained, 'but we still owe them our respect.'

'Why? What amazed me was the way we accepted his rudeness. We all looked on quietly, as if his behaviour was somehow admirable. What's he done to deserve such reverence? Why should a good man like Farazin be so desperate to impress him?'

His outburst surprised even Terrel himself – he hadn't been aware just how high his feelings were running – and Kerin was clearly astonished. Even Ysatel was quiet now, and the boy began to think that he might have gone too far.

'I . . . I'm sorry. This isn't my land. I have no right to question your beliefs.'

There was a long pause.

'You've every right,' Kerin said eventually, 'if you're speaking the truth.'

'It's just that I don't understand,' Terrel said, trying to explain. 'Why did he come here? What is he collecting?'

'Recruits, possibly.'

'For the sharaken?'

Kerin nodded.

'I'm only guessing, though,' he went on. 'No one's ever been sure what they want.'

Terrel thought back, wondering whether the contact had been some kind of test – and knowing that if it was, then he and Talker had both failed it.

'Would Davi have known that?' he asked.

'He might have guessed the same thing,' Kerin replied.

'Do you think that's why he disappeared?' Ysatel asked, her eyes wide.

'Would they have taken someone so young?' Terrel asked.

'Maybe.'

'Then I'm *glad* he wasn't there.'

CHAPTER NINETEEN

Although the sharakan and his assistant left the next morning, another short month was to pass before Farazin would talk of what he and the visitors had discussed. During that time, the sky-watcher became a virtual recluse among his own people, keeping to his hut, poring over charts and muttering to himself. Terrel was not the only one who tried to talk to Farazin, but no one succeeded. Everyone was given short shrift, and told that they'd learn all they needed to know when he was good and ready.

That time did not come until many days had passed, and by then most of Fenduca's inhabitants had begun to dismiss the sharakan's visit as an irrelevance, something that had had no effect on their lives – beyond the fact that there had been no gatherings since then, and no prayer-flags had been set for the most recent full of either the Amber or Red Moon. Although this in itself was not so unusual, many villagers would have begun to feel uneasy if the situation had continued for much longer. It therefore came as something of a relief when Farazin finally emerged from his self-imposed isolation.

The gathering was held, as the last had been, on the open ground outside the sky-watcher's hut and, as instructed, many of those who came were carrying flags, the coarse material wrapped around wooden poles. The strips of cloth had once been white, but were now varying pale shades of grey or brown – the legacy of the symbols and messages which had been daubed upon them in the past. These markings had all relayed questions, hopes and pleas, and as they faded through the action of the wind and rain, the prayers were sent heavenward until the flags were used again.

'I thought this would be an appropriate time to tell you what I have learnt,' Farazin informed them, when everyone was present, 'because tonight the Dark Moon will be full.'

After all the recent uncertainty, this news was greeted with nods of approval and expressions of relief, but with no real apprehension. Everyone knew that the other three moons were all less than half full, which meant there was little danger of a new tremor – and it was good to know that the sky-watcher was once more sure about what was happening in the heavens. However, what Farazin went on to say left many of the villagers feeling very uncomfortable.

In essence, this was a more detailed description of what Terrel already knew about the suddenly erratic behaviour of the most enigmatic of the moons, but the sharakan had evidently been no more able to explain these supposedly impossible changes than the seers on Vadanis had been. All Farazin could offer was the vague and – to Terrel – unsatisfactory comment that 'something in the dream-world above' had altered.

'I'm sure the sharaken will work it all out eventually,' the old man concluded, looking round at the rows of puzzled faces. 'The dictates of the lore haven't changed that much yet, and I can advise you now if you're unsure about anything. In the meantime, we can play our part here. This is a time of omens. Pay attention to your dreams tonight, and come to me if there's anything significant in their images.'

'Isn't the Amber Moon new tonight?' someone asked.

'Exactly,' Farazin responded. 'Ordinarily the Amber Moon is the most influential when it comes to configuring our dream space, but it's precisely because it's at its weakest that tonight is important. The Dark Moon is at its strongest, and this is therefore the best opportunity to study its mysteries without interference from the Amber. Who knows, we may even discover its secrets before the sharaken do.' He was smiling as he spoke, and his last words were greeted with muted laughter.

'Is that what the sharakan was hoping to collect when he came here?' Azian asked. 'Our dreams?'

Farazin glanced at his fellow elder, then nodded.

'In a way, yes.'

'Is that why he wanted to see Terrel and Talker?' Cutter asked.

'I suppose so,' the sky-watcher replied, 'but their kind of trading was of no use to him.'

'That's good,' one of the healers' former patients declared. 'We don't want to lose them.'

This remark was greeted with some good-natured

laughter and several nods of agreement – which made
Terrel feel uncomfortable. Few of the villagers were aware
of his intention to leave them before the year was out. In
fact, he'd been growing more and more restless for some
time. He'd been in Fenduca for almost four median
months now, and in one sense was content enough. His
talent for healing and his acceptance into the Mirana
family were both sources of comfort and a little pride,
but he was aware that he hadn't made any progress
towards getting back to his own home. Indeed, he had no
real idea how to start going about it. All he knew was that
he had to try.

'Why did he want to see our Davi, then?' Frasu, the
boy's father, asked.

'I don't know,' the sky-watcher admitted.

Davi had returned home almost as soon as the sharakan
had left. The boy had come to no harm during the day
and night he'd gone off on his own, and when asked where
he had been – and why he'd left in the first place – his
answers had been vague and evasive. He'd claimed that
he couldn't remember where he'd slept, and explained
his absence by saying simply that he'd 'just felt like it'.
Frasu and his wife Erena had been too relieved by his
return to press him further, and no one else had got much
from the child. Davi had resumed his duties as Talker's
guide – something that delighted the healer, but did not
please the boy's parents. Terrel thought that they believed
Talker might be leading their son astray, and he had done
his best to persuade them that the partnership was not
only worthwhile but also a positive force for good.

There had been a few very minor tremors recently –
including one that Farazin had predicted near the full of

the Red and Amber Moons – but there had been no serious repercussions. Nor had there been any more mudslides. With the onset of spring, the weather had been improving steadily, which meant that the ground – even on the abandoned east bank – was becoming drier and less treacherous. However, the warmer air brought with it a huge increase in the number of insects that could bite or sting the unwary, and also made it more difficult to store food for any length of time. Because of this, there had been an increase in minor illnesses. Terrel and Talker had both been kept busy – and Terrel was glad the blind man had not been deprived of his 'eyes'.

'Will the sharakan come back?' someone asked.

'I've no idea,' Farazin replied honestly, 'but I don't suppose it'll be any time soon. After all, the last visit was over six years ago.'

Terrel happened to be looking at Davi when the sky-watcher gave this answer, and he was not surprised to see the boy smile. Whatever he had told his parents, there was no doubt in Terrel's mind that Davi's absence that day had been deliberate.

'We should prepare the flags now,' Farazin said, 'so that we may dedicate them at the shrine before noon.'

The gathering broke up into family groups, each attending to their prayers. A few were able to make the inscriptions themselves, but most took turns in quietly relating their wishes to the sky-watcher, who transcribed them onto the cloth. It was a time-consuming process, and Terrel heard Farazin grumbling that his fingers were not as nimble as they used to be. He wished he could have offered his help, but although he was more or less fluent in his hosts' spoken language, he had grasped only the most rudimentary elements of the Maculian alphabet. So he kept himself apart, feeling like an outsider once more, as the flags were finished. The ceremony was completed when the poles were planted in the earth around the carved stone that acted as a shrine to the Dark Moon.

The banners fluttered and snapped in the wind as Farazin intoned the final words of the ritual. As Terrel saw Kerin and Ysatel look skyward, following the flight of their prayer, he knew they were seeking protection for their unborn child, and he added his own heartfelt plea for the baby's safe arrival.

Ysatel's health remained good as her pregnancy progressed. She was hardly affected by morning sickness, and seemed to be revelling in her condition. When some of the more experienced women told her that she would find the whole process wearisome and frustrating long before she came to term, she just nodded solemnly, then smiled as soon as they were gone. This was her miracle, her chance when all hope had gone – and she was determined that nothing was going to spoil it.

Even Kerin recognized how well she was doing, how robust and clear-eyed she had become, and he was less overprotective now, allowing her to go about her own business. In truth, as she had predicted, this suited him well enough too. During Farazin's self-imposed absence, Kerin had become the elders' leader by default, and it was he who had suggested and then implemented a plan to replace the fish-pool as soon as possible. This was now ready – a deep basin of solid rock that had been formed beneath a small cliff when a new stream had scoured away the soil inside. This natural cistern was on the western side of the river, away from the layers of mud, and Kerin had taken advantage of the land's new contours. It had taken only minor adjustments to make the pool perfect. It was now fed by a small waterfall – the stream that had formed it having been diverted – and the exit channels were too shallow to allow any fish to escape. As yet the pool was empty, but Aylen and Olandis were away at the time of the gathering, seeking out the wolf-fish.

The brothers were not the only villagers missing from the gathering. Cardos, the young man who'd been convinced that the soldiers were responsible for the mudslide, was also absent. No one thought anything of this; he was an impulsive and sometimes wayward individual who often hunted, or visited other villages, on his own. But their attitude changed rapidly that same afternoon, when they found out where he had gone.

The first indication that something was amiss came when the gate in the new fence below Raven's Crag was opened, and a group of soldiers came through. Led by Janizar Yahn, they marched to the natural vantage point at the top of the cliff overlooking the new fish-pool. Once there they could be seen by most of those at work in the river, and by a good number of people in the village itself. One of the closest huts to the fence was the infirmary and, at the sound of swords clashing on shields, Terrel left his work to see what was happening. Talker and Davi came out too, and a few moments later Ysatel strode up the path to join them.

'What's going on?' she whispered. 'What does *he* want?'

'He hasn't said anything yet,' Terrel replied.

By then, everyone had stopped whatever they were doing and were waiting, looking up at the janizar. Having got the villagers' attention, Yahn seemed in no hurry to explain his presence. He looked around, a small contemptuous smile on his face.

'I warned you people!' he shouted eventually, his bull-like voice carrying easily over the sound of running water. 'But you couldn't leave well alone.'

No one knew what he was talking about until the soldiers behind him parted ranks, and a bedraggled figure was pushed forward.

'We fished this young fool out of the Demon's Cauldron last night,' Yahn told them. 'I'm not sure whether he was trying to hide from us, or to steal some of the king's treasure, but that's not important. He has paid for his trespassing.'

Cardos stood, eyes downcast and hands bound, saying nothing. The matted blood in his hair and clothes, and the livid bruises on his face and arms, were testament to just how he had 'paid' for his crime. He swayed on his feet, as if he might fall at any moment, and seemed quite unaware of what was going on about him.

'I am a merciful man,' Yahn went on, 'so I'm going to let this vermin live. But the next one who tries anything so stupid will not meet with such leniency. I suggest you learn from his example.'

So saying, the janizar lashed out, landing a back-handed blow with his mail-clad fist in the centre of the prisoner's face. The gesture seemed almost casual, but fresh blood gushed from Cardos's ruined nose as he fell back into the arms of the guards who had been standing behind him. A few of the watching villagers gasped, but most remained silent, their eyes burning with horror and anger.

'You can have him back now,' Yahn said, signalling to his men.

The soldiers took a step forward, dragging Cardos with them, and then pitched him over the edge of the platform and onto the rough slope that lay to one side of the small cliff. His unconscious body tumbled awkwardly down the steep bank, and came to rest in a crumpled heap next to the pool. He lay quite still, and for a few moments no one else moved either.

'Don't you have a healer among you?' Yahn asked sarcastically. 'I think he could do with a bit of help!'

Terrel was about to step forward, but Ysatel's hand on his arm held him back.

'I don't like this,' she whispered. 'Why aren't the soldiers going?'

Terrel turned and saw the anxiety in her eyes. He had long since learnt to trust Ysatel, to listen to what she said, but this seemed to be something he *had* to do. If he couldn't use his talent to help someone like Cardos, what was the point of having it in the first place? He was about to say as much to her when he saw that it was too late. Davi had already set off, guiding Talker to the stricken man.

'Let them do this,' Ysatel hissed urgently. 'Stay where you are.'

Reluctantly, he did as he was told, and watched the latest act in the drama unfold. As Davi and Talker reached their patient and knelt beside him, Terrel became aware that some of the soldiers were laughing.

'*This* is your healer?' Yahn exclaimed, looking down in astonishment.

Talker was now touching one of Cardos's bloodied hands, and he and Davi exchanged a few quiet words.

'Hey, Killian!' the janizar called. 'What are you doing?'

At the sound of what was evidently his real name, Talker turned his face towards the sound.

'Darkness laughing,' he said clearly. 'Wings come.'

'I see that rockfall's robbed you of more than your sight,' Yahn remarked.

Talker turned his attention back to the injured man.

'What's he talking about?' Yahn shouted.

No one answered him.

'Boy!' he yelled, then waited until Davi glanced up at him. 'Is he really a healer?'

'Yes he is!' Davi replied, fiercely indignant.

Cardos's eyes fluttered open, and he groaned weakly.

'So I see,' Yahn said thoughtfully.

At a signal from the janizar, four soldiers set off down the slope, leaping nimbly from rock to rock, and before anyone could react they had reached Talker and hauled him to his feet. Although the healer looked bewildered, he didn't struggle, and it was left to Davi to put up any resistance. The boy flailed ineffectually at one of the guards, who swatted him away like a troublesome insect. Davi fell to the ground but jumped up again almost immediately.

'Leave him alone!' he cried, as the men who held Talker's arms began to drag him away. 'He's blind! I'm the only one who understands him. He can't do anything without me.'

'Very well then,' Yahn replied calmly. 'We'll take you too.'

Until that moment, the villagers below had all been

watching the scene in frozen silence. Now, as another soldier grabbed Davi and swung him onto his shoulder, there was sudden movement. Erena ran forward, her voice locked in a continuous high-pitched wail – the most desolate, desperate sound Terrel had ever heard.

'They'll kill her,' Ysatel breathed.

'We have to do something!' Terrel said, but he was trapped by the same paralysis that gripped the rest of the onlookers.

By the time Erena reached the bottom of the steep slope, the soldiers were almost at the top, but she did not give up the chase, scrambling over the boulders like a frightened mountain goat. Seeing her, Davi stretched out his arms in mute appeal.

Ysatel looked around desperately, but no one else – not even Frasu – was moving.

'Come on,' she said. 'We can't let her do this alone.'

'No!' Terrel exclaimed. 'You should—'

She brushed him aside and set off in pursuit. Terrel went after her, only to stumble as his twisted foot caught on the side of a large stone. He fell heavily, winding himself, and lay there, gasping for breath and trying to ignore the shooting pains in his legs. When he was able to look up, the soldiers had regained the platform, but Erena was almost there too. She was sobbing now, crying out incoherently in answer to her son's calls for help.

The fourth soldier glanced at his commander, who simply nodded and made a flicking gesture with his hand, as if to say 'Get rid of her'. The guard turned to face the woman, while his colleagues went on with their new prisoners, rejoining the main party and heading up the slope towards the gate. Yahn remained where he was, coolly regarding the entire scene.

The soldier had not drawn his sword – either because he felt it beneath him to use his blade on a woman, or because he had some scruples about doing so – and when she reached the ledge, he merely tried to shove her down again. However, he had underestimated the agility her desperation had granted her, and she twisted past him, leaving him waving at thin air, and ran on after her son.

Yahn's intervention was swift and brutal, a lightning-fast blow that caught the side of Erena's head and sent her crashing to the ground. The janizar's face was set in an expression of disgust as he beckoned to the remaining guard and turned to head after his men. He had gone only a few paces before his ears were assailed by a second furious screaming. Ysatel flew at him like an avenging demon, and such was the speed and ferocity of her assault that he almost fell. As it was, he had to rely on one of his men to drag the attacker away, the two of them staggering backwards towards the cliff edge.

Yahn glared at her, touching his cheek where her nails had drawn blood.

'Throw her over,' he barked, then turned and stalked away again.

Ysatel's charge had finally brought the rest of the villagers to life. Many of them were moving forward now, but when they saw the soldier spin round and thrust her over the edge of the precipice, they froze again. Time seemed to stand still as Ysatel appeared to hang suspended in midair for a long moment. Then movement and sound returned in a rush as she plunged towards the pool.

'No!' Terrel screamed, his helpless denial echoed by

the same cry from further away as Kerin – who had been
working much further down river – tore along the western
bank.

The sunlight seemed to flicker and dim, and everything in Terrel's world became a blur. There was a deep
rumbling noise, as if the mountain itself was growling,
and he shook convulsively, as though there were sparks
jumping in his blood. His legs would not move.

Ysatel's body appeared limp as it fell, and she made
no attempt to protect herself from the impact. She hit
the water side on, with a clap of sound that echoed all
around. The splash made a small explosion that glittered
in the sunlight, and she disappeared below the surface.

Terrel forced himself to hobble towards the pool, too
numb and horrified to even think. At first he could only
just see the roiling surface of the water, but as he climbed
it became clear that Ysatel had not resurfaced, and his
panic increased. He was vaguely aware that others were
converging on the pool, of voices crying out, but nothing
seemed real, nothing registered.

In the next moment the whole world went mad.

The pool exploded in a vast shimmering fountain of
light and foam, scattering water for hundreds of paces in
all directions, and hurling twisted flashes of spray far into
the sky. And yet it all happened in total silence. The only
sound came later, as the water fell back to earth, pattering
on the ground as an impossible rain shower.

The sudden jolt of finding himself soaked to the skin
helped Terrel set aside his fear and amazement, and he
stumbled on over the slippery ground until he came to
the rim of the pool – where he was met with yet another
incredible sight. The hollow in the rock was now

completely dry. Not a single drop of water was left any-where within its contours, and even the small waterfall that usually fed it was silent and dry.

Ysatel lay – utterly still – at the bottom of the inden-tation, and Terrel threw himself down beside her. Her eyes were closed, but the expression on her face was impassive, almost serene, and he could see no obvious injuries. But that meant little. She was unconscious, and it was possible that she had sustained severe internal damage. Some distant part of Terrel's brain registered the fact that her clothes and hair were not even damp, but he concentrated on trying to find out if she was all right.

When he took her hand, his sight began to blur again, as though an unnatural shadow had fallen over his eyes, and his heart began to pound wildly. His skin tingled uncomfortably.

Ysatel's chest rose and fell almost imperceptibly, and her pulse was equally faint, but at least she was alive. Terrel closed his own eyes, and willed himself to use whatever healing talent he possessed. Moments later, he was moving in a different, invisible realm, exploring, reaching out . . . But she was beyond him. The joint dreams were still there, but they were muted now, almost hidden. He persevered, and knowledge came gradually, seeping into his consciousness with infinite slowness. Ysatel's lungs were clear, her heart had set a new pace but was still beating, her mind was distant but intact. She had no real need of his help, even if he had been able to offer any.

'Ysy? Ysy!'

Terrel opened his eyes at the sound of Kerin's voice,

and saw that Ysatel's husband had joined him, kneeling at the other side of the unconscious woman, while a large group of villagers was crowding round the rim of the empty pool.

'Is she all right?' Kerin was cradling Ysatel's other hand in his own.

'Physically she's unharmed, and so is the baby.'

'Thank the heavens,' Kerin sighed heavily. 'So how soon will she wake up?'

'That I can't say.' Terrel knew now what had happened. He had seen it before, after all. 'But it may not be for some time,' he added with a heavy heart. 'She's become a sleeper.'

CHAPTER TWENTY

'Why did she do it?' Kerin asked. '*Why?*' The hurt and bewilderment in his voice made Terrel's heart ache, and he wished he had the answers his friend was seeking.

'I don't know,' he said miserably. He had not told Kerin of Ysatel's actions before the fateful encounter. He was already plagued by guilt over the fact that she had held him back, correctly suspecting the soldiers of treachery. And he still could not work out why she had been so anxious to protect him and risk Talker and Davi instead.

'It's not just her,' Kerin went on. 'Although the moons know that's bad enough, but it's the baby too. She's wanted one for so long . . .' He ran out of words, and Terrel saw that he was fighting back tears.

Terrel felt like crying himself, but knew that that would only make his friend feel worse. At least now they were alone, so that Kerin was able to let some of his emotions show. When they'd been in the empty pool, with so many people looking on, and when Kerin had carried his comatose wife back to their hut, he'd behaved with great stoicism, determined not to betray any sign of weakness. Terrel had been the only person he'd allowed inside with him, and the rest of the villagers had drifted away slowly, discussing the day's incredible events in low voices. Many of them did not know about the sleepers in the cave, so Terrel's diagnosis had not meant anything to them, but the few that did were grim-faced and silent.

Ysatel now lay on Terrel's bed in the smaller of the hut's two rooms. Placing her there had been instinctive – it was where they went when there was illness to defeat. Her appearance had not changed, and neither had her condition. All Terrel's efforts had done was confirm that she was slipping further away from him.

'What's happening to her?' Kerin asked quietly.

'She's being protected,' he replied, offering the only crumb of comfort he could find. 'She won't come to any harm.'

'How can you be sure of that?'

Terrel had been struggling with the problem of how much to tell Kerin, but realized that he had to try to explain. He owed them that.

'There are strange forces in the world, forces nobody understands,' he began, 'but they're shielding Ysy from danger. If they weren't, don't you think she would've been hurt by her fall, or maybe even drowned? But the protection comes at a cost. I don't understand it, but I've seen it happen before.'

For the first time since he'd laid his wife down, Kerin looked up and stared at Terrel.

'Something similar happened to a friend of mine, back

on Vadanis,' the boy said in answer to the unspoken question. 'She was being attacked, and was saved from certain death by a force no one could explain.'

'And then she became a sleeper?'

'Yes.' Terrel was tempted to tell Kerin that his wife might not be lost to him completely. Perhaps Ysatel would be able to return in a different guise, as Alyssa had done. But he said nothing, remembering that the only other sleeper he'd known who'd been able to do this was the seer Lathan – and then only after instruction from Elam. There was no guarantee that *all* sleepers were capable of such transmutations, and he did not want to raise Kerin's hopes unrealistically. And the poor man would probably think Terrel was quite mad if he tried to explain the process – unless Alyssa returned so that it could be demonstrated in action. Terrel desperately needed to talk to her – and Elam – in order to glean more information about Ysatel's condition. He also wanted to confirm his own suspicions about the elemental's involvement – even though the idea that it could affect events in Macul when the Floating Islands were so far away was hard to credit.

Kerin's concerns were more immediate.

'How long ago did that happen?' he asked.

Terrel thought back, calculating.

'About nine months.'

'Moons!' Kerin breathed. 'The baby . . . Your friend hasn't woken up yet?'

'No.'

'But she will, eventually?'

'We have to believe that,' Terrel replied, wishing he could just have said 'yes'. 'But there's no way of knowing when it'll be.'

A look of horror replaced the pleading in Kerin's eyes.

'The sleepers here have been like this for more than ten years. I could be an old man before Ysy wakes up.' He swallowed convulsively. 'And what about the baby? Could it survive that long?'

'She's protected too. From what Farazin told me, it seems the people in the cave have aged very little in all the time they've been there. Maybe time slows down for them.' Terrel was grasping at straws now, but Kerin was desperate for any degree of hope.

'That's true,' he said. 'I knew one of them before, and he's hardly changed in appearance.' He paused, and his puzzled expression dissolved into misery once more. 'But it's not natural. I couldn't bear it if she . . . Perhaps it would've been better if she'd been killed. That way at least I'd know.'

'Don't say that!' Terrel cried. 'Don't *ever* say that.'

Kerin's face registered sudden shock, as if he had been slapped.

'What am I saying?' he mumbled. 'Moons' blood. This is all too much for me.'

They were silent for a while, each trying to control their emotions.

'The fact that she was saved means she's special,' Terrel said eventually. 'Even more special than we knew.' He'd been puzzling over this aspect of the mystery, but he had no time for further speculation now.

Kerin nodded.

'I love her,' he stated simply.

So do I, Terrel thought, but knew that it was neither the time nor the place to put such a sentiment into words.

'I lost another wife, another daughter,' Kerin added softly.

'I know. Ysy told me. It's one of the reasons this baby means so much to her.'

'So why did she do it?' Kerin asked, returning to his original question.

This time Terrel knew he had to make some attempt at an answer.

'I think it was instinctive,' he said. 'She knew Davi was special, but when she saw his mother's distress it connected to her own feelings, as if she imagined it was *her* child in danger, the one growing inside her. And she simply reacted. It's illogical, I know, but emotions often are. The injustice of what she was seeing affected her personally, and she just *had* to act.' It was the best he could offer and, even though he knew that none of it made much sense, it seemed that Kerin was taking him seriously.

'She always put others before herself,' he said, as if he'd only just realized this. 'Me, thc boys . . .'

'Even me,' Terrel added. 'And I was a stranger.'

'Not any more. You . . .' Kerin hesitated, evidently feeling uncomfortable about finishing the thought. 'You will stay and help me look after her, won't you?' he asked instead.

'I'll stay as long as I can. But the main reason I want to get back to Vadanis is so I can go to my friend, to try to help her.'

Kerin nodded reluctantly, acknowledging the prior claim on Terrel's loyalties.

'Besides,' the boy added, 'this is beyond my healing. You'll be able to do as much for her as I can.'

'I won't let them put her in the caves,' Kerin declared abruptly.

This possibility hadn't even occurred to Terrel, but he was not familiar with all the customs and superstitions of Macul.

'I'm sure it won't come to that,' he said, hoping this was true.

'Maybe these forces will let her wake up soon anyway.'

Terrel said nothing to dash this optimism, even though he did not share it. He thought that, in his heart of hearts, Kerin probably didn't believe it either.

'I still don't understand what happened to the water,' Kerin said, changing the subject again. 'Did you have anything to do with that?'

'Me?' Terrel was taken aback by the question, but then he recalled some of the whispering he'd heard as they made their way back to the hut. 'No. I'm not a sorcerer or a sharakan. I don't even know where my healing comes from.' He could see now that, faced with inexplicable events, the villagers might have wondered about the only person in Fenduca who had demonstrated arcane powers of any kind – but the idea that he might be capable of such a feat was ludicrous, and he was surprised that Kerin had even considered it.

'But *something* happened,' Kerin said.

'I think it was the same forces.' Terrel recalled the elemental's panic – which had bordered on madness – when it had been threatened by a deluge of water. It was another reason for him to believe it must have been involved in Ysatel's fate. 'They react violently to water,' he went on, picking his words carefully, 'and emptying the pool was the only way of saving Ysy from drowning.'

'I've never seen anything like it.'

'I don't suppose many people have,' Terrel commented, remembering the stream flowing *uphill* in Betancuria. Although the water here had been flung aside as if propelled by an incredible explosion, the two events had defied both nature and logic. Perhaps finding the person it was trying to protect surrounded by what it thought of as a magical substance had confused the elemental and caused it to react so wildly.

'And it was so quiet!' Kerin exclaimed. 'You couldn't believe what was happening.'

That had indeed been the eeriest aspect of the whole scene. But what had amazed Terrel more than anything was the fact that the power that hurled the water into the sky had not only left Ysatel perfectly dry, but had also done not the slightest damage to her body or even her clothes. The forces involved had been precisely controlled – at odds with the apparent violence of their action.

As Terrel was preoccupied with these thoughts, he was startled by a sudden bark of laughter from Kerin. It was not a happy sound.

'I don't know whether the Dark Moon's listening or not,' he remarked bitterly. 'Did it hear our prayer or reject it?'

Terrel had no answer to that.

Kerin was not the only one who was distraught after the events of that afternoon. Frasu and Erena were also in a terrible state. Terrel went to see them as soon as he felt able to leave Ysatel's bedside, and he found Davi's parents close to breaking point. Although Erena had recovered from the janizar's blow with nothing worse than a lump above her right ear and a nasty headache, the loss of their only child was utterly devastating. They had no idea when – or even if – they'd ever see Davi again. In Frasu's case at least, their anguish was combined with pent-up rage and guilt that manifested itself in an inability to keep still. While his wife lay propped up in bed, trying to move her head as little as possible, he paced around the hut, muttering to himself.

Terrel's first concern when he arrived was to see that Erena was all right physically, and his healing instincts soon confirmed that she had suffered no lasting damage and helped her to deal with the lingering pain. After that there wasn't much he could do to console them, but he felt he ought to say something. As he considered various alternatives, he wondered if they were blaming him for not going to Cardos's aid himself, but he soon found that their main complaint was directed at Talker instead.

'We *knew* something bad would come of Davi being with that man,' Erena said quietly.

'The two of them did a lot of good, though,' Terrel pointed out.

'And look where it led!'

Terrel tried to convince Davi's parents that they were laying the blame at the wrong door, that it was Yahn and the soldiers who had been responsible for the terrible events.

'But none of this would have happened if Davi hadn't been with Talker in the first place, would it?' Frasu said.

Once again, Terrel had no answer.

It was only when Terrel returned to the Mirana household and checked on Ysatel's progress that he recalled

Farazin's advice to take note of his dreams that night.

Some people were not going to dream at all; Kerin was intent on sitting up all night with his wife, even though Terrel tried to persuade him to get some rest. The boy would have liked to keep the vigil too, but his healing efforts that day had left him close to exhaustion, and he knew he would have to sleep at some point. Even so, it felt very strange to be alone in the larger of the two rooms – Olandis and Aylen had still not returned – and he lay awake in the unfamiliar bed long into the night, replaying the events of the day in his head.

The abduction of Talker and Davi was yet another sign of injustice in a land where those who held any sort of power – whether it was the king and his soldiers, or the sharaken – seemed to have little or no regard for the welfare of the common people. That was bad enough, but it was Ysatel's fate that occupied most of his thoughts.

He told himself that it was possible that something else, and not the elemental, had been responsible – but all his instincts rejected that idea. The parallels with what had happened to Alyssa – potentially fatal danger averted by extreme, supernatural phenomena, but at the cost of becoming a sleeper – were too obvious to ignore. And Alyssa was convinced that whatever had protected her – and protected her still – originated from the elemental. Terrel was more familiar with that strange creature than anyone else alive, but even he had no idea how or why it did such things. What made Ysatel – and Alyssa before her – worthy of its guardianship?

That word rang alarm bells in Terrel's head. Was it possible that the elemental was the Guardian of the Tindaya Code? This was a question he was not remotely qualified to answer, and once again he hoped that Alyssa and the ghosts would return soon so that he could discuss it with them.

Setting that disturbing train of thought aside, he returned to the possible similarities between the two women. Was it something intrinsic to their minds? Perhaps even a type of madness? Ysatel had been completely sane, as far as he knew. There had been some uncharacteristically eccentric behaviour since she'd become pregnant, but that was hardly the same as Alyssa's peculiarities. Talker had seemed much more like Alyssa at times, but he had *not* become a sleeper. In fact, only a very few people were chosen – if indeed the process was as deliberate as that – and both men and women had fallen into comas. Apart from Ysatel and Alyssa, the only ones Terrel knew about were Lathan and the trio in the caves, but he thought now that there must be more elsewhere. What did they all have in common?

The only link he could think of between Ysatel, Alyssa and Lathan was that he himself had been there when they'd fallen asleep – although in Lathan's case he had not known this at the time – but he had been many miles away and little more than an infant when the three prospectors had succumbed on the black mountain, and this seemed to rule out his being a direct influence.

Even so, he could not help brooding on his own role in events, thinking of the similarities between what had happened to Ysatel and Alyssa, and wondering if his presence had been partly instrumental in their fates. And if so, had he been a curse or a blessing? Were all the people he came to love doomed to become sleepers? Or was it possible that they'd have died if he hadn't been there?

Could it be that *his* presence had made the elemental notice the two women? No matter where the protection came from, it had to be directed somehow. After all, most people in deadly peril were not saved in this manner – if 'saved' was the right word. And if the elemental was going to be influenced by anyone, Terrel knew it was likely to be him.

Flummoxed by another set of questions he couldn't answer, Terrel yearned again for Alyssa and her entourage. After all, he thought, they really *ought* to come now. If what had happened was not another step along the unknown road, then what *was* it?

Just before he finally fell asleep, Terrel remembered that he'd received dream-messages from Alyssa soon after she'd become a sleeper – messages that had reassured him that she was all right, and would wait for him. He'd found this enormously comforting. Would the same thing happen with Ysatel? Or would her messages – if she was able to send any – be directed to Kerin? And if so, would he need a link to her, like Alyssa's ring?

Terrel was determined to explore every possibility – both while he was awake and while he was asleep. He let himself drift into the world of dreams, his heart filled with a mixture of hope and fear.

Far above, the invisible shadow that was the Dark Moon passed silently across the slumbering sky.

CHAPTER TWENTY-ONE

It began with an image that could only make sense in a dream. A group of people were flying up into the air from a mountaintop, because there was a hole in the sky and they were needed to weave the cloth that was to patch it. After that it got *really* strange.

Terrel was one of the flying people, but suddenly he was alone, and instead of looking up to find the elusive hole, he was gazing down. The land spread out below him like a map – but a map designed by an insane cartographer. Rivers ran as straight as the flight of arrows, ignoring the contours of the terrain. Mountains were revealed as hollow, collapsing in on themselves as they melted, so that rock bubbled and spat like stew in a cauldron. Towns and villages were mere patches of pestilence, black markers of a plague that infected the earth itself. There was just one place that was different, that glittered and shone like a bright jewel cast into a pigsty.

There was an extra darkness moving within this unreal

night. At first Terrel thought it was the shadow of the
Dark Moon, but he soon realized that this was impossible. Looking at it made him feel cold. He was touched
by an inexplicable fear, and a sense of separation that was
wrong. He tried to warm himself, to guide the darkness
to safety, but he was enveloped by swirling clouds and
felt rain lash down below him, driven forward on a new
wind. Blind now, he was assailed by new torments – a
familiar, childlike panic, a malicious sense of amusement,
and then a searing pain in his chest that left him gasping
for breath.

He awoke, bathed in a cold sweat, with the mocking
words of the enchanter still sounding in his ears.

*Still alive, I see. It's a pity such resilience should have
been wasted on you. Not that it matters. I have other things
to amuse me now. Enjoy your travels, Terrel.*

He was not able to answer, rendered mute as he had
been so many times before, but this time it was different.
He knew a little about the enchanter now. He had a sense
of him, some knowledge – though incomplete – of his
motives and abilities. Terrel knew his enemy's status, his
heritage and title. And his name.

By the time Terrel staggered from his bed, he had decided
that he would not tell Farazin about his dream. It seemed
much too vague and ominous to mean anything to the
sky-watcher – and in any case, it had had nothing to do
with the Dark Moon. Besides, he told himself, I've got
more important things to think about.

He stumbled over to the connecting doorway, rubbing
the sleep from his eyes, and saw that Ysatel had not
moved. He hadn't expected anything else, but was still

disappointed. Kerin had finally fallen asleep where he sat, his mouth open and his neck bent at an awkward angle. He would be stiff when he woke, but Terrel decided not to disturb him. He would need as much rest as possible to help him through the next few days. Instead, the boy pulled on some clothes and went out into the cool air of dawn.

Does knowing his name help?

Terrel spun round, and saw a seagull alight on the roof of the hut.

Alyssa!

The bird's glinting eyes were fixed upon a point above Terrel's head, and he knew that she was 'seeing' remnants of his dream – the after-images that hung there like clouds, and which were visible only to Alyssa, until they dispersed and blew away upon the wind of a new day.

I'm glad you're here, he said, not wanting to talk about dreams.

You did your best, she told him. *It wasn't the right time.*

What? Terrel was confused. Was Alyssa still talking about the dream, or was she referring to his efforts to revive Ysatel? But he didn't get the chance to ask her, because at that moment Elam walked out through the wall of the hut.

So you got your sleeper after all, the ghost remarked.

Looks like it, Terrel replied, then glanced up at the bird.

Her spirit is wandering, Alyssa confirmed.

Is there any way of telling when she'll wake up?

No.

Terrel hadn't really expected anything else.

Can she do what you do? he asked. *Borrow the body of an animal, I mean?*

I don't know.

Could you teach her? Terrel asked Elam. *Like you taught Lathan?*

I'd have to find her first, Elam replied.

For a moment, Terrel didn't understand what his friend meant, then realized that Elam was referring to Ysatel's spirit, not her physical form.

You found Lathan, he pointed out.

He came to me. Or rather, he was brought to me. Anyway, why d'you want her to come back as an animal?

I'd like to talk to her. And so would her husband.

I think we'd need more of a reason than that, Elam said doubtfully.

She could be important, Terrel claimed.

What makes you think so?

This 'voice' had come from behind him, and Terrel turned to see that Muzeni and Shahan had materialized next to the turf-banked fire.

Because of the way she became a sleeper, he said.

Tell us more, Shahan demanded.

Terrel told them what had happened, in as much detail as he could remember, and – for once – none of them interrupted him. When he finished there was a thoughtful silence, and then Muzeni made the obvious comment.

It does bear a remarkable similarity to what happened to you, my dear.

Only in some respects, Alyssa replied.

The reaction to water is interesting, Shahan said.

Did anything happen on Vadanis? Terrel asked. *I mean, if the elemental was directly responsible for this, there might have been some effect there, don't you think?*

Not that we're aware of, Shahan answered, *but then now that the islands are back on a safe course, no one is paying much attention to such matters.*

Most people are trying to pretend the elemental doesn't exist, Elam commented. *And that nothing happened.*

You can't blame people for wanting to return to their ordinary lives, Muzeni remarked. *Some of us don't have that choice.*

Elam laughed.

That's an odd thing for a ghost to say, don't you think? he remarked.

Would any other ghosts have a connection with Ysatel? Terrel asked. *One of her own family, perhaps? Might she be able to make contact that way?*

This means a lot to you, doesn't it? Elam said.

Yes.

We'll see what we can find out, Shahan promised.

Thank you.

Terrel had sat down, leaning against the wall of the hut, when he had begun his tale, and the seagull had flown down to settle on the ground nearby. The ghosts were ranged about them, both seers still standing, Elam – typically – lying full length on the dew-damp grass. With his head resting on his hands, he seemed at ease and content, and Terrel envied him his composure.

You look relaxed.

Being dead helps.

Not all of us can afford to be so idle, Muzeni commented acidly.

That's right. Elam replied calmly. *Only those with a clear conscience.*

Why have you all come? Terrel asked quickly, wanting to forestall any quarrel. *Do you have something to tell me?*

There have been several new developments in reinterpreting the Tindaya Code, Shahan answered.

Is it possible that the elemental is the Guardian? Terrel asked.

You see, Elam put in. *I told you he's not as stupid as he looks.*

That is one of the theories being whispered about in Makhaya, Shahan said. *You can imagine how it's being received by Jax and his mother.*

My mother, Terrel thought, but didn't say anything. It still seemed too incredible, too remote.

Adina's claim to be the Mentor was always feeble at best, Muzeni added, *but she's a dangerous woman. Most of the clowns at court wouldn't dare annoy her.*

Which makes it all the more remarkable that these theories are being voiced abroad at all, Shahan went on. *Of course, the official line is still that the prince is the Guardian, but in private even Kamin is taking some of the new ideas seriously.*

What made them change their minds? Terrel asked.

The Dark Moon's antics have increased the confusion over certain sections of the Code – parts which seem to indicate that the Guardian isn't human, Muzeni said. *Which attribute divine powers to him.*

Or her, Alyssa said.

Muzeni gave her a long-suffering look.

I doubt we need to worry about the sex of the elemental, he told her.

But I thought the Guardian was supposed to be born on the night of a four-moon conjunction, Terrel objected. *The Ancient's been around for much longer than that.*

So everyone believed, Shahan conceded, *which is why many are still upholding Jax's claim.*

And why you come into the picture, Muzeni added.

But the theory goes that the creature might have been awoken *that same night*, Shahan explained, *after being inert for however long it's been down there.*

As if it were a sleeper, Terrel said quietly.

Alternatively, it's being argued that the references to the confluences are about the Mentor, not the Guardian, Muzeni said. *I'm not convinced, but as a rationalization it's attractive enough for facile minds.*

And it does at least fit with your role in averting the islands' crisis, Shahan went on. *You were the one who acted as go-between, advising both the elemental and the seers about what needed to be done.*

You think I'm *the Mentor?* Terrel asked incredulously.

It's one possibility, Muzeni replied.

To Terrel, that sounded even worse than being the Guardian. Being expected to be a hero was one thing; at least you got told what to do. Being responsible for prompting another's heroic actions was a very different matter.

Of course, as far as Vadanis is concerned, it was Jax, not you, who communicated with the Ancient, Shahan reminded him.

But no one's really sure about anything, Elam commented, summing up the entire situation in one sentence. *They can't even agree among themselves on* how many *Mentors there are supposed to be!*

There may be more than one? Terrel exclaimed hopefully. If this was true, then he might not have to work alone after all.

Some passages do seem to be contradictory, Muzeni admitted. His tone dampened whatever optimism the boy had been feeling.

Wonderful, Terrel muttered. *So what does all this mean for* me? *Do you have any more idea about what I'm supposed to do?*

Not yet, Shahan replied. *But, as we told you before, it seems clear that your participation is not yet over.*

Terrel was about to restate his determination to return to Vadanis as soon as possible, but he was distracted when he saw Kerin emerge from the hut. He was stretching and groaning softly in between yawns, and didn't see Terrel at first. He clearly had no idea that there were three ghosts only a few paces away. In fact, it was the seagull that first caught his eye, and he glanced at the large bird in surprise before noticing the boy and nodding in understanding.

'Another new friend?'

'You could put it that way,' Terrel replied, hoping Alyssa wouldn't fly away. There was a great deal he still wanted to discuss.

'Ysy's just the same,' Kerin said. 'She hasn't moved at all.'

'I know.'

'It's a nightmare.'

Not really a nightmare, Alyssa commented, obviously taking the prospector's remark out of context. *He dreamt about fish with long whiskers flying in the air.*

'I had the strangest dream last night,' Kerin remarked.

Terrel almost responded that he knew about it already, but managed to hold his tongue.

'Perhaps you should tell Farazin,' he said, seeing the old man coming down the path towards them. 'He's on his way here now.'

The new arrival proved too much for the seagull and, much to Terrel's dismay, the bird flew away. The ghosts faded from sight, Elam waving in silent farewell.

'Any change?' Farazin asked.

Kerin shook his head.

'And you're certain she's become a sleeper?' the sky-watcher asked Terrel.

'Yes. I'm sure.'

Farazin nodded.

'These are strange times we live in, old friend,' he said, putting a consoling hand on Kerin's shoulder. 'Strange times.'

As the two men went inside to look at Ysatel again, Terrel remained where he was. He was suddenly very tired, his entire body feeling heavy and lethargic. His life had indeed become stranger than he could ever have imagined – and nothing the ghosts had just told him made it any easier to cope with.

CHAPTER TWENTY-TWO

Terrel never found out whether Kerin told Farazin about his dream of the flying fish. He didn't tell the sky-watcher about his own nightmare, but he was aware that many villagers visited Farazin during the day.

At dusk, when Kerin and Terrel were sitting down to a cheerless meal together, the old man approached them. He enquired about Ysatel, nodding sadly when told that there had been no change, then asked to speak to Terrel alone.

'I'll go and sit with Ysy,' Kerin said immediately. He took his bowl into the hut, while Terrel waited, wondering about the ominous tone of Farazin's request. A few moments later, they heard the low murmur of Kerin's voice.

'He talks to her,' Terrel explained.

'She may be able to hear him,' Farazin commented, 'even if she's unable to respond.'

'It'd be nice to think so. What do you want to speak to me about?'

The sky-watcher sat down beside the fire, wincing at the protest of his elderly joints.

'Did you dream of anything last night?' he asked once he was settled.

'Nothing of consequence.'

Farazin paused, apparently wondering whether to accept the boy's answer at face value, then decided not to press the point.

'Would it surprise you to learn that almost everyone in Fenduca dreamt about you last night?'

'Me?' Terrel was astonished.

'That in itself is not really so surprising,' the old man went on. 'You've become a significant figure in our lives, after all, and given your role in yesterday's events, it's not hard to see why you should've been on most people's minds. The interesting thing is that more than half of them dreamt about your leaving us.'

'I've never hidden the fact that I want to go back to my own homeland,' Terrel said, feeling slightly defensive.

Farazin did not respond, and his silence was worrying.

'What?' Terrel asked nervously. 'What is it?'

'Have you ever considered that your journeying might not be over yet?' the sky-watcher said.

Not you too, Terrel thought dismally. The hints dropped by Shahan and Muzeni had been bad enough, but when his new neighbours added their voices to the argument, even his own faith began to waver.

'I see that the possibility has occurred to you, at least,' Farazin said, noting the boy's stricken expression.

'Did the dreams tell you where I'm supposed to be going?' Terrel asked.

'No, nothing specific. The only common thread was that you were heading inland.'

'But they're just dreams,' Terrel objected. 'They don't *mean* anything.'

'We can't trade as the sharaken do,' Farazin admitted, 'but when conditions are favourable, even people of no appreciable talent are able to share elements of the greater vision. As to the meaning of dreams, we each have to seek out our own.'

Terrel understood little of what the sky-watcher was saying, but the implications of his words were clear – and unwelcome.

'It's surely significant,' the old man went on, 'that our dreams should have been linked on this particular night. It would seem that your fate is somehow connected to the Dark Moon.'

'How is that possible?' Terrel asked, his mind recoiling from the idea.

'The moons affect us all.'

'Of course, but surely only in a general sense.'

Farazin considered this for a time before responding. 'It'd be my guess,' he said eventually, 'that destiny has already touched your life, Terrel. You wouldn't be here if it had not. You wouldn't be a healer. I won't pry into your secrets, but ask yourself this. Is it possible that there is something else you must do before you can go home?'

Terrel said nothing for a while, wishing he could have denied the possibility outright. He was disheartened by the fact that he could not.

'Why *must* I do anything?' he said eventually.

'Men have been asking themselves that question down

all the centuries,' Farazin replied. 'It's one of the things that makes us what we are.'

In the silence that followed this philosophical observation, Terrel heard Kerin speaking again. His voice was too low for his words to be understood, but the love and hope and sadness they contained humbled Terrel. He was not the only one who had a quarrel with fate.

'Did the dreams tell you *when* I might be leaving?'

Farazin shook his head.

'Time doesn't mean much in the dream-world.'

The boy sighed, realizing that a part of him did not *want* to leave Fenduca. He had found an acceptance here he'd never really known before. He'd become part of a family. If it hadn't been for Alyssa – and his promise to her – he might even have been content to stay. The idea of his leaving the village for any other reason seemed stupid and hurtful.

'I can't leave now,' he muttered. 'Not with Ysatel . . .'

'What happened with Ysatel might have been a sign,' Farazin said. 'And you said yourself you can't do anything for her here.'

A sign, Terrel thought. How could it be a sign? And then the rest of what the sky-watcher had said registered, and he looked up.

'You think that by going somewhere else I might be able to help Ysy?'

'I can't be sure, but . . . it's . . .'

It was not lost on Terrel that if he was able to help one sleeper, then he might be able to help others – including Alyssa. And Farazin's hesitancy made the boy jump to another conclusion.

'Did *you* dream anything?'

'Yes. But on its own it probably means nothing.'

'Tell me anyway.'

'I saw you travelling into the mountains of the interior,' Farazin replied. 'To join the sharaken.'

Terrel sat alone for some time after Farazin had gone, thinking about the old man's words. His first reaction had been that the idea of his attempting to join the sharaken was ridiculous, and would serve no purpose – even in the unlikely event of his succeeding. The Collector had shown no interest in the sleepers, so why should the addition of one more make any difference? And then he had told himself that not even Farazin had been sure about the interpretation of his dream; it might just have been a selection of random, meaningless images from the sky-watcher's own mind. However, the correlation between the dreams of the other villagers was harder to set aside, and Terrel couldn't dismiss them out of hand – especially as many of the locals had only just become aware of the existence of the sleepers in the cave. But Terrel did not see why this should have led so many of them to dream about *him*. There had to be a link somewhere.

Once again he hoped that Alyssa and the ghosts would return, so that he could confront them with this new evidence and see what they made of it. But that was something else he had no control over.

Olandis and Aylen looked down at the half-full pool, and frowned.

'What happened here?' Olandis wondered aloud.

'Is it all right?' his brother asked.

Even in the pale light of dawn, it was obvious to the

two young men that the pool had recently been emptied. However, there was no sign of why or how this had been done. It seemed as if the small stream that fed it was slowly filling it again, but they were reluctant to trust their precious cargo to the water if there was any chance that they'd be left high and dry again later. It had taken the young men several days to capture just two wolf-fish, and the last part of their journey – carrying one each in heavy, water-filled jars – had been made even more difficult by the fact that they'd been travelling by moonlight. Having reached Fenduca at last, they'd gone straight to the pool rather than to their own hut, in order to release the fish into their new home.

'Looks fine as far as I can tell,' Olandis said, peering at the rock. 'No cracks or sink-holes.'

'The level's rising again,' Aylen added. 'Shall we put them in?'

Olandis looked around to see if there was anyone nearby who might be able to give them some advice but, unusually, no one was yet stirring.

'Yes,' he decided. 'They need fresh water, and it'll be easy enough to catch them again if we have to move them.'

Once released from their confinement, the wolf-fish began to explore their new domain, their antennae bristling with curiosity. The brothers watched for a few moments, then turned away and headed down the hill.

'Gate'll know what happened,' Aylen said. 'He'll do whatever's necessary.'

Olandis nodded wearily.

'We've done our bit,' he said. 'All I want to do now is sleep for about two days.'

*

'How could you let this happen?' Olandis cried.

When confronted with the disaster that had befallen their stepmother, the two brothers had reacted in markedly different ways. Aylen had become silent and withdrawn, apparently unable to speak, and barely reacting even when told of the bizarre circumstances of Ysatel's fall. Olandis, on the other hand, seemed to have been seized by a terrible fury.

'You know what she's like,' Kerin said. 'I tried—'

'Not hard enough,' his son cut in. 'You're her husband. You're supposed to *protect* her.'

'It wasn't his fault,' Terrel protested. 'If anyone was to blame it was me.' He had been listening to the argument between father and son with a growing sense of guilty despair.

Olandis turned to glance at him.

'Keep out of this,' he said dismissively. 'This is family business.'

With those few thoughtless words, Olandis cut away the temporary foundations of Terrel's life, and his belief that he had become part of the Mirana family was exposed as mere wishful thinking. When it came to a crisis, he was an outsider once more. He did not try to interrupt again, knowing that anything he said now would be useless.

'Well?' Olandis demanded, glaring at his father.

'I could no more turn Ysy into a caged bird than I could fly to the moons,' Kerin replied. 'You know—'

'What I *know* is that she was pregnant.'

'And she still is! She's going to wake up sooner or later.'

'How can you know that?' Olandis asked. 'My mother didn't.'

The moment of absolute stillness that followed this outburst seemed to last for ever. The accusation implicit in Olandis's words drained the colour from Kerin's face, and when he finally spoke his voice was small and tortured.

'That was different.'

'How would you know?' Olandis muttered. Even he seemed shocked by his own declaration, but he was still burning with righteous indignation. 'You weren't even there.'

'Olandis?' Aylen said in a quiet, warning tone, but this was not enough to deter his brother. A dam had burst somewhere deep inside him, and he was helpless to stop the deluge now.

'I watched her fading away,' he said, 'wondering all the time where my father was, why he didn't come home and make everything all right again. And after she died and the elders wouldn't let us go and see her any more, I held the baby in my arms and told her that we'd look after her. Then she stopped breathing too, and I couldn't help. I didn't understand what I'd done wrong. I didn't understand anything. I was seven years old. *Seven*.'

Terrel was appalled to see tears running silently down Kerin's face, tears that he made no attempt to hide or wipe away.

'That's enough,' Aylen pleaded softly, but once again Olandis ignored him.

'Didn't you learn anything from what happened to Aryel?' he asked, seemingly intent on twisting the knife now that he'd driven it into his father's heart. 'Is this how you honour her memory? By *repeating* the whole thing?'

Terrel would not have believed Olandis capable of such

cruelty and – even after hearing about the traumatic events of his childhood – could not understand why the sorrow he had expected should have turned to such vicious rage. In the end it was to that rage, and not to the injustice of Olandis's claims, that Kerin responded.

'Get out,' he grated, in a cracked and bitter voice. 'Get out of my house.'

'Oh, I'm going,' Olandis replied with equal fervour and disdain. 'You think I want to stay here?'

So saying, he turned on his heels and strode from the hut into the incongruous sunlight of a new day. A moment later, before either of the others had had a chance to say anything, Kerin also turned away and went back to his vigil at Ysatel's bedside.

Aylen and Terrel were left numb with horror, each seeing his own shock reflected in the other's eyes.

CHAPTER TWENTY-THREE

'You're both as stubborn as each other!' Aylen was trapped halfway between anger and dejection.

'Just leave it, Chute,' Kerin said. 'This is between me and your brother. I know you mean well, but it won't help. Olandis will come to his senses in his own time.'

'Will he? One of you has got to make the first move. Or maybe you'll just never speak to each other again. Is that what you want?'

'I told you to leave it, boy.'

'He'll probably end up marrying Elyce.'

'If that's what he wants,' Kerin stated coldly.

'You know it isn't!' Aylen exclaimed. 'But he's got to live *somewhere*, and he's quite capable of doing it just to spite you.'

Pain flashed in Kerin's eyes, but he just shrugged, as though the actions of his elder son were of no interest to him.

Several days had passed since the argument between Olandis and his father and, true to his word, Olandis had not returned home. He was now living with his would-be sweetheart and her family, an arrangement that would normally make their eventual marriage a foregone conclusion. Elyce had been delighted by his apparent change of heart, caring little for his reasons. Even though Olandis was clearly unhappy most of the time, and had been treating her with little consideration – and at times almost with contempt – she was quick to display their new attachment to all and sundry. Her sometimes thoughtless comments had done nothing to heal the rift between Olandis and his father.

Terrel was dismayed by this state of affairs, but – heeding Olandis's warning that this was *family* business – he had made no attempt to mediate between the two warring parties. Instead, as on this occasion, he had merely been a silent onlooker as Aylen tried to bring what was left of his family back together.

'He doesn't even love her,' Aylen said now. 'That's obvious to everyone except Elyce. He's being cruel to her too, and that's not like him, is it?'

Kerin shrugged again, as if disavowing any knowledge of his son's character.

'Just give him a chance,' Aylen pleaded. 'An opening.'

'He can do anything he likes. I'm not stopping him.'

'I give up,' Aylen muttered, waving his hands in the air. 'I'm going to work.'

After he left, Terrel desperately wanted to say something, but the look on Kerin's face and the lingering atmosphere of antagonism kept him quiet.

*

In contrast to earlier times, the Mirana home had become a cold and lifeless place. With Olandis gone, Ysatel still deep in her coma, Kerin brooding and Aylen helpless to do anything about it, there was little Terrel could do to lighten the mood. Not even Aylen seemed willing to talk to him any more, and Terrel could not help wondering if he was being blamed in some way for what had happened. As a result he could only look on in misery as the family he had once thought to be invulnerable tore itself apart. He didn't want to believe that this was inevitable for *all* families, but the conclusion seemed inescapable. If these things could happen to such a tight-knit unit, what hope was there for the rest of humanity?

As time passed, the person he missed most was, of course, Ysatel. It was she who had first made him feel that he belonged in Fenduca and, as someone who'd never had a real home – or family – of his own, that had been enormously important to him. Now she was gone, beyond even the reach of his talents, and Terrel was bereft.

Ysatel's almost lifeless body still lay in the hut's small side-room. No one had yet suggested moving her to the cave with the other sleepers – Terrel dreaded to think what Kerin's reaction would be if they did – and the boy had thus been able to monitor her progress as best he could. He visited her each morning and evening, trying to ignore the habitual look of hope Kerin gave him as he came in. He always took her hand, but although he occasionally felt a tentative connection, these moments were only fleeting and uninformative – and they were growing weaker. She was fading gradually from his waking dream, and Terrel knew that eventually she would become like the men and woman in the cave, and that he would then feel nothing at all when he touched her. For a moment he wondered whether it would be the same with Alyssa, in spite of her being able to come to him in another form.

Alyssa had been a sleeper now for more than three-quarters of a year, which – while it was a lot less than the unfortunates in the cave – still seemed an age to Terrel. The thought of her spirit fading, and his losing contact with her, was unbearable.

There had been no sign of Alyssa and the ghosts since their visit on the day after Ysatel's fall. Terrel had long since given up trying to think of anything he could do to *make* them come, and had resigned himself to simply waiting. In the meantime, he continued his healing work in the village, although that gave him less satisfaction than it had once done. The fact that he could do nothing for Ysatel – something he suspected Kerin secretly resented – made his other achievements seem almost pointless. Nevertheless, those he treated were still grateful, and the gifts he earned went some way to supplementing the household's meagre income.

However, one of his patients was unable to give him anything in payment. Cardos was slowly recovering his health – although his face would always be disfigured – and as he had no family, he had been staying in the infirmary. He had refused to talk about his time on the mountain, and after the events precipitated by his return, most people wanted little to do with him. Apart from Terrel, and occasional visits from some of the village women, the only person who went to see him regularly was Aylen – and he always left when Terrel arrived, and wouldn't discuss what had passed between them.

One of the few things Terrel was grateful for was the

fact that Farazin had made no more mention of the villagers' dream predictions, or of a possible meeting with the sharaken. If the Collector who had visited Fenduca was a true representative of the mystics, Terrel wanted nothing to do with them – and certainly did not want to travel to their mountainous retreat in Macul's interior. Their lofty attitudes seemed to him to be almost as bad as the venal greed displayed by the country's rulers. Neither seemed to have any regard for the general population, and Terrel could not help comparing them to the equivalent authorities in the Floating Islands. It was true that the imperial forces and the seers paid little attention to the troubles of the common people of Vadanis, but at least their attitudes had not been actively pernicious.

These thoughts were enough to make Terrel feel even more homesick – until he remembered that the Emperor was actually *his father*, and that the seers had been among those responsible for his abandonment as a baby. After that he decided that all governments must be as vile and corrupt as each other.

The spring rains returned that afternoon, bringing with them renewed worries about a further mudslide. Rumours had been circulating that the soldiers were preparing another 'accidental' avalanche, but as there was nothing the villagers could do about this – even if it were true – they went about their business as usual. After everything that had happened to him, Terrel was beginning to understand their fatalism.

He was hurrying down one of the village paths, resigned to getting soaked before he reached the shelter of Kerin's hut, when he was hailed from one of the nearby buildings. This was a ramshackle place, whose owner – a one-eyed man called Arbanas – made a precarious living selling the ale he brewed himself, wines and spirits he bought from travellers, and occasionally even some food. The quality of his merchandise was mediocre, and because Terrel had had an aversion to alcohol ever since his experience in Tiscamanita – when he'd got so drunk that the enchanter had been able to control his body as well as his mind – he had never been inside before. However, the man beckoning to him now was a well-dressed stranger, and the prospect of getting out of the rain made Terrel hesitate. Going back to the Mirana home no longer held much attraction, so he went over to the ale-house and stepped inside.

'You're Terrel, aren't you?'

As the stranger let the protective canopy fall back over the doorway, the only illumination in the bar came from two sputtering candles, and it was hard for Terrel to make out many details. The place was almost empty, and the air smelt stale.

'Yes, I'm Terrel. Who are you?'

'My name is Bezaki Antin, but most people call me Rider. Can I buy you a drink? Or what passes for a drink in these parts,' he amended with a grin.

'No, thank you.' Terrel knew of Rider by reputation. He was one of the merchants who came regularly to trade with Cutter, always arriving on horseback with two other mounted men acting as his bodyguards.

'Very wise. Arbanas here has tried to poison me on more than one occasion.'

'I'll succeed one of these days,' the landlord commented gruffly from the depths of the room.

'Good health to you too,' Rider said, laughing.

'What do you want with me?' Terrel asked.

'Well, I've completed my trading with my dear friend Cutter,' the merchant replied. 'And I've paid my respects to Farazin. I'd normally have left by now – there's not much else to keep me in Fenduca – but it's too late in the day to start journeying again, so I've some time on my hands. It's been suggested that you might be able to offer more original and intelligent conversation than most people here.'

'These people are my friends,' Terrel pointed out.

'I meant no offence,' Rider said quickly, still smiling. 'But you're new to this region, aren't you?'

Terrel nodded.

'And to be honest,' the merchant went on, 'I was curious to meet the healer everyone's been talking about.'

'Well, now you've met me,' Terrel said shortly. The man seemed affable enough, but his slightly conde-scending manner was beginning to irritate the boy. Bezaki Antin obviously liked the sound of his own voice, and Terrel doubted that he would gain much from any conver-sation.

'I'll be straight with you, Terrel,' Rider said, his expression earnest now. 'I don't believe in things I can't see and touch, and you don't look like much to me, but too many people have been singing your praises for me to ignore it completely. One of my servants has injured his shoulder.' He waved a hand at two burly men sitting in a dingy recess at the end of the room. 'The stupid oaf doesn't even know how he did it, but he can't raise his right arm above chest height. That's his sword arm, which makes him about as effective a bodyguard as a blueriver duckling. I was wondering if you'd work some of your magic on him – for a suitable fee, of course.'

Terrel hesitated for only an instant before replying. He was learning that being a healer carried its own obligations, and now that he knew the true reason for Rider's invitation, he wanted to end the encounter as quickly as possible.

'All right. Which of them is it?'

'Draven, get up here.'

The bodyguard stood up and walked over to them, eyeing Terrel with some suspicion. Like his master, he was clearly sceptical about the healing process.

'Give me your hand.'

Draven hesitated, then – looking distinctly embarrassed – laid his calloused fingers on the boy's outstretched palm. Making a connection was something that now came naturally to Terrel, but on this occasion he met more resistance than was usual, and he put this down to the man's lack of belief. But the pain in Draven's shoulder was real enough, and Terrel shuddered involuntarily when he reached it. The injury itself was not really serious – it would have mended in time – but while it lasted it was not only agonizing but debilitating too. He dealt instinctively with the pain, enabling the patient to control it himself, then moved his attentions to the joint, noting where the problems lay and adjusting the play of muscles so that they caused the least possible discomfort. It was not a cure, but it was the next best thing. Terrel withdrew his hand.

'Try it now.'

Draven did so, flexing his arm, then raising it gingerly, before lifting it above his head. His expression as he did so was almost comical, and his amazement was echoed on his master's face.

'Moons!' Rider exclaimed heartily. 'If he'd tried to do that earlier today he'd have been squealing like a stuck pig. You really are a healer, boy.'

Yes, I am, Terrel thought, with some satisfaction. And I can do it even when someone has no faith in me.

'It'll be stiff and sore for a while,' he told the guard, 'but you'll be as good as new in a month or so.'

'Thanks,' Draven said quietly.

'That's all you can say?' Rider demanded.

'That's all that's necessary,' Terrel said.

'I'm sorry I doubted you,' the merchant told the boy. 'I've never seen anything like it.' He dug into his belt-pouch and picked out four stones. 'Will one of these do for your fee?' he asked, holding them out.

'Any of them.'

'Then choose one.'

Knowing that this was another of Rider's games, another test, Terrel was tempted just to pick the first one that took his eye. But then he resolved to make a considered choice. Kerin and his sons had taught him a little about the relative values of their finds, and he owed it to them to get as much as he could from Bezaki. The merchant could afford it, after all.

In the end he settled on a dull-coloured, irregularly-shaped nugget that promised a good yield of metal within.

Rider nodded approvingly.

'Not just a healer, I see,' he commented. 'Most novices would've gone for something prettier, but you've chosen the best of the four.'

Terrel pocketed the stone, feeling in no need of the merchant's flattery, and turned to go.

'You're wasted here, Terrel. Why do you stay?'

'I don't have much choice.'

'A man of your talents would be welcome anywhere, and you could earn much more than a few stones.'

'I'm not interested in that.'

'Such selflessness!' Rider exclaimed, half mocking.

'Besides,' Terrel added, 'when I leave here, I'm going home.'

'And where is home? I haven't been able to place your accent.'

'I come from Vadanis. It's one of what you call the Cursed Islands.' He found that he was childishly pleased to note the shock that registered on Bezaki's face.

'No wonder,' the merchant said, then paused. 'Getting back there's going to take some doing.'

'I know when the islands will reach the closest point to the coast of Macul.'

'Even so, you're going to need a ship willing to make the trip.'

'Do you know where I might find one?' Terrel asked, belatedly realizing that a traveller such as Rider might well be a source of useful information.

'The nearest place would be Tanggula,' the merchant replied, 'but I doubt many of the captains there would want to attempt such a voyage. And how would you pay their passage-fee?'

'Where *is* Tanggula?'

'About forty miles southwest of here. The best route is via Fenia Rybak, but even that's not easy. Have you ever walked that far?' Rider glanced at Terrel's twisted leg.

'Many times.'

The merchant nodded, showing little surprise at the boy's claim.

'Perhaps we could come to some arrangement,' he suggested, 'so that you could ride . . .'

'I'm not ready to go yet.'

With that, Terrel left the ale-house, ignoring Bezaki's final attempts to persuade him to stay a little longer. He was feeling a surge of confidence now that he knew where to go when the time came. It was not much, considering the voyage he intended to make – but it was a start.

The following morning brought another piece of good news. Unseen by all but a few prospectors working in the upper stretches of the river, the gate in the fence opened and two figures were ushered through without ceremony. Talker and Davi had been returned.

The child's parents claimed him as soon as he reached the village, and for a time would let no one else near him. Talker was as incomprehensible as ever, so it was not until late in the afternoon that Terrel found out what had happened. Frasu came to see him, and grudgingly admitted that he'd been unable to get anything from his son apart from the fact that Davi wanted to see Terrel. When he reached their hut, Erena was reluctant to let the boy out of her arms – as if she feared that Terrel's mere presence would lead to her son being taken away again – but Davi wriggled free. Even then he was reticent, obviously finding it difficult to talk, and Terrel began to wonder if the little boy had been badly treated by the soldiers.

Eventually, though, Davi confided in him, the child's words spilling out in a rush. Talker, he said, had lost his gift. He hadn't been able to heal any of the soldiers or miners, and this upset Davi greatly. Terrel tried to get him to go into more detail, but he clammed up again – and then Frasu made it clear that the interview was over.

Terrel made his way to the infirmary, where Talker had been installed. He found the blind man kneeling over Cardos's bed, nodding silently over the sleeping patient, and in that moment Terrel knew that Talker's gift had not been lost. Somehow, in the midst of the soldiers and miners who had abandoned him earlier, he had found a way to hide his talent. There was no telling how or why he had done this, but it meant that in some ways Talker was an even more remarkable healer than Terrel himself.

'Did you talk to Davi?' Aylen asked.

'Yes,' Terrel replied. 'He didn't say much, though.'

'Did he hear anything about a possible avalanche?'

'I don't know.'

'I had a bit of good luck today,' Aylen remarked, grinning as he changed the subject. He dipped a hand into his pocket and took out a stone about the size of a hen's egg. It had a smooth, almost polished surface, which glowed in swirls of blue, silver-white and violet, with a few tiny sparks of orange glittering within its depths. It was as though a particularly serene moment of sunrise had been frozen in stone, and even to Terrel's largely untutored eye, it was obvious that it must be both very rare and extremely valuable.

'Not bad, eh?' Aylen commented, seeing Terrel's awed expression.

'It's beautiful.'

'It's a fire-opal,' Aylen told him grandly. 'I bet the

miners would be sick if they knew they'd missed this. It's exactly what I needed. Don't say anything to Gate yet, will you? I want to surprise him.'

Terrel expected Aylen to reveal his find that evening, but he didn't, and the atmosphere in the hut remained as depressing as ever.

The next morning, Kerin and Aylen had already gone out when Terrel awoke and, after checking on Ysatel, he made his way to Davi's home. As he approached the hut, Aylen came out, but he strode off before Terrel had a chance to talk to him.

Despite Terrel's pleading, Davi's parents flatly refused to let the boy resume his partnership with Talker, and Terrel went on to the infirmary. Cardos's condition had improved overnight, and Terrel was in no doubt that this was because of Talker's presence.

Without his 'eyes', the blind man was effectively confined to one place, and Terrel was determined to try to remedy this. He took Talker with him on his subsequent trip around the village, but the arrangement proved impractical. He did not have Davi's knack as a guide – or as a translator – and no one had any need of Talker if Terrel was there. By midday he had taken the blind man back to the infirmary, having decided to try once more to change Frasu and Erena's minds about allowing their son out of their sight.

He was on his way to their hut when he met Aylen again.

'You'll help them, won't you?' Aylen said abruptly.

'Who?' Terrel asked, taken aback by this unorthodox greeting.

'Gate and Olandis. They're going to have to forgive each other eventually.'

'Of course. I'll do anything I can, you know that. But—'

'Good man,' Aylen cut in. 'I've got to run. No peace for the wicked.' He dashed off, evidently in a hurry. As Terrel watched his fleet-footed progress, he felt clumsy and confused.

He was not to realize the significance of their brief conversation until that evening, when he returned to the Mirana house to find Kerin sitting alone in the main room. The expression on his face was so desolate that for a moment Terrel thought something had happened to Ysatel, but a glance into the inner room told him that her condition was unchanged.

'What's the matter? What's happened?'

For answer Kerin held up his clenched fist.

'If I hadn't seen it written down in his own hand, I'd never have believed it,' he said.

Terrel saw that he was holding a crumpled scrap of the material used for making the family's prayer-flags.

'That's all he left apart from this.' Kerin opened his other fist, and Terrel saw the fire-opal glittering on the palm of his hand.

'Aylen?' he said stupidly.

'He's gone to the mountain,' Kerin said. 'To take the king's wages.'

CHAPTER TWENTY-FOUR

Overnight, Kerin had become a wraith. Before Aylen's departure, there had been a spark of defiance in his misery, even in the midst of all his troubles, but now that had been snuffed out. The prospector was a silent figure, forlorn and without hope. He'd lost everything – his wife, his unborn daughter, both his sons – and nothing in his life held any meaning.

Terrel watched him fading, knowing he could do nothing. Kerin refused to discuss his family, and simply ignored the boy's efforts to console him. Farazin was among several of the villagers who had tried to comfort him, but none of them met with any success either. The only person Kerin would talk to was Ysatel, and then only when he thought there was no chance of his being over-heard. Terrel occasionally caught a few mumbled words when he returned to the hut, but he did his best not to eavesdrop, recognizing the private pain in Kerin's voice. The fact that he chose to talk only to someone who could not respond was in itself symptomatic of the tragedy that had befallen him.

When he was able to tear himself away from his vigil at his wife's bedside, Kerin returned to his place in the river – he had to work, after all – but even a good find did not dent his gloom.

Terrel also noted that he had made no attempt to sell the fire-opal. 'It's exactly what I needed,' Aylen had said. Terrel hadn't understood what he'd meant at the time, but it was clear enough now. Yet even though it was obvious that Aylen had meant the stone to provide his father with some much-needed income, Terrel understood why Kerin wanted to hold on to his last link with his son.

'What do you expect me to do?' Olandis asked.

'You could come home,' Terrel suggested.

'This is his home now,' Elyce said, and took Olandis's hand.

As always, Terrel felt inhibited by the girl's presence. She had a knack of always being there whenever he tried to talk to Olandis, and her possessiveness was demonstrated in her every word and action.

'He's suffered enough,' Terrel insisted. 'And he needs you.'

'Then why won't he say so himself?'

'Pride, stubbornness . . . who knows? Does that matter? He's still your father.'

'You think I'm being cruel, don't you?'

'Would talking to him be so difficult?' Terrel asked, avoiding a direct answer to the question.

'He won't listen.'

'He might now.'

'Now that Aylen's gone, you mean?'

'You're all he has left.'

'I don't suppose he's even stopped to consider *why* Chute left.'

'He won't discuss it with me,' Terrel replied, 'but I'd guess he's thought of little other than his family recently.'

'He's driven us all away,' Olandis stated bluntly.

'You can't mean that!'

'Can't I?'

Terrel had spent some time trying to fathom Aylen's motives for leaving. He had explained nothing in his farewell note, but no one believed that Chute had simply been tempted by the regular wages of a mine-worker. Most people thought that he'd gone to be the villagers' spy in the army camp, to warn them of more avalanches or of any other threats from the military. Others had even speculated that he might be planning to incite a revolt among the miners – something Olandis had discussed with Terrel during their fishing trip two months earlier. But no one had suggested that Aylen had simply wanted to escape from his family home – until now.

'Kerin needs a reason to forgive himself,' Terrel said quietly, not knowing what else to say.

'And you want me to give it to him?'

'You're the only one left who can.'

'And if what he's done is unforgivable?' Olandis asked, his dark eyes filled with painful memories. 'What then?'

Terrel trudged up the path to the infirmary, wondering gloomily if it was his own baleful influence that caused families to tear themselves apart. He was so sunk in

memories of Ferrand's farm that, when he was hailed, he
did not know who had called out or where they were.
Looking round, he noticed Cutter standing with a
stranger, presumably another of the travelling merchants
he dealt with.

'Can you spare us a moment, Terrel?' Cutter called,
beckoning him over.

Terrel made his way across to them, more than a little
surprised. Although he was on good terms with Mitus
now, they rarely had much to say to one another. He had
never set eyes on the other man before.

'This is Masiuk Ilona.'

Terrel and the merchant nodded in greeting, each
weighing the other up.

'Is it true Kerin has a fire-opal?' Cutter asked, revealing
his reason for speaking to the boy.

'Yes. Aylen found it before he left.'

'Do you realize how valuable it might be?'

'He won't part with it.'

'Why not?' the merchant asked. 'I can guarantee him
an excellent price.'

'If it's a good stone,' Cutter added, 'it could make his
life a lot easier. He could—'

'He's not interested,' Terrel said.

'You're sure?' Masiuk queried.

'Talk to him yourself if you don't believe me.'

'We've tried,' Cutter admitted, shrugging. 'He won't
even show it to us.'

'Then there's nothing I can do.'

'We could make it worth your while,' the merchant
suggested.

'Leave him alone,' Terrel said, angry now. 'And leave

me alone.' He was about to turn and walk away when the merchant spoke again.

'You're from the Cursed Islands, aren't you?'

'Yes.'

'And you intend to return there?'

'When I can,' Terrel replied. 'Why? Do you know any of the sea captains in Tanggula?'

'Most of them.' It was not a boast, merely a statement of fact.

'Masiuk knows everyone, everywhere,' Cutter remarked with a grin. 'And he's always first with all the gossip. He's just been telling me about some monster that the king's got locked up in Talazoria.'

Terrel froze, all thoughts of ships fleeing from his mind.

'A monster?' he asked shakily.

'Some say it's a demon,' the merchant said with relish, 'a creature so vile no man can look on it for long without his blood boiling or turning to ice.'

'What does it look like?'

'I've not seen it myself, but I've heard they're calling it Anetek-Vori.' He explained that this meant 'the rock that walks' in the wanderers' tongue.

'And you say it's locked up?'

'Walled up, rather. Inside the old fortress. Apparently Ekuban's turned it into a new entertainment for his court.'

'How?' Terrel asked, his sense of dread increasing.

'He sends convicted criminals inside, and sees what happens,' Masiuk replied. 'So far none of them have ever come out again.'

'Eaten alive,' Cutter concluded. 'That sounds like the sort of entertainment Ekuban would enjoy.'

'If the creature's that powerful, you wonder why it hasn't tried to escape,' the merchant added.

'Is there a moat around the fortress?' Terrel asked.

'Yes. How did you know that?'

'Just a guess.'

The more Terrel thought about the rumour, the more worried he became. It sounded so like the initial gossip that had surrounded the monster in the mines at Betancuria that he couldn't help thinking the creature at Ekuban's court must be an elemental. At first he wondered if the Ancient had somehow followed him, but rejected that idea. Given its fear of even relatively small amounts of water, there was no way it could have crossed the ocean. The conclusion was therefore obvious. There was a second of its kind.

And if that were true, a number of other things began to make much more sense. For a start, it meant that the sleepers here – including Ysatel – were linked to the elemental in Talazoria, and not to the one on Vadanis. So it was hardly surprising that his efforts to find a connection between Ysatel and Alyssa had been largely unsuccessful. On the other hand, if the second creature *was* afraid of water, it seemed likely that there would be some other similarities between the two. However, the one in Betancuria had looked nothing like a rock – walking or otherwise.

Terrel shook his head as if to clear it. The world had been confusing enough before this!

He'd walked away from the village, looking for somewhere to be alone with his thoughts, and his vantage point on a nearby hillside gave him a good view of the black

mountain in all its bleak, imposing majesty. There had
been times in his wilder flights of fancy when he'd
wondered fleetingly if another elemental had had something to do with the emergence of the mountain, but he'd
dismissed the idea – partly because it seemed absurd, and
partly because the ghosts had been able to come to him.
They had not been able to get within twenty miles of
Betancuria, held back by a force that none of them could
explain. But the theory didn't seem quite so ridiculous
now. It was possible that the elemental *had* been there
when the mountain grew – when the earlier sleepers had
fallen into their comas – but that it had subsequently
moved away.

Terrel recalled a conversation about the water level in
the area rising, and wondered whether this might have
been what had driven the creature away. Although this
made sense, he couldn't imagine how it had come to be
captured in a distant city – if that was indeed the case.
He knew, from hard-won experience, that not all rumours
were true. However, they had to begin somewhere, and
a horrible suspicion was growing in Terrel's mind. How
long will it be, he wondered, before someone starts telling
me that destiny's calling for me to go to Talazoria?

The voice of the cloud was deep and sonorous, like the
muted rumbling of thunder.
  'Omens.'
  'I'm sick of omens,' Terrel said.
  'Omens are important here.'
  'You mean dreams.'
  Terrel was flying again. He found nothing strange in
the fact that he was talking to a cloud, but he wished it

would release him from its clammy embrace so that he could see. He knew the land was below him somewhere, remembered from moonlit glimpses, but it was invisible now. And there was magic in the air.

He couldn't control the weather. No one could.

Cruel laughter made him doubt his own reasoning, as the veil of wind-blown mist parted. The soaring eagle's view of Macul made him momentarily dizzy, and he saw movement where there was none. The darkness below shivered.

This is fun, isn't it! The enchanter's voice was gleeful. *We make a good team, you and I.*

We're not a team, Jax. We never will be.

The enchanter hesitated, evidently caught off guard.

So, you've realized at last, he commented eventually. *It took you long enough. And we* are *a team, whether you like it or not. How else could I be here, unless you invited me? How else could all this have happened? Watch.*

As the remote presence withdrew, Terrel felt a mixture of relief and foreboding. The diseased land below him flickered dully, one jewel outshining all the rest. He flew on, drawing closer, sensing the fearful darkness at its heart.

Talazoria rose like a beacon in the endless night, its facets capturing all the pale moon-rays and turning them into rainbow-coloured fountains of light. The city glittered and blinked like a million stars, too elaborate to be beautiful but awe-inspiring nonetheless. Terrel stared, torn between astonishment and guilt, as the internal trembling began.

Even though he knew it was coming, the sudden wave of destruction still shocked him to the core. One moment the city was intact, the next it was being ripped apart by a convulsive, lurching series of violent tremors, each one more explosive than the last.

Terrel would not have minded any form of justice, however brutal, that turned Talazoria into rubble, but he knew that this was not the end of the devastation. Like ripples spreading out from a pebble thrown into still water, the earthquake tore across the landscape, levelling mountains, uprooting forests, and flinging lakes and rivers into the sky.

Was this happening? he wondered.

Time doesn't mean much in the dream-world.

Would it happen?

And was there anything anyone could do to stop it?

The rock and earth of Macul turned to liquid, flowing like dark water and crushing every living thing in its smothering embrace.

Terrel awoke from the nightmare just as the black mountain had begun to disintegrate, burying Fenduca beneath its suddenly murderous bulk. All around was quiet and still, but the dread did not leave him – and something Alyssa had said a long time ago sounded in his head again as if she were there beside him.

Dreams are sometimes meant to show us things.

CHAPTER TWENTY-FIVE

Dreams are sometimes meant to show us things.
Especially here.

Terrel looked around, not sure whether he was remembering Alyssa's voice or whether she was actually there.

I told you that ages ago.

Alyssa? His hopes were rising, though he still couldn't see her.

Who else are you expecting?

Where are you?

We need to talk, away from prying eyes.

Terrel saw a flash of brilliant colour outside the hut, but it was moving too fast for him to see what it was. Although he didn't understand her comment about prying eyes, he was too pleased to even think of arguing with her.

The old stones? he suggested.

All right.

I'll be there as soon as I can.

*

By the time Terrel reached the glade, Alyssa and the ghosts were already there, apparently deep in conversation. They were so intent on their silent discussion that they weren't aware of his approach until he was almost upon them, and he was able to catch a little of what they were saying.

That would be an incredible coincidence, don't you think? Muzeni said.

Too incredible, Shahan agreed.

Then why did he see it? Alyssa asked.

And even if it is *connected*, Elam added, *what's he supposed to do about it? Terrel can only tell when earthquakes are coming. He can't prevent them.*

You're absolutely sure it began in the city? Muzeni asked.

Alyssa leant forward from her perch, her long bill stabbing towards the ghost in an unmistakable gesture of annoyance. The bird that housed her spirit was the most beautiful Terrel had ever seen, its plumage a mixture of bright blue, yellow and a deep rust red, with black stripes around her neck and across her eyes. He had no idea what it was.

Of course— she began.

It started in Talazoria, Terrel said.

They all turned to look at him, the ghosts' expressions betraying some relief.

What did you do, take the scenic route? Elam asked, grinning. *Or did you stop for breakfast on the way?*

I got here as soon as I could, Terrel replied. *The only thing I stopped to do was get dressed.* He had also glanced in at Ysatel and the still-sleeping Kerin before he left, but he saw no need to mention that.

Thank goodness, Elam commented. *Even as a ghost I'm not sure I could stomach the sight of you naked this early in the morning.*

Alyssa's been telling us about your dream, Shahan said, directing the conversation back to more serious matters. *You say the city is called Talazoria?*

Yes. It's the capital of Macul. Unlike many of Terrel's dreams, the images had stayed clear in his head as the day began.

We've been trying to work out if this is significant, Muzeni said. *If it might be some sort of prophecy.*

Or warning, Shahan added.

Or if it means you ate too much cheese last night, Elam said.

Can't you be serious, just for once? Alyssa chided.

Elam bit back the flippant comment that had evidently sprung to mind, and shrugged instead.

I'm simply trying to keep some sense of proportion, he explained. *We're talking about a* dream *here. It doesn't have to mean anything.*

I don't think I'm a prophet, Terrel said, settling himself on one of the ancient stones. *But the Amber Moon was full last night, and* all *dreams seem to be important here.*

Do you have any idea what prompted this one? Shahan asked.

The rumours, probably.

What rumours?

In the past it had always been the ghosts who passed information on to Terrel but now, for the first time, it was the other way around. As soon as he realized this, Terrel had the feeling that what he was about to tell them would probably affect their interpretation of his vision.

It's being said that Macul's king has captured a monster, he began – and knew instantly that he had their undivided attention. He repeated everything Masiuk had told him, and added some of his own conclusions – all the time watching the calculation on the faces of the two seers.

A second elemental, Shahan said quietly when Terrel had finished.

That would explain a lot, Muzeni muttered.

Do you still think the elemental is the Guardian? Terrel asked.

It's a possibility we can't rule out, Shahan replied.

But that means there's more than one of them too! Alyssa exclaimed.

Did you lot get anything *right when you translated the Code?* Elam enquired.

It would explain all the different landscapes that are mentioned, Shahan said, ignoring Elam's barbed comment.

Do you know when the creature here became active? Muzeni asked. *Could it have been at the last confluence, on the night you were born?*

I don't know, Terrel replied, thinking. *If it was responsible for the black mountain, that might have been around then. But I don't think that would prove when it woke up. The Ancient was in the mines for a long time before anyone noticed it.*

It would be worth investigating, even so, Shahan said.

I'll ask Kerin.

What do you know about Talazoria? Muzeni asked.

Not much. I don't know anyone who's actually been there. Apparently Ekuban, the king, is obsessed with precious stones and metals. Even the buildings are supposed to be decorated with—

The jewelled city! Muzeni and Shahan exclaimed simultaneously.

There was a sinking feeling in the pit of Terrel's stomach.

It's in the Code, isn't it?

Shahan nodded.

We always thought that section was either a poetic reference to Makhaya or just a flight of fancy.

A parable, Muzeni explained pedantically.

What does the Code say about it?

It's another of the places where the Guardian and the Mentor are supposed to join forces.

Nothing about an earthquake?

I don't remember anything specific, Shahan answered, glancing at Muzeni.

There are apocalyptic passages throughout the prophecy, the heretic said vaguely. *I'd have to check . . .*

You still think Terrel's dream was a warning? Elam asked.

Terrel is part of the prophecy, Shahan replied. *It seems reasonable to assume that his experiences may have some bearing on its interpretation.*

All right, Elam said, his voice taking on a practical tone for once. *Assuming this elemental is in Talazoria, and that it is going to start an earthquake, what would prompt it to do something so violent?*

Water, Alyssa stated.

It's surrounded by a moat, Terrel confirmed. *And Ekuban may well be tormenting it without realizing what he's doing. It's possible the elemental will be driven past the point of madness by what's happening to it – and we know just how powerful it could be.*

They were all silent for a while, each contemplating the possible consequences of their discoveries.

Well, Elam said eventually. *There's one way to find out for certain if there really is an elemental there.*

The others looked at him.

One of us, he said, indicating his fellow ghosts, *has to try to go to Talazoria.*

Of course, Muzeni agreed, turning to look at the bird. *Can you help us with that, my dear?*

Why do you need help? Terrel asked. The ghosts had apparently been able to visit various places on Vadanis on their own – apart from Betancuria, of course.

We're linked to this world in various ways, Shahan explained, *to our own former lives, if you like. Outside those realms we require the services of a guide.* He nodded towards Alyssa.

I'll let you look through the windows, she agreed.

Thank you, my dear, Muzeni said, then turned back to Terrel. *However, whatever the outcome of our experiment, it seems certain that you will have to go to Talazoria.*

Terrel had been waiting for this.

Are you sure? You told me yourself that there's probably more than one Mentor, so why does it have to be me? This isn't even my homeland. There could be someone else here already.

Then why did you *have the dream?*

Look, Terrel replied, uncomfortably aware that he was beginning to sound desperate, *I don't know how long it'll take me to get to Talazoria. I probably wouldn't arrive in time, and it's almost certain I wouldn't be able to get back to the coast in time for the return of the islands. I'd be stuck here for another year! This is someone else's problem. The earthquake won't even affect Vadanis.*

The two seers exchanged glances.

I'm not so sure that's true, Shahan stated earnestly. *If the tremor is as severe as Alyssa described, it's not going to stop when it reaches the coast. At the very least, it would create a massive tidal wave.*

And if that happened when the islands were on this side of the ocean, Muzeni added, *the results would be catastrophic. Apart from the damage done by the wave itself, it could knock the empire off course again.*

I'm afraid there's good reason to suspect that any major quake here would be desperately serious, Shahan went on. *Macul is part of a fixed land mass, and that makes it more vulnerable. The islands are fortunate they're able to move as this minimizes the impact of any tremor. In effect, they shift and flex to absorb the blow. That can't happen here, and the forces will build up until something has to give way. When it does, the results will be extremely violent.*

I thought all the destruction, the giant waves and everything else, was supposed to be at the next conjunction, Terrel persisted. *After seventy-five years, or whatever it is now.*

That's what most people thought, Shahan conceded, *but it doesn't mean something can't happen earlier. We've already had to avert one crisis in order to prevent the devastation of the islands. It's possible we may need to do so again.*

And you are *here, Terrel,* Muzeni pointed out. *This might be why.*

Terrel knew by then that this argument was not one he was going to win. Alyssa remained silent, and when he glanced at Elam, his friend could only shrug.

I'm not going until it's certain I have *to,* he said, using up the last vestiges of his defiance.

It will be your decision, Muzeni assured him. *We can only offer advice.*

Terrel looked at the long-dead heretic, suspecting him of dissembling, but the old man seemed genuine enough.

We'll find out what we can, Shahan added.

When . . . when will you . . . Terrel asked hesitantly.

As soon as possible, the seer replied. *But you'd better start making your preparations now. We don't know how much time we've got.*

All right. He felt his shoulders sag in defeat, and was overwhelmed by a sudden wave of homesickness. *What's happening on Vadanis?* he asked quietly. *Is everything all right there?*

All seems well, Shahan replied. *No one's found out why the Dark Moon is behaving the way it is, but the islands are definitely back on course, and they're hardly rotating any more. The consensus is that the lodestone principle is reasserting itself.*

Now that they don't need to do anything, Muzeni added, *most people are content simply to wait. Complacency is rife – even among the seers – now that they think they're safe.*

Of course, Jax is using his new-found status to make life miserable for those around him, the seer put in. *But that was only to be expected.*

He's still invading my dreams, Terrel said.

Really? That shows a tenacity that seems out of character. Was he in the vision of the earthquake?

Yes. He said we were a team.

And are you?

No! Terrel replied without thinking, angry that Muzeni should even ask the question. *I don't know what he was doing, but I wanted no part of it.*

Do you think he might have something to do with the destruction? Shahan asked.

I don't see how.

He's a weather-mage, Alyssa stated.

They all looked at the colourful bird, but she chose not to expand on her remark. Terrel saw again the tornado that had almost killed him and Alyssa at Betancuria. He remembered the clouds of his dreams, the rain below – the magic in the air. Was it possible that Jax was using the weather to torture the elemental? Could he somehow have been involved in the events that had led to the creature's imprisonment? And if so, had he done so as part of a *team*? The idea that he himself might unwittingly have been part of such an undertaking filled Terrel with horror.

The others were silent too, caught up in their own speculations, and it was left to Elam to end their reverie.

I think we should investigate this brother of yours, he decided. *See what he's up to. It's a long time since I visited Makhaya.*

Agreed, Shahan said. *Muzeni and I will return to our study of the Code. You can follow the prince.*

Wait a moment! Don't go yet, Terrel implored them. *Do you remember what we talked about last time? About Ysatel?*

Your sleeper, Elam said, nodding.

Did you find her?

No. But Alyssa did.

I had help, Alyssa said.

I told you the bird-girl has friends in high places, Elam commented.

Will she be able to do what you do? Terrel asked Alyssa.

Not yet. But I may be able to arrange something else.
What?

A tree has as many branches under the ground as it does above.

I'm glad you cleared that up, Elam remarked, laughing, then caught sight of Terrel's puzzled expression. *What? You didn't expect a straight answer, did you?*

Terrel said nothing. He was still trying to decipher Alyssa's cryptic words. As he was thinking, all three ghosts vanished.

Do you have to go too? he asked quickly.

Alyssa did not reply, but the bird remained where it was. A moment later another bird flitted down to join her. It was small and dowdy by comparison, with a mottled brown back and wings, and white breast feathers, but it was eerily beautiful in its own way. It had appeared suddenly, as if it too were a ghost.

Ysatel? Terrel asked hopefully.

There was no response, but even though he could hear nothing, Terrel sensed some sort of communication between the two birds. To his disappointment, the newcomer flew away again after a few moments of this silent conversation.

Who was that?

A treecreeper, Alyssa replied. *They walk differently too.*

And they follow ghosts, Terrel thought, remembering something she had told him during one of her earlier visits.

Can you stay with me for a while? he asked.

I always stay with you, she responded, as if this should have been self-evident.

Terrel was about to contradict her, but thought better

of it. He would just make the best of what time they did have.

If I have to go to Talazoria, you will come with me, won't you?

If you want me to.

Of course I do! We really are *a team.*

There are some dreams I want to see, Alyssa told him, changing the subject abruptly.

Where?

In the village.

Won't they have blown away by now? The day was already over an hour old, and most people would have been awake for at least that long.

Not all of them, she answered. *At least I hope not.*

All right, Terrel said, getting to his feet. *Let's go. Do you want to fly, or ride on my shoulder?*

Does anyone in Fenduca keep hives?

Not that I know of. Why?

Because I'm a bee-eater, she replied. *For some reason, not all bee-keepers take kindly to my presence.*

CHAPTER TWENTY-SIX

'So you're thinking of leaving us?' Cutter asked.

'I don't want to,' Terrel replied, 'but I may have to.'

'I always thought you'd go home eventually. What made you change your mind?'

'A lot of things. Including what happened to Ysatel.'

'You think you'll find someone in Talazoria who can help her?'

'In a manner of speaking, yes. How far is it to the city?'

'Must be three hundred miles at least.'

Although Cutter obviously thought that this was a tremendous distance, Terrel found that he was actually relieved. He had feared it might be far more. He'd travelled much further than that on Vadanis.

'What's the best way to get there?'

'I'd head for Aratuego first,' Cutter advised him, pointing to the northwest. 'Then you might be able to hitch a ride with one of the merchant convoys heading inland. After that I've no idea.'

'How long do you think it'll take?'

The big man shrugged his broad shoulders.

'It depends on how you travel.'

'What's the best I can hope for?'

'I've heard it said that a dispatch rider can make the trip in little over a short month,' Cutter replied. 'But people aren't going to be lining up to offer you a fresh mount at each outpost, are they? You'll be lucky to do it in double that.'

Terrel's previous experience made even this estimate seem wildly optimistic. He'd be travelling in completely unknown territory, with few resources of his own. What was more, he had no idea what he was supposed to do at the end of his journey, nor how long this would take. However, he'd worked out that in order to get to the coast in time to try to return to the islands, the whole trip needed to last no more than seven median months – which didn't seem to be beyond the bounds of possibility. And the sooner he went, the better his chances would be.

Terrel realized, with a sinking heart, that he was already assuming he was going to Talazoria. Everything pointed to that conclusion.

'I'll be sorry to see you go,' Cutter said.

'I'll be sorry too,' Terrel responded, 'but I don't seem to have any choice. At least Talker's back in the village now, so he'll be able to go on with the healing.'

'As long as he can find someone to guide him.'

'I'll see to that before I leave,' Terrel promised. 'Thanks for your help, Cutter.'

'No problem,' his former enemy replied. 'Just do me a favour. Try to get Kerin to change his mind about that fire-opal before you go.' Mitus was smiling as he spoke, and Terrel half grinned in response, knowing such an attempt would be pointless.

As he went on his way, Terrel thought of the encounters that had occurred earlier that day. Obeying Alyssa's request, he had taken her first to Davi's hut. The little boy had just woken up and, after rubbing his eyes in disbelief, he'd been entranced by the colourful bird on Terrel's shoulder. Alyssa had spent the time studying the air above Davi's head, but wouldn't tell Terrel what she'd seen in the child's dreams. Her only comment had been – *He has the moons on his eyes* – and she'd refused to explain what that meant.

Their next port of call, again on Alyssa's instructions, had been the infirmary, where she'd spent a much shorter time examining the remnants of Talker's dreaming. Then, to Terrel's dismay, the bee-eater had taken to the air and flown away. She simply ignored his pleas for her to stay, and – as usual – had left without giving any indication of when she might return.

After that, once he'd recovered his wits and overcome the sadness prompted by her abrupt departure, Terrel had gone to speak to Kerin. He had found the prospector pacing listlessly about the hut, and had asked him about the timing of the emergence of the black mountain. But he'd learnt nothing conclusive. Eventually, Kerin had wandered off to the river – after one more look at Ysatel's unmoving form – and Terrel had gone in search of Cutter.

Now, having done all he could in the way of research, he could only wait, and wonder what the others would come up with.

*

Well, there's definitely an elemental in Talazoria, Elam stated.

Terrel had not had to wait long. The bee-eater and her ghostly retinue had returned the next morning.

It was like Betancuria, Shahan confirmed.

But stronger, Elam added. *We couldn't get within fifty miles of the place.*

So it's more powerful than the other one? Terrel said. It was a frightening thought.

It would seem so, Muzeni muttered.

You don't sound very sure.

It may not be as simple as that, the heretic admitted.

Why? What do you mean?

The two seers glanced at each other, each apparently hoping the other would speak first.

It's difficult to explain, Shahan began.

Quantifying subjective impressions is always tricky from a scientific point of view, Muzeni added. *We . . .*

What they mean is, Elam cut in, *although the effect of the forces on us was the same, it didn't* feel *the same. Some of it felt different, but some of it was identical – as if the two creatures were working together.*

Is that possible?

How are we supposed to know? My guess is there's some sort of link between them.

As if they were twins? Terrel whispered.

You could put it that way, Elam said, understanding his friend's disquiet. *But to me it seemed almost as if they were somehow part of the same being.*

Although Terrel wanted to dismiss this idea out of hand, Muzeni nodded in apparent agreement.

Our young colleague has admirably conveyed the feelings

we all experienced, the heretic said. *There were . . . reson-ances . . . I don't know how to express it more accurately. In some sense, the two entities may be one and the same.*

But they're hundreds of miles apart, Terrel objected.

This is a form of life we have never encountered before, Shahan pointed out. *There's so much about them that is a mystery. However, if our supposition is correct, the conse-quences could be far-reaching. Most obviously, it means that the bargain you made with one you also made with the other.*

Terrel was stunned.

That's ridiculous!

The divisions between individuals simply may not exist for them, Muzeni ventured.

Terrel found himself struggling with the implications of this theory. If it were true, it would mean that his inno-cent offer of friendship was to have repercussions that went far beyond the problem he had been trying to solve on Vadanis. He felt as if he'd been duped.

But that means . . . he began.

It means you have to start all over again, Elam completed for him.

Terrel glanced at his friend.

Why do we get lumbered with all the lousy jobs? he quoted, taking them back to an incident at the haven when they'd been forced clean out the stables. It seemed like another lifetime – another world.

Come on. It's not that bad, Elam said. *At least the elemental doesn't produce any manure.*

Terrel grinned, but then Shahan brought the dis-cussion back to more serious matters.

You may be the only person who can contact the Ancient, the seer explained. *The one here has apparently been killing*

*the prisoners sent into the fortress, just as the miners were
killed in Betancuria. And the creature there chose to befriend
you. So it follows that you may be the only one who can
prevent disaster.*

Your actions saved the islands, Muzeni added. *There's
a chance you might be able to save Macul.*

And you have the amulet.

*I suspect your journey's not over yet, whether you like it
or not.*

Terrel waved the two old men to silence with an impatient gesture, wishing they'd stop trying to persuade
him of his duty, his destiny. He turned to Alyssa, who
hadn't said anything for some time.

Do you sense a connection between the two elementals?

There are no walls in their rooms, she replied.

Do you feel a link to the one here – as a sleeper, I mean?
he asked, hoping that making the question more personal
might prompt a less enigmatic answer.

No. Not yet.

But the sleepers here . . . Ysatel . . . ?

Yes. Their fates depend on the creature in Talazoria.

So you see, Terrel, Muzeni began, *it really is—*

It's all right, he cut in. *I'll go. I don't really have much
choice, do I?*

The ghosts looked relieved.

If I leave soon, Terrel went on, *there's a good chance I
can get to the coast in time. I'm still coming back to you, Alyssa.*

I know, she responded simply.

They looked into each other's eyes for a few heartbeats, the bird's black orbs contrasting with the boy's
crystalline light. His promise was repeated and accepted
again in that look.

Did you find anything more in the Code about the jewelled city? Terrel asked, turning back to the seers.

There was one piece that intrigued us, Shahan said. *The commonly accepted translation is, 'Beware the golden way, the silver steps deceive, Until the royal day, the diamond moons believe.'*

I had no idea you astrologers could be so poetic, Elam commented.

What does it mean? Terrel asked.

It's in the form of an instruction – or a warning – to the Mentor, Shahan told him. *The trouble is, because it's couched in poetic terms, the exact meaning isn't clear.*

And anyway, you think it might not have been translated correctly? Terrel guessed.

Muzeni nodded.

The first couplet is straightforward enough, but the second is open to several interpretations. 'Royal day' could just as easily be rendered as 'important time', and 'diamond moon' might simply be about anything to do with a source of light in the sky.

So how is this supposed to help me?

We don't know, Shahan admitted. *But the reason we think it's relevant is because when the Mentor is mentioned later in the same passage, he's supposed to be accompanied by a flying creature.*

A bird? Terrel asked, glancing at the bee-eater.

So I'd better be careful what shape I choose when we get close, Alyssa remarked calmly.

Just bear the passage in mind, Shahan concluded. *It might make more sense once you get there.*

Is there any reference to an earthquake? Terrel asked.

We couldn't find anything specific, the seer replied, *but we haven't had the opportunity to check all the sources yet.*

*There are several mentions of large waves 'from the west',
though,* Muzeni said. *One passage calls them 'mountains of
water'. But it's hard to tie any of them down to a definite
time.*

A quake here is unlikely to be part of the islands' prophecy,
Shahan explained. *Though the resulting tidal waves* would
be. *I think we have to take your dream warning seriously.*

*But you said the Code contains descriptions of lots of things
that don't exist on Vadanis. So why wouldn't the earthquake
be in there too?* Terrel was confused – but it had occurred
to him that if it wasn't in the prophecy, then it might not
be going to happen. His dream could be wrong.

*We think the places and events that don't seem relevant
to the Empire are related either to the Guardian's exploits or
to the Mentor's observations,* Muzeni explained. *The foreign
aspects of the Code couldn't exist unless he – or they – experience something directly.*

*So if the quake does take place, I won't see it? How could
that happen?* In his dream, the devastation had engulfed
the entire land. It was only after he'd asked the question
that Terrel thought of one possible explanation. He would
see nothing if he was already dead.

We don't know, Shahan admitted. *This is all new to us,
so a lot of it is speculation.*

You're not exactly being very reassuring, you know, Elam
remarked.

I'm sorry, Terrel, Shahan said. *We're doing the best we
can.*

It was the first time either of the spectral seers had even
come close to displaying any degree of humility – and
perversely, this made Terrel feel worse, not better. He

wanted them to be arrogantly certain they were right. That way he could feel confident about taking their advice.

We did find something else that points to your journey, Muzeni said. *It refers to 'a path guided by the dreams of many'.*

The villagers all saw me going inland.

Exactly.

I thought you said that was on a mountaintop? Elam said, looking puzzled.

That's what it appeared to say on first reading, Muzeni conceded dismissively, *but all translations have to allow for some degree of inexactitude. There is a prominent mountain here, after all.* He gestured towards the mass of black rock that towered above them. *Do you have a better explanation?*

I was on top of a mountain myself recently, Elam stated, blithely ignoring the heretic's challenge.

I thought you were going to see what Jax was up to, Terrel said.

That's what I was doing. The prince had gone to Tindaya.

Why? Terrel felt a sense of foreboding at the news. *What was he doing there?*

I've no idea. As far as I could tell, he was just wandering about, looking at the ruins.

An enchanter's whim? Alyssa suggested. *Or a hero's pilgrimage?*

They all looked at her, but she did not expand upon her remark.

I wasn't able to stay long, Elam went on, *so I didn't learn much. I'll do better next time.*

They have to go now, Alyssa said, stabbing her beak towards the ghosts.

Before he vanished, Elam pulled a face and tugged at an imaginary forelock. The seers simply accepted their fate.

I don't want to confuse the issue, Alyssa said.

For once, Terrel was not sorry to see the ghosts disappear. It felt as if the time for talking was over.

Are you going too? he asked.

Not yet, she replied. *There's something else we have to do first.*

CHAPTER TWENTY-SEVEN

'Does this have anything to do with my father?'

'Indirectly, yes.' Terrel was not going to start lying to Olandis now. That would only make things worse. 'But I want you to come for your own sake, not his.'

'Olandis doesn't have to do anything he doesn't want to,' Elyce said belligerently. She had come down to the river bank with Terrel after he'd called at her hut.

'I know that,' Olandis snapped. The girl looked crest-fallen, but although Terrel felt sorry for her, he had more important things on his mind.

'There's someone I want you to meet,' he went on. 'You won't have to say or do anything, just listen. And you can walk away again at any time if you want to.'

Olandis looked at him steadily, but there was uncertainty in his gaze now as well as suspicion. Terrel's evident sincerity was obviously having an effect.

'This is the last thing I'll ever ask of you,' the boy added. 'I'll be leaving Fenduca soon.'

Olandis nodded slightly, his expression grave, as if he had been expecting this.

'You saved my life once,' Terrel reminded him. 'I'm trying to repay part of that debt now. Please come. You'll always regret it if you don't.'

'What could be so important . . .' Olandis began, then shrugged. 'All right. I'll come.'

'I'll come with you,' Elyce said quickly.

'No,' he told her shortly. 'Go home. This isn't for you.'

Terrel was aware of the venomous look the girl flashed at him then, but he could feel nothing but relief. He had done his part. All he could do now was hope that Alyssa was able to live up to hers.

Davi was lying on his stomach, studying an ant trail, when the bird landed in front of him. He knew instantly that it was a treecreeper, but he'd only ever seen them in the woods before – and never as close as this! Although it seemed awkward on the ground, it didn't appear to be injured in any way. They were usually shy and secretive creatures, but this one seemed to be staring straight at him, ignoring the scurrying insects, and when its delicately curved beak opened, the thin call held a note of appeal.

'What do you want?' Davi asked softly, keeping very still in case any sudden movement scared his unexpected visitor away.

The bird repeated its shrill cry – seeee – and shuffled a few paces to one side, its long tail dragging in the dirt. Its jerky movements reminded Davi of those of his mouse. Slowly, he raised himself up onto his knees and then stood up. As he did so the treecreeper rose into the air, fluttering up in a spiral that mimicked the strange way it climbed up and around the tree trunks of its normal habitat. Davi expected it to fly away, but it remained nearby, flitting towards the forest and then returning, calling every so often.

'Do you want me to come with you?' he guessed, taking a few steps after the bird.

Immediately it flew a little further in the same direction, and Davi followed. He looked round once to see if his mother was watching, but she was nowhere to be seen. His parents had become gradually less vigilant as the days had passed. They could hardly keep him a prisoner, and because they both had work to do, they'd contented themselves with making Davi promise not to go to the infirmary or to speak to Talker. They hadn't said anything about not going to the woods.

When they finally arrived at the glade – Davi had guessed their destination some time earlier – he found several people there already. He only had time to notice that there was a bee-eater perched on Terrel's shoulder before the healer spoke.

'Don't be nervous, Davi.'

The small boy looked around, and wondered why he should be nervous. Even the new voice in his head was kind and gentle. He wondered where the treecreeper had gone.

'Tell Kerin and Olandis what you see,' Terrel instructed, pointing towards the centre of the group of ancient stones.

'You mean the lady?'

'There's no lady here,' Kerin stated.

'Yes, there is,' Davi insisted. 'She's come to see you.'

'What's going on?' Kerin demanded, looking at Terrel.

'If this is some sort of joke . . .' Olandis muttered, anger simmering in his dark eyes.

'Davi can see things we can't,' Terrel told them. He knew that the ghost was there, but all he could see was a vague, shimmering outline. 'What's her name, Davi?'

'She didn't say.'

'Then tell us what she looks like.'

'This is ridiculous,' Olandis hissed.

'Just listen,' Terrel said forcefully.

'She looks nice,' Davi said, with a happy smile.

'What colour is her hair?' Terrel prompted.

'Yellow. It's very long. And her eyes are green.'

Terrel saw the ghost's shape flicker, and Davi took a few steps towards her.

'She has a ring,' he said, 'with lots of blue stones, like a star. And there's a brown mark on her arm that's the same shape.'

As the boy spoke, Terrel watched Kerin and his son. They were frozen where they stood, several paces apart. Both faces reflected a mixture of shock and disbelief.

'Will she tell you her name now?' Terrel asked.

'Aryel?' Kerin breathed, answering the question himself.

'It can't be!' Olandis exclaimed, but he sounded uncertain, his anger replaced by fear – and by a little hope.

'She says "Follow your heart. If you do that there can be no regrets",' Davi announced.

Olandis looked stunned, and Terrel knew he was remembering the words from his own childhood.

'And she called you "Thunder",' Davi added.

'No one's called me that since . . . since I was a boy,' Olandis said, his voice no more than a whisper.

A little of the colour that had drained from Kerin's face was seeping back now.

'Is she . . . a ghost?' he asked.

'Yes,' Terrel replied. 'Her spirit is here.'

Kerin nodded, signalling that he no longer needed any convincing of that fact. Davi had not been born until long after Aryel had died, and the accuracy of his description had been very persuasive.

'Can I talk to her?'

'She can hear you,' Davi answered. 'I'll tell you what she says.'

For a few moments this prospect stilled Kerin's nervous tongue. He looked lost and frightened, prey to a dozen different emotions. When he finally spoke, it was to utter the words he'd never had the chance to say, the words that had festered inside his heart for twelve years.

'I'm sorry, Aryel.'

It was no more than an agonized croak, but in the stillness of the haunted glade that was enough.

'She says you don't have to tell her that,' Davi reported. 'She's always known.'

'Can you forgive me?' Kerin whispered.

'There was nothing to forgive. If you'd known what was happening, you'd have come back. I knew that.' Davi was now simply repeating what Aryel told him, word for word.

Kerin's eyes were brimming with tears, and his next words were tentative, as if he was having to force himself to speak.

'You . . . and . . . and . . . the baby?'

'Her spirit was never fully formed in your world. She's moved on. After today, I'll be able to as well. I didn't know it before, but I was waiting for this.'

Kerin seemed to have forgotten that it was Davi's voice he was hearing. He was staring transfixed at the spot where the ghost stood – and Terrel wondered whether he was able to see anything of his first wife's spirit.

'Then . . . you are . . . well?' the prospector stammered.

'We are well.'

Kerin hesitated again.

'There's so much,' he began, 'so much . . .' He glanced round as a racking sob interrupted his halting words. Tears were streaming down Olandis's face.

'It wasn't your fault, Thunder.'

'I know that,' Olandis said, his voice that of a confused child.

'You did all you could. It wasn't your fault,' Davi repeated, his words carrying a mature sincerity that did not belong to a five-year-old.

'It was never your fault,' Kerin said. 'I never blamed you.'

'I blamed myself,' Olandis said, trying to wipe away his tears.

Prompted this time by Alyssa, Terrel intervened again.

'Aryel doesn't have much time. She has something else to tell you.'

'What?' Kerin asked.

'Ysatel.'

'I like her,' Aryel told him.

'You've met her?' Kerin exclaimed with renewed astonishment. 'But—'

'She is wandering. Not in your world or mine. But she *will* return to you, Gate. Your love is worth a little patience, isn't it? She deserves that – and more.'

'You . . . you . . .' Words failed him.

'Be happy, Kerin.'

And then the glade suddenly felt empty.

'She's gone,' Davi said, as he looked round at Terrel.

'Come on,' Terrel said, as he walked forward and took the boy's hand. 'You did very well, but we'd better get you back home now, eh?'

They left Kerin and Olandis clasped in each other's arms, their murmured words mingling with their tears.

From that time on, Terrel knew that he was truly free to leave. The wounds of the past had been healed a little. The scars would always be there, but the pain-filled memories would be allowed to recede now.

A day and a half later, as dusk set in, Terrel knew that this was to be his last night in the village. He would be leaving at first light the next day, and he'd already made his round of farewells. Most of the villagers were sorry to hear of his departure, but when he explained that he was following the path of his dreams, they all understood that he was doing what he had to do. One visit was particularly important. He had been to see Davi's parents, and had persuaded them to let their son resume his partnership with Talker. He had told them nothing of the events in the glade, but had simply praised the boy's remarkable talents. Although they had initially been less than enthusiastic, Terrel's heartfelt pleas had eventually won them over. Davi had been overjoyed, and had dashed off to give Talker the news. Terrel had grinned to see such eagerness, and first Erena and then Frasu had eventually smiled too.

That evening, after sharing a final meal with Kerin and Olandis, Terrel began to feel the familiar mixture of excitement and dread that had accompanied his earlier travels.

'All set, then?' Kerin asked.

Terrel nodded. His few belongings had been placed in the backpack that was a gift from Olandis, and he'd memorized some detailed instructions about the first part of his journey.

'I didn't want to leave you alone,' he said.

'Now you don't have to,' Kerin replied, glancing at his son. Olandis had told Elyce that he was moving back to his own family. He was ashamed of the way he had treated her, and had tried to be as gentle as he could, but he'd been resolute in the face of her tears.

'At least I understand why you have to go,' Kerin added. 'And you know you'll always be welcome back here.'

'I know. And I'm grateful for all you've done for me.'

'Here,' Kerin said, holding out a cupped hand. 'Take this.'

Terrel saw the fire-opal on his palm, and shook his head.

'No. Aylen meant that for you – and for Ysatel.'

'But you'll need money for the journey.'

'I've managed before. I don't want it, Kerin.'

'If you don't take it, he'll just go on and on,' Olandis said. 'You know how stubborn he can be.' Father and son exchanged wry grins.

'No,' Terrel repeated. 'Thank you, but no.'

'He'll probably hide it in your pack if you won't take it,' Olandis added.

'Please, Terrel,' Kerin said. 'If you succeed, and it helps Ysatel, that will be worth more to me than a hundred of these.'

Terrel had told them of some – but not all – of his reasons for going to Talazoria.

'Aylen would say the same if he were here,' Olandis said.

'I'm not going to win this argument, am I?' Terrel said resignedly.

'No,' Kerin agreed, placing the stone in the boy's outstretched hand.

Some time later, as the others were preparing to go to bed, Terrel told them he was going for a walk. The sky was clear, and both the Amber and White Moons were just past full, so there was enough light for him to make his way through the village. Scar's barking turned to nervous whining when he recognized the scent of the visitor trying to rouse his sleeping master, and the dog slunk into a corner when Cutter ushered the boy inside and lit a candle.

The haze of slumber left the trader's eyes instantly as soon as he saw what Terrel had brought him.

'How did you persuade him?' he asked, rolling the fire-opal in his fingers. Even in the gloom the stone smouldered with a cold flame-light.

'I didn't. He gave it to me, for my journey.'

'Really? But you go tomorrow, don't you? I don't have enough—'

'Can you give me an advance?' Terrel cut in. 'Anything

that'll be readily accepted when I'm on the road. I only
want a fraction of its value.'

'I have some coins,' Mitus said doubtfully, 'but no
more than a tenth of its worth.'

'That'll be fine. Give the rest to Kerin when you sell
it.'

'All right. If you're sure that's what you want.'

'I'm sure.'

Cutter fetched the money and handed it over.

'Kerin will receive a fair price, you have my word on
that.'

'Thank you.'

Terrel returned to the Mirana home with heavier
pockets, but with a lighter heart.

It was time for the last of his farewells.

When he got back to the hut, Kerin and Olandis were
asleep, and Terrel went into the side room and sat down
beside Ysatel. He talked to her for more than an hour,
and even though she did not react to his softly spoken
words, he thought that maybe – in some realm – she
might be able to hear him.

He told her about his reasons for leaving; the rumours
of a monster in Talazoria, and the subsequent realization
that there was an elemental there – a creature on which
her own fate, as well as Alyssa's, might well depend; the
enigmatic directions of the Tindaya Code and his
'bargain' with fate; the communal dreams of her fellow
villagers; and Farazin's comment that there might be
something else Terrel must do before he went home. He
told her about Kerin and Olandis's reconciliation, and
reassured her that his own skills were no longer needed

now that Talker and Davi were able to begin healing again – and now that there were wolf-fish in the pool to warn the villagers of earthquakes.

The one thing he did not tell her was his dream about Macul's destruction. If that was real, nothing he could say would help. And if it wasn't, then there was no need to mention it.

'I know you'll come back to Kerin one day,' he concluded, 'just as Alyssa will come back to me. I'm doing all this so it can happen as soon as possible.'

After that, Terrel slept fitfully for a few hours. In his mind he was already on his way, and his body was eager to follow. It was still dark when he rose, collected his pack and crept out into the last of the night.

He felt some guilt about sneaking off before anyone was awake, but found that he couldn't face the idea of more goodbyes. Several of the villagers had said they'd come to see him off, and some had volunteered to go with him the first part of the way – offers he had refused, saying that he'd rather travel alone from the start – and the idea of escaping while everyone was still asleep was appealing.

At the edge of the settlement he paused, looking back for the last time.

'Goodbye,' he said quietly, then turned and took his first steps on the path of his dreams.

When the sun rose, his lopsided gait had already carried him several miles from Fenduca, following the unknown road.

PART TWO

THE UNKNOWN ROAD

CHAPTER TWENTY-EIGHT

Terrel stood at the crest of a high pass. The climb had been long and arduous, and even at this altitude the air was warm, but that was not what had brought him to a standstill. The sight before him had almost literally taken his breath away.

He was looking down on an almost featureless white plain, dazzling in the summer sunlight. It was entirely ringed by mountains, so that its boundaries were sharply defined, and on the far side he could clearly see the V-shaped gap between two jagged peaks which contained the track he'd been advised to head for. The trail could be no more than a handful of miles away, and yet reaching it now seemed both hazardous and daunting. Terrel had been travelling for nearly three median months, and during that time he had seen many incredible sights – but he could never have imagined anything like this.

As he watched, the luminous plain bulged and shifted slowly, as if it were alive, boiling and bubbling like a giant's cauldron. Although Terrel's most recent companions on the road had told him what to expect, he hadn't really believed them – until now. They had tried to persuade him to go a different way – to make the long detour to east or west – but Terrel wanted to get to Talazoria as quickly as possible. He was footsore and weary, and the prospect of a short cut, no matter how perilous, had been too attractive. He had stood by his avowed intentions, going on alone, but now – too late – he began to question the wisdom of his decision. Having come this far he had no choice except to go on, but he would not be crossing this shining landscape; he would be travelling *below* it. The white plain was made of clouds.

It's always like that,' Barker had claimed. 'No matter what the weather's doing above or around the valley, the cloud is always there.'

Terrel had taken this for a storyteller's embellishment, and he'd said as much at the time. However, Barker – the most voluble of his fellow travellers – had been insistent.

'No, it's true. It's like a blanket, and it's always dark under there.'

'And the people who live there are really strange,' someone else had added, provoking general agreement from the group. '*Really* strange.'

Terrel had finally forced them to admit that none of them had actually been down into the valley, and although his scepticism had not altered their conviction that the place was cursed, he'd been able to dismiss much of what he had been told as mere hearsay. The valley's climate, he had concluded, might well be a little odd, but it couldn't be as peculiar or as dangerous as they'd alleged.

Now, gazing across the bright expanse below him, he was not so sure. The impenetrable layer of cloud was incongruous and unnatural. Above the mountains the sky was a uniform shade of blue, and the sun's rays were hot on Terrel's head and shoulders, but a steady breeze blew through the pass, making the day's warmth bearable. All these factors should have meant that any mist would clear, either from being burnt away or dispersed by the wind, and yet it was obvious that this was not going to happen. The surface of the false plain rippled and swirled, but beneath that blinding facade there was a hidden stillness. And beneath that . . .

Terrel pushed the thought aside, refusing to be influenced by Maculian superstition. It was just cloud. And the valley was only a few miles across. He might even reach the other side before sunset.

Having no other option, the boy set his aching legs in motion again. Even then, he hesitated when he reached the edge of the bank of fog. Wisps of moisture seemed to reach out towards him, like transparent grey tendrils. He felt their coolness on his skin, pleasant after the heat of midday, but ominous at the same time.

Taking one last deep breath, as if he was preparing to dive into the waters of an unknown sea, Terrel finally stepped forward. He began his descent into perpetual gloom.

At first, as the white turned to grey about him, he was virtually blind. The mist seemed to cling to him, making every step a tentative voyage into the void. Before long he had lost all sense of direction and half expected to leave the cloud again, having gone round in a circle. Only the fact that the ground beneath his feet still sloped downwards gave him the confidence to continue. The path he was following – if he was indeed still on the path – remained reasonably smooth, and although it was damp, he was in no real danger of losing his footing as long as he was careful.

Eventually, to his great relief, the fog thinned a little – and because his eyes had adjusted to the half-light by then, he was able to look at his surroundings for the first time. He *was* still on a trail, made up of hard-packed earth and stones, in which a few tufts of brown grass were growing. To either side, boulders glistened dully. Beyond that all the boy could see were shadows. He could hear the distant sound of running water, but apart from that the silence was total, as if the cloud muffled sound as well as light.

Tiny droplets of water had formed on his hair and clothes, and his skin felt chilled and damp. Shivering, he stopped to take a jerkin out of his pack and pulled it on before going forward again. Tall shadows loomed out of the mist, and as he drew closer he realized they were trees. Compared to those he'd seen in the forest near Fenduca and elsewhere, they were stunted and sickly-looking. Their trunks and branches were twisted, and seemed very pale in colour, until he saw that they were covered in lichen. The bark beneath was almost black, but the leaves were of such a soft-hued green that they appeared almost silver. Although the trees were virtually still, water dripped from them constantly, creating a soft pattering on the ground below – the only sound to break the silence. No birds sang here; no forest creatures rustled in the sparse undergrowth. The grey wood was one of the most unnerving places Terrel had ever visited, and he hurried on, wanting to leave its shadows behind.

The path was soft now, almost springy, but at least he could see where he was putting his feet, and the way ahead looked clear enough. By the time he'd left the trees behind, the visibility had improved again, but what was now in view was not much more inviting. Even though Terrel knew it could only be an hour or two past noon, it was so dark beneath the lowering roof of cloud that it felt like the hour after sunset, and the landscape revealed by the dim light looked bare and forlorn. There were patches of spiky grass, some bracken and a few straggly bushes, but they all seemed drained of their natural colour, and the earth between them was bare and littered with dark stones. To Terrel it was a wonder that *anything* grew there and, in spite of what he'd been told, he began to wonder if anybody could possibly live in such a bleak and oppressive terrain. Indeed, he could not understand why anyone should *want* to. He had been in the valley for less than two hours, and already he couldn't wait to get out again.

The fact that the path he was on existed at all was proof that someone at least visited the area, but he had seen no sign of habitation. He went on, hoping he was still heading north, straining his eyes to peer through the gloom and listening for any unusual sounds. Instinctively, he moved as quietly as he was able, and when the constant dampness in the air made him cough, the noise seemed frighteningly loud, almost impious.

After a while, the trail veered sharply to the left and plunged into a narrow defile. Until then Terrel had found it easy to navigate the constant slow incline, but now he was forced to scramble, using his good hand to steady himself as he made his way down over slippery, tumbled boulders. Small pools of water, narrow crevices and spongy patches of moss added to the pitfalls, until he began to wonder if he had lost the path altogether. However, his perseverance was rewarded when the ground finally levelled out once more, and he was able to walk normally to the lower end of the ravine. There the terrain opened out again, but he could see no more than a few hundred paces in any direction before the darkness and residual mist made everything a blur. As a result, the dilemma that now confronted him appeared insoluble. The trail split into three – and none of these paths continued in the direction he had been travelling. Terrel rejected the route which turned back and climbed up the hill to one side of the ravine, but there was nothing to choose between the other two, which went off at angles to left and right. Straight ahead there was only an area of marshy scrubland, and beyond that, he thought he could see the dark glint of open water.

He was glancing around, hoping for some clue to help him decide which way to go, when his attention was caught by one of the boulders that flanked the entrance to the ravine. There seemed to be something unnatural about it. He went closer, and saw that one face of the black rock had been artificially shaped, smoothed so that it presented a flat surface that was angled up towards the cloud above. Not only that, but it had been inscribed with a complicated pattern of grooves and holes. Wavy lines crossed from left to right, set at various angles so they intersected each other in places; cup-like circles were surrounded by shallower spirals; and there were also several small x-shaped crosses etched into the stone. Terrel could make no sense of it at all, but the carvings were too precise and elaborate to be anything other than a deliberate design. What was more, there were several patches where the surface of the stone was shiny, as if it had been polished.

'Do you consult the jasper?'

Terrel started so violently at the sound of the voice that he almost lost his balance, and as he stretched out a hand to steady himself, his fingers landed on the carved stone. He glanced round to see who had been able to come so close without him seeing or hearing a thing, and saw that the newcomer was a girl – who was looking at his hand in wide-eyed horror.

'Not there!' she exclaimed. 'Not there!'

Terrel lifted his hand away from the rock, and wondered what he'd done to alarm her so.

'This is a *touchstone*,' she told him, but then her disapproval was replaced by a look of astonishment – and something more.

'You're . . . you're the Messenger,' she stammered. 'I'm so sorry . . . I . . .'

Still bemused by the manner of his reception, Terrel could not think of what to do, and just stared at the girl, astonished by her strange appearance. She was as tall as he was, but so thin that even his twisted frame seemed solid and robust by comparison. She was dressed in a simple tunic of dark woven cloth, her black hair was cut cruelly short, and her eyes seemed too big for the delicate

features of her face – but it was her skin that held his
disbelieving gaze. It was the colour of chalk, paler than
any flesh he had ever seen. Even the dead bodies he'd
pulled from the mud at Fenduca had had more colour.

'I did not know,' she said now, apparently recovering
her composure. 'Forgive my disrespect.' She spoke in the
Maculian language, but her words seemed stilted and
formal. More surprising still, she went down on one knee
after she had spoken, and bowed her head in apparent
deference.

'Please get up,' Terrel said, feeling distinctly uncomfortable. 'You haven't offended me. I was startled by your
approach, that's all.'

The girl looked up, but stayed where she was.

'It is you who should forgive me,' he went on. 'I'm
not familiar with touchstones or your ways.' He was afraid
he had somehow broken some strange taboo.

'That is of no matter. You are the Messenger.'

'I'd prefer it if you called me Terrel. That's my name.'

'Silverlight,' she breathed in delight.

'Is that your name?'

She laughed at that, adding to his confusion.

'No, that's what your name means in the before-
tongue,' she explained. 'My name is Imana.'

'Please get up, Imana,' Terrel repeated, stretching out
his good arm to help her stand up.

To his astonishment, she took his hand in both of hers,
and gently kissed the tattoo, before allowing herself to be
drawn to her feet. She seemed as light as thistledown.

Terrel stared into the girl's huge eyes. Her irises were
of the palest blue, and the pupils within them were vast.
She was gazing back at his own eyes with unabashed

curiosity and wonder. Unlike many of his fellow country-
men on Vadanis, few people in Macul had reacted with
horror to Terrel's crystalline orbs. Most soon seemed to
get over their initial surprise, and regarded them with a
mixture of interest and unease. But no one had reacted
like Imana.

After a few moments, they stepped apart. It was only
then Terrel realized that – through their contact – his
instincts had been able to confirm that she was healthy.
On anyone else, he would have assumed that such a
complexion meant they were seriously ill, but that was
not the case here. She was *meant* to be this pale.

'Why did you call me the Messenger?'

'The jasper tells of your coming,' she replied. 'From
long ago. We all know the signs to look for. I never
thought it would be me.'

'What signs?' he asked, though he thought he already
knew.

'Your eyes, and the rings of life,' she replied, pointing
to the markings on his hand. 'And you come from the
burning lands.'

The fact that he was evidently part of some local legend
– and yet another prophecy! – provoked mixed feelings
in Terrel's heart. It was reassuring in one sense, because
it showed that he was *meant* to be there. On the other
hand, it complicated matters. His journey to Talazoria
had already taken much longer than he would have liked,
and he wanted no more distractions on the way. He had
the uncomfortable feeling that the Messenger was probably supposed to *do* something in the valley.

'Come,' Imana said. 'The elders will want to meet you.'

His suspicions deepening, Terrel prepared to follow

her down the right-hand trail, only to have her halt suddenly.

'What am I thinking?' she exclaimed.

Terrel could see that the girl was both excited and nervous as she returned to the touchstone and lightly pressed the tips of her fingers to each of the shiny places in turn. It was immediately clear what must have produced their polished appearance; this was obviously a ritual that had been repeated many thousands of times.

'Now we can go,' she declared eagerly.

'Should I do the same?' he asked, gesturing at the stone.

'It would honour us,' she replied, her pale face glowing with pleasure.

'Is there an order in which I should touch the points?' He couldn't remember the sequence she had used, and was afraid of making another mistake.

Imana nodded, and stood at his side indicating the moves he should make. Her own small hand was trembling as she did so. Terrel felt nothing unusual in the cool surface of the rock, but a strange feeling of satisfaction swept over him when he'd finished, and he began to wonder if there really was some magic hidden in the patterns of the touchstone.

Then they set off together down the path, and Terrel found, to his surprise, that his legs no longer felt weary. Imana offered to carry his pack, but he refused. It was light enough, but she looked so frail that he didn't want to burden her. As they walked she kept glancing at him, half shy, half fascinated, as if reassuring herself that he was still there.

'Where are we going?'

'To the elders.'

'In your village?' he guessed.

'In *the* village,' she replied. 'Inside the day-stones.'

'Is it far?'

Imana shook her head, but did not elaborate.

Their path curved round so that – as far as Terrel could judge – they were heading roughly northwards again. He could only see a short distance in any direction, but he did make out the still surface of a lake to their left.

'I'm on my way to Talazoria,' he ventured. 'Do you know the way there from here?'

Imana looked confused, and a little frightened, by this idea.

'Is that in the burning lands?' The city's name obviously meant nothing to her.

'It's beyond the clouds, yes,' Terrel replied. 'On the far side of the valley from where I came in.'

'I know nothing of the burning lands,' she said, sounding worried.

'Is something wrong?'

'The jasper . . .' she began, then faltered. 'You must talk to the elders.'

After that she increased her pace and, recognizing her unease, Terrel saved his breath for the task of keeping up with her. The light was growing even dimmer now, and he guessed that – far above – the sun was sinking towards the western mountains. His eyes were adjusting slowly, but the change didn't seem to affect Imana at all. He presumed that having spent her entire life beneath the cloud – incredible though that notion was – her eyes would be enormously sensitive to even the lowest levels of illumination.

After a while, a small flapping shape appeared in the distance ahead of them. It soon resolved itself into the figure of a little boy, running towards them along the path, his footsteps thudding softly in the gathering gloom. When he was close enough to see them clearly he came to a sudden, skidding halt, and stared. His skin was just as pallid as Imana's, and his eyes looked even bigger in his small face. His expression was a mixture of awe and horror.

'Are you burnt?'

Terrel smiled.

'No. I am quite well.'

'This is the Messenger, Brin,' Imana said impatiently. 'What are you doing beyond the day-stones so late?'

'I can run fast,' the boy retorted defiantly.

'Then run back and tell Tavia that we're coming.'

The child hesitated for a moment, apparently considering what to say next, then turned around without a word and ran back the way he had come. Imana sighed.

'My brother is hopeless,' she said apologetically. 'It's because he's the youngest.'

'How many of you are there?'

'Three hundred and seven.'

Terrel laughed.

'I meant how many brothers and sisters do you have?'

'Oh. Just me and Brin.'

Terrel thought about this.

'Did you mean Brin is the youngest of all of you, of everyone in the village?' The boy had looked to be about four years old, and it seemed unlikely that there was nobody younger than that in such a large community.

'That's right,' Imana confirmed. 'All the others . . .

Well, you must know about that.'

Terrel was about to deny any such knowledge when he was distracted by the sight of two large stones, one on either side of the path. Their shape and position gave the impression that it was not a natural formation, and he half expected to see their surfaces carved with more patterns. However, as they passed through the monolithic gateway, he saw that the rocks were unmarked.

'Are these the day-stones?'

'Yes,' Imana told him. 'We're safe from the darkness now.'

Terrel was bursting with unspoken questions, but he didn't want to burden his companion with endless queries, so decided to wait until he met the elders.

After walking for perhaps another half mile, he saw the first signs of the village. From a distance, the single-storey houses were just dark shadows in the mist. No light shone from any lamp or window, and it was so quiet that Terrel wondered if the place was deserted. However, as they drew closer he was able to make out more details, and he eventually realized that groups of people were standing quite still and in perfect silence outside each building. They all watched intently as Imana and Terrel went past, heading towards the centre of the settlement, but no one spoke or waved in greeting. It was one of the oddest, most intimidating experiences of Terrel's life.

Imana led him to a small wood-built hut, which was entered via a porch. The room inside had a door but no windows, and it was so dark that Terrel only saw the single occupant when she moved. The old woman rose stiffly to her feet and looked at the newcomer.

'Tavia-lan,' Imana said in a respectful tone. 'This is Terrel, the Messenger.' The girl had stayed on the porch, and was now hovering in the doorway.

'I am honoured to meet you, Terrel,' Tavia said. 'This will be your home.'

'My home?'

'Where you will sleep,' she explained, 'until the jasper oracles are fulfilled.'

Terrel did not like the sound of that, but he was given no chance to protest.

'You have the healing in you,' Tavia went on. 'I can feel it. But for now we must rest. The darkness is almost upon us. There is food here,' she added, pointing to a half-seen table. 'And your bed is prepared. We will consult you in the morning.'

With that Tavia left him, touching Imana on the forearm as she went out. The girl nodded, but said nothing. Terrel put down his pack and investigated his surroundings. The food turned out to be bowls of various nuts and vegetables, none of which were familiar to him. He ate a little, finding the tastes bland, but did not have much of an appetite. The darkness outside was now almost complete, and it would clearly be absurd to think of trying to continue his journey in such conditions. He thus had little choice but to take up Tavia's offer of a night's rest. Taking out his blanket, he wrapped himself in it as he lay on the pallet, and tried to calm his thoughts enough to go to sleep.

It was only when she moved slightly that he realized that Imana had not left, but was curled up in the doorway like a guard dog.

'Imana?' Terrel called softly.

There was no reply, and he assumed that she was already asleep. As he lay there, lost in speculation, Terrel's apprehension grew. For all his hosts' benevolent and even reverent behaviour towards him, he could not escape the feeling that he was in fact their prisoner.

CHAPTER TWENTY-NINE

Terrel dreamt that he was on an island. It seemed comforting at first, but then he realized that it was a cold place, formed within a circle of giant standing stones and surrounded by a sea of darkness. Then he saw that the darkness itself was an island, encircled by a dazzling white ocean which moved slowly in tides that held no reason.

He awoke shivering, in a darkness so complete that he feared he had gone blind. As his panic subsided, he told himself that the night down here – without moon- or starlight – would be pitch black. He had only to wait for dawn – or what passed for dawn in this valley.

Before he fell asleep again, he reflected that this place was indeed like an island in a way, cut off from the mainland by a sea of cloud.

When Terrel next awoke, a feeble grey light was filtering in through the open doorway. It was barely bright enough for him to see the far side of the room, but outside there was noise and movement. For the people of the village, the day had evidently begun in earnest.

Imana came in, carrying two bowls which she set on the table.

'Good morning, Mess— Terrel,' she said with a shy smile. 'I've brought your breakfast.'

Terrel went to look at the bowls, but could not identify their contents. The food appeared pale and insipid, and his expression must have betrayed his distaste.

'You must eat,' she told him. 'Food is strength.'

'What is it?'

'Tymar paste and nepp roots,' she said proudly. 'The finest.'

Reluctantly, Terrel tried a little of each. The paste was like watery porridge, and the sliced roots were crisp but equally tasteless.

'I like them best together,' she said.

'Sit down and share it with me,' he suggested.

Imana smiled, glanced round to see if anyone was watching, then sat on the stool next to Terrel's. At his urging she took a piece of root and dipped it in the paste before popping it into her mouth and chewing with apparent relish. Terrel followed suit and found that the combination did indeed make it slightly more palatable.

'Does the cloud never lift?' he asked after a while. 'You've never seen the sky? Or the sun?'

'No!' Imana appeared quite horrified by the idea. After a few moments, she asked, 'Have you really looked at the sun?'

'Well, I haven't looked *directly* at it,' he replied. 'That would hurt my eyes. But I've seen it many times.'

'It would kill any of us,' she whispered. 'Burn and kill us without mercy.'

Terrel found that he believed her. The people of the valley had obviously adapted to their home, and in that world of ever-present shadow it was easy to see how the sun might become a terrifying, almost mythical being. Too much exposure to its heat and light were harmful even to those in the upper realms. For the men and women here it might well prove deadly. And yet it was not the absence of the sun that Terrel found most difficult to comprehend. A world where the sky was permanently screened also meant that no one down here had ever seen *the moons*.

The phases of the four moons had influenced almost every aspect of life on the Floating Islands and, until now, the same had been true of everywhere Terrel had visited in Macul. Although their methods of observation, their rituals and laws, varied in their details, the people of Macul also obeyed the dictates of the sky.

Their country was bigger than Terrel could ever have imagined. He had travelled almost the entire length of Vadanis, which was the largest of the islands by far, and yet it could have been lost many times over in any one of Macul's provinces. Cutter's estimate of the distances involved in his proposed journey had been wildly inaccurate, and Terrel had found making his way to Talazoria an extremely difficult task. The only straightforward part had been the very first – the long walk from Fenduca to Aratuego. After that, he had sought and received a good deal of advice along the way – much of it contradictory. At Aratuego he had been told of three main trading routes to the capital city, all of them sounding very complicated, with different people advising him that their choice was clearly the best. Thereafter, each decision he had made only seemed to make his progress even more complex, and he'd begun to despair of ever reaching his elusive goal.

During his travels, Terrel had encountered many wonders: a sacred waterfall where lunar rainbows turned the night into an enchanted realm; an entire mountain which had been carved into a single colossal sculpture by an unknown race who were long gone; a forest so vast and deep it had threatened to swallow him whole, and which had contained the remnants of a lost city, abandoned and overgrown – now only a magnificent relic of a vanished civilization; hot springs surrounded by white stone deposits that looked like frozen waterfalls; a plateau that was criss-crossed with deep fissures, each of which had to be traversed on swaying rope bridges. He had seen pools where gases bubbled up from the rock, fires that burned brighter than anywhere else, and lakes that were studded with stone towers of improbable shapes. He had visited a town that made even Fenduca look solid and prosperous, for the simple reason that each spring the meltwaters from the nearby mountains would rise and the floods would carry the entire settlement away. These same waters brought the chance of wealth, so people returned year after year in spite of the obvious perils. 'Some always stay too long,' one prospector had told Terrel with a shrug.

All these things and more had amazed and fascinated him, but he'd never lost sight of his original intent, always moving on, drawing slowly closer to the jewelled city.

Somewhere along the road – he had no idea where – he had spent his fifteenth birthday. It had passed unnoticed and uncelebrated, and he'd only realized that he was a year older when midsummer's day had come and he had still not reached Talazoria.

In all that time, he had not seen Alyssa and the ghosts once. During his more optimistic moods, he took this to mean that his progress along the unknown road was satisfactory, and that he therefore had no need of their guidance. At other times their absence depressed him, and made him wonder if they had abandoned him – or if they were simply unable to find him. Neither possibility was comforting.

At least what he had to do was clear in his mind, and he was able to concentrate all his efforts on getting to Talazoria. What would happen when he eventually succeeded was a different matter, and one he didn't want to consider until the time came. However, as his journey dragged on, he began to long for his friends, for some companionship.

By the time Terrel reached the valley, he knew that if there were to be any more delays, he would have little or no chance of returning to the coast within the allotted time span. If that happened, his return home would have to wait another year, and this was something he could hardly bring himself to contemplate.

Terrel's promised meeting with the elders took place almost as soon as he'd finished eating. There were eight of them and, to his surprise, they were all women – and at least two of them did not look very old. It was another sign of how this place was set apart from the rest of Macul.

The gathering took place in the open air. After Tavia had completed the introductions, they all sat on benches round a circular table, in what Terrel assumed was the central square of the village. No one interrupted their discussion, but many people – men, women and children – watched from a distance even as they went about their normal business. Terrel noticed that some people looked horrified – presumably by the sight of his dark skin – but he had little attention to spare for the onlookers. He was anxious to learn what the elders expected of him – and to determine when he'd be allowed to go on his way. With the coming of the muted daylight, he had considered simply walking out, heading in the direction he hoped would lead him to the northern pass. His best guess was that the village was more or less at the centre of the oval-shaped valley and, if he was lucky, he might have emerged into the sunlight in an hour or two. But he had rejected this idea. It would have seemed ill-mannered, and he was still hoping that his hosts would help him to find the correct route. In any case, he had not yet heard what they had to say – and he wasn't even sure that they would have *allowed* him to leave.

'This is a joyous day,' Tavia began. 'One we have been awaiting for many years. The Messenger has come, and the oracles will be fulfilled at last.'

'Are we to accept him as our leader without even testing him?' one of the younger women asked. Terrel recalled that her name was Amie, and that she hadn't smiled when they were introduced, but had simply nodded her head in greeting.

'Do you doubt his identity?' Tavia asked, looking surprised.

'No. He is the Messenger.'

'Then—'

'How can any man, especially one so young, under-stand our problem?' Amie cut in. 'Let alone solve it?'

'It is my belief that Terrel is a healer,' Tavia said. 'The rest does not matter.'

'*Are* you a healer?' a grey-haired elder called Zelgren asked, looking at the boy.

'Yes.' Terrel had been following the exchange intently, bewildered yet again by the reference to himself as their putative 'leader'. He had been waiting for a chance to speak, and took the opportunity they'd offered him. 'But many illnesses are beyond my powers. I don't know whether I'm the Messenger or not, but I have to tell you that I cannot stay here long. I have sworn to travel to Talazoria as soon as I can. If I fail in that, the conse-quences for all of Macul will be disastrous.' He glanced around at the faces ranged about the table, and saw both shock and uncertainty in their expressions.

'Is this the voice of the oracle?' Amie asked sharply.

'The jasper cannot lie!' someone else retorted.

'It was not meant to be this way,' Tavia commented, in a tone that betrayed her disappointment.

Terrel was not yet sure which way he wanted this de-bate about his identity to go, but having made his position clear, he felt he ought to offer some sign of cooperation. It was possible that he might be able to do what they wanted and still meet the extended terms of his bargain with the elemental.

'I will help you all I can,' he said. 'But, as I told you, my time is limited – and I can't understand your problem unless you tell me what it is.'

Tavia looked around at her companions and received nods of agreement from all except Amie, who merely shrugged, her white face impassive.

'For the last four long cycles, our women have been afflicted by a mysterious illness,' Tavia began. 'During that time, all the children born here have either been dead at birth, or have been so sickly that they died in infancy.'

Terrel's heart sank. Such a terrible disease would surely be beyond his skill.

'So Brin really is the youngest here,' he said quietly.

'He's the last one to survive,' Tavia confirmed. 'None of our efforts to counteract this plague – or even to discover its cause – have met with any success. And now it seems that some women of childbearing years have become barren. If things go on like this, our community will simply grow old and die.'

For a few moments Terrel was too horrified to speak, but he knew they were expecting him to say something.

'Are any women still becoming pregnant?' he asked eventually, desperately trying to hide the embarrassment he felt at having to ask such a question.

'There are only six at present,' Tavia replied. 'Most of them in the later stages. We'll take you to see them when you're ready.'

'Do they seem well?'

'Outwardly, yes. That's the most mystifying aspect of this epidemic. The mothers have all seemed to come to term in perfect health, and yet their babies have still been afflicted. If there was any *obvious* problem, we might have been able to treat it. There are those among us who are skilled with herbs and essences, but the women show no sign of needing such treatment, and we have been able to do nothing for the children once they are born.'

The more he heard, the more Terrel became convinced that it would take something greater than his nascent talents to overcome this disease.

'I watched my first-born fade away before my eyes,' the youngest of the group said quietly. 'And I could do nothing to help her. Now I don't know if I'll ever get the chance to try again.'

'You will, Liana,' Tavia told her gently. 'That's why the Messenger has come to us.'

Terrel had been deeply affected by the wrenching sadness in the young woman's voice, but the sympathy he felt had to be weighed against logic. It was possible that the price of averting an even greater tragedy would be to leave this one unsolved. He couldn't afford to stay more than a few days at most – even that was longer than he'd originally intended – but he could at least put what time he did have to good use.

'Did anything happen here four years ago?' he asked. 'Did any strangers visit you who might have been carrying the infection? Or did you change the way you grow your food?'

'No, nothing like that.' Tavia hesitated. 'But . . .'

'But what?'

'The ground shook,' Liana said.

'An earthquake?'

'Yes,' Amie confirmed. 'It was a bad one, but we can't see how that would have had such an effect on our health. There were a few injuries, but they soon healed.'

'But this was the only unusual occurrence at that time?'

'Yes,' Amie admitted. 'The tremor was unexpected.'

'So you usually know when to expect them?' Terrel asked, wondering how they were able to achieve this when they had never seen the moons.

'It is all part of the jasper,' Tavia answered. 'Such things were laid down long ago. The patterns of the oracles are constant in this.'

'Unless we are upon the time of change,' Zelgren commented. 'That too was prophesied.'

Terrel almost told them about the Dark Moon then, but realized it would mean nothing to them. He could not help wondering whether the elemental's influence might have had something to do with the seemingly fateful earthquake. If that were the case, could it even be in some way responsible for the women's illness? Although the idea seemed far-fetched, the notion that the elemental had created the sleepers had also seemed absurd at first.

'Tell me more about the jasper,' he said.

'We'll do better than that,' Tavia said. 'We'll show you. Come.' She stood up, and everyone else followed her example. She led them all to the outskirts of the village, to where a large black boulder lay. As Terrel expected, one part of it had been sliced away to leave a flat plane, which was inscribed with more of the marks he had seen the day before. This one also had a section of hieroglyphs above the other signs, and he saw a familiar symbol in their midst.

'The rings of life,' Tavia said, noting the direction of his gaze. 'Just like those marked on your hand.'

'And the inscriptions around it are in the before-tongue?' Terrel guessed.

'They are. It is here that your arrival was prophesied,

many generations ago. Now that you have come to us, you will be our leader. We will do whatever you say.'

Terrel wondered what their response would be if he simply said 'Let me go', but he kept the thought to himself.

'Our future is in your hands,' Tavia told him solemnly. 'I hope you are ready to accept the responsibilities of destiny.'

CHAPTER THIRTY

As Terrel entered the room where the six pregnant women were waiting for him, his first impression was not of ill health but of fear – and he thought initially that he might be the cause. The women all looked surprised and anxious as they stared at him, and he realized that although they might have seen him before – either the previous evening or during the elders' meeting – this was certainly the first time they'd seen him close to. Apart from his 'burnt' skin, the fact that he was both male and young, and that his limbs were obviously deformed, probably did nothing to inspire confidence in his abilities. He suspected that this was not how they had pictured the Messenger. However, he soon realized that although they were apprehensive about his presence, the real source of their fear came from within.

Knowing that every baby born during the last four year had died was bound to terrify them – and the knowledge that they carried inside them not only their own hopes but those of an entire community could not have made their situation any easier. Terrel remembered Babak telling him that the human mind was a wonderful physician and, by the same token, it seemed logical that it could also be the reverse. If these women believed that their babies would be ill – and they had plenty of reason to believe just that – then it might well become a self-fulfilling prophecy. Conversely, if they could be given sufficient faith in him, it was possible that he might be able to allay their fears and thus change their fates. A curse only worked if its victims believed that it would. This had been another of the pedlar's maxims – but Terrel could hardly tell the women that. It would be tantamount to claiming that all those who had lost their children had done so deliberately. Their circumstances made this group of women particularly vulnerable, and he knew he would have to be very careful in what he said.

'This is the Messenger,' Tavia announced. 'His name is Terrel, and he is a healer.'

None of the women said anything, but Terrel saw a little flicker of hope in their eyes. He began to feel uncomfortable under their combined scrutiny. At fifteen years of age, the last thing he wanted was to be surrounded by a lot of obviously pregnant women. It had been different with Ysatel, because he had come to know – and love – her, but the boy found these bloated strangers vaguely repulsive. He was not entirely ignorant about sex – at least in theory – but its subtleties were still a mystery to him, the subject of unfulfilled longings. Being presented with such plentiful evidence of others' amatory exploits both embarrassed and unnerved him. Something of this must have shown on his face, because the youngest of the group – a girl who could not have been much older than Terrel himself, and who stood slightly apart from the other five – grinned suddenly.

'*This* is the Messenger?' she queried. 'I'll bet you haven't even been with a girl, have you?'

Terrel blushed as she smiled knowingly.

'That is entirely irrelevant,' Tavia snapped. The girl's lack of reverence had clearly annoyed the elder, but the other women were trying to hide their smiles.

'Not everyone's such a quick learner as you, Esera,' one of the expectant mothers remarked pointedly.

'No,' the girl agreed. 'They're not clever enough.'

'Getting yourself pregnant wasn't exactly clever, was it?'

'Quite right. I am to be pitied,' Esera responded sarcastically. 'Especially as I haven't been able to get my man to marry me.'

'She won't even tell us who the father is.'

'She probably doesn't know,' another woman suggested, provoking laughter among her companions.

'Oh, I know,' Esera said, apparently quite unperturbed by their taunts. 'Worthless toerag. I wouldn't marry him even if he *did* ask me,' she added, staring defiantly at Terrel.

'Enough!' Tavia exclaimed. 'This is a serious occasion.'

Terrel had the feeling that the women were just trying to mask their own nervousness, and he was about to say something to that effect when Tavia turned back to him.

'What happens next, Terrel?' she asked, in a businesslike manner. 'Will you examine them?'

The older women looked slightly alarmed at this, but Esera just gave him a measuring glance, her eyebrows raised.

'I'll only need to hold your hands,' he blurted out, blushing furiously again.

'That's what they all say,' Esera replied, and a couple of the others giggled.

'Young lady,' Tavia began, rounding on the girl. 'If you can't—'

'It's all right,' Terrel cut in, utterly humiliated but knowing that he must try to take charge of the situation. 'I know I'm not what you imagined when you thought of the Messenger, but I *am* a healer, and I'll do everything I can to help you. I'd like to get to know you all better, but I don't have much time, so I'll just do the best I can. Will you help me?' He had been looking from face to face as he spoke, but as he finished his gaze came to rest on Esera, and stayed there.

She looked uncertain for a moment, but then smiled and nodded.

'How could we refuse such a generous offer?' she said, and despite all that had gone before, Terrel felt a sudden conviction that under different circumstances the two of them could have been friends.

'Very well, then,' Tavia said, sounding relieved. 'Who wants to go first?'

After only a slight hesitation, it was Esera who volunteered.

'It might as well be me. I'm already beyond the daystone ring, after all.'

'What does that mean?' Terrel asked.

'It means I'm not entirely respectable,' she told him. 'Being *examined* by a strange man can't do my reputation any harm.'

Tavia frowned disapprovingly, but Terrel was grateful to the girl for trying to lighten the mood. He moved forward until he was standing in front of her, but made no attempt to touch her.

'How long have you been pregnant?'

'Three cycles. I'm the latest recruit to this band of swollen bladders.'

'And you don't feel unwell?'

'I feel fine. We all do.' She was serious now. 'That's what makes this so strange. I mean, we all get emotional sometimes – angry or sad for no reason – and until recently I felt sick every morning, but that's normal, isn't it?'

Terrel nodded, trying to think of something else he could ask in order to delay the fateful moment, but he'd run out of ideas.

'All right,' he said. 'Are you ready?'

Esera nodded and, for the first time, she looked very young and rather frightened.

'There's nothing to be afraid of,' he reassured her. 'I won't hurt you. Take my hand.'

As his dark fingers closed over her pale ones, Terrel fell, unresisting, into the waking dream. It had become such an easy, natural process that he closed his eyes and smiled, recalling a similar welcoming sensation of warmth and peace when he'd checked on the progress of Ysatel and her baby. That had been a draining but rewarding experience and, feeling more confident now,

Terrel began to look for the small dream within another, the echoes of a new life.

It took him longer than expected, and when he finally succeeded, the shock of contact almost made him cry out. Far from being serene and comfortable, the unborn child's dreaming was chaotic – full of pain and a kind of morbid exhaustion, as if it were already being asked to fight a battle that was beyond its strength. When Terrel instinctively tried to lessen the hurt, the dream fragmented, becoming even more difficult to pin down. Shafts of agony, like bolts of fire, sliced through the dream-space; pools of sucking darkness swirled and eddied; and, far away, someone screamed. Everything Terrel did only seemed to make matters worse and he withdrew, defeated, knowing that he had been right. The illness that was tormenting the unborn babies was beyond his healing – beyond even his understanding.

As his fingers uncurled to release Esera's hand, he felt numb as well as bewildered. He found that he couldn't even find the strength to open his eyes, and knew he was about to collapse. He did not feel himself falling, but a moment later knew that he was on the floor. The last thing he heard before he became entirely oblivious of the outside world was Esera's voice.

'Well,' she said. 'I've never had *that* effect on a man before.'

When Terrel regained consciousness, he found that he was lying on the bed he'd slept in the night before. He had no idea how much time had passed. It was quite dark outside – but that meant little here. He groaned as he remembered the dream within a dream, and as he did so, movement near the door told him that he was not alone.

'Are you all right?' Imana's pale face appeared out of the gloom like a small ghost. 'Is there anything you want?'

'No. I'm just tired.'

'The elders will want to speak to you,' she said anxiously. 'Shall I fetch them?'

'Not yet. Why are you looking after me?'

'I've been assigned to tend to you.' She sounded half timid, half proud. 'To assist you in any way I can.'

And to be my watchdog? Terrel wondered.

'It's because I was the one who found you,' she added by way of explanation.

'Will you sleep here again tonight?' he asked.

'Yes. On the porch.'

'Then you must arrange for a proper bed. You can't sleep on the floor like that.'

'I'm used to it.'

'Either you arrange it, or you'll sleep on my bed and *I'll* sleep on the floor,' he insisted. His own pallet was hardly a luxurious resting place, but it was better than bare boards.

'All right.' Her solemn expression gave way to a brief, shy smile.

'Can I ask you a question, Imana?'

'Of course.'

'What exactly is the darkness you talked about, the one outside the day-stones?'

The girl looked taken aback, but she recovered quickly.

'It's forbidden.'

'I know that. But why?'

'Evil spirits walk in the darkness.'

'Ghosts?'

'No. They are not human. Anyone who meets them is either killed or driven mad.' Her voice was trembling now, and Terrel decided not to press her further. He stored the information away, looking ahead to the time when he would leave the valley – whether his hosts liked it or not.

'Shall I bring the elders now?' she asked earnestly. 'They wanted—'

'Tell them I can't see them all,' he said quickly. He couldn't face the prospect of being interrogated by the entire group. 'I'd much rather just talk to one person.'

'I'll tell them,' Imana said, and practically ran from the room.

'That doesn't sound too good,' Amie said.

Terrel had just finished telling her all he could remember of his encounter with Esera. He had been surprised that it had been Amie and not Tavia who had come in response to his message, but as they talked he began to appreciate the younger woman's keen intelligence and practical mind. She seemed to have set aside her earlier scepticism about his healing abilities, and was listening attentively to everything he had to say.

'It's not,' Terrel agreed. 'I've no idea what we're dealing with here, and I'm almost certain I won't be able to help.'

Amie looked grave, but said nothing.

'I can stay two more days at the most,' Terrel went on. 'I'll do everything I can during that time, including examining the rest of the women, but I can't promise anything more. And after that I *will* have to leave.' The time he was wasting was already weighing on his mind, and giving himself a deadline made it easier to plan his actions – and he wanted to be as open and as honest as he could. 'Will the elders agree to let me go then?'

'We may be powerless in this,' Amie replied. 'Such matters are the province of the jasper.'

'Yes, but surely it's you who interpret the oracles? By itself the jasper is meaningless.'

'No. Many things are fixed, so that no interpretation is necessary – or possible. There are many cycles within the jasper. The alternation of light and dark, the long cycle that is called a year in the burning lands, and many more. It is from these that our lives are regulated, and our fates foretold.'

In spite of the fact that he was still anxious to discuss his departure, Terrel was intrigued.

'Does the jasper include the cycle of the moons?'

'It would seem so,' Amie replied, 'although no one knows now how this comes about. We've been asked this question before by outsiders. They find it strange that we could respond to something we cannot see.'

'So do I,' Terrel admitted.

'Isn't it possible that the world contains means of communication other than light?'

'Of course. There's sound, for a start.'

'And what about things beyond our so-called normal senses?' she went on. 'Perhaps we respond to such powers. Your moons may talk to us in ways we don't understand – perhaps in a manner to which we are uniquely sensitive.'

Terrel considered this for a few moments before he spoke again.

'One of the moons has changed its nature recently.'

'I thought as much,' Amie said. 'I believe this is why you are here, Terrel. To help us understand this time of change. And to survive it.'

CHAPTER THIRTY-ONE

True to his word, Terrel did everything he could over the next two days to try to heal the babies' mysterious ailment. To save him time and effort, the women came to see him in the guest hut one by one. On each occasion, he encountered a similar pattern to his experience with Esera. The women themselves seemed perfectly well, but the embryonic children inside them were in torment. Terrel approached their dream-space with more caution than he had done earlier, finding ways of protecting himself from the worst effects of the onslaught of bewildering and sometimes terrifying images that bombarded his questing mind. Even so, it was still a gruelling task and, although he did not collapse again, he was forced to rest between sessions to try to recover his strength.

Through it all, he learnt little that he had not already gleaned from his contact with Esera. One thing that did become clear was that the further into the pregnancy the woman was, the more bizarre and alarming was the baby's dream-world. But that in itself did not help Terrel come any closer to a possible cure. Overall, he became more and more convinced that his efforts were doomed to failure – and that impression was confirmed in dramatic fashion when he saw Parina, the woman whose pregnancy was nearest to completion. By enlisting Amie's help, and by comparing their respective methods of measuring time, Terrel knew that Parina's baby was due in approximately one median month. When he entered that dream-space, he was almost overwhelmed. It was not the rush of pain or the inexplicable sights and sounds that defeated him; it was the huge, suffocating weight of fear that consumed the emerging mind of the child. It was as though the baby knew it had been condemned to die, and was awaiting its birth as if it were its own execution. Terrel had no anti-dote for such unreasoning terror, and he was forced to withdraw before he too was dragged down into that fatal whirlpool of despair. He was left gasping for breath, his face sheened with sweat – which did nothing to soothe Parina's already frayed nerves. He glossed over what he had seen, wanting to spare her the details, but she knew that something was very wrong. In a sense, the most remarkable thing of all was that Parina – and the other women – seemed quite unaware of what was going on inside their own bodies.

In between the examinations, Terrel rested, sleeping when he could. He ate the food Imana brought him in mechanical fashion, without really tasting anything. He spent the rest of his time brooding, hoping for – but not expecting – a solution, and wondering about his own appointment with destiny. Each evening Amie came to speak with him, first to discuss the day's findings, and then to talk about anything else that seemed appropriate. She had told him that there were six touchstones in the valley, and that they were all consulted – about everyday matters – on a regular basis. It reminded Terrel of the way the farmers on Vadanis had consulted their almanacs. She had also told him a little of the valley's history, its sporadic contacts with the outside world, and its inhabitants' way of life. In return he told her about his healing – even demonstrating it on one occasion by relieving her headache – about his journeying, though not the specific reason for it, and about his time in Fenduca. The one topic they avoided was that of Terrel's impending departure.

As dusk approached on his third day in the valley, Terrel was sitting at his table, eating something that Imana had informed him was fish from their lake. He would not have recognized it as such from the strange taste, but it made a welcome change from the bland, vegetarian diet of his previous meals.

To one side of the table was set a dish of oil in which a floating wick burned, spluttering and wavering as it gave off a pungent smell and what was – to Terrel – a feeble light. He had asked if he might have a lamp, but the villagers had never heard of such a thing, and Imana had explained that although their communal fires were used for cooking and the provision of warmth in the winter, they were kept banked and carefully controlled. Torches were used only in exceptional circumstances, because the light from open flames hurt their eyes. Terrel had countered by saying that he wasn't used to such constant gloom – even at the height of the day – and that he was unnerved by the total darkness of the night. The oil-dish candle had been a compromise, but even then the women who came to the hut were careful not to look directly at the flame, often shading their eyes with a hand.

Imana appeared as soon as Terrel had finished his meal – she always seemed to be there the instant anything needed to be done – and took the plates away. As the girl left, Amie came in, and went to sit as far from the candle as possible.

'How are you feeling?'

'Weary,' Terrel replied. He'd had a second session with Esera that afternoon, just to see whether anything had changed since the first time. It hadn't, and although he hadn't fainted – Esera had congratulated him on that – his efforts had left him drained.

'Did you learn anything new?'

'No.'

'So you still think you can't help us?'

'I wish it were otherwise, but this is quite beyond my scope. No ordinary illness could possibly affect the babies in this way and yet leave the mothers unscathed.'

'So what is it?'

'I've no idea.'

'You must have *some* theory.'

'I have two,' he conceded, 'but they're both going to sound very far-fetched.'

'I would think it would need something far-fetched to explain our problem,' Amie said. 'Tell me.'

'The first concerns the earthquake four years ago. It's possible it was caused by a very unusual force,' Terrel said, picking his words carefully, 'and that the aftereffects are lingering on even now.'

'What kind of force is this?'

'No one really understands it,' he replied truthfully, 'but it's been responsible for other tremors, and it may well be again.'

Amie gave him a measuring look.

'And the other idea?' she asked.

'The Dark Moon. We know that the moons affect a great deal of what goes on on Nydus, and that's still true here, even though you can't see them. Maybe it's responsible for the time of change, and some previously unknown malign influence is creating this illness.'

'You're right. They are far-fetched.'

'And there's nothing my healing can do about either.'

'So what can we do now?'

'I don't think I can be the Messenger you've all been waiting for,' Terrel said, 'but I have an idea where he might come from.'

Amie looked sceptical.

'Where?'

'Have you heard of the sharaken?'

To his surprise, Amie began to laugh.

'What's so funny?'

'We *have* heard of the sharaken,' she told him, 'but they don't come here. Some would say they cannot.'

'Why not?'

'One of our legends tells us that long ago the sharaken created the darkness that surrounds our land, and set the cloud above us to hide their creation from the world. Ever since then, this has been a forbidden place for their kind.'

'So they've never been to the valley?' Terrel queried, trying to work out the implications of what he was hearing.

Amie nodded.

'But you're not the first to suggest we should try to contact them.'

'Really?'

'This is another part of the jasper oracles. At each turning of the dark in the long cycle – you would call it mid-winter – we elect an "advocate". In the past, this was a purely ceremonial title, given to a man who made a symbolic journey to the edge of the cloud. However, over the past three years it's carried a more onerous burden. The chosen man has to leave the valley in reality, and try to summon the sharaken to help us. They leave in winter, when the dangers of the sky's burning are minimized, and their protective clothing is the best we can devise, but the hazards are still great. To be chosen is an honour, but it's the honour of sacrifice. None of the three has ever returned. We no longer expect them to.'

The cold-blooded manner in which Amie spoke chilled Terrel to the bone.

'You do all this because of a myth?' he said incredulously.

'We do none of it lightly,' she replied. 'Our situation is desperate. Too many children have died.'

Terrel had been appalled by what he'd heard, but it occurred to him now that this new knowledge had presented him with an opportunity, a possible way out.

'I could go!' he said eagerly. 'I could be your advocate. I'd have a much better chance of succeeding than one of your own men, and you wouldn't have to wait until winter. I have to leave tomorrow anyway.'

Amie looked surprised, then concerned, then she shook her head.

'That won't be possible.'

'Why not?'

'You have to stay here,' she stated simply.

'Even if it's against my will?' he demanded, getting angry now. 'Are you threatening me?'

'No.' She sounded weary and resigned, but infuriatingly calm. 'This is also part of the jasper.'

'Now you're just hiding behind words!' He had thought there had been the beginnings of respect and even friendship between the two of them, but now Amie's apparent intransigence had thrown all that aside. 'How are you going to stop me leaving? By force?'

'We won't have to,' she replied sadly, steadfastly meeting his gaze. 'You *are* the Messenger, whether you believe it or not. And the valley won't let you leave until the oracles are satisfied.'

Terrel pulled the straps of his pack over his shoulders and picked up the still-burning candle, listening for any sound from the porch. Outside the night was jet black, and all was silent. He moved slowly towards the doorway, praying that the floorboards would not creak and that he would not stumble. As he passed Imana, she sighed and fidgeted in her sleep and he froze, but then she grew quiet again, her eyes still closed.

Using his clawed right hand to protect the candle flame as best he could, Terrel made his way to where the rushlights were stored, took two, then crept towards the edge of the slumbering village. He hadn't had the chance to explore since he'd arrived, but he'd noted as much as he could. He had decided to head first for the touchstone the elders had taken him to see, and then continue on in the same direction in the hope of finding a trail going north.

Once he was clear of the houses, and no one had raised the alarm, he paused to light the first of the torches. When it was burning steadily, he extinguished the candle and left it on the ground before going on, moving faster now that he had a little more light and didn't need to be so quiet – though he was aware that the torch made it more likely that he would be seen if anyone did happen to wake up. The light from the flames seemed very bright, but it still didn't help him to see very far. Shadows jumped and flickered around him in alarming fashion.

As he passed the touchstone, Terrel thought he heard a noise behind him, but he couldn't see anything, and decided that it had just been his imagination. He had learnt that the day-stone 'gate' by which he had entered the villagers' domain was part of a complete ring around the settlement, and he knew that once he was past that he'd be safe from any pursuit. The villagers' own superstitions would keep any would-be search party inside the circle until daybreak, whereas he was willing to risk the darkness beyond – inhuman spirits and all. It might well be his only chance of escaping. In spite of what Amie had told him, Terrel believed that the people of the valley would become his gaolers if they thought this was the only way to meet the demands of the jasper.

His hopes rose when he saw another pair of huge monoliths ahead of him. This was surely another gate, and the chances were there'd be another trail on the far side. He was only a few paces short of the stones when he was startled by another sound behind him. He turned round slowly.

'Terrel?'

Imana emerged from the night, shielding her face with her hand. It occurred to Terrel that the rushlight might not only help him to see where he was going; given the sensitivity of the villagers' eyes, it could also be used as a weapon against them. But he immediately felt ashamed of the thought, and knew he could not use the light in such a way.

'What are you doing?' Imana asked plaintively. When he did not answer, she added, 'Don't go.'

'I have to.'

'But the darkness—'

'I can't help here. I'm not the Messenger, and I've promised—'

'You'll die. And I'll get into trouble.' Her voice wavered. She was obviously distraught, and close to tears.

'I'm not going to die,' he told her. 'And no one will blame you.'

'Yes, they will,' she sobbed. 'I was supposed . . . to . . .'

'I'm sorry, Imana. I have to go.'

'No, *please*.' It was no more than an anguished whisper.

Feeling appalled by his own callousness, Terrel turned away from her and strode through the gate, his heart pounding.

The damp breeze came first, then the fog closed in so thickly that – even with the light of the torch – Terrel could barely see his own feet. The trail had initially led him over level ground, then had begun to climb gently – which he'd taken for a good sign – but then he'd found himself among ghostly trees, and it had no longer been clear whether he was on the path or not. He'd gone on, hopeful still, until the mist enveloped him.

He paused, considering his options. He could continue blindly, feeling his way ahead, reasoning that as long as he was still going uphill he would be making progress. Although the first torch was burning low now, he still had the second, and that ought to give him time to go a considerable distance. Alternatively, he could stay where he was and hope that the fog would clear. He could even wait for daylight. He ought to have enough of a head start on the villagers to make good his escape from the valley before they caught up with him.

His clothes were damp now, and he shivered. The decision to go on was influenced as much by his need to keep warm as by anything else.

Some time later, Terrel began to wonder if he was being foolish. He'd been forced to light the second torch, but because the fog was still dense, it hadn't really helped his progress. The trail was just a distant memory now, and at one point he found himself with no choice but to go downhill again, even though he was as certain as he could be that he was still heading in the right direction. It was only when he saw the standing stones looming up out of the mist ahead of him that he knew it had all gone horribly wrong.

He couldn't tell whether the monolithic gate was the same one he'd left from earlier, but he was sure it must be part of the day-stone ring – which meant he had somehow gone round in a circle. He turned around, and – with dread in his heart – set off again, hoping at least to put some distance between himself and the village so that he might be able to escape when daylight returned. He knew now that there was no chance of the torch burning long enough for him to complete his journey during the night.

A little while later, Terrel's skin was touched by an icy, burning cold and, inexplicably, the rushlight went out. Terror clutched at his chest, threatening to paralyze him completely. In the total darkness, he felt as though he might go mad. And then, as quickly as it had arrived, the cold was gone – and the torch was burning again.

Almost panicking now, the boy stumbled on, only to find himself coming to the edge of the lake where – paradoxically – the mist was less thick. But even that was dispiriting. The lake was to the *south* of the village.

Disorientated and close to despair, he turned again and made one last effort to break free of the spell that seemed to be entangling him. The fog closed in again, and a slow-rising, moaning sound – that seemed to come from all around – reminded him of Imana's tales of evil spirits. In the end it came as no real surprise – and even something of a relief – when he found himself approaching another massive standing stone. Finally admitting defeat, Terrel re-entered the day-stone circle and, as the rushlight burned down to its last glowing embers, he made his way back to the village.

He found Imana sitting on the porch. She had obviously not raised the alarm.

'Are you mad?' she whispered fearfully.

'No.' And I'm not dead either, he added silently.

'I hoped you'd come back.'

'I didn't have any choice,' he said as he went inside and laid his pack on the floor. All of a sudden he felt unbelievably tired.

'I won't tell anyone,' Imana volunteered.

Terrel nodded, not really caring one way or another. *The valley won't let you leave.* It seemed that he was bound by the jasper oracles after all.

CHAPTER THIRTY-TWO

At first the dream was the same as before. It began with omens and ended with the devastation of the earthquake – except that it *didn't* end there. Still flying, Terrel jumped back in time and saw the jewelled city from a different angle, another perspective. As the violent series of tremors spread out from the centre, he hovered over the mist-filled valley and saw – to his amazement – the waves of destruction part and flow around it, like the ripples of a stream dividing to pass on either side of a boulder. Even as the mountains that ringed the valley trembled and fell, the blanket of cloud – and the land beneath it – remained unaffected.

Terrel was still trying to work out what that meant when another new element was added to the dream. Jax's earlier words had come from Terrel's own memory, but now the enchanter was there in person once more – and the tone of his voice was nowhere near as gleeful as it had been before.

Who are you? How dare you—

Another voice, remote and barely audible, was speaking too, but the words were lost amid the rushing sounds of the dream's passage.

What do you mean, this is another test? Jax demanded angrily. *Why should I care?*

Terrel knew that the prince had misunderstood. The unknown voice had been speaking to *him*, not to Jax.

Alone? the enchanter shouted. *Good. Then leave me alone!*

The interloper spoke again, and this time Terrel heard him clearly. The message came as a terse command, in a voice that seemed vaguely familiar but which was obviously under considerable strain.

Look up.

After that there was nothing but silence, and all Terrel could do was obey. Tearing his gaze from the raging progress of the earthquake below, he looked up into the night sky.

He found himself staring at the Amber Moon. It was full, beautiful and bright in all its glory. Then the sky blinked, and the Amber was replaced by the White Moon. At first Terrel thought that it too was full, but then he noticed the slight inequality in the curve of its sides, and realized that it was three or four days short of its time of greatest influence. A moment later the scene changed again, as if a veil had been thrown over the boy's eyes and then drawn away to reveal a different portion of the heavens. This time it was the Red Moon, the merest crescent silver resting on a quilt of stars. The last of the four – and the last of the dream – was, inevitably, the Dark Moon. Terrel expected to see nothing, and was unprepared for the vision that greeted him. The Dark Moon was surrounded by a glowing halo, a shifting crown of light that stirred memories as well as a sense of wonder. He was not sure if it was a true eclipse – he was floating in the sky himself, after all – but he knew it was another omen, another message.

When Terrel awoke, he was so tired that it felt worse than if he hadn't been to sleep at all. His terrifying nocturnal adventures and then the dream had combined to leave him totally exhausted, but with the coming of a new day he knew he would not be able to rest for long. He lay where he was, aware of the village beginning to stir outside the hut, and tried to fit the pieces of the puzzle together. As his conscious mind caught up with the memories of his unconscious imagery, he was sure of one thing at least. This dream had definitely been meant to tell him something.

Terrel realized that the most curious aspect had been the ability of someone other than the enchanter to invade his thoughts. The stranger's presence had clearly antagonized Jax, and the most likely explanation was that the outsider had been using the link between the twin brothers to pass on a message of his own. Which meant that the message probably came from Vadanis.

Thinking back over what he'd heard, Terrel guessed that the reference to 'another test' – if this did indeed apply to him – had probably come from the seers. After all, they'd tested him on previous occasions, in order – he presumed – to assess his suitability for his role as the Mentor. The challenge this time must surely be the plight of the valley women and their babies. It didn't seem fair that he had to keep proving himself time and time again but, thinking back over all his journeyings, it was obvious that he'd only ever been able to move on once he'd healed certain ills – Kativa's misery, the Ancient's threat to the islands, the rift between Kerin and Olandis – and if that was the case, he would have to solve the problem here before he'd be allowed to leave. The events of the previous night fitted with that theory precisely – which was dispiriting, because Terrel still had no idea how to go about his latest task. What was more, it also appeared that this was a task he would have to complete alone.

For the first time, the boy realized that he had not seen a single animal in the valley – which meant that he was effectively cut off from Alyssa and the ghosts. There was still the possibility that Alyssa would be able to bring some creature in from the outside, but her aversion to water in all its forms would make her reluctant to enter the cloud. Because of this, it made sense that his friends might have tried to contact him in another manner.

That led him to think about what exactly they'd been trying to tell him and, a moment later, Terrel was sitting up in bed, his weariness forgotten as the significance of what he'd seen became crystal clear. He had been shown the precise alignments of all four moons at the time of the earthquake, and – while such a combination might not be unique – the chances were that it would occur only once in the next year or so. If he could calculate when that would be, he would know exactly when the catastrophe was due to take place – and thus be aware of how long he had to try to prevent it!

Almost as soon as he reached this conclusion, Terrel's

sudden feeling of exhilaration began to fade. He was stuck in this shadowed valley, where even true daylight was a half-forgotten memory. He had not seen the sky – day or night – for three days now, and wasn't likely to for some time to come. Nor could he even recall what the phases of the moons had been before he'd walked down into the cloud.

Terrel sank back onto his pallet, feeling cheated and depressed again. It was even more urgent now that he fulfil his obligations as a healer – and as the Messenger – so that he would be able to leave this cursed place. His dream had given him no help with that – rather the reverse, in fact. It had simply confirmed that he was on his own and could expect no help.

The boy felt incredibly frustrated now – especially when he realized that he knew whose voice had told him to look up. Although Terrel did not understand how his friend had managed it, he was in no doubt that the message had come from Elam.

'So what do you want to do today?' Amie asked.

'Nothing.'

'You're not thinking of trying to leave us, then?'

'No.' Terrel chose not to elaborate, and his visitor did not pursue the matter.

'Your arrival gave us new hope,' she said. 'I didn't think you'd let us down.'

Amie had come to see him much earlier than usual, and Terrel was still lying on his bed, staring morosely at the ceiling. When he did not respond to her comment, she tried again.

'You're a healer. Don't you think you owe it to—'

'Don't lecture me,' he cut in. 'I'm aware of my responsibilities.'

'Are you?'

Terrel was saved from having to answer this by the appearance of Imana in the doorway, rubbing at her eyes.

'I'm sorry,' she said, yawning massively. 'Do you want some breakfast?'

'No, thanks.'

'You slept late,' Amie remarked, glancing at the girl. 'That's not like you.'

Imana looked flustered and uncertain. Terrel knew that she had kept her promise, and hadn't told anyone about his attempted flight. She had even retrieved the candle and disposed of the remnants of the burnt-out rushlight before she'd gone back to bed. He was grateful for her discretion, but he didn't want her to have to tell any lies on his behalf.

'I disturbed her during the night,' he said. 'I had a dream.'

'Really?' Amie said curiously. 'What about?'

Terrel was about to describe some of the things he had seen – in the hope that the elder might be able to help him decipher their meaning – when an idea struck him with the force of a thunderbolt. He didn't need to see the sky to witness the procession of the moons. The jasper could tell him!

He threw off the blanket and lurched out of bed, heedless of the fact that he was dressed only in his underclothes.

'You told me the jasper oracles include the cycles of the moons,' he said breathlessly as he began to dress hurriedly.

'Yes,' Amie replied, smiling at the boy's appearance and sudden change of attitude.

'Will you show me?'

'Of course,' she said. 'Is it important?'

'Remind me again,' Amie said patiently. 'The Dark Moon was new?'

'Yes.'

'How could you tell, if you can't see it?'

'Because there was a solar eclipse. That can only happen when a moon is new.'

Terrel had told Amie about part of his dream as they'd walked to the first of the touchstones – saying only that he believed he had been shown the configuration of the moons so that he'd be able to tell when a possible disaster might occur. She had tried to get him to elaborate, but he'd avoided her questions, and had insisted on concentrating on calculating the timing of his supposedly prophetic vision.

'And the Amber Moon was full?'

'Yes.'

Amie traced some more of the wavy lines on the stone. Her fingers hovered over the surface without touching it. This was the fourth touchstone they'd consulted, and the process seemed so complex that Terrel had begun to despair of ever getting the answers he needed. Each oracle appeared to contain only a part of the complete solution.

'Now we're getting somewhere,' Amie murmured to herself. 'We have to narrow it down to this set of intersections. You said the Red Moon was almost new?'

'Yes. One or two days old, no more.'

'Hmmm.'

'What?' he asked anxiously.

'Tell me about the White Moon again.'

'It was almost full, but not quite,' Terrel repeated, trying to remain calm. 'Three or four days short, I would guess.'

'You're certain it wasn't full?'

'I think so,' he said, beginning to doubt his own memory. 'Why?'

'There are two sets of intersections in the jasper that match your observations closely. The first of these will be quite soon.'

'How soon?' he asked, his heart sinking.

'Thirty-nine days,' Amie replied, after a moment's calculation. 'Here, look.' She pointed to a section of the carved patterns, but Terrel couldn't make any sense of them, even though she'd tried to explain their workings to him several times. 'The only thing is that the White Moon is full then, as well as the Amber. That's why I wanted to know if you were sure.'

'I don't think that can be right then,' Terrel said hopefully. 'What about the other two?'

'The Red Moon would be two days old, which fits, and the Dark Moon one day old.'

'That's wrong too. It has to be new for an eclipse.'

'Yes, but I'm having to amend that cycle to take the time of change into account,' Amie said. 'We can't be sure that the Dark Moon is completely accurate.'

'Oh.' Terrel's doubts began to resurface. 'When's the next set of intersections?'

'Much further off,' she told him. 'Almost half a long cycle. Here.' Her finger moved to another part of the stone. 'If I've got the adjustments right, the Dark Moon would be new then, but as I said, we can't rely on that totally. The Amber is full and the Red is one day old, which is what we want.' She paused, working something out. 'And the White Moon would be three days short of full.'

'That's a much better fit,' Terrel said eagerly.

'Yes, but the only significant difference from the earlier date is the White Moon. It's crucial.'

Terrel closed his eyes, trying to see the dream image again. Every time he attempted to do this, he saw the tell-tale variation in its shape, the distortion of its nearly perfect circle. And yet it seemed so small a difference on which to base such an important conclusion.

'It wasn't full,' he said eventually. 'I'd swear to it.'

'Then that has to be the answer.'

'Exactly how long is it till then?'

Amie spent a little time counting cycles and checking the relevant markings.

'It's two days before midwinter,' she said. 'One hundred and sixty-four days from today.'

Terrel let out a sigh of relief. His mission to Talazoria was not as urgent as he'd thought. Unless he'd made a horrible mistake, he had some time to spare in order to try to help the people of the valley. There need not be any more escape attempts – at least for a while.

'Now will you tell me what this is all about?' Amie asked.

CHAPTER THIRTY-THREE

'What do you see when you look inside me?'

Terrel thought for a moment, wondering how best to describe the waking dream.

'I can sense things,' he explained. 'It's as if I'm dreaming about what you and the baby are feeling, even though I'm awake.'

'Yes, but what's it *like*?' Escra persisted. 'Can you tell what I'm thinking?'

'No. It's more what you're feeling. And it's not really specific.' Terrel hesitated, wondering how to explain it. 'It's symbolic, I suppose, but the symbols tell me whether you're healthy or not.'

'And is it the same for the baby?'

'Yes.'

'Will you look now, and tell me what you see?'

'All right,' he said, trying to hide his reluctance. Although the women knew that what he saw wasn't good, he had avoided giving them specific details about their babies' suffering.

'Will you be all right out here?' Esera asked with a smile. 'I'm in no condition to carry you back to the village if you faint.'

They were walking in the woods outside the day-stone circle. Several days had passed since Terrel and Amie had consulted the jasper, and Terrel had spent most of that time with Esera. There were several reasons for this, the most obvious being that he now thought of her as a friend. She was the closest to his own age and, despite her teasing, he was comfortable with her. She was also the most mobile of the six pregnant women, and the dreams of her unborn child continued to be the least violent of the group – making them the easiest for him to study.

'I haven't done that since the first time,' Terrel said, feeling only slightly defensive. 'I'm not likely to start again now.'

'So I don't make you go weak at the knees any more?' she asked, looking at him with soulful eyes.

'Do you want to do this or not?' he said, grinning. 'Give me your hand.'

Esera did as she was told, and for a moment Terrel glimpsed the fear beneath her bravado. Then he closed his eyes and made himself concentrate. Finding the diseased echoes within the dream was easy enough now, but stopping himself from being absorbed by the enervating waves of agony still required a degree of vigilance. For the time being at least, he had to be an observer, not a healer.

This time the internal darkness held a palpable sense of menace. It was like no dream Terrel had ever encountered, and yet all at once he found himself remembering the ordeals he had suffered before his birth. This dream had the same sense of *memory*, of reliving the past – and it held the same kind of unreasoning hatred. He was blind too, not in the thunder of the red sea, but in absolute blackness. At first Terrel thought it was like the sudden darkness that had doused his torch on the night he'd tried to escape – but then he realized that the echoing spaces of the dream felt more like being trapped in some vast cavern, or in the mines at Betancuria. He moved on, driven by fear, *underground*. Evil flowed above and all around, and he felt the need to protect himself, to escape. But there was no way out. He was engulfed by panic, and struck out wildly. The dream-world shifted, and he fled, leaving only hatred behind.

As Terrel emerged from the contact he was trembling, but he had a new set of observations to add to his growing hoard.

'You don't look quite so burnt now,' Esera said, her concern obvious. 'Are you all right?'

'I'm fine.' He was not really surprised to hear that his face was paler than usual. The baby's fear had infected him too.

'What did you see?'

He described his experience as best he could – but because he didn't want to worry her, he toned down the violence of the emotions he'd felt.

'That's new, isn't it?' she commented, when he'd finished. 'Do you know what it means?'

'Are there any caves under the valley?' He knew from his travels that there were many systems of caves and tunnels, as well as underground rivers, in various parts of Macul.

'Not that I know of.'

Terrel looked down at the ground at his feet, wondering whether the dream might have originated – perhaps four years ago – in a cave hidden beneath where he now stood. That might explain why this particular examination had felt so different.

'What are you thinking?' Esera asked.

'You remember that force I told you about, the one that might have been responsible for the earthquake here?'

'The elemental, you mean?'

Terrel nodded. As he had grown more at ease in Esera's company, he had fallen into the habit of thinking out loud, using her as a sounding board for his ideas. Although he hadn't told her about the exact nature of the elemental, he had described a little of what it could do.

'I'm beginning to think it really could be the cause of this illness,' he said.

'Does that mean you'll be able to cure it?' she asked eagerly.

'I don't know yet. Let me explain my theory first, and then tell me what you think.'

They began walking again, threading their way between the dripping trees.

'Suppose the elemental *did* pass through here four years ago, but it travelled underground,' he began. 'I told you before that it both hates and fears water, and so this valley, with all the cloud and mist and the lake, would have seemed like a terrible place. So it moved away as fast as it could, and because it's very powerful, that caused the tremor. But what if it somehow left a residue of its presence here, some part of its power?'

'Like a curse?'

'Exactly! I'm sure it wasn't meant to be a curse – more

likely it was intended as a warning – but it might have acted like one.'

'And that's what hurting the babies?'

'Inadvertently, yes.'

Esera thought about this for a few moments.

'This residue?' she asked. 'It's still in the ground here?'

'Yes. At least I think so.'

'Then it's hopeless. We can't escape the soil we live on, and we can't ever leave the valley.' Esera looked as miserable as he had ever seen her.

'It's only a theory,' he reminded her.

'If it's in the land itself, why does it only affect the babies and not the rest of us?' she asked, recovering a little.

He had asked himself this question many times, puzzling over it for hours. He had talked it over with Amie and the other elders, without ever reaching any definite conclusions. Now he believed he had hit on something that might explain the apparent anomaly and, even though he knew Esera was hoping to disprove his theory, he owed it to her to be as honest as he could.

'What's the main difference between the babies and the rest of you?'

'Umm,' Esera said, adopting a feeble-minded expression. 'They haven't been born yet?'

'Exactly,' Terrel said, grinning. 'Which means they have very little awareness of the outside world. All the light and sound that we see and hear, everything that our senses tell us about – they don't have that. Everything they experience comes through their mothers.'

'And *we're* not making them ill, because we're healthy.'

'That's right. There isn't even any connection between your dream-space and theirs. But what if there are other forces in the world, that they *can* experience directly without reference to you?'

'Are there such things?' she asked.

'Yes, things we perceive somehow, without using our external senses,' Terrel replied, remembering a conversation he'd had with Amie on this very subject. 'And what's more, I believe the elemental uses these forces in the same way we use *our* various abilities. If something it did warped the natural environment here, then that could be the source of the curse.'

'I still don't see why—'

'A wise man once told me,' Terrel went on, 'that a curse will only work if the victim believes in its potency. By the same token, if someone is sure they won't be affected, then they won't be. You and the other women – and everyone in the valley for that matter – know that your home is not an evil place. You see that every day of your lives, and even if the elemental's curse is telling you there's vile magic all around, you have the evidence you need to ignore the suggestion.'

'But the babies don't!' Esera exclaimed.

'If the curse works on them directly, that's *all* they know,' he said, nodding. 'They have no one to tell them otherwise, no evidence to contradict a false assumption. The warning is all they understand.'

Esera was clearly impressed by this argument, even if she didn't like its implications. But she still had one more objection.

'So why don't the babies who are born alive recover? Once they can see that the outside world isn't as bad as they thought, shouldn't they be able to set the curse aside like we do?'

'I'm not sure,' Terrel admitted. 'But I would guess they're so exhausted and ill from the pregnancy, and so frightened about what's going to happen to them, that they don't have the strength or willpower to survive – even if they realize the curse isn't real. They just fade away,' he added, remembering Liana's poignant words.

The two friends had come to a halt at the edge of the lake, and Esera gazed out over its calm surface, a faraway look in her eyes.

'So if all this is true,' she said, 'what can we do about it?'

'That's what we have to decide next,' Terrel replied, wishing he could give her a better answer.

'Well, it makes perfect sense, as far as it goes,' Amie commented that evening. 'But it's still only a theory.'

'I know,' Terrel said, 'but it's the best I can come up with.'

'What made you abandon your ideas about the Dark Moon? Wouldn't that control some of these unseen forces?'

'Yes, but if it was responsible for the illness, you'd expect there to be some variation in the patterns of the babies' dreams, depending on the moon's cycle – and there isn't any, as far as I can tell.' The latest new Dark Moon predicted by the jasper had already passed without affecting Terrel's findings. 'It'll be full again six days from now,' he added, 'so I should be able to confirm it then.'

'Fair enough.'

'If anything,' Terrel went on, 'from what I've learnt with Esera, the dreams seem to vary depending on *where* we are in the valley. I'm going to work on that.'

Amie nodded, observing a new sense of purpose – a new maturity – in the boy.

'There's something else that I think argues against the Dark Moon being the culprit,' Terrel added. 'I can't be sure when its aberrations began, but I've got a feeling it wasn't as long ago as four years. Its time of change certainly didn't have any effects on my homeland until much later than that.'

'The jasper tells the same story here,' Amie stated.

'So the Dark Moon can't have provoked an *unexpected* earthquake four years ago,' the boy concluded.

'That's only relevant if you're sure the tremor and the illness are connected.'

'I think they are. Don't you?'

'I still find it hard to believe,' Amie replied. 'But I'm beginning to trust your intuition.'

Soon after the elder had left him, Terrel realized that his own moon-dream – as he thought of it now – *had* given him a clue about the source of the illness. If the massive earthquake had been instigated by the elemental, then it made a kind of sense for the valley to have been spared. The Ancient may have realized that it was different from the land surrounding it, perhaps believing that the valley had already been destroyed by the curse and so there was no need to do so again. Although that part of Terrel's dream may have been symbolic, it still made it seem more likely that the elemental and not the Dark Moon was the cause of the disease.

It was nearly dark outside, and Terrel thought better of pursuing Amie. His news could wait for another day. Ever since he'd realized that time was no longer such a pressing problem, he'd had no more thoughts about trying to leave just yet. There was no question of making another attempt at night – his blood ran cold at the very thought – and he was convinced that even if the villagers would let him go during the day, the fog would not. The cloud layer separating the valley from the outside world would remain an impenetrable barrier until the time was right.

Knowing that he had to solve this problem himself, with no guidance from Alyssa and the ghosts, had concentrated his mind effectively. And he also felt a personal responsibility now. His friendships with Esera and Amie meant that he cared about what happened to them and their community. And though he still hated the lack of sun and sky, he had even begun to appreciate the place itself a little. He was determined to earn his title, to prove his worth as the Messenger.

But this was presenting him with an apparently insoluble dilemma. Now that he believed the valley's curse stemmed from the elemental in Talazoria, he had another reason for wanting to make contact with the creature. Indeed, it might be the only way to restore the babies to health. Unfortunately, as the Messenger, he was forced to stay in the valley. He couldn't leave until he healed them. And he couldn't heal them unless he left. His unknown road seemed to have come to a dead end.

'There must be another way,' he muttered, talking as much to himself as to Esera.

'You'll find it,' she said loyally.

'It'd better be soon, then,' he replied. 'Parina hasn't got much time left.'

They were taking their morning walk together, a habit they had fallen into. However, there was a greater purpose about today's stroll. Terrel had already checked on her baby's dreaming several times, each in a different place, and had found several minor variations – but no comfort. Now the two friends had returned to the lakeside, one of their regular haunts.

'I always feel calm here,' Esera said, looking out over the expanse of dark water. 'Peaceful.'

The day was the brightest Terrel had experienced in the valley. Although the layer of cloud above was as thick and unyielding as ever, the air below was relatively free of mist, and they had been able to see much further than normal. The air even felt warmer than usual.

'It is nice here, isn't it?' Terrel agreed.

'Mmm,' Esera murmured. 'Romantic.'

Terrel was mortified to find heat rising in his cheeks. He tried to turn his face away, but – true to form – she noticed anyway.

'There's so much colour in your face already, I don't see why you need any more,' she remarked, making matters worse. 'Don't worry,' she added, smiling. 'Just because I let you hold my hand doesn't mean I have any designs on you.'

'What would you want with me anyway?' he said, trying to laugh off his embarrassment.

'There's more to a man than his physical appearance,' she told him.

That's easy for you to say, Terrel thought. Esera seemed beautiful to him now, in spite of her pallid complexion. But he kept this opinion to himself.

'And I bet you'd make a much better father for this baby than its real one,' she added.

Terrel was astonished by her comment, and he had no idea whether she was being serious or not. He blushed again, hating the way he was betrayed by his own skin.

'Oh dear,' Esera said, looking at him. 'Poor Terrel. I'm sorry. Perhaps we shouldn't come to the lake any more.' Then she frowned. 'What is it? What's the matter?'

Terrel was lost in a memory that had been summoned by her casual words. All of a sudden his awkwardness was forgotten, and he reached out and grabbed her hand.

'Come on,' he said, setting off along the shore and pulling her along with him.

'Where are we going?' she asked, laughing.

'I'm going to take you out in one of the fishermen's boats,' he told her.

CHAPTER THIRTY-FOUR

'You want us to do *what*?' Tavia exclaimed.

'It's not as crazy as it sounds,' Terrel replied. He was so excited he could hardly keep still.

'I think you'd better explain why you believe this is a good idea,' Amie said calmly.

Terrel and the elders were sitting around the outdoor table once more, but this time – at Terrel's request – the other villagers were all gathered there to hear what was being said. He wanted everyone to be part of the decision; if they agreed to his proposal, they would all be involved, one way or another. An extra bench had been provided for the more heavily pregnant women, but Esera was sitting next to Terrel, and was clearly enjoying her role as one of the central figures in the proceedings.

Terrel gave the villagers a brief version of his reasoning about a curse that might have become embedded in the very ground of the valley, and told them why he thought this would affect only the unborn babies. For once he did not feel nervous or awkward speaking in front of so many people, even though he knew they were all hanging on his every word.

'The only real clue we had about the nature of the curse,' he went on, 'was the fact that it seemed to vary in intensity, depending upon where you were in the valley – but it wasn't until Esera told me how she always felt calm and peaceful when she was near the lake that I began to get an idea. If I'm right, the curse was aimed not at you, but at the water – and the greatest concentration of water here is in the lake.'

'But surely that would make the curse more powerful there,' Amie said.

'You'd think so, but in fact the reverse is true. Don't forget, this force is coming from underground. So if someone is out on the lake, it would have to come *through* a considerable depth of water to reach them – and I don't think it can. When Hellin took Esera and me out in his boat this morning, I looked into her baby's dreams. They were peaceful for the first time – just as they ought to be.' He paused as a buzz of conversation ran around the gathering.

'And how did *you* feel?' Amie asked Esera.

'There was no real difference,' the girl explained. 'Except that for the first time in ages I wasn't worried. I was just calm and happy. I didn't know why until Terrel explained it to me.'

'After that I wanted to be sure,' Terrel said, taking up the story again, 'so Hellin and I took each of the other five women out onto the lake in turn. The results were all the same. In themselves they didn't feel much change, but what I saw of the babies convinced me that their condition improved dramatically.'

'So all this supposition rests on what you saw?' Amie commented. 'Nothing else?'

'That's right,' Terrel admitted, 'but I'm sure what I saw was genuine.'

'And he *is* the Messenger,' Liana added, her eyes bright with new hope.

'Did the babies' illness return once they were back on land?' Amie asked.

'Yes,' Terrel replied. 'Almost immediately.'

'I'd be glad to go out on the boat again,' Esera offered, 'so Terrel can repeat his examination.'

'Me too,' Parina added forcefully. 'I'm the one who's got the least time left. I'm already convinced the Messenger's instincts are correct, but if you want more proof, I'll do whatever you like.'

'There's one more thing,' Terrel said. He had wondered whether to even mention this last point of his argument, and if he'd been in any other country he would probably have kept quiet. But all dreams were important to the people of Macul. 'I realized this morning that I'd been here before. In a dream. It was a long time ago, when I was many miles away from here.' In fact he'd been in a prison cell in Tiscamanita, wondering if he was going mad. 'At the time I thought it was just a scene from my imagination, but I know now that I saw this place – the dripping trees, the mist, the lake. I even saw some of you,' he added, glancing at the row of pregnant women. 'And you were in a large wooden house built upon the surface of a lake.' He did not add that the same dream had also contained other equally improbable images and landscapes. That was something he didn't even want to think about at the moment. 'I think we have to try to build you that house.'

'I think so too,' Esera stated boldly.

'We all do,' Parina added in her role as spokeswoman for the other mothers-to-be.

'*Can* it be done?' Tavia asked, looking round at some of the faces in the crowd.

It was Hellin, the fisherman who had become a ferryman for the earlier part of the day, who answered.

'It can,' he stated simply, his gruff voice carrying the weight of knowledge.

Tavia nodded, then glanced at each of the elders in turn.

'Are we all agreed?' It was a rhetorical question by then, and received no answer. 'Then let's do it!'

The rest of that day passed in a blur of activity. Hellin and his group of fellow craftsmen asked Terrel to join them, and they discussed a seemingly endless list of questions concerning the building of 'the hospice', as it was now called. This was the first time he'd had extensive dealings with any of the men of the valley, and because they all had vastly greater expertise in practical matters than he did, he felt completely out of his depth. Nevertheless, his opinion was sought frequently – and his contributions were listened to attentively.

By an unspoken agreement, Hellin had assumed the role of coordinating the project, and Terrel worked with him most of the time. Others came and went, beginning various preliminary tasks or seeking out information needed by the planners. Several of the elders were involved too, and their advice was taken into account. Everyone in the village – even the children – seemed to be helping somehow, and Terrel marvelled at the way his original idea had galvanized the entire community.

During the course of their discussions, it was agreed that Hellin and Terrel, with Esera's help, would choose the exact site for the hospice. The plan was for the three of them to take to the water in the fisherman's boat, and for Terrel to monitor the condition of Esera's baby while they were afloat, to see whether there was any advantage to one spot or another. The assumption was that the deeper the water below the hospice the better the protection would be, so the building should be as far from the shore as was possible within the bounds of practicality. It was also decided that it should float upon the surface of the water rather than rest on stilts driven into the bed of the lake. As Terrel pointed out, they wanted to try to avoid any direct contact between the hospice and the ground below. No one knew how the curse was transmitted, but if water *was* the barrier, then they did not want to leave any gaps in their shield. This arrangement would also have the advantage of mobility, as they'd be able to move the hospice from one place to another if they encountered any unexpected problems at the chosen site. They also had to decide how the building should be tethered to the shore. Any system of ropes would leave it at the mercy of wind and currents – gentle though they generally were – and would mean that the only way to approach or leave the hospice would be by boat. The alternative was to build a wooden walkway, which *could* be supported by stilts – at least for the first part of its length. If this was sturdy enough it would effectively anchor the hospice in place, and would allow the women – and anyone visiting them – to simply walk to and from the building.

As for the size and design of the hospice itself, the only obvious criterion was that it had to be large enough to house six women, with scope for more if the experiment was successful. At Hellin's insistence, Terrel described as much as he could remember from his dream, but he deferred to the carpenters and boatmen when it came to deciding on details. It was already clear to him that the community possessed all the necessary skills to complete the project – and, more importantly, they were also displaying the enthusiasm and determination that would be needed to carry it through.

At the same time, arrangements were put in place to begin gathering the necessary raw materials. It was obvious that, first and foremost, they were going to need a great deal of wood. Various groups were detailed to fell trees, ready for cutting and shaping, and two empty huts were to be taken apart, so that the planks and beams used in their construction could provide mature timber for the hospice. Some of the boatmen were detailed to gather the necessary oils and other substances needed to make the wood waterproof, while others agreed to take the pregnant women out onto the lake in their craft, so that they could spend as much time on the water as possible before their new abode was ready for them.

As evening came, and darkness put an end to their frenetic activity, Terrel was feeling tired but elated. The plans were already much further advanced than he had expected. Even so, it was clear that building the hospice was going to be a major undertaking, and with Parina's baby due within a month, it was going to be a race against time. However, such was the spirit of optimism that Terrel felt all around him that he was sure it was a race they were going to win. And even though his physical limitations meant that he would not be able to help with the actual labour, it had already been made perfectly clear that the villagers regarded his part in the process as not only necessary but crucial. He had actually begun to *feel* like the Messenger.

Imana often ate with him now, and it was during their meal that night that an innocent question from the girl drove a wedge of uncertainty into Terrel's burgeoning confidence.

'When the hospice is finished, the women will spend as much time there as possible,' she said. 'That's right, isn't it?'

Terrel nodded.

'Ideally they'd spend *all* their time there while they're pregnant,' he said. 'And possibly some time after their baby is born.'

'So they'll be there at night?' Imana queried.

'Yes. Of course.'

'But the lake is outside the day-stone circle,' she said, sounding confused. 'What about the darkness?'

Terrel froze, a piece of nepp root halfway to his mouth.

'I never thought of that.' If the women had to come ashore each night, the benefits of the hospice might be greatly reduced – or even lost altogether.

'I'm sure you and the elders will sort something out,' Imana said blithely as she began to clear their plates away.

Remembering his own unnerving experiences with 'the darkness', Terrel could only wish that he shared her faith in him.

*

After brooding for much of the night, Terrel went in search of Amie at first light. The villagers were already busy, and the boy dreaded having to tell the elder that all their efforts might be in vain. He found her organizing means of collecting and distributing food, but one look at his face convinced Amie that they needed to talk in private, and she led him to her own home. The rest of her family were already at work.

'Imana's told me about the darkness,' Terrel began without preamble. 'The lake is outside the day-stone ring.'

'Yes. I wondered about that.'

'And you didn't say anything?' he said, amazed by her apparent calm.

'This project has brought us all together,' Amie replied. 'Even if it doesn't work as well as you hope, it's got to be better than nothing. It's a relief just to be able to *do* something at last.'

'But if the women are terrified of the darkness,' he protested, 'that might harm the babies.'

'Then maybe we'll have to bring them ashore at night. Or we'll think of another solution.'

'What other solution could there be?'

'Perhaps the darkness doesn't affect the area over the lake,' she suggested. 'Perhaps we'll find a way of counteracting it even if it does. We could reassure the women by having others stay there overnight before they do.'

'Who would be willing to do that?'

'I'd be happy to volunteer. So would Esera, I'd bet. And there'd be others.'

'I could do it too,' Terrel offered, ashamed that he had not said as much immediately.

'That would help,' Amie said, smiling. 'This is the Messenger's business, after all.'

'We could have torches,' he said, becoming a little more enthusiastic now.

'Fire brings its own dangers,' she pointed out, 'but it's worth considering.'

'Perhaps I could stay out at the hospice *with* the women . . . in another room or something. Do you think that would help?'

'And perhaps some of their husbands could be persuaded to stay with them too.'

'We'd better tell Hellin to make it bigger,' Terrel remarked.

'You see,' Amie told him. 'It's not so bad when you start thinking about it. And if we fail, at least we'll know we've tried.'

CHAPTER THIRTY-FIVE

After ten days of intensive activity, the hospice was declared ready for habitation. This in itself was a reason for celebration, and the fact that it occurred on a day already deemed propitious by the jasper – and which Terrel realized coincided with the full of the Red Moon – reinforced the general mood of optimism. There were still trials to be faced – not least the first night outside the day-stone circle – but an important step had been taken in the search for a cure to the babies' ills. The women and their escorts walked aboard their new home at midday, watched by the entire population of the valley. Terrel and Esera brought up the rear together, completing the slow-moving procession, and they stepped onto the walkway to a gradually swelling round of cheers, whistles and applause from the spectators.

'You should turn round and take a bow,' Esera told him, grinning. 'Or wave, at least.'

'Don't be silly. If I try that I'll probably fall in the

water.' Although the walkway was protected by railings on either side, Terrel was not confident of his balance on the gently swaying boards. 'It wouldn't look too good if the Messenger drowned himself, would it?'

'I'll save you,' Esera promised – and Terrel had the feeling that, pregnant or not, she would probably do just that.

'Actually, I *can* swim,' he said, as they walked on. 'I tend to go round in circles, but I can stay afloat.'

'Let's hope the same is true of this place,' she remarked, looking ahead.

The hospice rested on a large hollow raft which had been sealed tight, trapping a layer of air beneath the floor. This gave it extra buoyancy, to support the weight of the dwelling above. The walls had been topped with a thatched roof and were surrounded by an open area which formed an extension of the walkway, so that it was possible to go all the way around the building without actually going inside. This area was also protected by wooden railings. The entire structure was surprisingly stable, a testament to the skill of those who had designed and built it. It also matched Terrel's dream image.

Inside, the one large rectangular room smelled of sap and oil. It was almost completely bare, containing just a row of eight beds. Other furniture and facilities were to be added as and when necessary, but for now it offered only the minimum of comfort. None of the women minded about this. They were simply delighted to be there.

During the construction of the hospice, the pregnant women had spent as much time in the boats as possible – an experience most of them had found awkward and unpleasant, in spite of the good it was supposed to do. Terrel had gone with them as often as he could, and had noted not only the almost immediately calming effect being on the water had had on the babies, but also – encouragingly – an apparently cumulative benefit. Even their dreams once they'd returned to land seemed a little less violent now. The full of the Dark Moon had also come and gone during this period, with no detectable change in the patterns of the dreams, and these two new sets of evidence made Terrel feel even more confident that his theory was correct. However, its first real test was to come that night.

All six women had declared that they wanted to remain in the hospice overnight. Any suggestion that someone else should test the risks first had been decisively set aside, on the grounds that because the entire project had been for their benefit, it was only right that they should be the ones to accept the corresponding dangers. Their recent shared experiences had given them a camaraderie – which even included Esera now – that Terrel found both admirable and quite moving. It also granted the women the sort of collective bravery that he could only hope to emulate, and even though they were clearly frightened – a lifetime's superstition was not to be discarded in a single day, after all – there was no question of them going back onshore once they'd been installed in their new accommodations.

Once that had been confirmed, the final decision was who was to stay with them. The five husbands all volunteered but, in a good-natured decision, this suggestion had been rejected by the women themselves – the general opinion being that the men would be more trouble than they were worth. It would also make the hospice too crowded. At that point it was hard to tell whether the men were disappointed or relieved.

It was eventually agreed that Amie would stay – she had honoured her earlier promise by volunteering to do so – and everyone took it for granted that Terrel would be there too. No one except Imana knew that the boy had faced the darkness before – and lived to keep the tale a secret – and Terrel tried to convince himself that what had happened to him then had been a warning, because he was doing the wrong thing, and that it would be different now. But he did not entirely succeed. The completely natural fear of the unknown malevolence in the night would not go away. As dusk approached and the other visitors took their leave, he began to feel very nervous indeed.

'Can't you sleep?'

Startled, Terrel looked up from where he was sitting, huddled against an outside wall of the hospice. Night had closed in some time ago, but he'd been restless and had got up from his bed to go outside. He had lit a candle, and its feeble glow was the only illumination, his only defence against the darkness. Even so, Esera found it uncomfortably bright.

'I think I'll stay out here for a while,' he told her. 'Just in case anything happens. You're the one who should be sleeping.'

Terrel had been surprised when the women had all fallen asleep that night, as an automatic response to the end of the day. The ingrained habits of a lifetime clearly outweighed their fears – and so far there had been nothing for them to worry about.

'I know,' Esera said, yawning. 'I'm not sure why I woke up.'

'Do you feel anything?' he asked quickly.

'No. I don't think the darkness is going to bother us.'

'Good,' he replied, hoping she was right. 'Go back to bed. I'll be in soon.'

Esera nodded, turned and padded softly back around the corner, heading for the doorway. The platform rocked gently in response to her movement, and Terrel went back to listening to the soft lapping of the water.

After a while he began to feel that there was something oppressive in the atmosphere. The air felt heavy against his skin and, strangely, it seemed to be growing slightly warmer. This was so unlike what he'd experienced on the night of his attempted escape that at first he felt more curious than afraid, but he strained his eyes nonetheless, hoping to make out something in the black void – and found, to his astonishment, that the night was no longer completely dark.

Far above him, there was a flickering deep within the ever-present blanket of cloud. It amounted to no more than a dull glow, a short-lived glimmering inside the enveloping grey, but even that seemed extraordinarily bright after the total absence of light that had gone before. Terrel stared up, thinking that it might be some kind of airborne lightning, and a few moments later a soft, distant rumbling confirmed his guess.

Although the air in the valley was always damp, Terrel had never seen any real rain fall there, and he wondered if that was about to change now. The storm intensified, becoming a little brighter and louder, but it was still completely contained by the cloud and no rain fell. Gazing upwards, Terrel wondered whether the remote violence in the sky reflected what was happening in the outside world, or whether it was simply part of the unique climate of the valley. He was so mesmerized by the now almost continuous luminescence that at first he didn't notice that he could see quite a long way across the lake, as it reflected the battle above. When he did look down, he gasped, and lost all interest in the lightning. Hovering just above the shimmering surface of the water were three black shapes, darker shadows upon the face of the night.

They had no form or features, and their only movement was a kind of slow undulation. Terrel had almost leapt to his feet and cried out a warning when he'd first seen them, but some instinct had held him back, and – even though his heart was hammering in his chest – he was glad now that he'd stayed still. The dark shapes were keeping their distance and Terrel sensed no malice from them, only a measure of curiosity and perhaps an ancient sadness, an unfulfilled longing. He did not know what they were or what they wanted, but one thing was clear. These amorphous creatures, like the ghosts, were of another world.

Was it the same world? he wondered. Was it even possible that Alyssa – and her friends in high places! – might have had some influence over them? Or could Ysatel's wandering spirit have been the one to curb their earlier enmity? Terrel had no way of knowing, and was given no chance to find out, because in the blink of an eye the strange beings vanished, leaving the boy wondering if he'd been hallucinating. The subdued lightning continued to flicker overhead, but now Terrel's view across the lake was uninterrupted. And he knew that Esera had been right. The darkness wasn't going to bother them that night.

The half-hidden storm soon petered out, leaving the darkness unchallenged except for Terrel's sputtering candle, and as he made his way back to his bed, he saw that the women were all sleeping peacefully, quite undisturbed by the noise of the passing storm. The rest of the night passed without incident – much to the relief and joy of all concerned – and in the morning Terrel found himself part of an impromptu celebration as everyone in the hospice greeted one another with open arms. Some of the hugs were clumsy, but they were no less genuine for that, with everyone caught between laughter and tears. Nor were the women any less demonstrative with Terrel himself. He was forced to endure a series of smothering embraces, but even though his embarrassment was plain, not even Esera teased him about it on this occasion.

Later that morning, after Terrel had checked on the progress of the babies, Amie went to report to the other elders and several visitors came to the hospice, eager for news. Terrel had said nothing to anyone about what he'd seen in the night, and all the talk was of how peacefully and enjoyably the time had passed. He escaped from the newly-crowded room, and went to sit outside in the same spot as before. Even now, when everyone else seemed to think that success was already theirs, Terrel knew that his job was not even close to completion; he would have to stay at least until the first babies were born.

It was a measure of his new-found self-confidence, as

well as his grudging acceptance of his destiny, that his long-delayed departure from the valley no longer filled him with gloom and frustration. He still had ample time to reach Talazoria, and if – once his task there had been completed – he was unable to make it back to the coast in time, then he'd be disappointed but would accept his fate and wait the extra year. Alyssa would wait for him. He knew now that the jasper was right. He was meant to be where he was.

A slight movement of the raft told him that he was no longer alone, and he was glad to see that it was Esera who joined him. She sat down beside him, and for a while they watched the placid, silver surface of the lake in companionable silence.

'If this works you'll be leaving us soon, won't you?' she asked eventually.

Terrel didn't say anything. He didn't need to.

'I wish you could stay long enough to see *my* baby born,' Esera added, sounding rather sad.

'So do I, but it's impossible.'

'And you're not going to tell me why, are you?'

'I made a promise,' he said. 'A lot of people are depending on me.'

Esera nodded, accepting this unsatisfactory answer as the best she was going to get.

'At least that means you won't see me when I'm as fat as the others in there,' she said. 'I can't believe I'm ever going to be that big.'

'You'll still be beautiful,' he told her.

A few moments later a small sound made Terrel look round, and he was dismayed to see that Esera was crying. After a brief hesitation, he put his good arm around her shoulders. He felt extremely self-conscious, but when she responded by leaning into him for comfort, he felt a wary kind of happiness. They remained like that, not talking, as Esera regained her composure – and even when she had dried her eyes, neither of them found any reason to move.

Eight days later, Parina went into labour.

CHAPTER THIRTY-SIX

Terrel came to with a slight headache and the vaguely uncomfortable feeling that he'd made a complete fool of himself. His senses had just recovered enough for him to realize that he was lying on the floor when Esera's face swam into focus.

'At this point I'd normally be saying something really sarcastic,' she informed him, 'but there's somebody here who's waiting to meet you.'

As she helped him to his feet, the memories came flooding back and he felt even more embarrassed – but then he saw the baby and forgot about anything else. He stared at the little face, its eyes screwed tight shut, at the small hands with their perfect, tiny fingernails. This living, breathing miracle was the result of all that pain and effort.

'It's a boy,' one of the midwives said. 'He *looks* healthy.'

It was only then that Terrel became aware of the

nervous air of expectancy in the room, and realized they were all waiting for him. He stretched out a hand, and gently touched the tip of his little finger to the baby's palm. The tiny fingers curled around it with surprising strength, and Terrel fell headlong into the most chaotic waking dream he had ever experienced.

He sensed longing and anger and pain, all of it over-laid with an almost overwhelming disorientation. Nothing made sense; everything was wrong. All sorts of alien sounds and smells assaulted him; light burned his eyes and the air chilled his skin and lungs. He fought for warmth and reassurance, finding them, amongst all the turmoil, in the comfort of the arms that held him. He clung to that slender lifeline as the unfamiliar sen-sations swirled about him.

Terrel rode the storm, trying to retain his own com-posure in the face of the onslaught. At first he was dismayed, certain that the illness had reclaimed the child, but as he gradually became accustomed to the tumult, he recognized the truth. How else could you expect a baby to react when it had just entered a completely new and probably frightening world? The important thing was that the earlier hatred and debilitating terror had gone. He could detect a few vestigial traces of the disease in amongst the other, natural emotions, but they were almost inconsequential and would fade with time.

'Is he all right?'

Parina's anxious voice broke the spell, and Terrel gently pulled his finger from the baby's grip.

'He's all right.'

'You're sure?' She looked drawn and exhausted, as well as apprehensive.

'He's confused and tired and cold,' Terrel told her, 'which I should think is normal when you've been through what he's just been through. But he's not ill. He's going to be fine.'

Although tears were welling in Parina's eyes, she allowed herself to smile then, and the look she gave the infant was so full of love and wonder that Terrel had to turn away, fearing that he too would start to cry – and thus humiliate himself for the second time that day.

'Fine healer you turned out to be,' Esera commented when they were alone. 'Fainting at the sight of a little blood!'

'It wasn't a little, it was a lot,' Terrel protested, but he still felt mortified. He could have claimed that it had been his own efforts – he'd been helping Parina control her pain – that had caused his collapse, but that would have been a lie. It had simply been caused by an unexpected squeamishness. He'd been the only male in the room – and he hadn't wanted to be there. But the women had all insisted that he stay with them, so he'd crouched at the head of Parina's bed, with her hand gripping his, while the two midwives went about their business. Amie and the others had been there too, but had kept out of the way. Terrel had tried not to look, but he couldn't help but be aware that there was something revolting going on. Long before the baby made its entrance into the world, the sounds and smells of Parina's ordeal had left him feeling nauseous and sweating profusely. The only other births Terrel had ever witnessed had been those of farm animals, and they – even the difficult ones – had seemed relatively simple affairs. This had been altogether different. What was supposed to be natural had seemed to him to be a most *unnatural* process. And the sight of all that blood had appalled him. In the end, to his shame, his own body had found a way to stop him having to see any more.

'At least it all turned out well,' Esera remarked, 'even if you weren't there at the end.'

'Yes, it did.' The glow of satisfaction Terrel felt at the eventual outcome could not be spoiled by the memory of his own shortcomings.

'We've beaten it, then,' Esera said. 'We've beaten the curse.'

'We've made a start,' he agreed, 'but that's all. What's happened here is wonderful, but it's hardly a long-term solution. Asking every pregnant woman to spend nine months in the hospice is going to put them and their families under a lot of strain. That's if there *are* any more pregnancies. This won't have done anything to help those women who have become barren. You can't *all* go and live over the water.' He fell silent then, hating the effect his words had had on Esera. She'd been bubbling over with excitement and happiness, but now looked solemn and downcast.

'I'm already beginning to feel like I'm in prison,' she admitted. 'All the others will be able to go home soon, but I've got ages to go. And even when my baby's born, I'll still have to stay out here, won't I?'

'Probably.' He had told Parina to stay in the hospice for a while before venturing ashore with her baby. He wanted to be sure that the child had at least begun to trust his own senses – rather than the feelings induced by the curse – before he returned to the land. 'But things *are* going to get better,' Terrel added. 'You know Hellin's already planning either to extend the hospice, or maybe even build another one. Either way, you'll all have more space at least.'

'That would be good,' she replied, nodding. 'We're a bit on top of each other at the moment. I mean, I like them, but we're all different. And now the baby's here, its crying's probably going to keep us awake.' She paused. 'At least he *is* crying. The last few didn't even have the strength to do that.'

'There are other possibilities too,' Terrel said, returning to the problem of Esera's restricted life. 'As long as you stay on the water, you'll be fine. You could go swimming, if you like. Or you could offer to help the fishermen. It would be a change for you, at least.'

'I might just try that,' she said, smiling.

'And there's a good chance you'll be able to go ashore occasionally,' he went on. 'Parina spent the majority of her pregnancy on land, and yet her baby recovered after just a few days on the water. Yours will certainly be better off than that. You just have to be careful.' The unborn babies had all been improving constantly during their time afloat.

'I'm not sure I'd want to risk anything unless you were here to check on the baby,' Esera said. 'And you won't be, will you?'

'I'll be here for a while yet,' he replied awkwardly.

'Will you come back?' she asked quietly. 'When you've kept your promise?'

'I'd like to, but it may not be possible.'

'I wouldn't want you to make a promise you couldn't keep.' She had seen the shadow that passed over Terrel's face when he thought about the future – but she also knew that he wouldn't tell her what was weighing on him so heavily.

'What I have to do when I leave here,' he began, confounding her assumption, 'may . . . may give me a chance to lift the curse completely.'

'Really?' she exclaimed, her astonishment plain.

'I'm going to do everything in my power to do just that.'

Esera did not know how to respond to this. Although she knew Terrel was serious, she didn't understand how he could make such a claim.

'Don't mention this to anyone else, will you?' he added. 'I just wanted you to know, that's all.'

'Are you going to see the sharaken?' she guessed.

'No. This is something else altogether.'

'But you could, couldn't you? You could be the new advocate.' The idea obviously appealed to her.

'Isn't being the Messenger enough?' he asked, with a hopeful grin.

'What's the matter? Don't you like titles?'

'Not much.'

They sat in silence for a while, looking out over the water from their usual spot on the platform.

'How will we know?' Esera said eventually. 'When you lift the curse, I mean. How will we know when it's happened?'

'You'll know,' Terrel replied. 'I'll find some way of telling you.'

Parina's baby, who had been named Nieto, made his first trip onto solid ground when he was twelve days old. Safe in his mother's arms, he was blissfully unaware that he was the focus of a huge amount of interest. Everyone wanted to see this child, the first to defy the curse and, in doing so, restore all their hopes for the future. Terrel went with them, occasionally monitoring the infant's dreams. Although he caught glimpses of doubt and fear as the forces that had tormented the baby for so long were reinstated, they were soon overridden by other, more direct sensations, and Terrel was confident that the infant would come to no harm. Even so, he suggested that Parina take her son back to the hospice after a few hours.

For Terrel, this had been the last big test, and he believed now that he would be free to leave whenever he wanted. Everything at the hospice continued to go well. There had been no signs of 'the darkness' since that first night and, far from going mad or dying, all those who had spent their nights outside the day-stone circle were prospering, so it looked as if his temporary solution was working as well as he could have hoped. However, the decision to leave was never going to be an easy one now.

He was pondering his options over his evening meal that day when Brin bounced into the hut, doing a kind of manic dance.

'I'm not the youngest any more!' he chanted happily as he bounded around the room. 'I'm not the youngest any more!'

Imana, who was also sitting at the table, looked stern, but Terrel smiled and shook his head, cutting off her rebuke. He could understand the little boy's elation and relief, and didn't want his sister to curb his high spirits.

Brin made a second circuit of the room, repeating his joyful refrain, then hopped out of the door and disappeared.

'I'm sorry about that,' Imana said, although even she was smiling now. 'He's hopeless at the moment.'

'I'd be excited if I was in his shoes,' Terrel replied. 'It can't have been easy for him.'

'I suppose not.'

Terrel had gone back to sleeping at the guest hut again several days earlier, in order to give the women a little more space. The hospice was now more homely and comfortable, with various alterations and additions having been made for the benefit of the residents. Esera had taken Terrel's advice and had been out with some of the fishermen, and she'd gone swimming most days too. None of the others had joined her so far, although they had looked on enviously at times. The overall atmosphere was much more relaxed, so Terrel's presence at night was no longer required. He'd been glad to return to the village.

His next visitor made a rather more dignified entrance than Brin had done.

'May I talk with you, Terrel?' Amie asked.

'Of course. Come in.'

'Shall I go?' Imana asked the elder, who looked at Terrel.

'Stay if you want,' he told the girl. 'I don't suppose we're going to be talking about anything secret.'

Amie nodded curtly, her expression betraying little.

'I'll come straight to the point,' she said. 'Some time ago you offered to be the next advocate. I'd like to accept your offer, if it still stands.'

Terrel stared at her in consternation.

'We're all enormously grateful for what you've done here,' she went on. 'The Messenger's work is done, but we both know this is only a temporary solution to our problems. The elders have agreed that our best chance of something more permanent is to appeal to the sharaken – and as you pointed out, you have a much better chance of reaching them than any of us. Will you do us this one last service?'

For a few moments no one said anything. For his own part Terrel didn't know *what* to say, and it was Imana who eventually broke the silence.

'Of course!' she exclaimed. 'You can travel in the burning lands. You have to leave soon anyway, so you can go to the sharaken on your way to Tala . . . Tala . . .'

'Talazoria,' Terrel said heavily.

'Yes. It's perfect!'

Throughout this exchange Amie had remained silent, watching the boy's face. Her own expression was calm, as always. Unlike Imana, she was not given to excessive displays of enthusiasm, but Terrel could nonetheless sense the hope behind her deceptively placid coun-tenance.

'You will do it, won't you?' Imana said, sensing his doubt for the first time.

'When would you want me to leave?' he asked.

'Well,' Amie replied, 'Jenna's baby is due any day now, and I think we'd all be happier if you stayed to see it born safely. After that it would be up to you. What do you say?'

'All right,' Terrel said. 'I'll do it.'

*

Jenna's baby, a girl, was born two days later. Once more everything went well, and this time Terrel managed to remain conscious – though he still found the whole procedure faintly repulsive. The baby howled from the moment she took her first breath, which made the midwives happy. However, a little while later the child – and everyone else – fell silent as a deep rumbling sound reached their ears. Then, in response to an exclamation from Esera, everyone turned to look out of the open doorway.

The water on either side of the walkway was dancing.

'Earthquake,' someone breathed.

As the hospice began to rock gently, Terrel and Amie glanced at each other across the room. All but forgotten in the excitements of the day was the fact that this was the time when both the Amber and White Moons were full, the day which had almost matched Terrel's dream.

A million tiny fountains rose and fell upon the surface of the lake. The walkway writhed like a living creature and almost buckled at one point, and beyond that the land trembled and groaned.

The tremor lasted only a short time, and did no great damage, but in Terrel's dream the valley had survived Macul's catastrophe. Although there was no way of telling what had happened in the outside world, Terrel knew he had to find out.

It was time to go.

In the end, finding his way out of the valley proved to be much simpler than Terrel had anticipated. He was able to follow the trail through the cloud layer easily enough, even when the fog was at its thickest. It made

him wonder whether he really would have been prevented from leaving before – or whether it had been
something he'd unconsciously decided for himself
because he'd known it was the right thing to do. Either
way, as the seemingly eternal grey relented, growing
steadily brighter as he walked on and up, he could not
wait to see the sky again.

When at last Terrel emerged into the outside world,
the daylight was glorious, but almost blinding, so that
he was forced to squint and shade his eyes. The sun's
heat was like a furnace, and the dry air seemed super-
naturally clear, so that the views to the distant mountains and along the steep-sided valley ahead of him were
breathtaking. It all presented such an incredible
contrast to the valley that he found he had to rest
frequently, and by the end of a day of only sporadic
progress he was thankful for the coming of nightfall.
He walked on for a while, finding even the moonlight
bright enough for his needs, before weariness forced
him to stop and set up camp. Even then he found it
hard to get to sleep. He had hoped to find Alyssa and
the ghosts waiting for him as he left the valley, but
there had been no sign of them so far. Now that he had
set out along the unknown road once more, he would
have welcomed their advice – but took comfort from
one piece of knowledge he had learnt for himself. It
had been immediately obvious that the earthquake of
his dream had not taken place. Yet.

Now, two days and a handful of miles later, as the
familiar aches and pains of a traveller's life were
reasserting themselves, his advisors still had not made
an appearance. He had met other travellers, who had

directed his steps so far, but he knew that the really crucial decisions were still ahead of him.

In the meantime, there had been plenty to occupy his mind. His latest round of farewells had been difficult. Although he'd known that he had to go – that he *wanted* to go – this had not made the partings any easier. Imana, Amie and especially Esera had become his friends, but the emotional attachment to the valley went beyond that in a way he didn't fully understand. Although he had only been there for just over a long month, and was departing of his own free will and as a hero, he could not escape the feeling that he was leaving unfinished business behind. He could rationalize this to a certain extent, of course. He was still hoping to be able to find a way of lifting the curse completely, and as their advocate – his status as such had been confirmed in a brief formal ceremony in the village – he carried with him their hopes for the future, but that still didn't explain his vague sense that there was something else he should have done.

He was also puzzled by the surprising fact that he'd received no internal warning of the recent earthquake. Was that because he had been over the water? Because he'd been concentrating on Jenna's confinement to the exclusion of everything else? Or was his talent fading as his healing skills developed? The only way to find out was to wait for another tremor – and Terrel was in no hurry for that to happen.

However, the question that had dominated his thoughts was a simple one – in theory, at least – and as he came to the spot where the trail he was following divided, his dilemma had become straightforward. Until that moment he'd been able to tell himself that there was still time, that the decision would be made for him by circumstance, that someone or something would give destiny a nudge in the right direction. Now, as he had known it would be all along, it was up to him. If he turned left, a well-defined track ran along the side of the precipitous river valley and once he had negotiated that, according to the advice he had been given, the route to Talazoria would be obvious. If he turned right, a path led up into a high pass, and thence into the mountains and the remote domain of the sharaken.

Terrel had been free to leave the valley – indeed he had gone with the people's blessing – but the manner of his departure carried with it an obligation to fulfil his duties as their advocate. Yet going into the mountains would make his journey longer and possibly more hazardous. It would certainly delay his return to the coast, which would mean having to abandon any chance of returning to the islands that year. And the longer he spent getting to Talazoria, the closer he came to the time of Macul's destruction. The earthquake was now only four months away, and Terrel had no idea how long the detour would take. He had responsibilities to an earlier promise, an earlier bargain. All the people of Fenduca, all the sleepers, indeed – unknowingly – all the citizens of both Macul and his homeland, were depending upon him. Shouldn't that commitment take precedence over his more recent undertaking?

Balanced against that was the hope that the sharaken might be willing to help the valley, and possibly even aid Terrel in his own quest. However, based on his only previous encounter with one of the mystics, Terrel was doubtful about either their willingness or their ability to do any such thing. Even if he was able to locate one of their fabled mountaintop palaces, it might well turn out to be a complete waste of his time and effort. There was a good case to be made for the argument that he would better serve the people of the valley by going directly to Talazoria.

But logic was not everything. And a promise was a promise.

The choice Terrel had to make now was whether to follow his head or his heart.

CHAPTER THIRTY-SEVEN

Until the fox arrived, Terrel had been able to convince himself that he'd made the right decision.

By then the brown hills, with their patches of scrub and cypress trees, had given way to steeper crags and pine woods. There had even been a few isolated vineyards on the lower slopes, the last sign of human influence on the landscape, but beyond that, beyond the last of the trees, the land was almost entirely barren and almost certainly uninhabited. Bare rock in varying shades of orange, white and ochre – all of them dulled by the ever-present dust – stretched out around him, turning to a uniform grey in the distance in the haze of the day and to shades of purple as night drew in. The trail was no more than an inter-mittent goat track here, broken in places by deep gullies of tumbled stones which were dry now but which must have been formed by winter torrents. Each ridge the boy crossed was higher than the last, the terrain gradually became more bleak and, despite the almost constant sunshine, the air grew colder. In the far distance, Terrel caught glimpses of vast white peaks, hanging frozen in the sky like glittering waves. Gazing at them in awe, he found it almost impossible to believe that they were so high that they were covered in snow even in late summer.

Terrel hadn't seen another human being for two days now. Indeed, he had hardly seen another living creature – just a few fast-moving lizards and the occasional bird wheeling in the sky far above. And yet it was here, according to all his informants, that the sharaken had chosen to reside. It was easy to see why the previous advocates had failed in their missions. This arid, sun-scorched region would be deadly to the people of the valley in summer, and winter would have brought intense cold as well as making any journey increasingly hazardous. As it was, Terrel was hoping that he would reach his destination soon, before his own strength – and his supplies – ran out.

His decision to make his way up into the mountains had been swayed by the memory of Aryel's advice to her son. He had followed his heart – and could only hope that he would have no regrets about doing so. And although he longed for the comfort of their company, the fact that Alyssa and the ghosts had still not appeared convinced him that he was on the right path. The alternative explanation – that they were now unable or unwilling to come to him – was simply too appalling to contemplate.

The fox, which came trotting out of a ravine at the side of the trail, looked quite out of place. Its fur was pure white, contrasting starkly with the dusty landscape. Terrel knew immediately that it was Alyssa, but his delight was dashed by her first words.

What are you doing here? she asked as she fell into step beside him. *You should be in Talazoria by now.*

I'm going to ask the sharaken for help. As he explained his promise to the people of the valley, Alyssa listened without interrupting. *Coming this way felt like the right thing to do,* he concluded, *and there's still plenty of time for me to get to Talazoria.*

So you got Elam's message, then? she asked.

Yes.

That's good. Muzeni and Shahan weren't sure it would work.

Where are *the others?*

They'll be here when the road next turns.

You mean it hasn't turned in all this time? Terrel exclaimed.

Only when we sent you the message.

So you knew that going to the valley was right, and that I had to help them. But what about afterwards? If I wasn't supposed to come up here, why didn't you stop me?

Why would a hero choose evil? she quoted.

I'm not a hero, he muttered. *And I never wanted to be.*

You are who you are, she replied. *Your choices are your own.*

Terrel was irritated by her evasiveness. She must surely have some opinions of her own. Neither she nor the ghosts had ever had a problem giving him advice in the past – so why was it all being placed on his shoulders now?

Many ghosts can't return to this world, she told him. *Most don't even want to. Even those who do aren't able to* all the time.

Terrel wasn't sure why she had chosen this moment to tell him something he already knew.

But it's been so long, he complained. *And they have you to guide them, don't they?*

We all follow our own instincts, Alyssa replied – and that, Terrel knew, was the only explanation he was going to get.

After a while they stopped to rest. They had reached the top of a ridge from where, to his great relief, Terrel was able to look ahead and see the landmark he'd been told to aim for.

Not far now, he said, as he took the last of his food from his pack.

How do you know?

See that spur over there? he replied, pointing. *The one with the rock shaped like an anvil? As soon as we pass that we should be able to see their palace.*

And then what?

I told you. I'm going to ask for their help. He cut a chunk from a loaf of hard bread with his knife. *Do you want anything to eat?*

No.

As Terrel chewed slowly, and drank a small amount of water from his dwindling reserve, he saw the ring, twisted round the tip of one of the fox's ears.

It's good to talk to you again, he said, reaching out and fondling the soft fur on her neck.

Alyssa gave him a warning glance.

Careful, she said. *I have fleas.*

As soon as they reached the top of the anvil ridge, the two friends were able to see the sharaken's refuge. From a distance it resembled a fortress rather than the palace Aylen had described. It sat upon a dusty mountaintop, and its massive walls were built of huge blocks of dull orange-coloured stone. Four squat towers were set at regular intervals around the walls, and each tower was topped by a curiously shaped roof. Terrel couldn't see any doors or windows in the forbidding facade, and he began to feel distinctly apprehensive about simply marching up to the castle and demanding entrance.

There are dreams here, Alyssa remarked. *Dreams inside the stone.*

That's what the sharaken do, Terrel explained. *They trade in dreams.*

And not reality.

Terrel took a few moments to work out what she might be implying.

You think this place isn't real? he asked.

It's real, she replied. *It's just not as it appears to be.*

What does that mean? Is it an illusion?

The moons rule everything here, she said, adding to his confusion. *Inside the circle.*

What circle?

They have their own form of the day-stone ring. Look.

Terrel looked, and on the far slope of the valley that separated their position from the fortress, he saw a line of paler colour. Although they were too far away to tell what it might be, it was clearly not a natural part of the landscape. The line stretched across all of the peak that was visible, and Terrel had no reason to doubt Alyssa's implication that it completely encircled the upper part of the mountain.

Do you know what it is?

A warning and a boundary, she replied. *Be careful when you cross it, Terrel.*

When I cross it? he asked, in sudden panic. *Aren't you coming with me?*

I'm not the advocate, she said. *I'll have to find my own way across.*

With that, ignoring Terrel's silent plea, she ran off along the ridge and soon vanished from sight.

Knowing that the sharaken's domain was protected by a warning circle did nothing to calm Terrel's nerves – especially now that he was alone again – but once he was close enough to see what it was, he became more puzzled than afraid. This ring, like the day-stones, presented no physical barrier to his progress. It was made up of endless ranks of prayer-flags. They were packed tightly in places, but elsewhere the gaps between the tall poles were wide enough for him to walk through easily. The printed banners were of all shapes and sizes, and although most of the material had been bleached by sun and rain, it was still possible to see that they had once been dyed in a variety of bright colours. The flags snapped and fluttered like loose sails in a strong breeze, the wind carrying their messages up into the infinite sky.

It was only when Terrel was almost upon this strange boundary that he saw the skeleton that lay sprawled on the bare earth only a few paces from the nearest flags. All the flesh was long gone and only a few strands of cloth remained, clinging to bones that had been bleached by the elements. Terrel's immediate response to this macabre sight was to wonder if it had been one of the earlier advocates. If so, it seemed particularly cruel that, having come so far, the man had perished in sight of his goal. Had he simply run out of strength, succumbing to cold, heat or thirst, or had his end been more sinister? It seemed unlikely that he would have died so close to the castle if he had gained an audience with the sharaken and was on his way home. So did that mean he'd been refused entry? Had he been repelled by force? There were no obvious signs of violence, but with such pitiful remains – and after such a long time in the open – that meant little. The only other skeleton Terrel had ever seen had been Muzeni's, and he'd been able to tell that the old heretic had died peacefully, smoking the pipe that the boy still carried in his pack, but there was no way of knowing how this man had met his end.

Of course, it was possible that it wasn't one of the advocates at all. Perhaps none of them had ever made it this far, and the bones belonged to another unlucky pilgrim. In any case, Terrel would never know what had brought the traveller to this lonely place, and even if he had, it would have made no difference to his own situation. He had no choice but to go on now.

He turned back to the prayer-flags, and saw that set amongst them were other, much shorter poles, embedded in the ground. These bore no messages, but were so beautifully and intricately carved that he was immediately intrigued. Drawn to one decorated with the shapes of a hundred tiny flowers, he stretched out a hand to touch the delicate wooden petals, only to shout aloud and jump back as a searing pain flashed through his arm. It felt as if his entire limb had been plunged into a fire.

Breathless with shock, Terrel could only stare at the innocent-looking carving as the agony subsided to a dull ache. By the time he could move his fingers again without wincing, he had realized what Alyssa had meant.

A warning and a boundary. This was another test. And if he was to have any hope of completing his quest, it was one he could not afford to fail. *Be careful* . . . Stepping forward again, he took a deep breath and then deliberately grasped the handle, enduring the burst of pain as best he could. This time he'd known what to expect, and so was able to deal with it more effectively, but he still gasped as the flames shot through his entire body. He was blind and deaf, but he clung on, refusing to let go. Eventually, after what seemed like an eternity, his torment suddenly stopped.

'Tell us why you are here.'

The voice seemed to come from far away, but Terrel heard it clearly. His determination had made them notice him at least.

'I come in search of help,' he replied, speaking aloud even though he was reasonably certain that mere thought would have sufficed. 'For myself and for the valley beneath the cloud.'

There was a pause while his answer was apparently weighed in the balance.

'This is a sacred realm,' the voice intoned solemnly. 'Do you swear to respect its covenants and obey its laws?'

'I do.'

'Release the message-handle now,' the voice instructed him. 'Complete your journey. The circle is open.'

He had passed the test.

Having threaded his way through the forest of prayer-flags, Terrel looked up the slope to the fortress and wondered what awaited him there after such an introduction. The final climb was steep, over bare rock and patches of scree, and he spent most of his time looking down at the ground, afraid of losing his footing. Any accident now and he would probably end up as the next forgotten skeleton on the mountainside. However, when he finally got the chance to look ahead, the castle walls looked even more imposing than before. What was more, he could still see no sign of an entrance. He groaned at the thought of having to scramble round to the far side in order to find the way in.

When he eventually reached the foot of the ramparts, he was sweating from the exertion of the climb, but the wind was much stronger now and it was bitterly cold. The boy shivered, the dampness on his skin suddenly feeling like a film of ice, and glanced around for any clue as to what he should do next. The nearest tower was about a hundred paces away to his right, and he was about to head towards it when a sound behind him made him look back.

Set in a shadowed recess in the wall, the two halves of a huge, semi-circular door were swinging back, apparently of their own accord. Too stunned to question the advisability of his actions, Terrel hurried towards the opening, seeing only a dark tunnel on the other side. A gust of warm air blew out, fragrant with the scents of herbs and flowers, as if to welcome him.

He stepped forward, wondering what kind of dream he was entering, and passed through a gateway that, only a few moments ago, he would have sworn did not exist.

CHAPTER THIRTY-EIGHT

The curving walls and roof of the tunnel were made of solid rock and, having committed himself, Terrel had nowhere to go but straight ahead. At first there was nothing but darkness ahead of him, but then a second pair of doors opened at the far end. They were perhaps forty paces away, which meant that the castle walls were massively thick. When Terrel was halfway through the tunnel, a dull reverberating thud behind him prompted him to look round. The outer doors had closed, once more apparently moving of their own accord. He went on, and came out through an archway into the sunlight again. The courtyard in which he now stood was empty and absolutely silent. Even the air here was still, the bitter mountain wind no more than a memory. Heady scents filled the boy's nostrils, even though he couldn't see any plants or flowers. There were several doors and passages leading from the inner walls of the yard, but – having no idea which of these he should choose – Terrel decided to wait where he was. He could see several parts of the internal structure of the castle now, and knew that it would be easy to get lost in what was obviously a many-layered labyrinth.

His patience was finally rewarded when one of the doors opened and a man peered out at him. He was shaven-headed and barefoot, and was dressed in a plain brown robe tied at the waist with a length of rope. Terrel was about to speak when the man beckoned and turned back the way he'd come, leaving the door ajar. Unnerved by his surroundings, Terrel silently followed his guide, wondering if this was a sharakan or merely one of their acolytes. They made their way along numerous passages and cloisters, crossed two more courtyards and climbed three different flights of stairs before eventually reaching their destination. The robed man opened a door and, still without saying a word, ushered Terrel inside.

Sunlight slanted in from high windows, showing an austere chamber that contained no furniture or decoration of any kind. Sitting cross-legged on the bare stone floor was an old man. He too was shaven-headed and dressed in a drab robe, but his expression was serene, and he had about him an unmistakable air of calm authority. Terrel guessed that this must be one of the sharaken's leaders, and wondered what he had done to warrant such a reception. This man displayed none of the high-handedness of the Collector who had come to Fenduca, and the boy's hopes rose a little. However, lying on the floor in front of the sharakan was a staff that looked uncomfortably like the message-handle on the mountainside that had been the source of so much pain.

His host made an open-handed gesture, indicating that Terrel should also sit down and he did so, not wanting to break the silence, but wishing that the old man would say something. He got his wish a moment later, but he was taken aback by the sharakan's words.

'I've asked for refreshment to be brought for you, but I assume your companions will make their own arrangements.'

Terrel glanced round – and saw the three ghosts standing behind him. So the road is turning, he thought. He was not really surprised that they had followed him here, though he couldn't help wondering where Alyssa was. But the truly remarkable thing was that the sharakan could see them too – and had taken their arrival in his stride.

'Yes,' Terrel replied simply. 'Thank you.'

The old man resumed his quiet contemplation, and even though he was bursting with questions, Terrel realized that certain formalities had to be observed, so he just sat and waited. His guide returned, bearing a wooden platter that held flat bread, cheese and a variety of fruit, plus a pitcher of water. While the chamber door was open, the white fox trotted in and sat on its haunches next to Terrel.

'Good,' the sharakan remarked. 'Now we're all here.'

How did you get in? Terrel asked silently.

Any palace has many entrances, Alyssa replied.

'The snow fox is a harbinger of good fortune,' the sharakan said. 'Such a creature will always find one of our entrances open, no matter what spirit rides in her.'

Terrel glanced at the old man in alarm. It seemed

there would be no point in trying to keep their secrets from him.

'You hear psinoma?' he asked.

'I am not familiar with that term, but I have studied the ways of thought. I can hear what is needful when the occasion demands it. However, among the sharaken it is considered impolite. We prize open communication.'

Terrel accepted the mild rebuke, but sought to justify his actions.

'My companions understand me when I speak aloud,' he explained, 'but they can only speak to me in thought. May they continue to do so?'

'If they will permit me to listen also.'

'Of course,' Terrel agreed readily, glancing round at the ghosts.

We would count it an honour, Muzeni said, with a small bow.

The sharakan nodded in acknowledgement.

'My name is Terrel.' The boy went on to introduce each of his friends in turn, then looked back at the old man expectantly. When there was no response, he asked, 'What should we call you?'

'My name is changing,' the sharakan replied mysteriously. 'It would probably be best if you think of me as Reader.'

Terrel nodded, and took a deep breath.

'I have two reasons for coming here,' he began.

'Not yet,' Reader decreed, holding up a hand. 'Eat first. Then we may talk.'

The boy's impatience almost got the better of his good sense, but he realized in time that the courtesies of hospitality had to be respected. He had sworn as much when he'd been granted entry. He began to eat, intending only to have a mouthful or two, but the food was delicious – better than anything he'd eaten in a very long time – and he found that he was ravenously hungry. As a result he all but cleared the platter, and felt much better for the meal. While he ate, the fox lay down, her nose between her forepaws, and appeared to go to sleep. The ghosts merely waited, displaying uncharacteristic stoicism at the delay. It was only as Terrel finished that any of them risked making a comment.

I think eating's one of the few things I miss, Elam remarked. *That looked good.*

To Terrel's surprise, Reader laughed.

'Food is strength,' the sharakan said, 'but it can be pleasure too.' He leant forward, picked up the carved staff and held it upright in his left hand, the bottom end resting on the floor. 'It is time,' he said, his expression serious now. 'Tell us of your two reasons, Terrel.'

'The first concerns the valley beneath the cloud that I mentioned before,' the boy began, assuming that Reader would be aware of his request outside the fortress. 'I was chosen to represent them, to ask for your help. I am the fourth advocate to attempt the journey. Did any of the others get this far?'

'No. Visitors here are rare. Not many come, and of those that do, few are judged worthy.'

Terrel had the impression that he was supposed to be grateful or proud – or perhaps both – to have been granted such a privilege. He was neither. If anything, his earlier dealings with the Collector and the ordeal of the prayer-flag ring had made him feel resentful, but the dignified presence and impressive demeanour of Reader were beginning to change that. It was possible that the sharaken were honourable men after all – which meant that he might have a chance of persuading them to aid his causes. However, he still owed it to the people of the valley to try to find out what had happened to their previous advocates.

'What happens to those who are not found worthy?' he asked, thinking of the skeleton outside.

'That is not our concern,' Reader answered, and for the first time Terrel heard a touch of the Collector's arrogance in the old man's tone. 'What is it the people of this place want? Do they wish us to take away the cloud?'

'No! That would kill them. But there are dark spirits there who turn their village into a prison at night. They say—'

'That we are responsible for these spirits,' Reader completed for him. 'Regrettably, that is true. Many generations ago, our trading released powers into this world that do not belong here. We chose to confine them to the valley rather than allowing them to roam free throughout the land. At the time it was thought that the place was uninhabited.'

'If your trading released them, couldn't it return them to their own world?'

'Alas, it is not as simple as that. Even if we had the strength to attempt such a feat, the darkness is now inextricably linked to the cloud. We could do nothing about one without affecting the other. Besides, this is ancient history, and your people seem to have adapted well enough to the presence of the spirits. I think it best for all concerned if we leave the situation as it is.'

Terrel had reached the same conclusion, and knew it was time to move on.

'The valley has a second, more serious problem,' he said. 'One that is recent in origin. There is a kind of force, some would call it a curse, seeping up from the ground below them.'

'That is not of our doing,' Reader stated.

'I realize that, but is there nothing you can do to help remove it?'

'A curse can only be removed by the one who placed it. Do you know who that was?'

'I can't be completely certain,' Terrel replied, 'but I believe I do. There is a strange creature which is now in Talazoria—'

'Anatek-Vori,' Reader cut in. 'The rock that walks.'

'You know about it?' Terrel exclaimed in astonishment.

'The White Moon brings us news of far places,' the sharakan told him. 'In her light, our dreams range far and wide. How is it that *you* know of this creature?'

Terrel did his best to explain, describing his encounter with the elemental on Vadanis as well as telling the sharakan everything that had happened since he'd arrived in Macul. It took a long time to tell the whole tale, but Reader rarely interrupted, and listened with unwavering concentration. The only times he asked for any further information was when Terrel related the images from his dreams and the conclusions he'd drawn from them. At the old man's insistence, the boy described each dream in as much detail as he could remember, but when he asked the sharakan if he agreed with his interpretations, Reader's answers were vague and noncommittal. Throughout his recitation, Terrel glanced at Alyssa and the ghosts every so often, to see whether they wanted to add anything to his narrative, but they left it to him. When he finally reached the end of his story, he waited for Reader to respond, but the sharakan's only reaction was to lay down his staff and then to become very still. The silence stretched until Terrel was almost at breaking point, and he was about to speak again when his host belatedly gave his verdict.

'It seems to me that your two tasks are one and the same. If you are indeed destined to prevent this elemental from destroying all of Macul, you should have no difficulty in persuading it to lift the curse on the valley.'

That made a great deal of sense, but Terrel began to wonder whether Reader had actually believed everything he had heard. That 'if' spoke of some doubts.

'Will you help me?' the boy asked.

'We have all heard,' the sharakan said, in a flat tone devoid of any emotion – and Terrel knew this was the only answer he was going to get.

With that, Reader closed his eyes – and all the other questions Terrel had wanted to ask flew from his mind. The old man's eyelids were tattooed with images of the real eyes beneath, and the effect was startling. The implication was that even when his eyes were closed – even when he was asleep or even dreaming – the sharakan still watched everything about him.

The door behind Terrel opened and his guide re-appeared, beckoning for the boy to follow him. Terrel picked up his pack, and as he left the room, he could feel the gaze of those painted eyes on his back. At the same time the ghosts vanished, but the white fox padded softly at Terrel's heels until they reached what were evidently the guest quarters.

I hate to say this, Elam commented, *but that guy was really spooky. Those eyes . . .* He shuddered theatrically.

I know what you mean, Terrel said.

The ghosts had reappeared as soon as Terrel and Alyssa had been left alone in the chamber assigned to them. The room was small, and the only illumination came from a barred window above head height and two skylights in the ceiling. Although this made it seem unpleasantly like a prison cell, the door had been left open and the bed was comfortable. There was also a table and stool in one corner, and a rug had been provided for the fox to lie on.

He didn't even blink! Elam added. *Not once in all the time we were there. That's not natural.*

At least he was prepared to give you a fair hearing, Shahan remarked.

Unlike the one who came to Fenduca, Muzeni said, nodding.

You were all very quiet in there, Terrel said. *Did I explain everything properly?*

You're the only one who knew the whole story, the heretic replied.

And we're not used to people being able to see us, Elam added. *It cramps our style.*

You did an excellent job, Shahan reassured Terrel.

Good enough to persuade them to help me?

I don't see why not, Muzeni replied. *If this earthquake hits, it will affect them as much as anyone else in Macul.*

Unless they have some way of protecting themselves, Terrel said. *We don't know how powerful their dream-trading can be.*

I doubt even their sorcery could compete with the sheer power of an earthquake, Shahan argued. *Defending themselves against that would hardly be as easy as creating a few illusions.*

Like the tunnel I came through?

The tunnel was always there, the seer answered. *The illusion was in making you think it wasn't.*

That's what I meant, Terrel said crossly. *I'm not completely stupid, you know.*

Even if they could keep this place safe from the quake, Elam said, *surely they'd want to save the rest of Macul too?*

You would certainly think so, Muzeni offered, *but I don't believe it's as simple as that. They don't appear to be a particularly benevolent group.*

Their social awareness does seem somewhat limited, Shahan commented sardonically.

The real question is, do we really want *their help?* Alyssa said.

As usual, her first contribution to the debate made them all look at her.

Why shouldn't we? Terrel asked. *I'll take all the help I can get.*

All magic comes at a price, she replied. *And you didn't need help in Betancuria, did you?*

I don't know what obstacles I'm going to have to overcome in Talazoria. I might not even be able to get anywhere near the elemental. But if some of the sharaken were with me, surely even the king's forces would have to take notice of them.

You think they'll travel with you? Elam queried. *They don't seem to get out much.*

I don't see how else they're supposed to help me.

Well, I don't think there's anything you can do about it tonight, Shahan said. *It's my guess that Reader is considering what you told him. Judging your case, so to speak.*

He said 'we have all heard', Terrel pointed out. *What do you think he meant by that?*

There was something odd about the staff he was holding, Elam said thoughtfully.

I had to use something like that when I was asking to be let inside, Terrel said. *I had a conversation with someone I couldn't even see. They call them message-handles.*

I think that although Reader was there with you, all the other sharaken were listening, Muzeni hazarded.

Terrel was glad he hadn't known that at the time. The interview had been daunting enough when he'd thought he was speaking to only one of the sharaken.

So they're all *judging me?*

You think they'll give him a fair trial? Elam asked. He had his own memories of legally sanctioned injustice.

We have no way of knowing, Shahan replied.

What do you think he meant when he said his name was changing? Terrel asked, not wanting to dwell on the outcome of any trial.

The moons rule everything here, Alyssa said.

Even their names? Elam looked incredulous. *That must get a bit confusing.*

The White Moon is new tonight, she replied, as though this explained everything.

So no news from afar, but a change of name? Elam

guessed. *And I thought* we *were the ones who came from a madhouse.*

I wonder what else changes whenever there's a new phase of one of the moons, Shahan said curiously.

And what are they making of the behaviour of the Dark Moon? Muzeni added.

Maybe we do, Alyssa said.

What? Terrel said, thrown by this apparently unconnected remark.

Have a way of knowing, she explained. *I can see their dreams. That's how they work, isn't it?*

They judge us by what they dream? Elam queried.

'*A path guided by the dreams of many*', Muzeni quoted. *Perhaps that didn't refer to the villagers in Fenduca after all.*

We're on *a mountaintop here, not next to one,* Shahan added.

I suppose all we can do is wait till tomorrow morning, Terrel decided, then glanced at the snow fox. *I don't think spying on them while they sleep would be a good idea. You don't even know your way around the castle.*

I know what's real, she commented.

Unlike me?

Alyssa did not reply.

Am I just seeing what they want me to see? Terrel persisted. *What would be the point of that?*

There are things here . . . Muzeni began, then fell silent as the fox gave a warning growl.

I preferred you as a bird, Elam told her. *Those teeth look altogether too sharp.*

I'd bite you if I thought you'd feel anything, Alyssa informed him.

I think it might be time for us to go, he responded. *Goodbye, Terrel. I don't think we'll be away quite as long this time.*

Make sure you're not.

The ghosts vanished, but not before Elam had made one last parting comment.

Be careful what you dream about tonight, he advised. *Alyssa may not be the only one who can see them here.*

CHAPTER THIRTY-NINE

You didn't tell me you'd fallen in love with her, Alyssa said accusingly.

Terrel had struggled into wakefulness to find the snow fox staring intently at the air above his head.

'What?' he mumbled. 'Who?'

Esera.

I didn't, he protested. *She was my friend, that's all.*

Do you always . . . Alyssa began, then obviously decided not to pursue the point. *Is that all you dreamt about?*

No. Far from it, Terrel replied. Reliving the time when he'd comforted the pregnant girl as they looked out over the lake had been only the last, inconsequential part of what had been a busy night. He was horrified by the fact that it had apparently aroused Alyssa's jealousy.

Then why is that all I can see? Alyssa asked.

I don't know. I woke up several times during the night. Maybe all the other dreams blew away then. At first he had not been sure what kept disturbing his sleep, but later in the night he'd heard noises coming from other parts of the huge castle. Bells had rung, and there had been the unnerving sound of clashing metal. It had almost sounded as if there was a battle going on. On each occasion, Terrel had expected voices to be raised in alarm, but instead the silence had been restored immediately. Such interruptions had not made it any easier for him to rest. Elam's parting comment had made him nervous enough as it was – and now Alyssa's evident puzzlement was making matters worse.

It doesn't work like that, she said, still gazing at the space above him, as if she could rediscover the after-images of his dreams by sheer force of will. *Why can't I see?* She was beginning to sound distressed. *What are you hiding from me?*

Nothing! Terrel exclaimed, upset himself now. *I wouldn't even know how. I—*

The fox looked down then, so that their eyes met for the first time, and Terrel knew they had both just reached the same conclusion.

They were *there*, Alyssa said. *But they vanished as soon as they appeared. The sharaken have stolen them.*

'It is our way,' Reader said. 'We can learn a great deal about someone from their dreams.'

'You don't consider such things private?' Terrel asked.

'Do you?'

'Yes.'

'And yet you allow Alyssa to look at them.'

'She's my friend. I have nothing to hide from her.'

'So you have something to hide from us?'

'That's not what I meant,' Terrel objected. He was

getting flustered now, and found it hard to express himself clearly. Everything in his current situation seemed to be set against him. He was back in the lofty chamber where he'd first met Reader, and the sharaken's leader was as imperturbable as ever. Terrel was facing him alone, because Alyssa had gone off on an unexplained mission of her own. Even the fact that the boy was now dressed in one of the brown robes – his own dust-filled clothes had been taken away for washing – made him feel uncomfortable. The coarse material chafed against his skin.

'You agreed to abide by our laws and covenants,' the old man pointed out mildly.

'Yes,' Terrel admitted. 'I had no choice. But no one told me what they were.'

'Would you want us to help you without satisfying ourselves that your cause is just?'

'No, but—'

'Forgive me, Terrel,' the sharakan cut in, 'but all men are capable of lying for their own purposes. Dreams show us the truth.'

Put like that, Reader's argument didn't sound quite so unreasonable, and Terrel's indignation began to subside.

'So what did you learn about me?' he asked reluctantly. His own memories of what he'd dreamt about had faded somewhat, but he still had a fair idea of the main strands.

'That your dreams match your waking tale,' the old man replied, 'as far as it goes.'

'Then you believe me?' the boy suggested hopefully.

'You have shown us only the past.'

'But not the future?' Terrel was thinking back over his fragmentary night. Scenes recalling events in Betancuria, at Havenmoon, and the day when Ysatel had become a sleeper had been interspersed with a repeat of the first time he'd flown over Macul. There had been the same arrow-straight rivers, the collapsing mountains and the plague-ridden land. He'd seen the extra darkness, felt the cold fear of separation in its wandering. But there had been no earthquake, no pattern of moons in the sky.

'Prophecy is an inexact skill,' Reader commented, echoing one of the seers' axioms. 'Your vision will require further study.'

Terrel was not sure he liked the sound of that, but he couldn't blame the sharakan for his caution.

'How will you do that?' he asked.

'We'll come to that later,' the sharakan replied. 'At the moment I'm curious. Why did you choose to drive the elemental to Talazoria?'

Terrel's instinctive denial died in his throat as he saw the dream in a new light. For some reason, the elemental had come to the surface of the land, into the open. That separation had been what was wrong, the source of its fear and panic, because it had then been at the mercy of the elements, of the magic in the air. *Why* had it done that? And why, once it was exposed to the cloud and rain, had it ended up trapped in Talazoria? It could only have been a deliberate act, a wilful piece of malice – and Terrel was in no doubt that Jax had been at least partly responsible for the Ancient's fate. And yet that was not the whole story. *We make a good team, you and I*, the enchanter had said in a later vision. It seemed that, unknowingly, Terrel had played a role in creating the very problem he was attempting to resolve. What was more, he doubted that even the prince would deliber-ately set out to cause an earthquake of such catastrophic destructive potential – but that was what they had done. Together.

'I did nothing intentionally,' Terrel said. 'I . . .' He hadn't mentioned his twin in his earlier version of events, and was at a loss to explain Jax's role now.

'The canals affected its course, and the rain,' Reader said, 'but there was human intervention too – and who else is the creature likely to have listened to?' The old man had been watching Terrel closely, gauging his reaction to the earlier accusation. He'd seen the hesitation and the changing emotions that spoke of the boy's inner conflict. 'But such an act seems out of character, if I am any judge,' he concluded.

'I think I was trying to protect it,' Terrel said, 'but something went wrong.'

Reader nodded. He knew this was not the whole story, but he was prepared to leave it at that for the moment. He got to his feet and signalled for Terrel to do the same.

'Come. It's nearly time.'

Nearly time for what? Terrel wondered as he followed the sharakan out into the corridor.

The parapet of the Dark Tower afforded a breathtaking panorama of the mountainous countryside around the fortress, but once Terrel had climbed up there, he had little time to admire the view. His attention was monopolized by the extraordinary structure that had been built within the crenellated walls. It was in the shape of a dome, reminding him of Muzeni's ruined observatory, but there all resemblance ended. This hemisphere was made almost entirely of glass, held together by a shining metal framework. In Terrel's world, glass was a rare and expensive luxury, and he had never seen so much of it in one place before. Nor had he ever seen such large and flawless panes. Each fitted into its bronze frame precisely, matching the curves of its neighbours to create the impression of a single enormous piece of glass. From a distance, Terrel had taken this to be a curiously designed roof, but now he knew it was much more than that.

The panes were not clear but tinted black, darker in some places than in others. Near the base of the hemisphere were various indecipherable markings in red, white and gold, which looked as if they were actually part of the glass itself rather than painted upon it. It was an awe-inspiring piece of craftsmanship, almost a work of art, but Terrel knew that it must also serve some purpose. A quick glance at the other three towers showed him that they were adorned with similar domes, each the colour of the moon they were dedicated to, and Terrel was in no doubt that each was used in ceremonies he could only imagine.

In the bright sunlight, the reflections from the dark glass made it almost impossible to see what was inside the dome, but he detected movement and assumed that there were other sharaken within.

'How do you like our shrine?' Reader asked, smiling at the boy's wide-eyed absorption.

'It's beautiful. I've never seen anything like it.'

'Your destiny is linked to the Dark Moon. You know that, don't you?'

Although this wasn't something Terrel wanted to admit, he knew it was true. It's been changing, he thought, and so has my life.

'Shall we go inside?' Reader asked.

Terrel could only nod, wondering what he had done

to deserve such an honour. The old man rapped on the glass with his knuckles, and a moment later one of the panes swung out and up, so that they were able to duck down and step through the low doorway thus created.

There were at least a dozen sharaken within the dome, some standing, some sitting on the floor. A few of them glanced at the newcomers, regarding Terrel with open curiosity and nodding respectfully to Reader, but most seemed to be in a state of trance-like meditation and paid them no attention at all. No one spoke and, now that they were out of the wind, the silence was almost complete. Once the door was closed again, the sunlight was muted too, the sun itself no longer dazzling but a bright orange disc high in the eastern sky. Those of the sharaken who still had their eyes open glanced towards it frequently. The others remained still, watching the world through the tattoos on their eyelids.

Intimidated by the silence, Terrel glanced at Reader, wanting to ask him what was going on, only to see that his elderly companion had closed his eyes. Looking round the dome, the boy was suddenly aware that he was the only one left with his eyes open.

It begins.

The unfamiliar voice spoke inside his head without the need of sound, and Terrel knew instinctively what it was referring to. A quick glance at the sun confirmed his intuition. It was no longer a complete disc. One of the moons – Terrel was in no doubt that it was the Dark Moon – had taken a small bite out of it, a bite that was slowly growing larger.

It was not a total eclipse, like the one he had witnessed at Tindaya. Indeed, if he had not been behind the partial protection of the dome, Terrel would not have been able to follow its progress at all. As it was, it was too bright to look at for long. However, at its greatest point, enough of the sun was covered to reduce its radiance considerably, and the temperature inside the glass canopy fell noticeably.

Terrel was intent on the spectacle above, and so he was unaware that all the sharaken had opened their eyes again. When he finally noticed this, he was unnerved to see that they were all staring not at the eclipse but *at him*. What was more, there now seemed to be another silvery light inside the dome, making up for the reduction in the sunlight.

And then he saw the reason for both the sharaken's amazement and the silver radiance. He raised his left hand, palm upwards, to see the miniature star of the amulet shining there like a magical beacon.

After that, it became clear that the sharaken had begun to take Terrel very seriously indeed. Nevertheless, it seemed that they were still not prepared to be rushed into any decision. That evening, presumably after conferring with his colleagues, Reader visited Terrel in his quarters and told him that they needed to study his dreams in greater detail. To that end, an oneiromantic ritual had been arranged. It would take place in two days' time, at the full of the Red Moon.

'What will it involve?' Terrel asked apprehensively.

'There's no need to worry,' Reader assured him. 'I will be sharing your journey. The exact form of the rite will depend upon our readings of the heavens, but this will be your chance to prove your worth once and for all.'

'What if I refuse to take part?'

'That in itself will answer most of our questions. But I don't think you'll refuse. Look inside yourself, Terrel. Have faith in your true character. If you can do that, you have nothing to fear.'

When the sharaken's leader had departed, Terrel turned to Alyssa, who was still sharing his room at night.

I have to do this, don't I?

I would trust you with my life, she replied. *Why should this be any different?*

The ceremony began, as Terrel had expected, inside the dome at the top of the Red Tower. The coloured glass turned the evening sky to a deep purple, in which the Red Moon rode in her full glory. Reader and Terrel sat facing each other in the centre of the gathering, next to a small, glowing brazier. The other sharaken were all crowded around the edge of the room. Alyssa was there too, her white fur turned pink.

At a signal from one of the onlookers, two men came forward, bringing with them a metal tripod and a silver bowl. They placed these so that the bowl was above the brazier, and immediately – even as the attendant withdrew – a strange scent began to rise into the warm air. There was a colourless liquid in the bowl but, as Terrel watched, it turned first milky white and then pale yellow. As soon as this transformation was complete, Reader leant forward and handed Terrel a small ladle.

'Drink.'

Terrel took the spoon with some misgivings. Although he wanted to ask what the peculiar concoction was, he knew that the answer wouldn't really make any difference.

He couldn't back out now. To do so would condemn him in the eyes of the sharaken.

Carefully, he dipped the ladle into the liquid, then brought it to his lips. The fumes seemed to fill his head, making him dizzy, and when he tipped the contents of the spoon into his mouth he almost gagged. The yellow fluid was only slightly warm, but it tasted incredibly bitter, and it burned his tongue and throat as he swallowed rapidly, hoping he would not choke. His eyes were watering as he handed the ladle back to Reader. The sharakan nodded his approval, and drank himself before insisting that the boy repeat his performance. In all both drank four times, by which time the bowl was almost empty.

'It is done.' Reader rose to his feet, and two of his colleagues came to stand beside him.

As Terrel tried to stand, others came forward to either side of him – and he soon understood why they seemed so anxious to be of assistance. As he got up his head started spinning and his legs almost buckled, but he managed to stay upright – in spite of feeling an odd sense of dislocation. It was as if the rest of the world was moving in slow motion. He tried to ask Reader what would happen next, but his lips and tongue were numb and would not work, so he simply let himself be led away.

Once back in his own room, Terrel was helped to lie down on his bed, and then his escorts departed, leaving Alyssa as his only company. The last thing he heard before he fell into a deep sleep was the sound of the door being closed – and then locked and barred from the outside.

*

When Terrel woke up, the early light of morning was filtering in through the skylights. His head and arm hurt, and his mouth was dry, but the worst thing was the horrible smell in the chamber, at once sickly and almost metallic. Then he saw that there was a dark sticky substance on his hands, and he began to feel ill. He could remember nothing of the previous night, and wondered if he had somehow cut himself while he was dreaming. His left forearm was beginning to throb painfully, and when he peered at it he saw a ragged tear in the skin. Dried blood was smeared around the wound, and a few fresh drops were oozing out even now.

He sat up gingerly, and saw his knife on the floor next to the bed. He had no idea how it had got there.

The snow fox lay curled up against the door, and it seemed odd that Alyssa should sleep later than he had. It was then – with a jolt of dread that hit him like a punch to the stomach – that he realized the fox was lying very still. His own discomfort forgotten now, he tumbled out of bed and knelt next to the animal. Its white fur was matted with drying blood, and there was a brown stain on the stone floor. Terrel's heart was in his mouth as he realized that the fox was beyond help. Its throat had been cut.

CHAPTER FORTY

It was only after he'd finished being sick that Terrel was able to begin thinking clearly. The horror he felt was compounded by the certainty that he must have been responsible for the death of the fox. But what terrified him most was the thought that he might have killed Alyssa too.

Forcing himself to return to the grisly remains, he examined the uppermost ear, desperately checking to see if the ring was there. Then he lifted the lifeless head to inspect the other ear, praying that he would not find anything. When he'd assured himself that the ring had gone, he felt a small measure of relief. If the link had still been in place, there would have been no hope. It would have meant that Alyssa's spirit had been unable to leave, and that she would be dead. It was even possible that her ghost might have been annihilated, or cast adrift in some spectral limbo, and so be lost to him forever.

However, his relief was only partial. He didn't know

what would have happened to the ring if Alyssa had still been within the fox when it was killed. Would it have disappeared as the animal – and Alyssa – died? The ring's absence was not conclusive proof that she had escaped. But it did at least allow Terrel a little hope. Even so, he knew he'd let her down. Alyssa had trusted him with her life, just as she'd said she would, and Terrel wondered if that trust had been misplaced.

He let the animal's head fall back and returned to his bed, his mind in turmoil. From a distance, the snow fox's body looked small and rather sad, curled around the wound that had robbed it of life, so that it looked as if it had just fallen asleep. Terrel knew better, of course, and he tried to remember what had actually happened. The last thing he could recall was being laid on his bed and hearing the key turn in the lock. That had been after the ritual. Bile rose in his throat again as he recalled the bitter taste of the liquid – and in that moment everything became clear. Whatever that vile potion had been, it had first intoxicated him and then rendered him unconscious – just as the wine and smoke had done at the festival in Tiscamanita. And then, just as had happened there, Jax had taken over.

Having accepted the chance to control not only his brother's mind but his body too, the prince would have been frustrated to find himself locked in a small room. If she had still been there, Alyssa would have regarded the interloper as her enemy; if she had left, then the fox would have been frightened and enraged by its inexplicable imprisonment. A confrontation had been inevitable. The Red Moon had been full – just as at Tiscamanita – and, whatever its supposed sphere of influence in Macul, the people of Vadanis believed that one of its effects was to promote violence. The wound on Terrel's arm was almost certainly a bite, and Jax had used the knife to retaliate in the most brutal fashion. And then, finding that he had nothing else to do, or possibly as the potion's influence had worn off, the prince had left – leaving Terrel to face the consequences of his actions.

Oh, Alyssa, I'm so sorry, Terrel thought. Why did I agree to take part in the ritual? Why? Please be alive, my love. I promise never to do anything as stupid ever again.

He continued to chastise himself for some time, holding himself very still to minimize the throbbing of his arm, and both longing for and dreading the moment when someone would come and unlock the door.

The atmosphere in the room was now more foul than ever, and Terrel forced himself to stand up on the bed, bringing his face level with the barred window so that he could breathe some fresh air. It was then that he realized Jax *had* found something else to amuse him.

The castle was covered in a deep blanket of fresh white snow.

'You say you can't actually remember any of this?'

'No.'

'Then how can you be sure this is what happened?'

Terrel was being interviewed by three sharaken – although only two of them had spoken so far. He didn't recognize any of them, though it was possible they might have been present at the eclipse or among the onlookers at the ritual. The one who was questioning him now was known as Eirenicon, and the other as Emptor, but Terrel thought that – like Reader – these were probably titles rather than their names. The silent one, the most intimidating of the three, simply watched Terrel, his cold black eyes never blinking.

'Something like this happened to me before,' Terrel replied. 'I told you. In a place called Tiscamanita.'

'A place we've never heard of,' Emptor reminded him.

'Look,' Terrel said, tired of repeating himself. 'I would never have done such a horrible thing. Reader must have told you how much the spirit inside the fox meant to me.'

'And yet it was killed by your knife,' Eirenicon stated.

'And it was your hand that wielded it,' his partner added.

'I'm not denying that,' the boy replied, 'but the enchanter was controlling me. How many more times do I have to say this?' The interrogation had been going on for a long time, and Terrel was weary and miserable – and becoming increasingly angry.

When the door of his evil-smelling room had been opened, the sense of shock among his hosts had been palpable. The body of the snow fox had been taken away for burial, and some of the acolytes had begun the unpleasant task of cleaning the chamber. Terrel's blood-stained robe had been removed, and in return he'd received his own clothes, which were mercifully free of any reminder of the night's events.

'The enchanter is your twin brother, whom you've never met, and who invades your dreams?' Eirenicon said.

'Yes! He can't make me do anything unless I'm very drunk or . . . None of this would have happened if you hadn't made me drink that evil stuff.'

The third sharakan spoke for the first time. Although his voice was soft, his eyes lost none of their intensity.

'Inanimate objects cannot in themselves be evil. It's how they are put to use that determines whether their effect is good or bad.'

Terrel wondered suddenly if this was the Collector. He hadn't seen his face or heard his voice when they'd met in Fenduca, but he felt the same sense of chilly emptiness about this man.

'Well, this was pretty bad, wasn't it?' Terrel said, then realized he was condemning himself with his own words. He wanted to shout at them. It wasn't me! It wasn't me! But how could he do that in the face of all the evidence? His only hope was in reasoned argument. 'Where is Reader?' he asked instead.

The two interrogators glanced at each other.

'He has not yet emerged from his dream-trance,' Eirenicon replied, his concern obvious.

'When he does, he'll be able to confirm what I've been saying, won't he?' Terrel said.

No one answered.

'What's the matter?' the boy asked. 'Is he dead too?' He had not meant this seriously, and he was stunned by the shocked reaction it provoked.

'We are not certain of his condition,' the Collector said after a short silence, 'but it seems unlikely that he will be able to corroborate your story in the near future. It's possible he now lives solely in the realm of dreams.'

'You mean he might never wake up?' Terrel exclaimed, aghast at the idea. 'Not ever?' Would that make him a sleeper? he wondered. Surely this was different.

'The moons will decide,' Emptor replied piously.

'And even if he does not,' Eirenicon added, 'the moons will provide us with an opportunity to join his dreams.'

'When?'

'Five days from now, at the full of the Amber Moon.'

'Do you really have to wait that long?' Terrel was anxious to leave the fortress, to continue his journey with or without the sharaken's promise of help.

'There is powerful magic involved here,' the Collector explained. 'Any man may wield a blade, but to bring snow on such a scale out of a summer sky is an enchantment to be reckoned with.'

'That wasn't me!'

'Your other self again?' the dark-eyed man remarked. 'Either way, we have to be sure. Five days is not so long to wait.'

It was only then that Terrel realized he had no choice in the matter. Whatever his wishes, the fortress would remain his prison until the sharaken decided he was free to leave. He was a suspect in a crime no one yet understood – and justice here had to wait upon the pleasure of the moons.

During the next four days, the sharaken did their best to ensure that Terrel did not *feel* like a prisoner. Whether this was because they genuinely believed him worthy of their trust, or because they couldn't conceive of any outsider constituting any real danger to them made no difference to the outcome. He was free to wander inside the fortress, and although no one mentioned the possibility of his leaving – and indeed he never came across any way out – his movements were not obviously restricted. He did not try to intrude upon private quarters, or to open locked doors, but he explored everywhere else with impunity.

He climbed all four towers, wandered through halls and cloisters, visited various shrines and places of study, inspected kitchens and store-rooms, and walked along several sections of the massive outer walls. He also went to the fruit and vegetable gardens, where seemingly endless supplies of food were grown. Not even the unseasonal snow – which had melted in a few hours, causing some inconvenient flooding – had affected the abundance of the gardens' produce. But although the air was scented with their fragrance, Terrel was never able to find the flower garden.

He witnessed his hosts in many of their activities – from such mundane tasks as drawing water from the wells or feeding their flocks of sheep and goats, to the more rarefied occupations that seemed closer to the life of a mystic. These included quiet periods of meditation and trance, as well as study of the heavens and of what they called the 'dream-oracles'. These, Terrel discovered, were records which had been kept for centuries, and which were added to each day – records of every important vision from every sharakan who had ever lived in the fortress. Endless rows of books and scrolls filled several rooms, and researchers pored endlessly over the sometimes fragile documents. Others were more intent on adding their own contributions to the libraries and, although most of these had come from normal dreams, some of the sharaken were prepared to go to extraordinary lengths to increase their chances of making a significant new discovery. Although food was plentiful, some of the mystics consumed nothing more than water, valuing it – according to one of Terrel's informants – not just for its cleansing properties, but also for its only partially understood magical qualities. A few employed even more extreme measures, depriving themselves of sleep for days on end in the hope that this would lead to revelations and augury. The most common technique used to keep them awake was to employ shifts of acolytes, who rang bells or crashed metal rods together as soon as their master looked as though he might fall asleep. This explained the noises that had disturbed Terrel's first night in the castle. Those who had not slept for more than seven days had sparks of madness in their eyes, but even then they did not flinch from their self-imposed tasks.

Terrel was also an onlooker at several rituals, including a complicated ceremony in which two acolytes were accepted into the ranks of the sharaken – a transformation symbolized by the shaving off of their hair and the application of tattoos to their eyelids. He never discovered what trials the young men had had to go through to prove their worthiness, or what privileges their elevation entitled them to, but it was abundantly clear that they were both overjoyed and honoured by their new status.

After a while, Terrel began to overcome his natural reticence, and he would talk to anyone he met, receiving a variety of responses – from friendly garrulousness to monosyllabic suspicion – but his overriding impression was one of austere reverence. These men had all given up the outside world – including any contact with women – for the sake of oneiromancy. Their dedication to their calling was impressive, and Terrel was struck by many outward similarities with the equally obsessive behaviour of the seers of his own homeland. Even though the astrologers there considered themselves to be scientists, while the sharaken thought of themselves as mystics, the practical consequences of their endeavours were often similar. Just as most of the affairs of the people of Vadanis were constrained by the dictates of the lunar cycles, so was every activity within the fortress community. All ceremonial occasions, periods of fasting, meditation, study and even sleep, were fixed according to configurations in the sky.

The one mystery that Terrel could not solve, in spite of all his investigations, was the reason behind the sharaken's way of life. What was the point of all their efforts? It was true that they sent occasional messages to the sky-watchers around the country, but – compared to the constant flow of information and decrees from the seers to the people of the Floating Islands – this seemed a vague and infrequent process. Beyond that, everything they did appeared to be inward-looking, academic exercises that were ends in themselves. Even the still enigmatic concept of dream-trading did not seem to have any practical application.

It was only when Terrel came across a familiar face in one of the courtyards that some of the answers fell into place. It took a few moments to place the acolyte, but when he did he called out and the young man stopped and looked round.

'You're the one who came to Fenduca with the Collector, aren't you?' Terrel said, walking up to him.

'What if I am?'

'I was there. I—'

'I know who you are,' the acolyte said shortly.

Although Terrel could sense the other man's hostility, he didn't know the reason for it.

'Do you still travel with the Collector?'

'No. Nor is he the Collector any more. We were both demoted because of you.'

'Me? Why?'

'We should have recognized your talent, the signs of power. We failed. I would have been a sharakan by now, but thanks to your duplicity, I've been apprenticed to the Keepers.'

'I did nothing—' Terrel began.

'You hid the star from us,' the young man cut in angrily. 'And you made sure the boy was nowhere to be seen.'

Terrel could understand the reference to the amulet, even though he hadn't hidden it deliberately, but he had no idea why he should be held responsible for Davi's absence. He was glad the little boy hadn't been there, but his disappearance had not been his doing.

'Don't look so innocent,' the acolyte scoffed. 'They'll all see the truth tomorrow – and then maybe I won't have to be a *gardener* any more.'

Terrel felt a wave of nervousness at the mention of the following day. That was when the Amber Moon would be full – and his fate would be decided. But his curiosity had been aroused.

'The Keepers are gardeners?'

'It's the lowest form of trading.' The acolyte paused, looking sceptical. 'Don't tell me you haven't noticed,' he added disdainfully.

'Noticed what?'

'That our tiny gardens produce so much food? That our wells never run dry, even though we're on top of a dry mountain? That the air inside the walls is always warm and full of the scents of flowers you can't see? For

someone with so much *talent*,' he said bitterly, 'you're
not exactly observant, are you? Or are you just stupid?'

His outburst left Terrel speechless. Was it possible that
the sharaken used their magic solely to make their own
lives more comfortable? Surely there had to be more to
it than that, something worthwhile, a long-term purpose?
In Vadanis, the Tindaya Code had provided such a
purpose for the seers, linking their work to the fate of the
entire population, but here the sharaken were isolated and
no such connection existed.

'Is that *all* you use dream-trading for?' he asked eventually. 'Nothing else?'

'Read the oracles,' the acolyte replied. 'If you can.'

With that he strode away, and Terrel wondered what
he had meant. His few glimpses of the sharaken's manu-
scripts had been enough for him to know that they were
beyond his comprehension – something the acolyte almost
certainly knew.

That evening, Terrel returned to his quarters – he'd been
assigned a new room well away from the one in which
the fox had died – feeling more apprehensive than ever.
Reader was still locked in his dream-trance, to the consternation of his fellow mystics, and no one could predict
what would happen when they joined him the next day.
The moment of truth was fast approaching.

During this period of waiting, Terrel had been hoping
that Alyssa would return to him in another form – to
prove that she was still alive – but she had not come, and
each day of her absence increased his anxiety. He'd even
begun to wonder whether the ghosts might have foreseen
some of the events within the castle, perhaps after noting

some clue in the Code, and that was why they'd been so reluctant to give him any advice. This didn't make much sense, but then not much did at the moment.

About the only thing that *was* certain was that his story was soon to become part of the dream-oracles. And it seemed likely that he would learn of Alyssa's fate at the same time.

CHAPTER FORTY-ONE

The change came over the castle slowly. The day had seemed like any other, but as dusk approached and the moment when the Amber Moon would rise drew near, all movement gradually came to a halt. Each sharakan had chosen his place to dream. Some gathered together in groups while others preferred to be alone, but they were all in the open air, in view of the sky. Each one sat in the same position – cross-legged on the ground, with their robes tucked in beneath them and their hands cupped together as if they expected to be given some offering. One by one they closed their eyes, so that their tattoos stared ahead of them.

The only exception to this was Reader who, accompanied by several acolyte attendants, was to be placed in the dome above the Amber Tower. His continuing trance made it impossible for him to sit as the others were doing, and it had been decided that the dome offered the best chance for his dreaming to become accessible to the other sharaken.

Terrel was very nervous, aware that his fate hung in the balance, but his curiosity outweighed his fear of disturbing the ritual. Unable to settle in his room, he wandered around the fortress, trying to keep as quiet as possible. He seemed to be the only one on the move. Even the acolytes had either retired to their own quarters or were reverently observing the night's events – without moving, and in absolute silence. Terrel's own sense of awe grew by the moment as he watched the sharaken all slip into a dreaming-state.

It was a clear night, and the Amber Moon had never looked more beautiful. When he first caught sight of it Terrel almost gasped, but he managed to stifle the sound as he gazed into the sky. He felt as if he could reach out and touch the golden sphere, which seemed to glow with an inner light of its own rather than merely reflecting the rays of the hidden sun.

Terrel had just entered one of the larger courtyards, and when he was able to drag his attention away from the hypnotic pull of the moon, he saw the largest gathering of sharaken so far. They sat motionless near the centre of the quadrangle, their bald heads glinting in the orange twilight. Eleven pairs of sightless eyes stared at the boy, and even though he knew they were only tattoos, the combined effect was both eerie and frightening. Terrel was just wishing that he could tell what they were seeing inside their dreams when all eleven men twitched simultaneously. It was only a small movement, a slight upward motion of the right shoulder and a corresponding jerk of the right arm, but the extraordinary thing was that it affected each of the sharaken in exactly the same way. They had all been responding to an unseen stimulus, and it was immediately obvious that they were all sharing the *same* dream.

After a few moments it happened again, but this time their left hands all clenched suddenly and then relaxed slowly once more. Then the sharaken were perfectly still again, as though their bodies had been paralyzed by an invisible force. The trance enveloped them all.

Terrel shivered, realizing that he was cold for the first time since he'd entered the fortress. The chill of the mountains had infiltrated the night air – but that was not all. He became aware of several unpleasant smells drifting on the sluggish breeze. The sweet floral scents had gone, and had been replaced by the odours of smoke, dust, sweat and rotting vegetation, as well as traces of another, even less palatable stench. It was as though the real world had reclaimed its hold on Terrel's senses – and that, he realized, was exactly what had happened. Now that they were enmeshed in the communal dreaming, the Keepers had evidently stopped trading, allowing the true nature of the place to reassert itself.

This realization quickly led to another, prompted by the thought that it was not only the warmth and smell of flowers in the air that had been produced by the dream-traders. Terrel began to wonder if he'd been able to trust *any* of his senses for the past seven days. The food he'd eaten had been real enough – but had it really tasted as good as he remembered, or looked as appetizing? Glancing around, he noticed other discrepancies. The stonework of several columns was crumbling in places, although it had seemed perfect before. Patches of dark green mould were spreading over one of the courtyard walls, and many of the flagstones were cracked or worn.

He knew that for the first time he was seeing the castle as it really was. *All* trading had ceased, and it was clear that Alyssa had been right. The sharaken's whole world was masked by a layer of illusion.

Thinking of Alyssa made the boy's stomach lurch violently, and for a few moments he felt nauseous again as he wondered what had happened to her. He had just realized that he might be able to leave the castle now – the gateways would no longer be hidden – but he knew that he couldn't go until he'd learnt all he could of Alyssa's fate. And yet the idea of simply waiting for several hours until the Amber Moon set again – when the joint dreaming would presumably come to an end – was intolerable, and Terrel wished again that there was some way of knowing what was going on *now*.

Maybe we do.

Hearing Alyssa's words again brought another pang of longing, especially as he realized that it had just been a memory and not her real voice. Nevertheless, it gave him an idea that both excited and frightened him. What if there *was* a way for him to see into the sharaken's dream-world? After all, as a healer he'd been able to experience many of the sensations of his patients' waking dreams. Why shouldn't he be able to glimpse at least a part of a real dream? Especially one as powerful as this?

Having made up his mind, Terrel knew that he could not approach the problem in haphazard fashion. He had to go to the best source of knowledge, to the heart of the dream. Turning abruptly, he left the courtyard and made his way towards the Amber Tower.

*

Without anyone to show him the way, it took Terrel longer than he'd hoped to reach the top of the tower, and when he climbed the final flight of stairs and came out onto the battlements, he was breathing heavily and plagued by shooting pains in his twisted right leg. Along the way, he'd noticed more signs that not everything in the castle was as it had seemed, but the amber dome still appeared perfect. The craftsmanship and eye for detail that had gone into its construction was genuine and needed no enhancement.

After taking a few moments to catch his breath, Terrel walked around the shrine until he found what he thought was probably the door. Because he had no idea how to open it from the outside, he was left with no alternative but to tap on the glass and hope that the acolytes attending to Reader would let him in. The moonlight wasn't bright enough to reveal anything inside the stained glass, but after he'd knocked the boy thought he glimpsed some movement. A few moments later he caught a few fragments of a whispered conversation. Although he couldn't hear what was being said, he guessed from the tone of the voices that some sort of argument was taking place. Without any of their masters to tell them what to do, it sounded as though the acolytes were unsure of themselves. Terrel rapped on the glass again and called out, putting as much authority into his voice as he could.

'It's Terrel. Let me in. This dreaming concerns me, and I wish to join Reader. We began this trance together. Let us end it in the same way.'

A short silence was followed by more whispering and then, somewhat to Terrel's surprise, the door was pushed open and he was able to step inside. There were four acolytes in all, none of them much older than he was, and they were all staring at him with fear in their eyes. He had no idea why they should be afraid of him, but he didn't really care about that at the moment.

Reader was lying on his back in the middle of the circular floor, his head resting on a pillow. His attendants had arranged his hands so that they rested on his chest, one on top of the other. The old man's face was peaceful, the tattooed eyes gazing up towards the night sky, and his breathing was so shallow that it would have been easy to imagine he was dead.

'I will sit with him,' Terrel said quietly, as one of the acolytes closed the door behind him.

He went forward and sat down on the floor. His damaged leg made it impossible to adopt exactly the same position as the other sharaken, but he did the best he could and tried to look properly reverent.

'Is this permitted?' one of the attendants asked nervously.

'I am part of the oracles,' Terrel replied. 'Reader would not have called me here if it was not permitted.'

His bluff seemed to work as none of the onlookers made any further objections, until – with his own nerve ends jangling – Terrel reached out and laid his own good hand upon the sharakan's.

'Wait!' an acolyte said. 'You must not attempt to influence the dream.'

'I wouldn't even know how,' Terrel replied. 'I'm here to observe, not to—'

But he got no further, because in that instant everything – the tower and its dome, the acolytes, Reader, even his own body – simply vanished. Terrel's vision spiralled

out towards the stars so that he seemed to be flying past
the moons, becoming part of their stately dance across
the sky. Simultaneously, he plunged down into the fires
that raged beneath the earth, down to the burning heart
of Nydus. Fighting to retain his balance – and his sanity
– amid such contradictory images, Terrel saw to his astonishment that there were traces of the Ancients in both
these alien realms, memories of their presence and their
passing imprinted upon the framework of existence. Their
swirling darkness had been converted into starlight and
into molten rivers of fire, but he recognized them
nonetheless.

Even though he knew he had glimpsed only a minute
fraction of the sharaken's dream, the boy found the
contact both breathtaking and terrifying. It bore no
comparison to the dreams he'd shared in his healing, and
he was certain this vision was not meant for him. He
clung on for a few moments, hoping in vain for something simpler, something that he could grasp and that
would give him a clue to Alyssa's fate. But it was hopeless, and he withdrew. As he lifted his hand, breaking the
link, the rush of sensations as the real world rebuilt itself
around him made him dizzy, and it took him a few disorientated moments to realize that even back in his own
realm, not everything was as it had been.

The first thing he noticed was that even though they
were still atop the tower, and Reader lay just as he had
done before, the dome was no longer there. They were
all exposed to the sky. The four acolytes were on their
knees, three of them with their heads buried in their
hands, cowering in an attitude of abject terror, while the
fourth looked up with an expression of awe-struck

wonderment on his face. Terrel followed his gaze and discovered, to his own utter amazement, that they were no longer looking at the heavens. The heavens had come to them.

The Amber Moon hovered directly over the tower, and seemed to be no more than a few paces above them. It was bright and astonishingly beautiful, the variations in its golden-brown colouring making it appear almost translucent, while the distinctive markings of its mountains and plains, its craters and ravines, were clearer than Terrel had ever seen before. Through his fear, he knew it could not be real – and yet how could it be anything else? Illusions were not so solid, so luminously perfect. Logic insisted that this must be a phantom, an exact replica, but logic had little chance in the battle against such wonder.

Instinct made Terrel wrench his gaze away from the mesmerizing sight and look around. Even though he'd expected it, the spectacle that greeted him was still spell-binding in its grandeur. Each of the other three moons was floating above their respective towers, each matching the phase of their real counterparts in the sky above. This was magic beyond anything he had ever seen before, and Terrel realized that the trading had not stopped. It had just been put to another purpose.

He watched and waited for what came next and, just when it seemed that this was to be the limit of the night's sorcery, a new drama unfolded. The entire sky flickered with a ghostly light, as if it were full of silent lightning, and in that moment the moons changed. It took Terrel only a few moments to realize what had happened. Time had slipped forward, so that the White Moon, rather than being halfway through its cycle, was now almost full; the Red Moon was no longer three-quarters full but a thin new crescent which was waxing rather than waning; and the Dark Moon – even though it could not be seen with normal eyesight – was now new instead of being just short of full. By then Terrel had no need to look up to confirm that the Amber Moon had remained full, because he knew what this set of phases meant. This was the configuration from his dream, the time – exactly one hundred days from now – when the earthquake would strike. The sharaken had received confirmation of his prophecy.

The lightning flashed again, and the illusory moons returned to their current phases before gradually fading from sight. As they disappeared, the glass domes made the reverse transformation, reconstituting themselves so that Terrel and his companions were encased once more. Somewhere below them, in the labyrinth at the heart of the castle, a bell began to ring. The acolytes slowly recovered their wits, looking around with a mixture of relief and bewilderment on their young faces.

Terrel was not really surprised to see that some considerable time had passed since he'd climbed the tower, and that the Amber Moon was now setting beyond a distant mountain range. The dream was over, and the sharaken's fortress was coming back to life.

'It's over,' Terrel whispered to himself.

'Indeed it is.'

Startled, the boy turned to see that Reader had sat up.

'And we have much to discuss, young man.'

CHAPTER FORTY-TWO

'Just tell me about Alyssa!' Terrel demanded. 'Is she alive?'

'I don't know how to answer that,' Reader said.

'Was she still there when Jax killed the fox?'

'We have no way of telling.'

'But I thought . . . You don't *know*?' Terrel was almost incoherent now, his frustration at boiling point. Being told that Alyssa was dead would have been devastating – the worst thing he could imagine – but being left in limbo was unbearable too. 'I don't believe this,' he muttered.

As soon as Reader had revived, the acolytes had fussed over him, preventing Terrel from talking to him while they assured themselves that the sharakan was all right. Then they had insisted on taking the old man back to his own quarters – which was where he and Terrel were now. Even then the boy had been forced to wait until several of the other sharaken had been in to see their leader. Terrel's increasing belligerence had finally gained him admittance, only for him to find that the one question he most needed an answer to was the one the dream had passed by.

'She means a lot to you, this spirit?' Reader asked. He had been taken aback by the boy's vehemence, and wished he could have set his mind at rest.

'Yes, she does.'

'Are you sure that's wise?'

'What do you mean? What are you talking about?' Terrel exclaimed. 'You don't even know her.'

'I know that she is not of our world.'

'She is. Or she will be soon, at least.'

'And I know that females of any race can be dangerous,' Reader added. He sounded serious, but there was an oddly wistful look on his face as he spoke, as if he wasn't sure that he believed his own words. 'They can distract you from the truly important tasks.'

More important than love? Terrel thought, but kept this question to himself. Instead he chose to ask another – one that had only just occurred to him.

'How old were you when you came here?'

'I was six years old,' Reader replied. 'Why?'

'No reason,' Terrel said. 'I just wondered.'

In fact he was feeling sorry for the old man, and wondering just how wise he could be if he'd spent so much time shut away from the world.

Outside the lamp-lit room, dawn was breaking. Terrel had not slept all night, but he still didn't feel tired.

'My belief is that Alyssa will return to you if she is able to do so,' Reader assured him. 'She is as devoted to you as you are to her. Can you be content with that?'

I already know that, Terrel thought. That's not what I'm worried about. He had taken some comfort from the prophecy within the Tindaya Code, which had foretold his arrival at the jewelled city with 'a flying creature'. Who else could that refer to but Alyssa? And if that were true, then she must be alive. But he also knew that the seers' translation of the Code had been inaccurate before. The thought of going to Talazoria alone was horrifying.

'The road must be turning now,' he breathed. 'If she doesn't come soon, maybe she never will.' He closed his eyes in anguish at the idea.

'What's that?' Reader asked, cupping a hand to his ear.

'Nothing.'

The old man sighed, adjusting his position among the pillows. One of the acolytes hovering nearby approached, but Reader waved him away.

'Don't you want to know the outcome of your petition?' he asked Terrel. 'That was your purpose in coming here, after all.'

'I already know,' the boy replied. 'The dream confirmed that everything I said was true, didn't it?'

'Not exactly. But it did confirm that you *believe* it all to be true.'

'And you don't?' Terrel asked, his confidence wavering. He had been assuming all along that the sharaken would help him. Now it seemed even that was not certain.

'*I* believe you,' Reader assured him, 'but some of my colleagues did not welcome your arrival, and have reservations even now. They are still consulting the oracles.'

'But I have to go,' Terrel protested. 'I can't afford to

wait any longer. Are any of you going to come with me?'

'That was never an option.'

'*What?*'

'We do not leave this place except by special dispensation,' the sharakan told him. 'These are granted by the oracles only for specific purposes of our own, not for the needs of others.'

'Then you were *never* going to help me!' Terrel exploded. 'So why have you kept me here? What has all this been about?'

'I didn't say we wouldn't help you. There are other ways for us to do that.'

'Such as?'

'We will watch over your journey and guide your path.'

'That's *it*? I've wasted all this time for that? I don't need a guide to get to Talazoria.'

'Don't be so sure,' Reader warned. 'Good advice should never be spurned.'

'Advice? Just how are you going to give me this advice?'

'Through one of these.' The old man pointed to the carved rod that was propped up against his bed.

'A message-handle?'

'It's that and more.'

'More?' Terrel queried.

'When my colleagues and I reach an agreement – as I'm sure we will eventually – you'll be able to speak to me through the staff,' Reader said. 'And when the situation demands it, you will be able to summon my image so that I may speak for the sharaken.'

'You'll be able to talk to anyone, not just me?'

'Exactly,' Reader confirmed. 'But do not think to abuse this gift, Terrel. We don't undertake such trades lightly, and the cost to us is high. You may only have a single chance to use it, so you must pick your moment carefully.'

Terrel nodded, already thinking ahead to his time in Talazoria. If he was able to get inside the royal court, even the king would surely be impressed by such a display – and the sharaken's words must carry some weight. His hopes began to rise, though he was still cautious.

'What if you don't reach an agreement?'

'Then I will personally do what I can,' the old man assured him, 'and hope that will be enough. I'm sorry I can't say more than that now.'

The anger that had sustained Terrel through the latter part of the night was turning to gloom now. Until he knew that Alyssa was all right, nothing could make him feel any better.

'You should rest now and sleep tonight,' Reader suggested. 'We'll prepare supplies for your journey, and you can leave at first light tomorrow.'

Terrel stood up, suddenly feeling utterly exhausted, and went to the door. There he paused and looked back at the old man.

'Thank you.'

'There's no need to thank me,' Reader said. 'You've earned our help.'

'That's not what I meant,' Terrel replied. 'I'll take your gifts, and gladly, but my thanks are for *you*. It's good to know that you at least believe in me.'

*

A day later, rested and well fed, his pack restocked with water and provisions, Terrel made his way through the tunnel beneath the fortress walls and out into the cold wind of the mountains. In his left hand he carried the intricately shaped staff that Reader had promised him. He didn't know what help – if any – it might provide, but he felt a little better for knowing he had earned it.

Desperately hoping that Alyssa would join him soon, Terrel set out on the last stage of the long road to Talazoria.

PART THREE

TALAZORIA

CHAPTER FORTY-THREE

Terrel stood on the roof of the barge, gazing to the west. Spread out below him in a vast panorama was a great plain, which stretched to the horizon. It was a patchwork quilt whose colours varied according to the different types of vegetation and settlements, but the most striking feature was the fact that the plain was sliced in half by the bright straight line of the so-called 'Royal Highway'. This was the last section of the canal on which Terrel had been travelling for several days and which would eventually carry him all the way to Talazoria. The setting sun was currently turning the surface of the water to the colour of burnished gold, emphasizing the unswerving line of the waterway. This was one of the impossibly straight 'rivers' of Terrel's dream, and for some reason, looking at it now made him feel uneasy.

On the other hand, the canal had provided him with an excellent – and effortless – means of transport and, for the first time since he'd left the sharaken's fortress, he could afford to relax a little, knowing that he would reach the city long before the earthquake was due. Before he'd met the bargee, a man called Drewan Lafis, and earned his passage by relieving the pain in his stooped and overworked back, Terrel's journey had been plagued by delays. The arrival of the autumn rains had hampered his trek from the mountains, and then the first signs of winter's cold had made the latter stages uncomfortable. Progress had been painfully slow, especially as his right boot – which had been made to fit the peculiarities of his twisted foot – was now chafing badly. His supplies had run out, and on several occasions he'd been forced to stop and earn his food by whatever means he could. Once they were accepted, his healing skills were always welcome, but his strange appearance and unusual accent always led to an initial period of suspicion and doubt which had to be overcome before he was allowed to prove himself – and that took time.

When he had reached the small town situated close to the canal, he'd gone to look at the man-made wonder but had been turned away by the sentries who guarded the perimeter of the way-station. Even after he'd met and been befriended by Drewan, Terrel was still not sure that he'd be allowed to travel on the barge. Technically, it was illegal to take passengers on board, and the soldiers who accompanied each waterborne convoy only bowed to the bargee's wishes when Terrel agreed to help some of them with their various ailments. After that, even though he was still regarded with some apprehension by a few of the military men, he had become an accepted member of the boat's crew. By then the wound on his arm had healed completely, and he had even taken his turn leading the horse that pulled the craft along, and occasionally wielding one of the long poles that helped to steer the barge as well as propel it. He managed the latter by jamming the pole under his twisted right arm and using his left hand to control it. Although he had felt awkward and clumsy at first, experience had soon improved his performance. The barge progressed at a steady but sedate pace, and Terrel no longer had to worry about whether he was taking the best route. Nothing could be more direct than the canal, and Drewan's estimate of their time of arrival in Talazoria meant that the boy had no need to hurry, even though almost two complete cycles of the Amber Moon had passed – which represented half the time available for the journey.

The barge was currently moored – along with several other craft – in a large artificial lake at the end of a high valley. This docking area was fed by several streams that ran down from the hills to either side. At the western end of the lake were the great wooden doors that formed the entrance to the first of a series of seven massive locks, which would transport the boats to and from the plain below. It was the largest and most amazing feat of engineering Terrel had ever seen – even more astonishing than the towering stone-built arches of the bridge – Drewan had called it an aqueduct – that carried the canal, its travellers and towpaths, over a valley that ran across its course. Terrel could hardly wait for the next morning, when their boat would travel down through the seven locks – an arduous and complicated manoeuvre which would take most of the day – so that he could see exactly how it all worked. After that, according to the bargee, it would take only a few more days of plain sailing until they reached their destination. Terrel preferred not to think about what would happen then.

The one aspect of travelling upon the canal that worried him was that it meant he was almost constantly upon water. Even though he still couldn't bring himself to accept that Alyssa might be dead, he had resigned himself to the fact that she would almost certainly not be able to join him on this particular journey. This conviction had grown in strength as time passed and she did not appear. However, Terrel never entirely lost hope, and because of that he'd been initially reluctant to commit his passage to the canal, knowing that – just as it had done in the mist-filled valley – the presence of so much water might make it harder, or even impossible, for her to approach him. In the end, with time pressing and a certain, easy passage to the city on offer, he'd decided that it was an opportunity he could not afford to miss.

Alyssa's continued absence was the main reason for him not wanting to look too far ahead. The prospect of encountering another elemental – and without her help this time – made Terrel feel both afraid and uneasy, but he knew he had to try to fulfil his bargain. Without Alyssa he was also unable to talk to the ghosts, of course, and he would have dearly welcomed their advice at this point of his travels down the unknown road. Before long, once the barge had gone a little way across the lowland plain, there would be no chance of the ghosts coming to him anyway. He would then be within fifty miles of the city – a distance that marked the extent of the elemental's unseen force.

During the earlier part of his journey, Terrel had used the message-handle to accept advice from another source.

Reader had discouraged the boy from talking to him too often, as it was tiring for both of them, but the sharakan's directions had been of use on several occasions – and the contact had made Terrel feel as though the entire weight of the endeavour did not rest solely upon his shoulders. Even when he did not send or receive messages, just touching the staff gave him a feeling of comfort and a measure of much-needed confidence. There was always a sensation of latent power, a potential source of help should he ever need it.

That had changed slightly since he'd come aboard the barge. His sense of the sharakan had become more remote somehow, as though the link between them was being stretched too thin. That was curious and a little unsettling, but as Terrel no longer needed the old man's advice for the journey, he didn't worry about this unduly. He had decided not to even try to contact Reader until he was in Talazoria – when the ability to summon the sharakan's image might prove vital.

Although he was glad to have it, the message-handle had proved to be something of an embarrassment. It was as long as Terrel was tall and, apart from a section a third of the way down – where he held it – its surface was decorated with meticulously detailed carvings of miniature flowers, leaves and berries, as well as other shapes he could not identify. It had attracted a great deal of attention from passers-by – far too much attention for the boy's comfort, especially as he wasn't sure how people would regard it – and him – if he admitted to having been given it by the sharaken. As a result he'd fallen into the habit of using the glamour to make the staff look like a perfectly ordinary stick, something a boy with a maimed leg might carry. He felt uncomfortable doing this, knowing that all magic had its cost – and that it might enable Jax to interfere with his life – but it still seemed worth the risk. As yet his twin had done him no harm, apart from a few cruel words in his dreams – and Terrel was used to that.

His dreams had been curious recently. Images of the Dark Moon, in all its aspects, had been linked with inexplicable messages that he usually only half remembered. He'd seen once more the majesty of the total eclipse at Tindaya, watched the black shape of the moon move across the lens of the telescope in Muzeni's ruined observatory, and stared in awe at its reflection at the ceremony in Betancuria – which had flickered with a swirling, rainbow-hued fire. He'd seen more fanciful images too, inspired by the haunting, almost poetic descriptions in Muzeni's lost journal, which pictured the Dark Moon as a bird of prey. And with all these visions he'd heard different voices, some of whom he recognized – such as Alyssa or Jax – while some were unknown to him. They had all seemed to be offering him advice. 'Don't try to dream within the dome,' and 'Move sideways first,' were two of the more memorable examples, but as Terrel couldn't decipher what any of them meant, and wasn't sure whether they came from friends or foes – assuming they really were messages and not pointless creations of his own subconscious – he decided to ignore them all. If these dreams were meant to tell him something, he hadn't the faintest idea what it was supposed to be.

'You never did tell us why you want to go to the city,' Drewan remarked.

Terrel and the bargee were sitting in the open stern section of the boat with the other member of the crew, a burly young man who was known as Odd. Terrel had yet to work out whether this was his real name or a due-name; although Odd was not the most intelligent person the boy had ever met, he didn't seem all that strange.

'There's some people there I have to talk to,' Terrel answered.

'Inside or outside?'

'What do you mean?'

Drewan took another swig of ale from the flagon he and Odd were sharing, then passed it to the younger man.

'There's as many live outside the walls of Talazoria as do inside,' he explained. 'And getting in's not so easy unless you know the right people. The likes of us only get in on sufferance, until we've delivered our cargo, and then we're sent on our way again.'

'Can't I come in with you?' Terrel suggested hopefully. He'd already been told that the canal passed directly through the city walls.

Drewan shook his head.

'You're not official, see. I can't risk that sort of trouble.'

'There must be other ways in.'

'There's gates,' the bargee agreed. 'But they don't let just anyone through.'

'You don't look right,' Odd added helpfully.

'Maybe they'll overlook that for a healer,' Drewan said.

'He still don't look right,' Odd repeated. 'The guards won't like that.'

'Too much at stake,' Drewan said, nodding.

'I don't understand.'

'There's three sorts of people in the world,' the bargee

informed him, 'and which you are means everything in Talazoria. There's the citizens, from merchants who're rich enough to own a house inside the walls, right up to the nobles and Ekuban himself. They can come and go as they please. Then there's the underlings, the domestics and soldiers and such like, the ones who do all the work inside and get to stay there so long as they behave themselves. Then there's the rest of us.'

'Peasants,' Odd said.

'Peasants,' Drewan agreed without rancour. 'Only a few of us ever get past the guards, and then only to do a specific job. Most people have never even seen the inside – and they're not likely to. Don't get me wrong, though. I'm not complaining. I do all right.'

Terrel had already seen that for himself. Many of the people of Macul lived in vile conditions. The deprivation he'd seen in Fenduca was far from unique. In fact, compared to some of the places he'd seen, the village beneath the black mountain had seemed positively prosperous. Drewan, on the other hand, had regular and reasonably well-paid work. If he disliked the fact that he was forced to spend his days under more or less constant scrutiny by the military, it was a price worth paying for protection against the envy of those less fortunate than himself. Apart from the soldiers who accompanied each convoy, the canal itself was guarded by manned way-stations at regular intervals along its length, and larger garrisons at places of particular importance – such as this series of locks.

'The city gets the best of everything.' Although Odd did not sound envious, Terrel could understand why others would be. It must be galling to see the best of all their produce – whether it be food, raw materials or precious stones – disappear into the seemingly insatiable maw of Talazoria, when many peasants barely had enough to eat. It was easy to see why the military escorts were necessary.

'That's the way of it,' Drewan said. 'I may not like it; but what can I do?'

'If enough people decided to fight against it,' Terrel suggested, 'a system as unjust as this would surely collapse.'

'Don't let the soldiers hear you talk like that,' the bargee hissed, glancing around nervously. 'I've stuck my neck out for you, and I don't want to end up in the stews.'

'Where?'

'That's what they call the encampments outside the walls.'

'Where all the beggars live,' Odd put in.

'Not just beggars,' Drewan said. 'Anyone who's got nowhere else to go. It's a pretty filthy way to live, even by the standards of the plain.'

'Lots of rats,' Odd confirmed sagely.

'Why do people stay there?'

'There's always a chance of getting a job,' Drewan replied. 'Even of becoming an underling. Maybe that only happens to one in a thousand, but people don't think like that, do they?'

'Some of them *do* get inside, though,' Odd remarked, with a malicious grin. 'For the entertainments.'

'That's no laughing matter,' the older man snapped, and Odd's face fell.

'Are you talking about the demon?' Terrel asked.

'That's the latest thing, apparently,' Drewan replied.

He seemed reluctant to say any more, and looked around again, but it was obvious that Terrel wanted him to go on. 'Ekuban's mad,' he said quietly, 'and he's infected the whole court so that now it's like an . . . an addiction. Before the demon came along, they'd have public burnings, hangings and beheadings, just for sport! Then some of the nobles started to compete against each other to devise better ways of torturing and killing for the king's amusement. The demon is just the most recent *entertainment*, but Ekuban's been using the people of the stews as his playthings for as long as I can remember. When there aren't enough criminals or heretics for the magistrates to condemn to death, he just gets the soldiers to round up a few people no one will miss from outside the city walls.'

'They're sent to their deaths for nothing?' Terrel breathed, appalled.

'Not for nothing,' Drewan replied. 'For being poor and stupid.'

That night, under the full of the Amber Moon, Terrel slept badly again, his nightmares haunted by disturbing images of blood and death. He also dreamt of the Dark Moon, seeing it this time as a great vulture that swooped down on black wings to tear at his flesh with its talons and curved beak. At the same time, a voice he didn't recognize told him to 'remember your sister'.

When he awoke from another vision – this time of being swept down in the churning waters of a giant cataract – he recalled the words, and found them as meaningless as all the other messages. He had no sister. At least none that he knew of.

*

The day began early, before dawn, because it was one of the superstitions of the bargemen that if all seven locks were not navigated between sunrise and sunset in a single day, back luck would follow the boat and her crew for a full year. Terrel helped with the preparations, and as the sun crept up over the eastern horizon, they set off.

The boy watched in fascination as Drewan's barge, together with three others, entered one lock after another, the giant doors opening and closing in sequence so that the water gushed down, sparkling in the morning light. With each lowering of the water level the boats moved on, coming ever closer to the plain below. All went smoothly, and by early afternoon they were down, and taking a well-earned rest at the mooring basin before beginning the last stage of their journey.

Looking back up the slope, Terrel couldn't help but be amazed that the transfer of these large vessels was even possible. He had been glad of the distraction – for a few hours he'd been able to forget about the dreadful things he'd heard the previous evening – but now, as Odd tethered their new horse to the lead rope and they set off again, he was forced to look ahead once more.

He was hoping that Drewan's tale had been exaggerated, that the way the city was run was not as vile as the bargee had suggested, but instinct told him otherwise – and nothing he saw for the rest of that day and all of the next made him feel any less pessimistic. The few people he glimpsed beyond the canal's perimeter fence looked ragged and dejected. Their settlements seemed even more drab and squalid than those he'd seen earlier in his journey and, what was more, they seemed to be getting worse the closer he got to the city. It was as though Talazoria's malign influence had sucked the land around it dry, leaving it without any pride or spirit, without even the possibility of any happiness or comfort. And if that were true here, Terrel thought, looking out as the depressing landscape slid slowly past, what must it be like in the stews?

'If those cretins at the way-station hadn't palmed us off with this stupid lame nag,' Drewan muttered angrily, 'we'd've been in Talazoria by tomorrow night.' He glanced at the boy and seemed to remember who he was talking to. 'No offence, Terrel. A man with a gimpy leg is still a man, but a lame horse is worse than useless.'

The barge had had to moor at the side of the canal only a short time after they'd set off that morning, and Drewan was not pleased. For Terrel, the enforced halt was less of an imposition. The closer he came to the city, the less he liked the idea of actually getting there. Even finding a way to get inside the walls – as he knew he must – now seemed like an impossible task. And if he managed that, all he had to do then was stop a mad king and a displaced elemental from driving each other to the point where the entire country was destroyed!

'You might as well stretch your legs,' Drewan suggested. 'It'll be a couple of hours at least until we get a replacement.'

Terrel took the bargee's advice, collected his staff, and made his way along the towpath. The morning was cool but dry, and after a while he climbed a grassy bank and sat down, deciding to try to talk to Reader. However, his greeting met with silence, and no matter how hard he gripped the staff or how much effort he put into his thoughts, nothing happened. He gave up, wondering dismally why the message-handle no longer seemed to be working. If the sharaken had abandoned him, then he had no allies left at all.

Lying on his back and gazing up at the sky, Terrel saw the pale crescent of the waning White Moon – the moon of logic and destiny – but it gave him no answers either. He could still see it when he closed his eyes and fell asleep; it followed him into his dream, which was made up of jumbled fragments of all the dreams from the last few nights.

Terrel woke to a painful stabbing at his left ear. He exclaimed in distress and flailed out with his arm, opening his eyes to a blur of black and white. The magpie, having succeeded in waking him, came to rest a short distance away and regarded him with jewel-bright eyes.

I'm not your sister, Alyssa said. *Why are you dreaming about her?*

CHAPTER FORTY-FOUR

'Alyssa!' Terrel cried. All of a sudden he felt joyful, tearful, lighter than air. The sheer relief of knowing she'd survived untied a huge knot in his stomach – which had been inside him for so long he'd almost forgotten it was there. *You're alive!*

Of course I'm alive, she replied. *No thanks to you, though.*

It wasn't me! he exclaimed.

I know that, stupid.

I had to take part in the ritual, he said, still stung by her accusation. *You agreed with me about that.*

I trust you, she said. *Not Jax.*

But he's part of me, Terrel said, admitting this to himself for the first time. *He's only really dangerous when I'm drunk, or . . . What happened?*

I saw the change – or felt it, rather – and I knew something bad was happening. Your eyes weren't right. I left just in time. She paused. *I felt her die, even so.* There was regret and anger, perhaps even guilt, in Alyssa's voice.

I'm sorry.

So am I. She had no choice, and I repaid her gift to me with death.

It wasn't your fault, he assured her. *We didn't know . . . We couldn't . . . What's done is done, Alyssa. We can't change it – and at least the sharaken agreed to help me.*

With that? she asked, glancing with obvious distaste at the staff that lay on the ground between them.

Yes. It could be important.

Let's hope so. If not, the fox's death was pointless.

Terrel wished that their reunion could have begun with a discussion of something more pleasant, but he was so glad to see Alyssa that he was unable to feel too much sorrow at the animal's end.

Is what happened the reason you've been so long coming back to me?

Partly, but I've been looking for you for the last few days. Now I can see why I couldn't find you, she went on, jabbing her beak towards the water. *I was only just able to get here this time.*

What do you mean?

There's a pulse to the water's influence, a pattern. I have to fit into it. There's a sickness here.

Like a curse? Terrel's fears about travelling upon water had been confirmed, but this extra ill omen was something he had not expected.

Yes. Don't you feel it?

No. I'm fine. He began to justify his decision to accept a ride on the barge, but even as he spoke he couldn't help wondering about the nature of his recent dreams – and the fact that the message-handle had seemed to lose its power. Was it possible that he *had* been affected by the curse, in ways he wasn't even aware of? And was the elemental responsible for any malign influence? From what Terrel could remember of his dream, the creature might well have passed this way on its unwilling journey to Talazoria. *I might not have got here in time if I hadn't used the canal*, he concluded. *We should reach the city in about two days.*

Sometimes easiest is not always best, Alyssa commented, *but you may as well carry on now.*

You will stay with me, won't you? he asked anxiously.

I'll fly alongside, she confirmed.

Terrel breathed a sigh of relief. He was no longer alone. *It's good to see you, Alyssa.*

There's another wind blowing, she replied.

Before he could ask what she meant, Terrel was distracted by the feel of something sticky running down the side of his neck. When he touched his skin, his fingers came away red and he realized that his ear was bleeding where she had pecked him.

'Ow!' he said, feeling it sting again. *What did you have to do that for?*

You're lucky, she replied. *This bird is evil. It tried to get me to peck out a lamb's eyes back there.*

Then why not choose a different bird?

I think maybe I need *to be nasty just now.*

Why?

Alyssa ignored his question and turned away, bounding across the grass in a series of long, springy leaps. Her tail swayed from side to side as she stared along the towpath.

There's a new horse coming. You'd better get back to the barge.

Terrel got to his feet.

Where are the others?

I haven't seen them for a while. And pretty soon they won't be able to join us.

And you'll be stuck as a magpie, Terrel pointed out. *Are you sure you don't want to find another bird while you still have the chance?*

The pulse is changing, Alyssa remarked, then flew off, chattering in the harsh manner of her kind.

Left alone again, Terrel made his way back to the boat and climbed aboard. They cast off as soon as Odd set the replacement horse in motion, and Terrel watched anxiously for Alyssa. He eventually spotted her flying a parallel course some distance from the water. She had to keep circling round to match the barge's ponderous pace, and after a while Terrel saw – to his amusement – that she had been joined by several other magpies. He gingerly touched his damaged ear, and thought that a whole flock of such belligerent birds would make a formidable army. He would certainly want them on his side in any battle.

When Terrel finally looked away from the birds, he turned his attention to the view over the barge's bows, wondering when he would get his first sight of Talazoria. Now that Alyssa had come back to him, some of his confidence had returned.

Had Terrel looked round, the sight he would have seen might have shattered his new-found optimism. Above the towpath, a few hundred paces astern, three ghosts were struggling against a powerful wind that tore at their clothes and hair, buffeting them so that they could hardly stay upright. They were fighting a losing battle against the ever-increasing force of a hurricane – but it was a hurricane that touched nothing in Terrel's world.

All three ghosts were shouting, but their words were blown away by the pressure of the unreal wind, and the boy heard nothing. Against such arcane power, not even psinoma stood any chance.

The old men were the first to surrender to the inevitable. Elam struggled on for a little longer, but eventually even his stubborn bravery was of no use. All three fell back, their failure reflected in their worried expressions, and then they vanished. Completely unaware of the drama that had unfolded behind him, Terrel sailed on, each moment bringing him a little closer to the source of the hurricane.

'Should I stay on the towpath?'

'Best not,' Drewan replied.

Terrel nodded. He had come this far on sufferance. The soldiers who had accompanied the convoy had accepted his presence, but the guards at Talazoria would not be so lenient.

'You're close enough now,' Drewan went on. 'You won't get lost. I wish we could take you further, but . . .' He shrugged.

'Good luck,' Odd said.

'Aye, good luck, boy,' the bargee said. 'Just watch your tongue when you get to the city. Not everyone will take kindly to some of your ideas.'

'I'll be careful,' Terrel promised. 'Thanks for everything.'

Now that the time had come for him to leave the barge, he felt a renewed sense of disorientation. Climbing over

the perimeter fence was difficult, and was made worse by
the fact that he knew several people were watching him,
but once he'd managed that – and had waved a last
farewell – he saw the magpie flying down to join him,
and this restored his spirits. Although he had seen her
from a distance, he hadn't spoken with Alyssa for the last
day and a half. Now they could go on together. It was
still very early in the morning, and – according to Drewan
– Terrel ought to be able to walk as far as the city walls
before nightfall.

Ready? Alyssa asked as she swooped past.

Ready for what? he asked.

A little thieving, she replied, and flew away again.

If anything, the stews were even worse than Drewan had
described. Clinging to the base of the uncaring walls of
Talazoria, the mouldering collection of dilapidated shacks
looked like some virulent fungus attached to the bole of
a giant tree. Everything and everyone there seemed to be
covered in filth and grime, and the air was so full of the
fetid stench of decay that at first Terrel found it hard to
breathe. Desperate poverty and all kinds of disease were
rampant, so that in spite of his twisted body, Terrel was
keenly aware of his relative affluence and good health.
There was more work to be done here than could be
managed by a thousand healers, let alone one, and the
boy was simply overwhelmed by pity and revulsion.

Many people watched as he went by, some looking at
him with fear or envy, but a few glared with unreasoning
hatred while others pleaded with him for alms. Terrel
felt very much the outsider, and knew it was only the
threat of his staff and his strange eyes that allowed him

to walk freely among these outcasts and beggars. He could scarcely believe that people lived like this – but it was only when he saw men and women fighting for the scraps of food that had been thrown out over the city wall amid a foul-smelling cascade of rubbish that he realized the depths of hopelessness and degradation they had reached. At that moment the boy thought he would never eat again.

By then he had been in the stews for more than an hour, working his way around the city walls, but as yet he had seen no sign of any gate. The only entrance so far had been the canal tunnel – and that had been some distance away, beyond heavily-manned fortifications. Terrel was beginning to despair of ever finding a way in, and had no idea where he was going to spend the fast approaching night. Just then the magpie dived down, then flew towards an open space a little further from the walls. When they'd first arrived, Alyssa had stayed close to Terrel, but some of the stew's inhabitants had thrown stones at her – presumably hoping to kill the bird for its flesh – and she had retreated to a safer distance. Having the advantage of flight, she'd been able to go *over* the city walls, and had done so in search of information. Now she had returned, and Terrel hurried across the patch of bare earth to join her.

It's like the cloud of a nightmare, she said, looking over at the jumble of hovels.

This place is worse than any nightmare, Terrel replied.

Quite a contrast to the other side of the walls, Alyssa noted. *It's beautiful in there.*

Where's the nearest gate?

Keep going the way you were. It's about four hundred

paces from here, but there are guards everywhere. What are you going to do? Just ask them to let you in?

Have you got a better idea? Terrel enquired.

'Where do you think you're going, son?'

'I've been summoned to the court,' Terrel declared.

The soldiers laughed.

'Really? Who by?'

'Lord Rekyar,' the boy replied, using a name he'd heard when eavesdropping on a conversation among the sentries.

'And what would he want with a deformed sewer rat like you?'

'I'm a healer. I'll prove it to you if—'

'Piss off, you little worm. Or you'll need some healing yourself.'

'I have to get inside. It's very—'

'You heard what the man said,' one of the other guards snarled. 'Clear off.' He advanced menacingly, his hand on the pommel of his sword, and as the boy turned and fled, their mocking laughter followed him into the night.

Terrel decided to make his next attempt in the small hours of the morning, when he hoped the sentries would be at their least alert. This time he was determined to advance by stealth rather than bravado – and he was now prepared to risk rather more than his dignity.

The great, iron-studded gates had been closed for the night, but the doors at either end of the side passage that went directly through the guardhouse itself were still open. A number of soldiers were on duty, though most of them were just lounging around, looking bored in the flickering light of the torches that burned in wall brackets. The smoke these torches gave off was scented with pine resin, which helped disguise the stink that drifted on the air from the nearest sections of the stews.

After his earlier failure, Terrel had decided to use the glamour this time. Although Alyssa had been unhappy about this, she had not been able to come up with an alternative suggestion. The possibility of attempting to alter his appearance to that of a respectable citizen, and then bluffing his way in, had been rejected as too complicated, and instead he'd decided to try to make himself invisible. He'd done this once before, on the wasteland above the mines of Betancuria, but on that occasion he had been standing still. This time he would have to move. He spent a few moments watching the play of light and shadow around the guardhouse, trying to imagine himself as just one more patch of unrecognizable darkness in the night. He crept closer, still keeping out of sight, and waited for Alyssa.

Now? she asked.

Now, he replied.

The magpies came swirling down, the sound of their harsh staccato chattering filling the air, and began to attack the main gate. They scrabbled for purchase on its ledges, wings fluttering in black and white, as they pecked at the wood in an apparent frenzy. After a few moments of this, guards started to pour out of the doorway.

'What the . . . ?'

'Have they gone mad?'

I am smoke and shadows, Terrel told himself. Smoke and shadows, nothing more.

He slipped past the first soldiers without them giving

him so much as a glance, and ducked quietly into the tunnel. He had to move aside when two more sentries ran past him, but he kept up his internal litany and neither of them paid him any attention. A few moments later, as the excited birds scattered into the night sky, Terrel stepped out into the calm air inside the city of Talazoria.

Smoke and shadows? the enchanter declared incredulously. *Moons! What are you up to* now?

CHAPTER FORTY-FIVE

Leave me alone, Jax.

But you invited me to watch, the enchanter said, and laughed. *And this isn't a dream, is it? This is real.* He sounded intrigued, and Terrel knew that the prince was storing up everything he saw for future use.

When are you going to get drunk again? the prince asked. *There's a lot more scope here than there was at that last place.*

Terrel wanted to be rid of the enchanter, and knew that his mind would remain vulnerable as long as he used the glamour, but he was still too close to the guardhouse for comfort. He began to run as best he could.

Your foot hurts, Jax commented. He sounded pleased.

Terrel tried to ignore him. He limped on, surprised by how much light there was in the city. There seemed to be lamps and torches burning everywhere, both on the streets and behind the shuttered windows of the buildings. More surprising still, there were a lot of people out and about – which would have been unheard of at that time of night anywhere else. The routines of Terrel's life had always been regulated by the hours of daylight, and even the largest towns he'd visited rarely had much activity after dark – and certainly not in the middle of the night. Talazoria, it seemed, was a law unto itself.

Even though it took him longer than he'd expected, Terrel eventually found a dark and quiet place to hide. As he released the glamour, the relief he felt was tempered by Jax's parting threat.

You'll have to go to sleep sometime. I'll be waiting.

It's just words, the boy told himself. He can put thoughts in my head and influence my dreams, but he can't *do* anything unless I've already lost control of myself. Terrel had no intention of getting drunk again.

Now that he had managed to get into the city, Terrel wondered what he ought to do next. He was hiding among some bushes in a small, shadowed garden, and was reasonably sure that he'd be safe there for the rest of the night – but he didn't want to risk sleeping, especially after his twin's final remark. His immediate problem was what to do at daybreak. There would no doubt be far more people on the streets then, and unless he was prepared to use the glamour again – which would both exhaust him and leave him prey to the enchanter – his appearance was bound to attract unwelcome attention. All the people he had seen so far had been well-dressed and well-groomed – and able-bodied. That meant he could have to act quickly, before he was caught and thrown out of the city.

It occurred to Terrel that if he was arrested by the guards, it was possible that he would not simply be returned to the stews. He might – and here the boy's heart raced as he sensed the beginnings of a plan – be found guilty of some crime, and condemned to be sent to the demon. If that happened, it would save him the trouble of having to find the elemental himself. His enemies would actually force him to make the very contact he desired!

There were risks, of course. His punishment might be something entirely different. They might execute him by a more conventional method, and – even if he wasn't killed – being thrown into gaol or exiled would be almost as bad as far as his plans were concerned. However, if what he'd been told was true, Ekuban was always looking for victims for his latest entertainment – and he was unlikely to turn down a volunteer!

Terrel was still wondering about this as the first light of dawn crept into the sky, and he decided to try to avoid capture for as long as he could – at least until he worked out what his chances were of reaching the elemental on his own. If, in spite of his best efforts, he *was* arrested, he would do his best to ensure that his sentence suited his purpose. In the meantime, he hoped that Alyssa would join him again soon. He needed her more than ever now. The little he had seen of the city was enough to show him that he could easily become lost, and he wanted her to help him find his way around.

Just as the watery daylight was becoming strong enough for Terrel to risk making his way out into the maze of streets, he got his wish. The magpie came gliding down, landed on the clipped grass nearby and bounded up to him. When she looked at him, she clicked her beak several times and lifted first one leg and then the other, waving them about as if she were trying to shake something off her feet.

Are you all right?

Doors don't have to open inwards, she replied. *How can you steal shadows?*

Alyssa? Terrel was worried now. He needed her to be rational. A long stay in the body of one animal or bird could bring her madness closer to the surface, but she had only been in the magpie for three days so far.

He's been here, hasn't he?

It took Terrel a moment to work out what she was talking about, but when he did he was glad she was making a little more sense.

Yes, but only for a while. He's gone now, he reassured her.

Don't let him come, she said. *You mend things. He destroys them.* There was both fear and revulsion in Alyssa's voice.

I'll keep him away, Terrel promised, even though the prince's threat was still fresh in his mind. *You and your friends did well. Thank you.*

You've no idea how difficult it was to get them all to fly at night! she exclaimed, apparently glad to change the subject. *I had to tell them there was food embedded in the door, just waiting to be stolen.*

Magpies like stealing things, don't they? Terrel said, smiling.

If thieves had a guild, they'd be the first to join up, she replied. *It's their one natural skill.*

Are they still here? he asked, wondering if he would need the birds' help again.

I can get them back if necessary, Alyssa replied nonchalantly. *What are you going to do now?*

Try to find the Ancient. Will you scout around for me, find out where the ruined fort is? And the palace?

Of course. Are you staying here?

No. Someone will see me sooner or later, so I'm going to have a look around.

Will you be all right? she asked. *You haven't had much rest.*

The sooner I get going now the better, Terrel said. *I don't want to sleep.*

As if to disprove his own claim, he yawned and his eyes closed of their own accord. He forced them open again.

Would it help if I pecked your ear again? Alyssa asked hopefully.

Terrel tried to appear confident, as though he belonged in the city, while Talazoria came to life around him. Most of the people he saw – in contrast to those who had been abroad during the night – were clearly underlings. Their clothes were generally of good quality but not showy, and most of them were obviously going about their business – sweeping forecourts, tending gardens and fetching food for their masters' households. Although the boy's presence attracted several questioning glances, no one spoke to him or raised the alarm. Terrel caught sight of several military patrols, but managed to keep out of their way as he moved further into the city. He was working on the assumption that most of the important buildings were likely to be near the centre, and when Alyssa returned she confirmed this, and told him that he was heading towards both the ruined castle and the king's palace. The two were situated next to each other.

Did you see the elemental? Terrel asked.

No, but I didn't stay long. I wanted to make sure you were going in the right direction.

And am I?

Yes. There's a big square nearby, and a lot of people are gathering there, she told him. *You might be less conspicuous in a crowd, and you'd have a chance to find out what was going on.*

Her advice was sensible, so Terrel continued on his way, with Alyssa flying ahead of him and acting as both guide and lookout. He was still the object of much curiosity, but no one seemed alarmed by his presence, and he began to wonder if the city really was as hostile to outsiders as he'd been led to believe. Because he was starting to feel light-headed from lack of sleep, he dared not use the glamour again. He would have liked to appear more presentable, and to disguise the message-handle, but he was afraid that if he did, Jax would take advantage of his vulnerable condition.

The closer he got to the heart of Talazoria, the more grand the streets and houses became. Manicured gardens surrounded enormous mansions, which were themselves decorated in flamboyant style, with statuary, gilded stonework and even jewelled mosaics on some of the walls. Such blatant ostentation was repulsive when set against the wretched poverty of the stews – and when Terrel saw a group of servants carting away a pile of garbage that included a huge amount of apparently good food amid the rubbish, he was appalled at such conspicuous waste. Talazoria was clearly a place where the fortunate few lived in pampered luxury. Drewan had told Terrel that even the king's dogs ate better than most peasants and, as with

several of the bargee's other tales, the boy had not wanted
to believe it. Now that he was inside the jewelled city,
such stories seemed all too plausible.

After a while, Terrel found himself moving within what
was now a constant flow of traffic. As well as those on
foot, there were some people on horseback, and others in
ornate carriages for whom underlings made way without
question. There were soldiers among the crowd too, but
they seemed preoccupied and paid the boy no attention.

By the time Alyssa told him that he was nearly at the
square, the sense of anticipation in the air around him was
reaching fever pitch – but although he had overheard
several snatches of conversation, he still didn't know what
was happening. As he finally emerged into the open space,
his attention was instantly drawn to an extraordinary
building on the far side of the square. Ekuban's palace was
the most elaborate, bizarre construction Terrel had ever
seen. Even on a cloudy day it glittered and glowed, each
surface displaying a whole range of vivid colours. There
were bulbous domes of shimmering blues and purples,
pointed turrets of red and ochre, wide roofs of glowing
orange and yellow tiles, and walls decorated in a variety
of exotic patterns. And everywhere there were touches of
gold and silver, as well as patches of brilliance that could
only come from precious stones set into the fabric of the
building itself. Even from a distance it was difficult to look
at the palace without squinting. On a sunny day it would
have been blinding. As it was, it was so garish that Terrel
felt the beginnings of a headache. Anyone who could build
such a monstrosity had to be mad, but if not, living there
would surely drive them insane.

Terrel switched his attention to the mercifully plain walls of the ruined fort next to the palace. He could see very little of the grey stones, just the jagged upper levels of what had once been a much larger building. In front of the ruin, on the edge of the square, stood three tall wooden towers, and Terrel could see people standing on the uppermost platform of each while others were climbing within the scaffolding below. Further away, presumably on the far side of the castle, were other similar towers. With a sudden sickening lurch of understanding, Terrel realized that these were grandstands, built to give a few observers the best possible view of the various spectacles within the elemental's prison. What was worse, there was obviously a great deal of competition for places on the platforms, which meant that something was going to happen soon.

Terrel made his way towards the fort without any real plan in mind, knowing only that he had to know the worst. He was soon engulfed by a densely-packed mass of people, the human tide now running strongly across the square. From closer to, the ruin was larger than he'd first thought, and it was evident that the original building had been an imposing edifice. The moat around it was wide and deep, but Terrel couldn't get close enough to see much more, and there was obviously no chance of clambering up onto the already overcrowded towers.

A new purpose had seized the crowd now, and the boy was swept along with it, first away from both the palace and the fort, then turning back to climb a small hill. This led to a slope of bare earth, which was covered with people crammed shoulder to shoulder. From this vantage point it was possible to see inside the fort, although it was a much more distant view than that afforded by the towers. However, no one seemed to be paying much attention to what was happening there. Terrel stared, trying to find some sign of the Ancient, but there was nothing like the swirling darkness he had encountered in Betancuria, and he assumed that the elemental was hiding. There was a buzz of conversation all around him, but he couldn't make out what was being said, and he glanced around, wondering whether he dared ask someone what was happening. He chose one of his neighbours, whose clothes were among the plainest he had seen, hoping that he would be the least likely to pay much attention to Terrel's own drab garments or his unusual staff.

'What's going on?'

'It'll be hours yet,' the man replied, without turning to look at the boy. 'Wish I'd brought something to drink.'

'I have some water,' Terrel offered, slipping his pack off his shoulder and taking out his flask.

'Thanks.' The man was obviously startled by the boy's crystalline eyes, but he accepted the water bottle nevertheless and drank gratefully.

'We've a long time to wait, then?' Terrel ventured.

'They're not going to feed the demon until noon. Didn't you hear the announcement?'

'I must have missed it. I only got to the square a short while ago.'

'You're lucky to get a spot like this then,' his informant commented. 'Especially as this is the last show for a while. After today they're going to be saving up all the prisoners for the festival.'

'What festival?'

The man gave him a strange look.

'Ekuban's name day, the day before Whitefire's Eve.'

None of this meant anything to Terrel, but he knew he'd already displayed rather too much of his ignorance, so he just nodded and said nothing for a while.

'That's an even longer time to wait then,' he commented eventually, his need to know more finally overcoming his qualms.

'Aye, a long month, more or less,' the man agreed, sounding resentful at having to endure such a long time between entertainments.

A horrible suspicion began to form in Terrel's mind as he worked out his dates.

'Whitefire's Day is midwinter, right?' he asked.

The underling shot the boy another suspicious glance. 'Of course.'

'My memory's not good today,' Terrel said, with what he hoped was a rueful grin. 'I had too much to drink last night.'

'I know that feeling,' the man said, his uncertainty replaced by a sympathetic smile.

Terrel was not sure whether he was pleased or horrified by what he had learnt. Closing his eyes for a moment, his memory took him back to the cloud-filled valley, and Amie's reply when he'd asked her when the day of the dream-predicted earthquake was. 'It's two days before midwinter,' she had told him. Which was Ekuban's birthday, the day of the festival.

Knowing that, it seemed very likely that this celebration, including the deaths of a large group of prisoners, was actually going to be the *cause* of the elemental's explosive rage. Terrel had to find a way of stopping that from happening, although as yet he had no idea how to

go about it. At least he had some time to consider his
options. After today's 'show' there were to be no more
for a while, which was a relief. On the other hand, the
idea of getting himself arrested was untenable now. Even
if the ploy succeeded, it would mean waiting until the
prophesied day of destruction before he would have a
chance to confront the elemental and try to avert a catastrophe. There had to be a better alternative.

As the sun climbed in the sky, and a few breaks in the
cloud made the day a little brighter, the sense of excitement in the crowd grew in intensity. Terrel felt their
blood lust as a kind of sickness, but there was nothing he
could do about it, and even he was curious to see when
the elemental would make its long-anticipated appearance.

As noon approached, Terrel saw that every vantage
point – every battlement, tower and window – in the
palace was crowded with colourfully dressed courtiers.
One particularly brilliant group seemed to be attracting
a good deal of attention, and Terrel assumed that the king
must be among them – but then he had no time to watch
the onlookers. A bell began to toll, marking the start of
the show, and a muffled cheer went up from the crowd.

Any bridges across the moat must have fallen into
disrepair long ago, and although it would have been
perfectly possible to have built a new wooden span, the
first of the condemned men was simply thrown into the
moat. He tried to swim back to shore, but guards held
him off with spears and he was eventually forced to splash
across to the other side. Once there he cowered on the
bank, while the spectators jeered and threw stones at him
until he finally began to climb the jumbled masonry of

the ruin. When he reached the top of the wall and stood still, his clothes dripping wet, the crowd of onlookers seemed to hold their breath. The man's terrified gaze swept the interior of the fort but he, like Terrel, obviously saw nothing unusual. More stones drove him on, but there was still no sign of the demon. The crowd murmured restlessly.

'Maybe it's down in the old dungeons,' someone to Terrel's left suggested.

'No chance,' his companion replied. 'The dungeons are full of water. They were flooded years ago.'

'Look!' a woman cried suddenly. 'There it is!'

At first Terrel couldn't see what she meant, but then something moved inside the ruins, and he realized that he'd been looking at the Ancient all the time. He had been searching for a writhing, amorphous mass – like the elemental at Betancuria – but this creature had evidently managed to make itself less conspicuous, blending in with its surroundings by disguising itself as a large grey rock. However, it had clearly become agitated – presumably by the approach of the prisoner – and when that happened its shape and colouring had begun to shift, making it visible to everybody – including its intended victim. The man tried to run, but he tripped and fell on the uneven surface, and a moment later a blur of darkness lashed out, distorting the scene so that it was impossible to see exactly what was happening. There was movement where there should have been none, shadows that were cast by thin air, and a hideous scream, sharply cut off. It was all over in an instant, but no less terrifying for that. One moment the prisoner was struggling to get to his feet, the next all that was left of him was a crimson mist, as his blood scattered and fell like a shower of bright red rain. Everything else – his clothes, hair, bones – had simply vanished.

Terrel was appalled, but all around him there were gasps not of horror, but of amazement and admiration, and there was a burst of cheering and applause.

'Not bad,' his earlier informant said, his eyes shining. 'It's always better when they make them swim across the moat first.'

I'll bet it is, Terrel thought, but he was feeling too nauseous to say anything.

I couldn't watch any longer after that. How many more died?

Three men and two women, Alyssa replied, sounding equally revolted. *The later ones were even worse.*

Terrel was not surprised.

The elemental is trapped with water all around it, he explained. *It's not even supposed to be in the open air, and it's full of rage and fear. Having those people approach it, especially with their clothes all wet, drives it mad and it lashes out. And the more furious and terrified it gets, the more violent it becomes.*

They were silent for a while, each wishing they could excise their memories of the 'show'. Hearing stories of what had happened to some of the miners in Betancuria was one thing; actually seeing it with their own eyes was something else altogether.

Did you try to talk to it? Alyssa asked.

I tried, but I was too far away – and I don't think it was listening anyway. But it's in dreadful pain. I didn't need to talk to it to know that. It's in constant torment.

Couldn't it use some of its power to escape?

Terrel shook his head.

You know the effect being near water has on them. It's on the verge of panic all the time, and it just can't think straight.

Do you think you could reason with it if you got closer?

Maybe. But I was only able to communicate properly with the other one when I was inside *it. I don't think this one is going to let me get that close.*

Especially not in its present state of mind, Alyssa agreed. *So what do we do now?*

Well, at least there won't be any more killings for a while. The Ancient may calm down. And if it doesn't, he added, glancing at his staff, *I'll have to try to make Ekuban see sense. If he won't listen to me, he should at least listen to Reader.*

Maybe you should try that first. The elemental might take days to calm down, and sooner or later someone's going to notice you're not a citizen. This place isn't exactly welcoming to outsiders.

So how do I get into the court?

I'll go and take a look at the palace, Alyssa replied, *then we can decide the best approach.*

After she'd flown away, Terrel wandered among the dispersing crowd, finding himself back in the central square. On the far side, beneath the outer walls of the palace, was a platform with several men standing on it. Some sort of announcement was being made and, joining many of the other spectators, Terrel went over to hear what was being said.

A red-faced man in ceremonial garb was reading aloud from a scroll. Terrel only caught the end of the proclamation, but that was enough to get the gist of it.

'It is therefore the finding of the judges' panel that these men are guilty of the crime of treason against the king and the land of Macul. The immutable sentence for this offence is death, and their executions will take place in due course in the manner laid down by the appropriate Royal Statutes.'

'But not until the festival?' one of the crowd called out.

'In this instance, that is correct,' the crier replied before turning away, his duties completed.

Terrel had not been paying any attention to this final exchange. As soon as the death sentences had been announced, he had looked across at the bedraggled group of prisoners whose wrists and ankles were manacled. When he saw the young man at the far end of the row, he could not believe his eyes. But he knew he was not mistaken. One of the condemned men was Aylen Mirana.

CHAPTER FORTY-SIX

Terrel stood quite still for some time after he'd watched Aylen and the others being led away, but then he became aware that several people – including a soldier – were looking at him, and he hurried on, picking one of the side streets at random. As the shock of seeing his friend wore off, he found it easy to imagine how he'd come to be there. When Aylen had left Fenduca to take the king's wages, he had clearly had an ulterior motive. He must have tried – and failed – to provoke a revolt among the miners on the black mountain. The charges against him, unlike many of the other prisoners Ekuban had sent to their deaths, were probably genuine. As things stood in Macul, Aylen almost certainly *was* guilty of treason. The fact that any man in his right mind would want to rebel against such a regime was no defence.

Aylen's situation gave Terrel one more reason to ensure that the festival never took place – or if it did, that its outcome was not the one he'd foreseen. To this end he worked his way around the square until he was able to approach the castle from another angle, deciding to continue his own investigations while Alyssa studied the palace. The moat was just as wide on that side, and there was no way across except by swimming – and Terrel already knew that he would stand no chance if he approached the elemental while he was wet. He had to try to contact the creature from where he stood. Psinoma usually only worked from relatively close range, and communicating with the Ancient was never going to be straightforward, so he didn't feel very optimistic – and although repeated efforts allowed him to form a vague picture of the elemental within, there was no direct exchange. What he learnt only confirmed his earlier impressions. The tormented creature was in agony, and in no state to listen to reason. It was much more likely to lash out and kill Terrel if he tried to get any closer. It seemed that approaching Ekuban's court was his only option.

That evening Alyssa informed him that under normal circumstances he would have no chance of getting even close to the palace, let alone inside. He had expected as much, and they spent some time discussing how to try to overcome this. The last of Terrel's food was gone, and the fact that he would soon have to resort to stealing made the situation even more urgent. But he couldn't help feeling that the plan they eventually decided on was hardly foolproof.

After Alyssa had flown away to roost, Terrel decided to try to talk to Reader, to see if he had any advice to offer. To the boy's delight, the message-handle responded to his call and he heard the sharakan's voice clearly, even if it was faint and a little wavery at times. The old man approved of Terrel's intentions, and promised to be ready should the boy need to summon him.

It's a propitious day tomorrow, Reader concluded. *The Red Moon will be new, and thus at its weakest. We can all be calm.*

Terrel thought this was oversimplifying matters, but he appreciated the sentiment and was glad the sharaken were going to support him. When their brief conversation ended, Terrel lay down beneath another garden hedge and fell into an exhausted sleep. He dreamt of the Dark Moon, its surface covered in diamond-bright swirls, shining down upon Talazoria. The strange light made the palace glitter like an enormous jewel, but the building seemed to be encased in a glass dome – a giant version of the structures atop the sharaken's towers – which held a fascination of its own. Terrel stared, unable to decide what it was or what it meant, and this time there were no words to help him decipher his vision.

The next morning Terrel stood in the square, gripping the message-handle tightly in his left hand, and stared at the palace again. This time there was no glass dome, just the same demented melange of shapes and colours. The platform where he'd seen Aylen was empty now, except for a couple of sentries who were watching over the square. To one side was the main entrance to the palace, with its doors – reputedly made of solid silver – standing open. A group of soldiers was on duty there, but the atmosphere seemed relaxed, as if they assumed that no one would be stupid enough – or bold enough – to try to enter uninvited. Terrel felt a sudden reckless determination to prove them wrong.

Which are you, then? Alyssa asked from above. *Stupid or bold?*

Terrel glanced up at the sky, no longer surprised by her ability to hear his thoughts.

Both, he replied. *Are you ready?*

Oh, yes, she answered eagerly.

You remember the signal? And exactly what to do?

You're in the hands of experts, she assured him. *Not that we have hands. Get going!*

Terrel took a deep breath, then strode forward as purposefully as he could, trying to ignore the soreness of his right foot. During his time in Talazoria, he'd come to realize that far from being a disadvantage, the unusual nature of his staff had actually helped him. As far as the citizens were concerned, a peasant would not own such a remarkable object, and therefore he must be worthy of a place in their city. As he neared the gateway, he brandished the message-handle energetically, and kept his eyes wide open so that everyone there could see that they too were out of the ordinary. Even though his heart was hammering, he tried to exude an air of self-confidence.

Several guards were aware of him now, and were watching his progress with some amusement. One of the sentries was about to challenge the boy when a whirring piebald shape flew past his head. He turned to follow its progress, and saw that it was not alone. The magpies descended in a chattering mob, each one drawn to a particular bright object in or near the palace gates, and the square was soon echoing to the sound of two dozen beaks pecking repeatedly at stone, plaster or wood. The guards all gazed at the onslaught, struck dumb by the birds' inexplicable behaviour. It was only when one of the magpies managed to dislodge a ruby that had been set in the eye of a statue, that the sentries began to react.

'Get rid of them!' the duty captain yelled. 'And don't let them take anything!' He drew his sword and waved it above his head in an attempt to scare some of the marauders away, while one of his men stooped to retrieve the fallen ruby – much to the annoyance of the bird who had flown down to claim its prize.

By then most of the soldiers were trying to fend off the magpies and, in answer to another shouted order, an archer had emerged from the guardhouse. He appeared to be at a loss at first, but then shot a couple of arrows at the insistence of his captain. He didn't come close to hitting any of the birds.

In the midst of all this pandemonium, no one noticed that Terrel had reached the gateway and was now standing under the arch.

'There is a plague upon this house!' he yelled, raising both arms.

At his words the entire flock rose into the air, only to come down again on the inner side of the wall and attack a new set of targets inside the palace. As the captain redeployed his forces and called for reinforcements, the battle moved on – and Terrel moved with it.

Which way now? He had forgotten Alyssa's instructions.

Go straight ahead, then climb the stairs to the right and go up to the third level, she told him. *There's a corridor there that leads to the inner ring. Once you're past that, the main hall is under the blue spire with the gold pinnacle.*

Terrel followed her directions, listening to the continuing sounds of the airborne conflict and keeping an
eye out for any guards. None of them seemed to be paying
him any attention, and a few even ran straight past him
on their way to help their colleagues. The magpies had
spread out now, attacking different parts of the palace at
random and driving the sentries to distraction.

When Terrel reached the inner wall, and had to pass
through a smaller gate where the sentries were still on
duty, a group of birds appeared at Alyssa's behest and
began to destroy a jewelled mosaic nearby. The soldiers
hesitated, not quite sure that they believed what they were
seeing, then they abandoned their post and ran to shoo
the raiders away – and Terrel walked unchallenged into
the royal inner sanctum. He soon reached the golden
doors beneath the spire, and knew that this was the
moment of truth. Until then he'd been avoiding confrontation; now he had to seek it out.

Be careful, Alyssa told him from somewhere overhead.
There's something not right here.

This is my chance, he replied. *Get your friends away now
before any of them get hurt.*

I can't, she said. *They're having too much fun to stop
now.*

Terrel grinned, in spite of the fact that his insides
seemed to have turned to liquid. He raised his staff and
slammed the heel into the golden door. He could sense
the shocked silence on the other side as the metal rever-
berated, and he struck again, even harder this time. At
the third blow the doors opened inwards, pulled by
unseen servants, and Terrel got his first look at the
Talazorian court. It took all of his remaining courage to

step forward and face a hundred pairs of curious eyes.

The hall was massive, with a cavernous roof, banner-strewn walls and a marble floor that was built on two levels. The outer part surrounded a sunken interior, with steps leading down on all four sides to a performance area below. There a man held a chain which was connected to a ring through the nose of a large bear, while three musicians sat to one side. Terrel's entrance had evidently interrupted their act, and the four men were looking up at him in disbelief. The area near the door was clear, but the rest of the upper level was filled with courtiers, and on the far side – raised above everyone else by a magnificent throne – sat the king. Terrel had expected Ekuban to be a dissolute old man dressed in colourful silks, but the king was young, well-muscled and extremely handsome. He was dressed more like a soldier than a courtier and, apart from a diamond-studded coronet, he wore no jewellery. His eyes, like everyone else's, were fixed on Terrel, and even though the king's face showed only amusement and a little surprise, the boy felt the madness in that gaze. He stood erect, staring back with all the bravado he could muster, but he was shivering inside. This was a man, he sensed, who would be capable of *anything*.

'After such an entrance, we expected at least a small army,' Ekuban remarked, breaking the deathly silence. 'And yet all we have is a crippled peasant boy.'

'I—'

'Did we ask you to speak?' His voice was soft, and his tone was deceptively mild, but it silenced Terrel nonetheless. 'Are your manners as deformed as your limbs? Give me one good reason why we should not feed your pretty eyes to Aygian's bear.' Ekuban waved expressive hands. 'You may speak now.'

'Your kingdom is under threat, Your Majesty.' Terrel's voice shook a little in spite of all his efforts.

'From you?' Ekuban laughed, and the rest of the courtiers joined in, taking their cue from their monarch. They were obviously pleased that the king had decided the intruder represented no threat and was allowing him to stay for his amusement value.

'No,' Terrel replied. 'From the creature you call the demon.'

'Our little pet?' Ekuban said, looking round in wide-eyed astonishment that provoked further merriment from his audience. 'Surely not. He is harmless to all but our enemies.'

'That will change if you go on as you are.'

Some of the onlookers gasped when they heard this provocative statement, but the king just smiled.

'Really?' he said, then paused, considering. 'You're clearly quite mad, but you've obviously gone to a lot of trouble to get here, so we might as well listen to what you have to say.'

Red-faced guards appeared in the doorway behind Terrel, but Ekuban waved them away, then gestured to the boy again.

'Begin.'

Terrel did his best to explain that the creature had been woken too soon, that it was not supposed to be above ground, and that water drove it mad.

'If it's not released it will start a great earthquake,' he went on, coming to the main point. 'An earthquake more violent than anything you have known before. All of Macul will be destroyed.'

'And how do you know this?'

'It's been prophesied in dreams.' Throughout his brief speech Terrel's words had been met with muted sounds of derision, but at the mention of dreams there was a brief hush. This was something they might take seriously, even here.

'Ooh, a prophecy. What fun!' Ekuban's sarcasm dashed the boy's hopes. 'I assume you know when all this is going to happen.'

'On your name day,' Terrel replied.

At this the king whispered an aside to some of those nearest to the throne, and mocking laughter spread quickly through the hall. Terrel didn't know what had been said, but – to his shame – he felt himself blushing.

'So,' Ekuban said, steepling his fingers and pretending to be in earnest. 'What must we do to prevent this disaster?'

'Don't send any more prisoners into the castle,' Terrel replied, answering the question even though he'd realized now that he had no chance of convincing Ekuban to take action.

'Leave the demon alone. Drain the moat and the dungeons so it can return to its proper place underground.'

'Is that all?' the king asked, feigning surprise. 'You don't want us to invite it to a celebratory meal? Or suggest that it marry our daughter?'

'The danger I've described is real. You'll regret—'

'We think not,' Ekuban stated flatly. 'You were entertaining for a while, but you're boring us now. You're only a peasant, so there's no reason to take you seriously. But even if what you say is true, we are in no danger here.

This palace might look like a work of art, but its foundations are sound – and we are protected.' He glanced at an old woman who stood next to the throne and who seemed vaguely familiar to Terrel, and she nodded, smiling slightly. 'Talazoria has withstood a great many tremors,' he went on, 'with only minimal damage. And if you think we're cancelling the festival because of what *you* think is going to happen, then you truly are mad.'

'Then at least let me talk to the creature,' Terrel pleaded, desperate now.

'You *want* to meet it?' Ekuban asked in surprise. 'You're either very brave or completely insane. Perhaps both.'

Some of the courtiers were whispering among themselves now, darting suspicious glances at the boy, but the king ignored them.

'Very well, you shall have your wish,' he decreed. 'You will go to the demon with all the others during the festival.'

'No! That will be too late. I'm not the only one who—'

'Silence!' one of the courtiers shouted. 'The king has spoken. This audience is at an end.'

Terrel turned to his last resort. Even as he called silently to Reader, he had a dreadful foreboding of disaster – but what else was he supposed to do? The sharakan's image flickered into being next to the boy, his ghostly hand grasping the message-handle just above Terrel's. Most of the courtiers gasped in wonder and fear, but one of them laughed abruptly. Terrel could not tell who that was, because he was looking at Reader in dismay. The old man was bent almost double, and was obviously in a great deal of pain. His eyes darted about, apparently searching for something he could not see.

'You really shouldn't try that in here, little brother,' the old woman said. 'My magic has always been more powerful than yours.'

Terrel realized in that instant why her face had seemed familiar. He also knew that there really *was* a protective dome over the palace – not of glass, but of sorcery – and that Reader's sister was responsible for it. What was more, it was somehow affecting the mystic.

'This sharakan is your brother?' Ekuban asked his elderly companion, his amazement genuine this time.

'I would recognize him anywhere,' the woman replied, 'even though he abandoned me when I was only eight years old.'

'Marika, please,' Reader croaked. 'You don't know what you're doing. This could . . .'

'Always jealous,' she commented as his voice died away. 'Even now.'

Terrel tried to say something, but his lips and tongue were frozen. In fact his entire body was paralyzed, as if he had been turned to stone. He couldn't even blink. Reader turned to give him a look that was full of regret, as his image faded and then vanished.

'Put him in the cells with the others,' Ekuban ordered. 'We'll save him for the festival, as we said. He might put on a better show than we first thought.'

Soldiers came forward and grabbed Terrel. One of them tried to take the staff, but jumped away, yelling in pain, as soon as his fingers touched the wood. No one else wanted to try after that, and in any case Terrel's grip was like iron and quite immovable. The boy himself was held rigid, every muscle frozen in place, and in the end the soldiers had to carry him out. They were all careful to avoid touching the message-handle.

Terrel couldn't even tell if his heart was still beating, and he felt sure he was about to die. He panicked, struggling uselessly against his internal captivity. A few moments later, when he realized he was not going to die just yet, he calmed down a little – but only a little. Even if everything else in his body was frozen, his brain was still working. He was able to think, and it was at this point, just as the bemused soldiers stood him against the wall of a prison cell, that he realized – too late – what the mysterious verse from the Tindaya Code had meant.

CHAPTER FORTY-SEVEN

'Eat up, lads. You're going to need all your strength tomorrow. It's your big day.'

The gaoler laughed as he went away, and for once the prisoners who shared Terrel's cell did not descend like a hungry pack of wolves upon the meagre rations. The imminence of death seemed to have robbed them all of their appetites.

The festival was only a day away.

Keeping track of time had been almost impossible for Terrel. Without the normal ways of measuring the hours and days – light and dark, the passage of the sun and moons, the rhythms of his own body – his attempts to do so had driven him close to despair. His utter physical helplessness, combined with an almost constant state of mental anguish, had meant that the time had passed with excruciating slowness. At first, when he'd still believed that his unnatural paralysis must either wear off or kill him, he had been alone in the cell. The only people he'd seen were the gaolers, who came to look at him occasionally and who left food he'd been unable to eat. Later, as the prison filled up with more men destined to play leading roles in Ekuban's show, he'd shared the space with others. Each batch of newcomers had inspected their strange cell mate, and one of them always tried to touch his staff, in spite of the warnings from those who had already seen what it could do. The pain it inflicted was severe, and left the victim's arm flopping uselessly at his side for an hour or more after the initial shock wore off.

Even without the message-handle, the other prisoners would have regarded Terrel with deep suspicion. His peculiar appearance, and the fact that he never moved, unnerved many of them – and those who had the courage to touch him found his flesh as cool and as hard as marble. No one had made any attempt to harm him, but they talked about him as if he were not there. Terrel couldn't blame them for that. He could still see and hear, but his fellow prisoners had no way of knowing that. He could even smell his surroundings, and he was aware of the hardness of the wall at his back, the smoothness of the wood that he gripped tightly in his hand, and the dampness of the air. But he remained completely immobile. Only his eyes moved – and they were all that kept the world from assuming he was dead.

With the arrival of his cell mates, it had become a little easier to gauge the passage of time. Their routine of eating and sleeping had given a pattern to the days, but all Terrel knew for certain was that a long time had elapsed. He was vaguely aware that the date when the

Floating Islands passed closest to the shore of Macul had come and gone. He'd known for some time that his chance of returning had vanished, but the absolute certainty was a further blow to his ravaged spirit. It was also an unwelcome reminder that when the earthquake struck, his homeland would still be dangerously close by.

Terrel had also been able to learn a little of what was happening in the outside world from the conversations between his fellow inmates and, occasionally, from the guards. Preparations for the festival were under way, and extra viewing towers were being constructed for the main event. A lottery had been organized to award places on these platforms, and the competition among the citizens for the winning numbers was fierce. In addition, Terrel had discovered that Aylen was being kept in an adjacent cell, together with his co-conspirators, and that his friend had heard about his predicament and was asking about him. On a few occasions the boy had even thought he'd heard Aylen's voice, but of course he had been unable to reply.

Remarkably, the only person he *had* been able to talk to was Reader. Now that they were outside the palace – the prison was on the other side of the square – the message-handle enabled them to communicate at intervals, depending on the relative influences of the moons. Terrel had been given new hope when he'd discovered this, but that hope had soon been dashed. The sharakan was a broken man, a shadow of his former self, and although he was able to talk to Terrel, there was nothing he could do to help him. The message-handle, he'd explained dismally, had been effectively destroyed by his sister's magic – which was indeed much stronger than his own. His image could not be summoned, and no trading was possible. In effect it had been paralyzed at the same time as Terrel. However, the boy's link with Reader, especially during his early solitary days, had probably been the only thing that helped him hold on to his sanity, and it had been during one of their remote conversations that he'd learned Marika's story.

As children, Reader and his sister had been inseparable. They had both shown early signs of remarkable abilities, but when a Collector had come to the village – when Marika was eight years old and Reader six – he had ignored the girl completely and spoken only to the boy, even though everyone – including the precocious children themselves – knew that Marika was the more talented of the two. When the sharakan had ridden off, taking Reader with him, the little boy had gloated over his triumph. Later he had come to regret it. During his many years in the mountains, he had tried to forget his sister, but he'd never succeeded. He had often wondered what had become of her. That he knew now had completed her revenge.

The other person Terrel wanted to speak to was, of course, Alyssa. However, she had not made contact – and he didn't know whether this was simply because she'd been unable to get into the prison, or if there was some other, more sinister reason. Now that so much time had passed, he assumed she must have been forced to leave the city. In Betancuria she had been a stonechat for about fifteen days, and that had put her under an enormous strain, damaging her health and accentuating her eccentric behaviour. If Alyssa were still in Talazoria,

she would have been a magpie for three times as long –
and Terrel wasn't sure whether she could have even
survived such an ordeal. There was always the chance
that she had left in order to rest in her own body, and
thus might return – either as a magpie or another creature. But time was running out.

The only thing Terrel had been able to do during his
incarceration had been to think – although few of his
thoughts had given him any comfort. He'd spent a great
deal of time brooding over the verse from the Tindaya
Code. The fact that he was now almost certain that
he'd deciphered its meaning gave him no pleasure.
'Beware the golden way, the silver steps deceive,' was
not, as he had thought, a reference to some part of the
jewelled city, but a warning against his mode of transport. He could clearly recall watching the setting sun
turn the canal the colour of gold, and the gushing water
of the locks were the silver steps. 'Until the royal day'
now seemed to be a straightforward reference to
Ekuban's name day, and the last line, the one that had
proved the most enigmatic – 'the diamond moon
believe' – he now took to be a link to his dreams about
the Dark Moon. The moon had sometimes been illumi-
nated by bright swirls of light, and at the beginning
and end of eclipses there was also a diamond effect from
the sun as it escaped from its shadow. This reasoning
had led him to reconsider the advice he'd been given
in those dreams. Although he'd forgotten most of it,
the meaning of what he *could* remember was now clear.
'Move sideways first' had been an instruction to leave
the canal. 'Remember your sister' probably referred to

Reader's sister rather than to any relation of his own, and 'Don't try to dream within the dome' was a warning whose relevance was now obvious. When he'd first heard it, he'd thought that it had meant the domes of the sharaken's towers. He realized now that it alluded to the sorcery protecting Ekuban's palace, and the dream in question had been Terrel's ill-fated attempt to conjure up Reader's image. He was still not sure whether the disastrous outcome of that experiment might have been caused by something that had happened earlier. Exactly *why* he had not been supposed to travel on the canal was not yet clear. Had it meant that the fluctuating curse Alyssa had talked of had somehow affected either him or the staff? Or was it because the presence of so much water had delayed Alyssa's arrival – and possibly that of the ghosts? Would they have been able to give him any advice about the possible pitfalls of his mission – pitfalls he had so spectacularly failed to avoid? Terrel had no way of knowing.

And unless something miraculous happened, he would probably never know now. The night that must fall soon was the last before the festival, and even if he was still paralyzed, Terrel knew he could expect no mercy from Ekuban – or the elemental – when morning came.

Terrel slept, with his eyes open.

Apart from thinking, the only other thing he'd been able to do was *dream*. He'd had frequent nightmares about being held in a vice-like grip by some unseen force, unable to move – even though all his friends were in terrible danger and needed his help. And he always woke, wailing silently, to find that the nightmare was all too real.

Dreaming that he *could* move was almost worse. It made the crushing disappointment of waking even more devastating.

Tonight he felt the Dark Moon rise, an invisible but tangible presence in the eastern sky, and sensed a new purpose in its flight. But no one, not even Jax – whose voice had tormented him on several occasions – came to give him any advice.

When Terrel awoke, the rank smell of fear filled the cell. The condemned men knew that this was the day they were going to die. No one spoke. They all avoided catching each other's eyes. Every sound from the corridor outside made them jump, as they waited for the guards to come for them. A few wept silently, while others only just managed to bottle up their impotent fury, but overall the mood was one of hopelessness and disbelief.

Footsteps sounded in the passageway, and the prisoners grew even more tense. Then a voice, from further away, echoed throughout the dungeon.

'Hey, Edo, come and look at this. It's amazing.'

The footsteps retreated again, and silence returned.

A few moments later Terrel felt an odd burning sensation in his left hand. At the same time he became aware of a new luminescence in the cell – a shimmering, dappled effect like sunlight reflected off running water. He also noticed that the other inmates were all staring at him.

At the edge of his peripheral vision, the boy saw that

the silvery glow was actually spreading from his hand, travelling along the entire length of the staff and making it shine as though lit from within. Terrel watched in disbelief as his fingers slowly uncurled, releasing their grip at last.

As the glowing message-handle clattered to the floor – with some of the prisoners jumping out of the way to avoid being hit – Terrel took his first shuddering gulp of air as he began to breathe again.

It felt as though his entire body was burning from inside – but he could move at last!

CHAPTER FORTY-EIGHT

Talazoria had never experienced a total eclipse before. Even the humblest sky-watcher had known that there would be an eclipse that morning, but no one had foreseen the fact that the Dark Moon would obliterate the sun completely. Being plunged into almost complete darkness in the middle of the day had a stunning effect on everyone in the city, including those who had gathered in the central square for the festivities. Silence fell over the celebrations.

Terrel looked round at his fellow prisoners, unnerved by their collective gaze. They in turn seemed to be afraid of him. The cold fire of the amulet burned in his hand even as the rest of his body came back to life.

'What *is* that?' one inmate whispered, clearly mesmerized by the talisman's delicate beauty.

Terrel hesitated before answering, partly because he didn't trust his tongue to work after it had been paralyzed for so long, and partly because he did not really know what to say. In the end he didn't say anything at all. Before he could decide how best to explain the miniature star, he felt another presence – and another question.

Had it been spoken in a human tongue, the nearest translation would have been 'Do you have the spiral inside you?', but the enquiry came not in words but in an enveloping sense of curiosity. With a sudden breathless surge of excitement, Terrel realized that – somehow – he was in touch with the elemental. He knew from his earlier experiences in Betancuria that he had no need to form specific answers. He had only to think of something and the Ancient would *know* as much as he did. However, the only way he could take advantage of this unexpected opportunity was to treat it like a conversation using psinoma. There were specific points he desperately needed to make – and he didn't know how long the link would last.

Whatever happens, you must stay calm. I know you're frightened and angry, but please, please, don't start an earthquake. Although Terrel could now sense the incipient madness beyond the curiosity, he also felt that the Ancient was still interested, so he sought to reinforce his message. *The people who are sent inside the walls mean you no harm. They are not to blame for your imprisonment. You don't need to hurt them.*

He sensed confusion now. Obviously some of what he said was beyond the creature's understanding, and he was wondering how to clarify his thoughts when he realized the elemental wanted to know who *was* to blame for its confinement inside the ring of magic – the same magic that the people always brought with them.

Who's to blame? Terrel hesitated, knowing that his own memories might already be betraying him. *There were a lot of reasons why you ended up here, but it's the people in the palace who are responsible for* keeping *you here.*

To his amazement, he heard the next question as if he were using psinoma with someone like Alyssa.

Within the circle of bright air?

Yes, Terrel replied, knowing that this meant the sorcerous dome. *I want to help you. I . . .* He stopped abruptly, aware that the link was gone. The amulet had vanished, and the glow of the message-handle was fading fast. Whatever had prompted the contact, it was over now – and Terrel had no idea whether or not he had convinced the elemental with his arguments.

Outside in the square, the light returned, the lunar shadow departing as swiftly as it had arrived. The dazzling ring of beads in the sky grew brighter still as the sun reclaimed its dominance of the heavens, but everyone knew they had witnessed an important and wondrous event. What they didn't know was whether the eclipse had been an omen for good or evil.

The power that had released Terrel from his paralyzed state had gone, but his body was still free. The spell was broken. He was back in the land of the living. However, unless he had managed to placate the elemental, he was not likely to remain there for very long.

There were sounds of movement outside the cell, and shouted orders. The guards were on their way to collect

the prisoners. This realization shattered the enchantment that had been cast over the cell, as the inmates
were suddenly reminded of the fate that awaited them.

'Are you a sorcerer?' one of them asked. 'Can you get
us out of this?'

Terrel shook his head.

'Any talent I have is as a healer,' he said. 'But I have
friends who may be able to help us.'

He looked at the message-handle, knowing that he
could not leave it where it was, but dreading the possibility that it might be used to trap him again. As he knelt
down and steeled himself to touch it, the other prisoners
cowered away, as if they might all be tainted by such
foolhardy behaviour. They watched nervously as the boy
gingerly stretched out his good hand and let the tip of
one finger brush lightly against the wood. He felt no
pain or paralysis. Encouraged, he felt its carved surface
with the rest of his fingers, then picked it up, still without
suffering any ill effects. He did not understand what had
happened, but the sorcery that had captured him had
been neutralized.

He stood up, gripped the staff tightly and called out
to the sharaken again, hoping that now they were outside
the dome the link could be restored.

Reader? Can you hear me? Reader?

There was no response, and Terrel wondered whether
the struggle between brother and sister had destroyed
the power of the message-handle. Even as his hopes
faded, he made himself try again, closing his eyes in
order to concentrate better.

I need your help, Reader. Please.

I am here.

Terrel didn't know what had shocked him most, the fact that someone had answered, or that the person who had done so was not Reader. This voice was quite different, emotionless and controlled.

Where's Reader? he asked, realizing as he spoke that the voice belonged to the sharakan he knew as the Collector.

Reader is dead. His mandates have passed to me.

Dead? Terrel was appalled.

His failure weighed heavily upon his spirit. Especially given the manner of his defeat.

Terrel was stunned and dismayed, but he had no time for grief now. He could hear squads of guards as they began to take prisoners out of the others cells, one group at a time.

I need your help, he said urgently. *We haven't got much time. The killings are—*

Is the elemental aware that Ekuban and his court are responsible for its predicament? the Collector cut in.

Yes. I've just been talking to it, but . . . Did you know that?

It was our reading of the oracles.

I'm not sure if I convinced it not to start the earthquake. You have to help me stop the festival and—

We will help you, Terrel, the sharakan cut in again. *I will gather my colleagues, but you must wait until the Amber Moon rises. We can do nothing until then.*

When will that be? Terrel asked, anxiety replacing his sudden hope.

An hour, no more. We must conserve our strength until then.

Can't you— Terrel began, but the contact had been broken.

He opened his eyes to find several of his cell mates looking at him, pleading silently for any sign of hope.

'We've got to delay things for at least an hour,' he told them.

'An hour?' one replied. 'I'd like to delay it a lifetime.'

'We might be able to do that if you can give me the first hour.'

'How?'

'I don't know. Just keep your eyes open for any opportunity.'

Outside the door, footsteps were approaching.

'The guards won't let you keep that now you can move,' another prisoner said, pointing to the staff.

'They won't have any choice,' Terrel replied, knowing he must keep hold of the sharaken's gift at all costs.

A key turned in the lock and bolts were drawn back.

'Right, you lot!' a guard shouted as the door opened. 'Single file, and no funny stuff, or I'll save the demon some trouble and slit you open myself.'

Terrel heard the cheering for the first deaths, and knew that his pleas had been in vain. The elemental was still reacting to what it perceived as an attack – and reacting in the only way it understood. And there was still no sign of the Amber Moon in the eastern sky.

The rest of the condemned men and women were now all in the square. They had been kept in small groups, and were heavily outnumbered by the guards who were escorting them, so there was no chance of anyone trying to escape or disrupt the proceedings. Terrel had racked his brain for a way of delaying the inevitable, but nothing had occurred to him. The only thing he had to be grateful for was the fact that, because of all the rest of the day's festivities – and the diversion caused by the eclipse – the show had not begun at the traditional time of noon but some hours later. This brought it much closer to the point when the Collector had said he would be able to help. However, to make up for lost time, Ekuban had instructed his men to send the prisoners across the moat in groups of five or six instead of singly. Terrel knew that the Ancient would be driven to extreme violence by these multiple assaults. The spectators, on the other hand, were wholehearted in their approval. Every tower was full to overflowing, people clung to every available vantage point, and the hill where Terrel had stood for the previous show was packed. Even in the square, where it was impossible to see into the castle, the crowds were massive. It seemed that everyone in Talazoria simply wanted to be close to the slaughter.

Terrel had at least managed to retain possession of the message-handle. He had done so by simply refusing to put it down or to let go – and when the sentries had tried to take it from him by force, the jolts of pain they'd suffered made their comrades less than eager to repeat the attempt. Their threats had had no effect, and some of Terrel's fellow prisoners had guarded his back to prevent a surprise attack. In the end the platoon leader had given in.

'Let him keep it,' he had said. 'A bit of wood isn't going to help him against the demon, is it? But if he tries to use it as a weapon, kill him, orders or no orders.'

Terrel was now beginning to wonder if the staff would help him in any way at all.

Another series of cheers went up as, out of sight, more prisoners were killed. The soldiers ordered Terrel's group to move forward, coming ever closer to their own doom, when a disturbance up ahead halted their progress. Terrel had spotted Aylen earlier, noting that – unsurprisingly – the young man looked haggard and ill. But Aylen had obviously not lost all his fighting spirit, because he was leading an escape bid. The prisoners were attacking their guards wildly, unarmed men against swords and spears. They had little hope of victory, but had evidently decided they'd rather die this way than surrender to an even worse fate. The battle was short and bloody, with most of the men either wounded or beaten senseless, but none of them was killed. The reason for this soon became all too clear.

'You don't get away that easily,' one of the soldiers told them when order had been restored. 'We've orders not to kill you scum. That's for the demon. But we'll be happy to beat the crap out of you again before it finishes you off. It's your choice.'

After that there was little chance of any more trouble. Terrel looked for Aylen, and when he found him he saw that his head and shirt were covered in blood – but it was impossible to tell whether this was his own or someone else's. He was helping one of his wounded companions stumble forward.

For perhaps the hundredth time, Terrel glanced at the eastern horizon, willing the Amber Moon to appear. More cheering signalled the fact that the show was continuing apace, and the boy began to feel sick to his stomach. A moment later, to his horror, he began to feel something else deep inside himself. It was faint and distant, but the internal trembling was an unmistakable signal. Terrel knew just what it meant.

The earthquake was on its way.

CHAPTER FORTY-NINE

Collector! Terrel cried. *It's time! You have to help me.*

The response was immediate, although at first it made no sense.

Is it clear? At last! Terrel? It's too soon.

The earthquake's coming!

Use the spiral, the sharakan told him. *Isn't that what the creature calls it?*

But—

We can't arrange another eclipse just for your convenience, the Collector said testily. *This is what the amulet is for.*

I don't know how—

Summon me, the sharakan cut in. *It's time we did some trading.*

But the Amber Moon— Terrel began, glancing again at the sky.

Has risen here, the Collector completed for him, *even if it's not visible to you yet. That is sufficient. Now do it!*

Terrel reacted to the command instinctively, repeating the appeal that had brought Reader to him more than a month earlier. As the Collector's image appeared beside him, the staff began to shine again. Although the internal light wasn't nearly as intense as it had been before, it was strong enough to make Terrel's fingers glow blood-red. The nearby prisoners and some of the soldiers fell back, amazed by the sudden appearance of the robed figure, while the crowds beyond the military cordon gasped and pointed, some edging away while others strained forward to see.

Terrel felt his mind drift into darkness, as if he were falling asleep, and in his waking dream he was vaguely aware of some sort of communication taking place – though he could not tell what was being said or even who was talking. And then his internal trembling began to recede a little. It was still there, deep inside him, and still ominous, but the threat seemed more remote now. This was something that hadn't happened before – the warning he was given usually only allowed him a few moments' notice – but he had never been in a situation like this before, and he was grateful for any scrap of good fortune. He returned to his senses to find the Collector addressing the crowd.

'This abomination must cease!' he cried, and for once his voice was passionate. 'I speak for all the sharaken. There must be no more killing.' He paused, aware that he had everyone's full attention now. All movement had stopped in the square, and even the people on the towers had turned their backs on the fort and were now looking their way. Temporarily at least, the show had come to a halt.

'You are meddling with forces you don't understand,' the sharakan went on. 'Have the moons taught you nothing?'

Terrel glanced round and saw that the Amber Moon had risen at last, but its arrival did nothing to quell the new doubts that were crowding into his mind. Although the Collector's words were fervent, there was something forced about their delivery, as if he were merely playing the role expected of him – reproducing the required emotion rather than feeling it. It was as though his attention was really elsewhere, and he was just marking time until the next important development.

'Can no one here answer me?' the sharakan asked, looking around. 'Then take me to someone in authority.'

A wide space had developed around the boy and his companion, and as yet no one had tried to breach it. Now, on an order from their leader, several guards rushed forward, their weapons drawn. The Collector smiled contemptuously, and the soldiers all fell to the ground, where they lay groaning and clutching their heads. The onlookers stared in awe, and the hush that had fallen over the arena was replaced by a spreading murmur as the news of what was happening passed through the crowd.

'Well?' the Collector demanded.

The platoon leader, whose men had been felled with such disdain, looked dumbfounded – and when, a moment later, a breathless messenger arrived, pushing his way through the throng, the soldier accepted his new orders gratefully.

'King Ekuban commands you to the palace,' he announced.

'Good.'

There was a disturbance at the edge of the circle, and Terrel heard someone calling his name. Aylen emerged from a group of prisoners, and pushed past the guards, who made only a half-hearted attempt to stop him.

'He's a friend,' Terrel told the sharakan quietly.

'Then he can accompany you,' the Collector replied as Aylen joined them. 'Escort these two to the palace,' he said to the platoon leader. 'I will join them there. Be sure that you keep them safe. They are still under my protection.'

'Yes, sir,' the soldier replied, deferring to the authority in the sharakan's voice.

Although Terrel hoped that Ekuban had finally seen sense – or was at least prepared to discuss the matter – the idea of going back inside the protective dome made him feel very nervous, especially as the Collector was not going to accompany them on the journey.

'Are you sure this is wise?' he asked quietly. 'Your dream-trading might not work in there.'

'It's all right, Terrel,' the sharakan replied calmly. 'Now that we're all working together, we're much more powerful than Reader was on his own.'

'Reader was working alone?'

'Unfortunately, yes. The fact that he was facing his own sister put him at an extra disadvantage.'

'Why can't you stay with us?'

'I'll see you inside,' the Collector stated firmly. 'Go quickly, and don't worry. This is what we wanted.'

And then the sharakan vanished before Terrel had a chance to say anything else.

'You have some interesting friends,' Aylen remarked.

*

'So, young man, we meet again.'

Terrel and Aylen had been escorted to a wide balcony which commanded an excellent view over the ruined castle. Ekuban had been waiting for them there, together with Marika and a large group of favoured courtiers.

'It seems we may have underestimated you. And you've brought a companion with you this time,' the king added, eyeing Aylen's bloodstained clothes with distaste. 'Is he injured?'

'I'm well, thank you, Your Majesty,' Aylen answered for himself. He made his words sound like an insult.

'I'm grateful for this second chance, Your Majesty,' Terrel said quickly. 'Macul is in grave peril. The demon—'

'Wasn't there a sharakan with you?' Ekuban interrupted. 'We should like to meet him.'

Rather nervously, Terrel called upon the staff and the Collector appeared again. To the boy's horror, he was bent double, just as Reader had been, and his face was contorted with pain. This time, however, Terrel himself was not affected and he knew he was not going to be paralyzed. Even so, the sharakan's evident distress was a terrible blow. It meant that Terrel had been right, and the dream-trading would not work inside the dome. They had walked into a trap.

'You seem to be in some discomfort,' Ekuban observed, smiling.

'You cannot . . . do . . . this. Do you know . . . who I am?' the Collector rasped, having to cling to the staff in order to stop himself from falling to the ground.

'We know who you are, Collector,' the king replied complacently. 'And we may do anything we please. What's more, you will have the pleasure of witnessing it all. You are in our domain now.'

'A trick,' the sharakan whispered painfully. 'S-sorcery.'

'If you wish to call it that,' Ekuban agreed affably. 'We're surprised you agreed to come here so readily. Of course the invitation was Marika's idea, not ours.'

The Collector's only response was a wordless snarl of agony and rage. The king strolled over to the wall at the edge of the balcony, then beckoned to his guests.

'Come. Join us as the show resumes.' He flicked a hand to one of the nearby guards, and orders were relayed onwards. A bell rang out, and cheering rose from the impatient crowds below.

'No!' Terrel cried. 'You mustn't do this. The demon will destroy everything.'

'We think not,' Ekuban said, laughing. 'Even demons would not dare spoil our birthday.' Some of his courtiers laughed at the witticism. 'Come here.'

Reluctantly, Terrel did as he was told. The Collector came with him, dragged along by the staff, and Aylen remained on his other side.

'Please, Your Majesty,' the boy begged. 'Don't—'

'Enough! Look, the next batch are in the moat.'

Collector, can't you do something? Terrel asked silently. There was no reply. The sharakan's eyes were closed, and he seemed oblivious to his surroundings, lost in his own private world of pain. An icy wave of despair engulfed Terrel as he watched six men reach the castle shore. As they dragged themselves from the water, it was obvious that some of them were injured, and he realized that they had been wounded in the fight Aylen had begun. Terrel glanced at his friend and knew, from his stony countenance, that Aylen was aware of this too.

'Acquaintances of yours, we believe,' Ekuban remarked, with a malevolent smile. 'Do you think they'll last long? Put on a good show?'

Aylen did not reply, but the muscles in his neck were knotted in tense fury. For a moment Terrel thought his friend was going to attack the king with his bare hands – and some of the guards obviously thought so too. They stepped forward quickly, but Ekuban seemed unconcerned.

'Do you wish you were with them?' he needled.

'I wish *you* were with them,' Aylen replied.

'A traitor's response,' Ekuban said, laughing. He appeared to be enjoying himself immensely. 'But we are protected. Your turn to meet the demon will come soon enough. For now, be content to watch.'

The grisly scene being played out inside the ruin came to a swift conclusion. All six men died within a few moments of each other, victims of unimaginably violent forces. Even as the cheering began to die away, another even larger group was forced into the moat and the cycle of horror continued, each increasingly spectacular death greeted with tumultuous applause.

Terrel felt his internal shaking increase. It was making him tremble physically now. The earthquake was coming this time – and there was nothing he or the Collector or anyone else could do to stop it. The first faint tremor shook the stones beneath the boy's feet, but no one else seemed to notice, their attention still fully occupied by the slaughter below.

A second, stronger tremor ran through the palace. This time no one could fail to notice it, and Ekuban glanced at Marika, uncertainty on his face for the first time. The sorceress looked perturbed.

'Stop the killing!' Terrel exclaimed. 'This is your last chance.' It may already be too late, he thought, but he owed it to himself and everyone else to try one last time. 'I told you an earthquake was coming.'

The king did not respond, but as cheers from the square indicated that more prisoners had been killed, a third tremor rocked the balcony.

This is it, Terrel thought. The end of everything. His terror was mixed with an intense sadness. He looked at Aylen, wishing he'd been able to see his other friends before he died, and wondered miserably which – if any – of the people he loved were going to survive this catastrophe. His failure, the fact that he had let them down, made him want to weep.

'What's going on?' Ekuban demanded.

'I don't know,' Marika replied. 'Something's . . .'

Terrel glanced at the Collector – and was amazed to see a small, secret smile on the sharakan's face.

What is it? What's happening?

It is certain, the Collector said, but Terrel had the feeling that he was talking to someone else.

Another tremor shook the palace, and screams and cries of alarm mingled with the sound of falling masonry. The Collector stood up straight, calm amid the panic, and Terrel realized that the sharakan's distress had been an act. The expression on his face was one of triumphant satisfaction. Ignoring the boy, the Collector turned to face Marika, who was now obviously terrified.

'Your talent is great, madam,' he told her, 'but you abused it. And you cannot stand against us.'

'Stop him!' Ekuban screamed. 'We demand—'

'Be quiet, you fool,' the sorceress ordered harshly. 'It's over.'

'We don't *need* your cooperation,' the Collector said, still speaking to Marika, 'but it will make it easier for all concerned if you do not oppose us.'

She nodded resignedly.

'Do what you will.'

'No! Traitor!' Ekuban launched himself at the woman, but he never reached her. Terrel could not be sure which of the magicians had thrown the king to the ground.

'What's going on?' the boy asked. 'What are you doing?'

The palace was shaking continuously now.

'Time to start dream-trading in earnest,' the Collector muttered to himself.

The sky turned green.

Almost at once Terrel knew what had happened. The Collector was using the sharaken's collective power not to defeat Marika's sorcery but to *reinforce* it. The dome was glowing now, visible even to the naked eye, but it was no longer protecting the palace. Instead of keeping the earthquake outside the royal domain, it was confining it *within* the dome. That was why the Collector had been so adamant that the elemental must be told who was responsible for its torment. He had wanted the creature to direct its fury at the palace and nowhere else. And now he and his colleagues were using all their magic to stop the earthquake from spreading to the rest of the country.

At the same time, Terrel noticed that a curious change was coming over all the people around him. The panic-stricken responses to the tremors had stopped, and most

of the courtiers were slumping to the floor. Even Aylen
had collapsed. If it had not been such a ludicrous idea,
Terrel would have said they were falling asleep.

You understand now? the Collector asked silently.

I think so.

We can be merciful. They will all die in their sleep.

And the rest of Macul will survive.

Yes.

Why aren't I asleep?

Because you have the handle.

Let me wake Aylen.

That would not be wise.

But we have to try to save him, Terrel objected.

The Collector did not reply – and finally the boy really
did understand.

*Reader's sacrifice was necessary for us to comprehend what
we faced,* the sharakan explained. *Yours is necessary to
defeat it. You have only to release your grip on the staff to
claim oblivion. The oracles will remember you, Terrel.*

Then the sharakan's image vanished, leaving Terrel
alone as the palace began to tear itself apart. He stumbled and fell as another tremor hit, but he kept hold of
the staff, and as he broke his fall it touched Aylen's pros-
trate body. He woke immediately and looked at Terrel,
fear and confusion in his eyes.

'What happened?'

'Take hold of the staff or you'll fall asleep again,' the
boy told him. 'The earthquake's destroying the palace,
but *only* the palace.'

'Then we'd better get out of here.'

'We can't. The dome that surrounds us is impenetrable
now. That's what's saving the rest of the country. The

sharaken had to get the message-handle in here to make sure of that.'

'And used you to do it?'

'Yes.'

'Then we're not dying in vain,' Aylen decided. 'At least Macul will survive, and Ekuban and all his cronies will be gone.'

And so will we, Terrel thought dismally, his mind conjuring up a picture of Alyssa. He wondered where she was now, and hoped she was safe. *Goodbye, my love*, he said. *Maybe we'll meet as ghosts*.

He did not expect an answer, and he received none. Terrel carefully took his hand away from the staff so that, at the last, he would not have to witness his own death.

CHAPTER FIFTY

Terrel dreamt he was back in Fenduca. He heard voices screaming, warning him, but there was no escape. The mudslide was a huge black tide that engulfed him even as he struggled, filling his mouth and nose, choking him. He was blind, but still the promised oblivion did not come. He felt cheated.

Terrel woke, still choking. The air was full of dust. A hand around his own was pressing his fingers against the contours of wood.

'Wake up, Terrel. I don't want to die alone.'

In the strange yellow light Aylen's face looked pallid, almost ghost-like.

'I keep hearing voices.' Aylen was having to shout over the tumult of the earthquake, the crack and slither of crumbling stone and the rattle of falling debris. Although it was impossible to see much through all the dust, it was obvious that the palace was collapsing about them. Terrel tried to speak, wanting to ask Aylen why he wouldn't let him sleep, but he could only cough instead.

'Voices,' Aylen repeated. 'In here.' He tapped the side of his head with his free hand.

Terrel was hearing them too, but he could make no sense of the raucous, incoherent screaming.

'Look!' Aylen cried, pointing northwards.

Part of the wall at the edge of the balcony had already fallen, and in that direction, away from the bulk of the dying palace, it was possible to see through the storm to the glowing yellow dome that encased its doom. And there, on the other side of the barrier, was a bird. It was fluttering in panic, hurling itself against the magical shield in a demented, futile attempt to get inside.

Alyssa?

The magpie's whirling attack became a little less frenetic, and the screaming stopped.

Terrel? Terrel! It can't end like this. It can't!

We can't get out, and there's nowhere to hide, he told her, the wrenching sadness he felt softened a little by the unexpected opportunity to bid her farewell. *Goodbye, Alyssa. I—*

No! she screamed. *Don't say that! You—*

The sun went out, cutting off her protest.

All three of them turned to look, but only Terrel knew what he was seeing. The second eclipse of the day was a scene straight out of Muzeni's poetic journal. The Dark Moon had returned, in the guise of a great bird of prey, the final, incontrovertible harbinger of death. Black wings blotted out the sun, and Terrel imagined the curved beak and the talons that he could not see, remembering more of Muzeni's words. *When she strikes, her speed and savagery will be unmatched, unmatchable*. He looked again for Alyssa, waiting for the end.

The sun's light returned, muted by all the debris in the air, as the giant bird changed course. As it did so, Terrel's perspective altered and he gasped, struggling to focus as the ground beneath him trembled and bucked like a living thing. He knew now that the creature was no incarnation of the Dark Moon, but it was like no bird he had ever seen. It was truly gigantic, and its plumage was not black but a shimmering mixture of scarlet and bronze, while its talons and beak were a dull yellow. Now that it was closer he could see that the bird's eyes had the metallic sheen of polished steel.

'What is *that*?' Aylen breathed.

Terrel thought he knew, but it was such an unlikely idea that he hesitated before answering. The description he'd read had been in a book in the library at Havenmoon – but that particular volume had been devoted to myths and legends, to creatures of the imagination.

'It's a caroc,' he replied eventually. 'It's supposed to be a mythical being.'

'Looks real enough to me,' Aylen commented in awe. 'What's it doing here?'

'I've no idea,' Terrel said, watching as the enormous bird wheeled about and began to fly directly towards them.

It's your turn to believe in me.

Although the voice that sounded in Terrel's head was not Alyssa's, it was still familiar. He was trying to place it when Aylen, his face a mask of astonishment, identified it for him.

'Ysy?' he exclaimed, his confusion obvious. 'Where are you?'

Ysy? Is it really you? Terrel asked, staring at the caroc in amazement.

I'm not the only sleeper, Alyssa told him, then turned to the newcomer. *Can you help them?*

I can try.

'What's going on?' Aylen cried. 'What are all these voices?'

But Terrel had no chance to answer, because just at that moment a section of the balcony crumbled and fell, and he and Aylen were forced to scramble away to stop themselves from being swept over the edge. At the same time, the huge bird flew straight into the dome – and instead of being repulsed, she passed through in a shower of orange sparks and a loud tearing noise.

From close to, her wings and body were so vast that they seemed to cover half the sky, but the bird's movements were controlled, almost delicate. In a single elegant manoeuvre she swept down to the ledge where Terrel and Aylen were clinging, and scooped one of them up in each monstrous set of talons. Terrel half expected to be crushed, but the grip of the giant claws was firm and oddly gentle. A moment later the rest of the balcony disintegrated.

Become part of me, Ysatel told them. *Part of the darkness*.

'What do you mean?' Aylen asked. 'What does she mean, Terrel?'

'Faith!' Terrel replied, shouting over the rushing air as they flew. 'We're going to escape!'

I'm not quite real here, Ysatel said. *But I'm real enough. You must be the same, Chute*.

'How . . .'

'We're going to escape!' Terrel yelled jubilantly. 'Just believe it!'

They crashed through the yellow dome in a second blaze of orange. Terrel and Aylen both released their hold on the staff, and it dropped back into the destruction below. Aylen screamed, but Terrel laughed as fire pulsed through his body – and then they were outside, in the cool, clear air far above the city.

Terrel? Aylen? Are you all right?

Terrel glanced across at the limp figure of his friend.

I'm fine, he replied. *And so is Aylen. He's just fainted, that's all.* He turned his head to see the magpie flying behind them, her wings beating furiously in the draught created by the caroc.

I'm alive, he said, hardly believing it himself.

I told you . . . Alyssa replied, but there was a catch in her voice, and neither of them was capable of saying anything more.

The giant bird was still climbing, taking them up to a height that made Terrel feel dizzy. Looking down, he watched the turmoil inside the dome as one shockwave after another pulsed through what little remained of the palace with ever-increasing fury. It was as though the elemental was determined to reduce the entire structure to dust. Every stone, every tile, every piece of wood and metal had to be pulverized before the mayhem would end. No living creature could possibly survive such violence. Their rescuer had arrived just in time.

How did you find us? Terrel asked.

Alyssa told me what was happening, Ysatel replied, *but it was Aylen who led me to you in the end. I knew his road was turning, and I couldn't let it come to an end. Not like that.*

How did you find the caroc?

There are worlds within worlds, Terrel. You must know that by now.

And you were able to get through the shield because you're not real in this *world?* he guessed.

They allowed me to become so, she replied, *to use one of the creatures of their realm.*

They?

The spirits in the cloud valley. Esera called them the darkness.

You met her? Terrel exclaimed in astonishment. *How did you get into the valley with all that water around?*

I didn't, Ysatel said, *but there is a link between us. It began because of you, your healing us when we were pregnant, but it was the night of dreams that made the real connection.*

At the full of the Amber Moon, a hundred days ago? he asked, recalling the sharaken's communal dreaming.

That's right. All Macul was affected one way or another, and there were many links forged that night. When you're a sleeper, dreaming is just about all you can *do, so I was part of it. And a good thing too*, she concluded. *Or I'd never have been able to come here.*

Thank you, Terrel murmured. The words seemed hopelessly inadequate, but he did not know what else to say.

I may have to land soon, Ysatel informed him. *Flying in my condition gets tiring after a while. Where shall I set you down?*

The caroc is pregnant too?

My eggs are almost ready to be laid, she confirmed, *but I'd better be back in my own world before that happens. I don't think your myths should become* too *real. Where do you want to go?*

Terrel looked down at the city, laid out before him like a map. People in the square were smaller than ants, most of them trying to get as far away as possible from the inexplicable events that had overtaken the palace. He could barely imagine the panic that must have gripped the citizens.

Then his gaze was drawn back to the dome. At first he thought he was imagining it, but the longer he stared the more certain he became, and the jubilation he had felt at his deliverance turned to horror. There was an irregularity in the colouring of the dome, a brighter patch on one side, which must have been where the caroc had smashed through. As he watched, orange cracks began to snake out from this weakened area, marking a fiery pattern over the surface of the shield. Inside it, the earthquake showed no sign of abating. If anything it was growing even more violent.

It's not going to hold, Alyssa said, putting Terrel's fears into words.

The Ancient's fury still raged. The palace was already devastated, but in human terms the elemental had no sense of scale. Like a man using a sledgehammer to crack a walnut, the end results were beyond control. The power it had unleashed was simply too great. Even the sharaken had underestimated what they were facing, and their efforts had been in vain. Now that their magic had been breached it was only a matter of time.

The dome would collapse and the earthquake would spread, destroying first the city, then the rest of Macul and possibly even the Floating Islands as well. Terrel's nightmare was coming true before his eyes. He would even see everything from the air – just as he had in his prophetic dream.

What's happening? Ysatel asked, anxious now.

There's only one chance, Alyssa said.

Terrel knew she was right.

Take me to the elemental, he told Ysatel.

CHAPTER FIFTY-ONE

As the caroc wheeled down in a steep, headlong spiral, Terrel thought that at least he would be dry when he approached the Ancient. The incongruous nature of the thought made him laugh out loud.

Don't get hysterical, Alyssa warned. *You're going to need to talk fast – and to do a better job of it than last time.*

They were directly above the ruined fort now, and Terrel could see a writhing vortex of unnatural shadows at its heart. The elemental's agitation was frightening to behold. Even if it tolerated his presence, getting the creature to listen to him was not going to be easy.

I can't go any closer, Ysatel announced suddenly, pulling out of her dive so quickly that Terrel was almost crushed by the abrupt deceleration.

What's the matter? he asked. *Doesn't it recognize you? You're one of its sleepers—*

It's not me. It's Aylen. It'll kill him if I go any closer.

Terrel glanced across at his still unconscious friend,

and knew he couldn't ask Aylen's step-mother to be the cause of his death.

All right, he said, looking down and gulping with terror at the thought that had just occurred to him. *Let me fall from here.*

What? Ysatel exclaimed. *We're too high. You can't—*

If the elemental accepts me, it'll break my fall, Terrel explained. *If it doesn't, I may as well be dead anyway. You have to believe in* me *this time, Ysy.*

Are you sure? she asked.

Yes! he replied, giving himself no time to reconsider. *Quickly. We don't have much time.*

The glowing network of cracks had now spread almost all around the dome.

All right.

The caroc's talons opened slowly, and Terrel forced himself not to cling to one of the huge claws. He let go and plummeted towards the ground, the wind whistling in his ears, his eyes tight shut. For a brief moment he blacked out, his terror overcoming his resolve, and it was only when Alyssa's voice sounded sharply in his head that he roused himself again – just in time to see the ground rushing up to meet him.

His screams were cut off as he was swallowed whole by the darkness. After a few moments of helpless, tumbling disorientation, Terrel realized that he was no longer falling, but was floating, weightless, within the swirling shadows. His return to the surface of Nydus had been cushioned, as if he had landed on the softest, deepest mattress on the planet, but he had no time to be thankful – for the second time that day – that he was alive. The fall had not killed him, and neither had the elemental, which meant that at least it was treating him differently from other humans. However, the Ancient was shifting convulsively, pulling him this way and that, and Terrel knew that this was an outward manifestation of its inner turmoil. Its long captivity, the tortures it had endured, and the ultimate, vengeful release of its pent-up fury had left it deranged and close to total madness. Even the creature in Betancuria, when it had learnt that the mines were about to be flooded, had not been as demented as this.

The boy realized very quickly that his presence had distracted the elemental, and that the boundless flow of destructive energy it was feeding into the earthquake had reduced a little, but it was not nearly enough of a change to prevent disaster. He had to try to calm its fears, to stop it from going completely insane. Terrel saw the spiral glowing brightly in the palm of his left hand and took courage from its presence, its fragile but potent beauty.

Your enemies are defeated, he began. *You don't need to do any more or punish anyone else. You're safe now. Please let the earthquake stop.*

He sensed that the Ancient was listening to him, evaluating his thoughts as well as his words, but the level of violence did not change. Its madness was not to be overcome so easily.

If the tremors spread outside the circle of bright air, Terrel said desperately, *they'll destroy everything. The water – the magic – around you will come even closer. If you stop now, I promise we'll empty the moat and drain all the magic from the caves beneath you. You'll be able to return underground. Please stop.*

On this occasion, the response was a brief moment of peace, which gave Terrel an equally brief surge of hope – but then the Ancient began to vent its rage again with renewed vigour.

Please. I made a bargain with your . . . brother. He did not know what other word to use. *With another of your kind. It accepted me as its friend. Won't you do the same?*

This time Terrel was aware of an intense curiosity, and the scale of the violence fell once more. And then the elemental's reaction came in the form of a simple, overwhelming command.

Show me.

How do I do that? Terrel wondered. His uncertainty registered with the Ancient and, fearing a return of its ferocious assault, Terrel began to talk again.

It's true, he insisted. *Your brother trusted me, and he's safe now. You can read my mind, can't you? Go ahead, look. You'll see it's true.*

Show me.

Ironically, inspiration came to Terrel from the most unlikely source. *You'll have to go to sleep sometime*, Jax had said. *I'll be waiting.* Terrel wasn't able to sleep now, but there was another way to let Jax in.

Summoning the glamour, the boy turned his eyes blue, and then – fearing that this might not be enough – he turned his hair purple and the skin of his hands green. He sensed the elemental's incomprehension, but it was another voice he was listening for now.

So you've finally gone completely crazy, Jax remarked. *Moons! That's quite a show! Where are you?*

I'm inside another elemental.

The prince laughed.

Are you just unlucky, or do you have a death wish?
Where are you? Terrel asked.
Makhaya. Why?
Do you remember being in Betancuria?
How could I forget?
Think about it. Please. Terrel was aware that the
Ancient was following the conversation closely, and
hoped it would be able to see into Jax's mind and find
confirmation there of what he'd been saying.

Why should I? the prince said, but the mere mention
of the episode had brought his memories to the fore, and
Terrel knew that that would be enough.

So you can be a hero again, he replied. *Even if no one
will know about it this time.*

What's the point of that? Jax asked.

Terrel ignored the question, because he had felt something extraordinary happening. The link he'd established
to his estranged brother, all the way to Vadanis, had
somehow enabled the elemental in Talazoria to reach out
to *its* brother in Betancuria. The nature of their communication was quite beyond his understanding, but he
knew it was happening. Between them, the two alien
beings were weighing up his sincerity and exchanging
information. Terrel sensed the panic and anger recede.
Even as his own link with Jax was broken, the elemental
in Talazoria overcame its immediate fears – of water, of
men, of its entire environment.

Whether it was new, or just an extension of the first,
another bargain had been made.

The terrified citizens of Macul's capital began to hope
that the worst was over. The monstrous bird that had

flown over their heads had finally gone, and the calamity that had befallen the king's palace seemed to be finished now. Inside the dome that had appeared from nowhere, the dust was finally beginning to settle.

CHAPTER FIFTY-TWO

That night saw the city in ferment, but by dawn the next day it was obvious to all but the most wilfully blind that the world turned on a new axis. All that was left of the royal palace was a vast pile of multi-coloured sand, and the dome that had once surrounded it had vanished back into thin air. Ekuban and his entire court were dead, along with a huge number of Talazoria's most important citizens and the majority of its high-ranking army officers. In a single day Macul had lost all its leaders, and that – together with the unbelievable manner in which they had met their end – should have been a recipe for chaos.

Indeed, the few soldiers who tried to keep order soon found that they lacked the necessary authority to do so. Many of them were overpowered by people who were no longer prepared to obey them. Others simply discarded their uniforms and became civilians again. Many underlings were now free, and a good number of those whose masters had survived were refusing to take orders from them any more, and were revelling in a heady new sense of freedom. To make matters worse, almost all the prisoners in the square had escaped, and there were even reports that people from the stews were forcing their way into the city. Rebellion was in the air, and in many places lawlessness was rife.

The one thing that kept the entire city from degenerating into anarchy was a series of events that took place at the old fort. When the boy with a limp and strange eyes had appeared on the ruined battlements, he had been the first person ever to emerge unscathed from an encounter with the demon. Not only that, but there were some who swore they'd seen him fall from the sky after being dropped by a huge red bird – the same bird that had later landed in the square and deposited another man on the ground. Most people who had not witnessed these amazing events found the stories difficult to believe, and even those who had found it hard to trust their own eyes. But the tales persisted, and a new legend was born.

However, no one could deny that the boy – some said he was the same one who'd summoned the sharakan earlier – was inside the moat and still very much alive. The few people who had been there to see him clamber over the walls were soon joined by many more, and he spoke to them all in a voice that was hoarse and weary – but which carried both an emotional appeal and a natural authority quite out of keeping with his slight frame and ill-matched limbs.

He told them that it was the demon who had destroyed the palace, and that it would tear their city to pieces unless they honoured the promise he had made and drained the moats that imprisoned it. Some of the onlookers decided that the boy was quite mad, and argued that the last thing they should do was set the monster free. But the majority were convinced by the stranger's evident passion, and all objections were set aside.

The work went on through the night, in the light of hundreds of lamps and torches. Artisans who had kept the city functioning for the benefit of others saw in this project a chance to stake their own claim in the future, and many other underlings – and even some citizens – threw themselves into the task until the work force grew to be several hundred strong. The undertaking provided a focus for the whole city, and its inhabitants embraced it, finding a sense of purpose amid all the mayhem.

Not everything went smoothly. There were some accidents and injuries, and in their haste, mistakes were made about where the water should go. There was so much of it, after all, and there was only a certain amount that could be absorbed by the city's canals and reservoirs. Some newly-dug ditches overflowed, flooding streets and cellars, but none of this was allowed to halt the progress of their enterprise. As morning came, the level in the moat had already gone down several paces, and every hour brought a further fall.

By then the boy was no longer alone. A small boat had been found from somewhere, and another man had rowed across to join him.

'You know what they're calling you?' Aylen said, after he and Terrel had greeted each other with a joyful hug.

'What?'

'The demon-master,' Aylen replied, grinning.

'Not exactly accurate,' Terrel commented, 'but I'm

not going to argue. Are you all right?'

'I'm fine. I just can't believe I passed out and missed all the fun. I remember the bird picking us up, but then the next thing I knew I was lying in the square with a lot of people staring at me. Was that really Ysy?'

'Yes.'

'Is she still here?'

'No. She had to go.' Both the caroc and Alyssa's magpie were gone, but Terrel had the feeling he had not seen the last of them.

'So, what did I miss?' Aylen asked.

Terrel gave him a brief version of everything that had happened, even as he continued to keep a watchful eye on the work that was going on around them.

'That's incredible,' his friend breathed when the boy had finished.

'If I hadn't been so stupid, I could have avoided a lot of this mess,' Terrel muttered.

'Are you *insane*?' Aylen exclaimed. 'If it hadn't been for you, all of Macul would've been destroyed by now.'

'Whereas now it's just going to be in complete chaos.'

'There are difficult times ahead,' Aylen conceded, 'but it's also a great opportunity for us. With Ekuban and all his cronies out of the picture, we've got the chance to start afresh. We can install a new system of government, one that's fairer to everybody. There are plenty of good men and women out there, waiting to build the future. I'm sure of it.'

Terrel could not help but admire his friend's idealism. It made him feel old and cynical.

'And you can be in charge of the whole thing,' Aylen went on. 'You can—'

'No,' Terrel cut in. 'This isn't my country, Chute.'

'But you're a hero!' Aylen protested. 'Look what you've achieved already,' he added, waving a hand at the people toiling below them.

'I have to leave.'

'You can't just walk away. Your influence could be vital. People will listen to you.'

'Everything I've done here has been because I've had no choice,' Terrel said calmly. 'But now I do. I'm not a leader. I'm fifteen years old, and I want to go home.'

Aylen was silent for a long time, but eventually he nodded.

'I can't say I'm not disappointed,' he said, 'but I understand.'

By midday the moat was all but dry, and Terrel and Aylen turned their attention to the flooded dungeons. Several artisans had been brave enough to join them. They were obviously still afraid of the now docile elemental, but nonetheless seemed eager to help. Terrel was about to discuss what they should do when the problem was taken out of their hands. Without warning, the water gushed from several outlets all over the castle, in defiance of the laws of nature. From there it flowed into the moat by a number of apparently impossible routes, and thence away to other parts of the city. Only Terrel knew that the Ancient, having learnt from its counterpart in Betancuria, was responsible for its own deliverance this time. He also knew that their efforts in draining the moat had cemented the trust between him and the creature.

'The demon will leave soon,' Terrel told his companions once the flow of water had stopped.

'Then our work is done?' one of them asked.

'Almost,' the boy replied. 'There's just one more thing I need to do. Aylen, will you come with me?'

'Me?' The young man looked understandably nervous.

'Come on,' Terrel said, and turned to walk towards the elemental without waiting to see if his friend was following.

'What are we doing?' Aylen whispered as soon as he caught up.

'The creature won't hurt you,' Terrel replied confidently, 'but if they see you come inside it—'

'*Inside* it?' Aylen exclaimed in disbelief.

'You'll become the new demon-master,' the boy continued calmly. 'When I've gone, that will mean the people will listen to what you have to say.'

'But—'

'There are good men out there,' Terrel said, overriding his friend's objection. 'And you're one of them. Take advantage of this.'

'All right,' Aylen agreed after a slight hesitation. 'As long as I don't die of fright first.'

'You won't.'

'What do I have to do?'

'Nothing. I'll do all the talking.'

The swirling darkness reached out to gather them in.

An hour or so later, the men who had watched the demon swallow the pair – and who had begun to wonder if they would ever see them again – witnessed their re-emergence. Aylen looked bewildered, and he was trying not to stumble as his legs got used to being back in the world he understood. Glancing round, he saw that

Terrel was not only unsteady on his feet but was weeping too.

'What is it?' he asked in dismay. 'What's the matter? What happened in there?' Although Aylen knew he had been measured in some way during his time inside the creature, he had not been aware of what had passed between Terrel and their host. Now it seemed that his friend was in some distress.

'It's too complicated to explain,' Terrel replied, trying to smile through his tears. Conflicting emotions played upon his face.

'At least tell me if you're crying for sadness or joy.'

'A bit of both,' the boy answered, wiping his face with his sleeve. 'Come on, Chute. The elemental will be leaving soon, and we don't want to be this close when it does.'

News of the last show that would ever take place in the old fort spread through the city. When the time came, the towers were crowded once more, and some of the braver spectators had even climbed onto the tumbled stones of the castle walls.

The ground shivered as the demon began to edge its way into a crevice, pushing rock aside as it tunnelled beyond the dungeons and into the earth below. The tremor was felt all the way to the city walls, but it did little damage. Talazoria had withstood much worse.

It was all over in a short time, and even though there had been no deaths – and not much spectacle – the audience went away satisfied.

A few hours later, another visitor left the city for the last time. Terrel was a wanderer once more. The Ancient had granted him his final wish, but there had been a heavy price to pay.

He walked through the night, following the unknown road again, but he was not heading towards the coast. Instead he was travelling north, and when midwinter's day dawned – even though the weather was mild enough – Terrel's heart felt as though it was frozen.

He could not go home, at least not yet. It had taken him a long time to accept this fact, and it had only been the elemental's intransigence that had overcome the boy's incredulous and distraught resistance. But in the end Terrel had bowed to the inevitable. He had to go on, not back. It seemed that his bargain of friendship had no end.

EPILOGUE

Esera sat with her baby nestled in her arms. She was waiting in the place where she had watched the lake with Terrel, but this time she was there for a specific reason. She often returned to the floating hospice, more out of habit than necessity now that the curse had been lifted. She had felt it go on midwinter's eve, more than a month ago, and her intuition had been echoed by the dreams of many others that night. Since then, as if to prove the point, three women had become pregnant.

The little girl wriggled in her mother's arms, and Esera pulled out the infant's most prized possession and held it in front of her. The baby's eyes lit up with delight and she gurgled, reaching a tiny hand towards the wondrous plaything.

Esera had never seen a bird, so she did not know what a feather was, but from the moment she'd seen it she had recognized the fact that it must have come from the great flying creature she had seen in her dreams. It was

bright red, except around the edges where it was tinged
with bronze. The delicate patterns of its construction
made the feather seem almost translucent, and it changed
colour as it moved. It was as long as Esera's forearm,
but so light that it almost floated in the air, and the baby
loved it, especially when her mother tickled her nose
with its tip.

Esera had found the feather in the place where she
was now sitting, the day before her daughter had been
born. At that time she'd had no idea where it had come
from. Now, thanks to her latest dream, she knew it had
been a present, meant for them both. And she knew who
had sent them the gift.

They came just before dusk, hovering over the water
some way out into the lake, as if they weren't sure
whether to venture any closer. There had been a time,
not so long ago, when Esera would have been terrified,
but that time was gone now. Standing up carefully, she
beckoned for them to come nearer. As the amorphous
shapes drew in, making the evening even darker around
her, Esera looked down at her baby, who was still
contentedly preoccupied with the feather.

'There's someone here who wants to meet you, little
one,' she murmured softly, then looked up to face the
darkness, unafraid.

The otherworld beings waited patiently for their
introduction, radiating a quiet sense of pleasure, and
Esera felt honoured to share her happiness with them.

'This is Terrella,' she said.

By then the boy who was often in Esera's thoughts was
far away, approaching the northern borderlands of

Macul. But he was no longer alone. Alyssa, in the form of a humble sparrow, was riding on his shoulder. The unknown road was about to turn again.

ICE MAGE

Julia Gray

The remote and wild land of Tiguafaya is on the edge of chaos. The manacing volcanoes that dominate the landscape grumble and threaten destruction. The repulsive fireworms, the marauding pirates and the ancient dragons grow bolder by the minute. The corrupt and ineffectual govermnent is paralysed and helpless in the face of all the dangers.

The country's only hope for survival lies with a group of young rebels known as the Firebrands. Led by the lovers, Andrin and Ico, and the half-mad musician, Vargo, the Firebrands are desperately fighting back. Using the once-revered but now lost arts of magic against the overwhelming odds, they are all that stand between Tiguafaya and total destruction.

Rich and exciting, powerful and engrossing, *Ice Mage* marks the arrival of a thrilling new voice in fantasy adventure.

FIRE MUSIC

Julia Gray

The stunning sequel to *Ice Mage* is a fast-paced fantasy adventure of war, magic and romance. The new government of Tiguafaya has finally brought peace to a people long suppressed by its tyrannical rules. But it may not last, for now a much greater power threatens the Firebrands – the mighty Empire to the north, whose emperor will not tolerate the Tiguafayans heretical belief in magic. However, the attempts to resolve the dispute by diplomacy will all count for nothing if the fire and lava shaking the ground cannot be controlled.

'A spellbinding storyteller' *Maggie Furey*

Orbit titles available by post:

☐ The Dark Moon	Julia Gray	£6.99
☐ Ice Mage	Julia Gray	£6.99
☐ Fire Music	Julia Gray	£6.99
☐ Isle of the Dead	Julia Gray	£6.99
☐ The Empire Stone	Chris Bunch	£6.99
☐ Transformation	Carol Berg	£9.99
☐ A Cavern of Black Ice	R. V. Jones	£7.99
☐ The Eye of the World	Robert Jordan	£6.99
☐ Colours in the Steel	K. J. Parker	£6.99
☐ Thraxas	Martin Scott	£5.99

The prices shown above are correct at time of going to press. However the publishers reserve the right to increase prices on covers from these previously advertised, without further notice.

ORBIT BOOKS
Cash Sales Department, P.O. Box 11, Falmouth, Cornwall, TR10 9EN
Tel: +44 (0) 1326 569777, Fax: +44 (0) 1326 569555
Email: books@barni.avel.co.uk.

POST AND PACKING:
Payments can be made as follows: cheque, postal order (payable to Orbit Books) or by credit cards. Do not send cash or currency.

U.K. Orders under £10	£1.50
U.K. Orders over £10	**FREE OF CHARGE**
E.E.C. & Overseas	25% of order value

Name (Block Letters) _____

Address _____

_____

Post/zip code:_____

☐ Please keep me in touch with future Orbit publications

☐ I enclose my remittance £_____

☐ I wish to pay Visa/Access/Mastercard/Eurocard

Card Expiry Date

